"I don't need a bride and there isn't 't happening." He grabbed the jail keys and shoved them n in his trouser pocket and stomped past her, spurs clinking along the hardwoods.

"I won't be home tonight, and it's your duty to protect her as sheriff." She was quick in rebuttal.

Sawyer balled his fists as she scurried toward the door ahead of him. How in the hell did she always back him into a corner? He folded his arms and uttered the one word he knew could stop her in her tracks. *"Mother."*

She spun on her heels, her blue eyes narrowing. Finally, he had her full attention. She didn't like being called anything but *Dodge,* and he had the sudden urge to protect his ears from retaliation.

"What kind of woman answers an ad like that anyway?" His knowledge of ordered brides was limited, though he'd seen a number head right back where they came from after a few days in Cheyenne.

"Her name is Rose Parker, and she's from New York City—well-educated from what I understand. I thought you might just enjoy a challenge."

Praise for Kim Turner

SAWYER'S ROSE was a finalist in the 2014 Georgia Romance Writers Maggie Award of Excellence for the unpublished historical category and received an Honorable Mention. The story was also a 2015 Golden Heart Finalist with Romance Writers of America.

Dedication and Family Acknowledgements

To my husband, Chuck,
for being my hero every single day.
And for my girls, Dakota and Shiloh,
so you will always know to follow your dreams.

~*~

Thank you Helen and Charles Turner for all the weekends in your home where I could write for hours at a time.

A huge hug for my Great Aunt Martha for reading. (Love you!)

To my sister Wendi (for reading) and to her family-Kyle, Whitney and Cole, for making family fun.

Thank you Mom and Dad for understanding the kid who always had a book in her hands. I love you both, and I am thankful you never bothered to censor the historical romances I was reading at a rather young age. Thanks for reading Mom, and no, I am not using a pen name.

Chuck, I am sure you never expected to play "Mr. Mom" this much, but you are darn good at it. I thank you and I love you.

Thanks to Dakota and Shiloh for putting up with a mommy who writes a lot of the time. I love you both forever and ever and always.

Acknowledgments

There are a lot of people who deserve a shout related to this story.

Maggie Worth, whatever made you take on a special needs case like me is still baffling, but thank you for teaching me this crazy craft and for believing in me when I didn't believe in myself.

A heart-felt thank you to Becke Turner for making sure my cowboys had the right horses and equipment and for reminding me that writing is indeed all about the journey.

Kim Simmons, when I started writing, I never expected that we would reconnect as if the years had not passed us by. This story is better because of you.

Every writer has an idol and Sherrilyn Kenyon you aren't only a friend, you have always been family.

And to Clare Roden, thanks for reading and keeping me sane with daily chats and support—wish you were closer than across the big pond.

Many thanks to Cheryl Hartsell, Stephanie Trietsch and Jillian Neal for the frequent critiques and for the chats on the rides to GRW meetings.

Thank you Jennifer McQuiston and Hildie McQueen, for the input at the Virginia Ellis Critiques.

And I truly thank The Wild Rose Press and Nicole D'Arenzio for taking a chance on me and this story.

Thanks also to the following people for reading and believing somewhere along the way: Diane Kitchen, Carol Opalinski, Sherrie Morgan, Dennie Garrett, Jewel Reed (R.I.P.), Scarlet Conner, Kelly Williamon, Lillie Farmer, Linda Abercrombie, Rachel Jones, Anita Tinsley & Angie and Stan Batchelor.

Prologue

North Platte, Nebraska 1863

Sawyer McCade urged his horse to a gallop to catch up to his father. This was the most important ride of his life, or at least it felt that way and he didn't want to miss any of the conversation. Mounted on the black stallion just ahead, Colonel John McCade led a small group of surveyors and investors further west, showing them areas of the Great Plains with potential ideas for developing cities and the railroads to connect them.

At seventeen, Sawyer held himself high in the saddle, riding alongside his father and the other men like he was truly one of them. The past few days together on the trail, his father had treated him as a grown man, allowing him to participate in the land discussions. He'd finally come of age, and the sense of pride he felt was enough to make him smile. Though negotiations were going well, the investors were reluctant to commit to the purchase. The War Between the States still raged full-force, limiting their available funds, making them think twice about acquiring land in western Nebraska. Land Sawyer's father owned.

Colonel McCade nodded toward Sawyer but spoke to Miles Rollins, a young senator from New York. "And my son would make a better leader than the lot of us. He runs the ranch, but wants to be a lawman and will make the finest."

"Ranching in this area must be profitable, but law—I think it would take quite a man to handle the law in western territories such as this." Senator Rollins darted a challenging glance toward Sawyer.

Sawyer held the man's gaze. He wasn't interested in the senator's continued remarks, but protecting peace and building the territory were respectable professions and something that would make his father proud. Little other than that mattered, though he was growing tired of the senator.

"You must be very proud to have sons to work with all this land you own," the senator continued looking back at the colonel.

"All four of my sons, even the youngest, are excellent cattlemen, riders and a better shot than any man I've ever led to war. They love this land and will serve the country well." The colonel answered proudly.

"Indeed. Yet the war continues, without you or your sons. Was your commission changed?" The senator's voice was innocent, but his implication was clear.

The colonel slowed his horse and eyed the senator without pause. "The war will end soon with the South's defeat. Look around you. With land such as this, unspoiled, would there not be enough so that all men, including those now kept as slaves, could own a plot of land where they could live, work and prosper?"

"With all due respect sir, slaves owning land?"

"Yet you serve the North in a fight to free such men. Would they not then have the right to their own property?" When the senator said no more, Colonel McCade continued. "I requested leave of my commission. The railroads must be built in spite of the war. As for my sons, only one is of age, but their fight is here—in the West, which *they* will settle."

Rollins pressed further. "And building the railroads and selling land fills your purse at the same time."

"I'm a soldier and businessman, Senator Rollins, just as you serve the government, but are here of your own interests." Colonel McCade smiled cynically and the senator nodded, allowing his horse to lag behind to wait for the other men.

Sawyer fought the urge to smile. His father had put the senator in his place. He had asked once about joining the war effort, he and his younger brother Wyatt. His father had forbidden any such idea, reminding them their war was at home, learning and enforcing the laws of the West.

Allowing his own horse to fall in behind the colonel's stallion, Sawyer took in vast prairies of green grass as far as the eye could see. Most of these men had never seen places like this, including the purple mountains in the distance which added to the view he would never take for granted. Large cliffs of dark gray rock hovered above them across the canyon, offering a bit of shade from the dreaded heat of mid-day. It was hard to think about a war going on back east when things around him were so peaceful.

Brett Morgan, his father's ranch foreman, rode up alongside him. "Tired of the cocky senator?"

"Just as soon kick his cocky ass," Sawyer grumbled, his gray eyes narrowing as he removed his hat and ran his hand through his thick dark hair.

"I know what you're thinking, and even if you *can* take down a man twice your size, let this one go. It'll be over soon enough." Brett chuckled.

"Father just wants to make the sale."

"Your father's a businessman, but he cares a lot more about what happens out here to the land than he does about the money. This is what he does. Listen, watch, and learn." Brett spat tobacco to the other side of his horse and looked at him again. "Go on." He nodded toward the colonel.

Sawyer spurred his horse ahead. Brett was right; he'd been allowed along on this trip to learn and that was what he needed to do. John McCade was in the business of showing political leaders and important government officials lands from Nebraska through Wyoming and Dakota Territories. It was no secret that he stood to make a great deal of money off expansion of the railroads, but it had never been about the money alone.

Sawyer lifted the reins and urged his horse onward, but just as he caught up, gunfire exploded from the north. Colonel McCade jolted in the saddle, clutching his chest with a groan. The men scattered, taking cover behind the rocks around them. Sawyer scrambled from his horse and grabbed his father. They fell to the ground, and the startled horse shied away with the commotion. Sawyer rolled and sat up, trying to make sense of what was going on. Blood. So much blood. He turned his father over. The white shirt was saturated crimson, and thick pools of coppery smelling blood soaked into the hard earth beneath him.

Colonel McCade opened his deep gray eyes and sucked in a shallow coughing breath. "Take...cover, son."

Sawyer yanked his shirt off and clamped it to his

father's chest. "No, I'm not leaving you."

Brett dropped beside them, his rifle poised in the direction of the gunfire.

"We gotta stop the bleeding." Sawyer's hands trembled as he increased the pressure on his father's wound.

"Who...was it?" Colonel McCade asked, his voice was fading.

"Lone horseman," Brett panted, still half-breathless. "Not sure."

Colonel McCade placed his hands on Sawyer's, stopping his efforts. "You *must*...learn the...law. Honor, not pride. The West will be settled...men like you and your brothers...will do it. Always remember, the...difference between justice...and revenge."

"Father?" Sawyer pressed harder, not wanting to say good-bye. He couldn't die, not like this. This wasn't supposed to happen.

"Keep your brothers together—always. Wyatt...needs direction, that quick temper. So...damn much like me." The colonel coughed with a slight chuckle. "Keep him grounded. All of you listen to Dawson. He's...very smart. You win him...he'll always have your back."

Sawyer nodded. Who had done this? His focus was lost, but he was listening to the words, taking the last of his father's voice to heart.

The colonel eyed Brett and gazed back at Sawyer. "Keep Evan out...of trouble. Mischief that boy, but a good...heart. He's a McCade, don't ever let him...forget that." His grip on Sawyer's hands weakened, and he closed his eyes.

"Father, you have to try." Sawyer's voice cracked

as tears streamed his cheeks.

"Your mother, heaven…help you boys." Colonel McCade opened his eyes again and smiled, his body shaking. "Dodge. I've always loved her…like no other. You find…that kind of love. Such…a good son, Sawyer." He touched Sawyer's cheek, meeting his son's gaze.

"Father?" The last breath of life drained from the man he had idolized his whole life. He pounded his fists against his father's bloody chest, willing him to live. But Colonel John McCade was gone.

A roar of deep guttural laughter echoed across the canyon, drawing Sawyer's attention. The lone horseman was no more than a silhouette as he rode in, circling closer. Sawyer ran toward his horse, only to be stopped by Brett, but not before he'd made eye contact with the man in the distance. The unknown rider gave a wicked smile, firing his rifle in the air, leaving behind nothing but his haunting laughter as he rode away.

Sawyer ripped himself from Brett's grip heading toward his horse once more. "I'll kill him!"

Brett gave chase and yanked him away from the frightened animal. "He'll kill *you*. This canyon's a trap for us all."

Sawyer struggled to gain his footing and jerked away from Brett, then realizing he had no chance at revenge, turned and fell to his knees beside his dead father. This couldn't be happening. He was supposed to bury his father when he was an old man. Not now. Not like this. He thought of Dodge and his brothers. How would he even tell them? Brett stood beside him, the other men in the expedition making their way closer.

"We'll bury him right here." Sawyer shook his

head. "He would hate for his body to be on display. *I'll tell my family.*" He would honor his father's wishes and his brothers would have no reason for revenge he would one day handle. "We're going to tell them we killed the man that did this—nothing more." He glanced up at Brett, who gave a simple nod of agreement.

Sawyer put one hand on his father's. He wiped his eyes, then removed his father's holster, the Union-issued revolver still cradled snugly in the leather. He stood and buckled the revolver low around his hips. While he wouldn't allow his brothers reason for revenge, he had no doubt he would avenge his father if it took him to his last breath on the earth. He stared in the direction where the unknown rider had long since vanished and gave a simple nod.

Chapter One

Cheyenne, Wyoming Territory, Fifteen Years Later

Sheriff Sawyer McCade tilted his hat back and stared hard at the woman before him. She was more than capable and no doubt sneaky enough, and it was apparent she had pulled it off.

"Dodge, why in hell would you do that?" He eyed his mother with caution but knew good and well she wasn't bluffing. She was always sticking her nose where it didn't belong, stirring up trouble of one kind or another.

She never flinched at the harshness of his tone, but glanced around the empty jail and back. "Because you're my eldest son and it's time you married and began producing my grandchildren." She placed a hand on her slender hip, not looking at all like anyone's fifty-five-year-old mother and much less like a *Dodge,* though she was both.

"Grandchildren?" He reached for his hat. So that was why she harped on him and his three brothers about settling down, not that one of them was listening.

"Yes and what would be so wrong with that?" Her eyebrows lifted, and the smile she gave him could have melted a bar of gold.

Grandchildren his right foot. He was all too familiar with the smug look on her face. She was hiding something, and it wasn't just the ordered bride.

She avoided his glare, spitting out a flurry of words. "She'll be on the afternoon train, and she's been several days getting here. Take her home to the ranch. She'll need a rest and a bath, so be nice enough to heat water for the tub."

"I don't need a wife. This right here isn't happening." He grabbed the jail keys and shoved them in his trouser pocket and stomped past her, spurs clinking along the hardwoods.

"I won't be home tonight, and it's your duty to protect her as sheriff." She was quick in rebuttal.

Sawyer balled his fists as she scurried toward the door ahead of him. How in the hell did she always back him into a corner? He folded his arms and uttered the one word he knew could stop her in her tracks. *"Mother."*

She spun on her heels, her blue eyes narrowing. Finally, he had her full attention. She didn't like being called anything but *Dodge* and he had the sudden urge to protect his ears from retaliation.

"What kind of woman answers an ad like that anyway?" His knowledge of ordered brides was limited, though he'd seen a number head right back where they came from after a few days in Cheyenne.

"Her name is Rose Parker, and she's from New York City—well-educated from what I understand. I thought you might just enjoy a challenge." She scuttled outside, pulling her riding gloves onto each of her hands.

Sawyer followed, rigid with anger and shaking his head. He should lock her up for being deceitful if nothing else. "You don't get to decide someone's fate

9

like that. You meddle too much." He caught her shoulder and wheeled her around, fully expecting that thump to the ear for his blatant disrespect. But her eyes softened.

"Sawyer, it's been what, twelve or more years? When are you going to let her go? I know you still wait." Her voice was little more than a whisper.

Sawyer winced as if an outlaw had rammed a fist right into his belly, the pain so intense he struggled to take a breath. It had been years. Fourteen to be exact, but who was counting? "I've *been* over it. Why do you keep bringing it back up?"

"Because, you haven't let go of her any more than you've let go of the pain of losing your father. Catherine's not coming back. Maybe the distraction of a good woman is just what you need."

She was right on both counts, though he wasn't about to admit it. He didn't need anyone, much less a woman, interfering with his work. "Keeping Cheyenne in order is distraction enough, and I have no intention of marrying some woman from back east." Catherine had made her decision long ago and he'd walked away for good, but that didn't mean he was going to marry some woman he didn't even know.

"Sawyer, I don't expect a marriage, but take some time to get to know her. You have a good heart. It's time you shared it with someone. Is wanting that so wrong of me?"

Sawyer growled under his breath, knowing it was futile to argue with the likes of Dodge. She always got what she wanted one way or another. "No, but did you ever think how unfair it is to this Miss Parker?" He fisted his hands once more. "She's going to be waiting for something that might never happen. What business does she have out here anyway?"

"Perhaps that's the first thing you should ask her." She placed a gloved palm to his cheek and walked toward her buggy.

"Yeah, right after I tell her this wasn't my idea." His belly clenched tighter, and his chest pounded. Somehow, Dodge was always right, and he cursed under his breath. He hadn't put Catherine behind him any more than he'd put away the demons haunting him over his father's death. Regardless, one woman could be more trouble than the worst gang of outlaws, and he wasn't looking for that kind of trouble.

He watched Dodge climb into her buggy and before he knew it, he found himself pacing outside the depot in wait of the bride he wasn't about to claim. He glanced at his pocket watch and sighed. The train from Council Bluffs was never late, and that it was today made him almost grateful. He shoved the watch into his vest pocket, secretly hoping the train had jumped its tracks.

He cursed to himself, still unable to believe Dodge had sent for a bride—for him. On second thought, he *could* believe it. Dodge was capable of anything. But why any woman would want to live in Cheyenne he hadn't a clue. It was no place for a civilized lady. Of course Dodge was an exception to the rule, but she could hold her own. Just look what she'd tossed his way—planned it all too well, including the part where she wouldn't be home. That meant she'd be with Brett Morgan, doing who knew what on his ranch adjoining McCade lands. Brett was a good man, but it was ridiculous for Dodge to carry on like she did. It caused talk, not that she paid it any attention.

Something wasn't right about this whole situation. He'd a mind to dump this mail-ordered-damsel at the hotel, but Cheyenne's only hotel was just as dangerous as a room at the saloon, and beyond a doubt no place for an unescorted woman from New York. Maybe he could pawn her off on one of his younger brothers. He shook his head. Wyatt was smitten with Tess Sullivan, the town doctor, though she wouldn't give him the time of day. And Dawson wouldn't work. No woman in her right mind would want to live in a cabin in the middle of nowhere with a husband who was never home. And surely not Evan. He might be interested, but he couldn't stay out of the local brothel to save his life.

Black smoke billowed in the distance, jerking him from his thoughts. The train hadn't jumped the tracks after all, and he was out of time to scheme. He kicked at the dirt, wishing there was a better way to release his frustration—a nice brawl with a gang of miners at the saloon would do. How was he to recognize this Miss Parker anyway? Worse yet, what would he even say to her? He watched in misery as the train rolled into the depot, steam blowing across the docks, stirring up dust. The noisy engine chugged to a slow and grinding stop. He thought about turning tail to run. But there'd be Dodge and his own conscious to answer to, and he didn't want to face either one.

The conductor placed a stepstool at the only car carrying passengers instead of livestock. Sawyer took a deep breath and watched as men and couples exited the train. After a time, he began to relax. Maybe she'd missed the train or changed her mind. Just as he'd begun to think he'd dodged the bullet after all, the conductor helped a young woman to the dock. She wore a fancy green dress that narrowed at the waist, and flared to a full skirt, not something he was used to seeing. Cheyenne women wore long calico dresses or simple blouses with long skirts. This woman's corset was tight enough that the tops of her breasts stirred up a thought or two he shouldn't entertain.

Rose Parker. It had to be. And she was beautiful, with a slight build, ivory skin, and blonde hair piled on top of her head. Her pale blue eyes smiled her thanks to the conductor, and for a moment he was so caught up he forgot to breathe. He gulped for air. She couldn't be more than twenty, but there was no way she was prepared for the world she had just stepped into. He watched as she sat on a bench and placed her bag beside her, glancing across town and then in his direction.

He froze, but then she smiled and drained what reserve he had left. Cursing Dodge one final time, he walked toward her on legs that didn't seem to want to move.

Her gaze fixed on his badge as she stood. "Sheriff McCade?"

He nodded, that being all he could manage for the moment. *Son of a bitch.* She was breathtaking up close.

"It's actually hard to believe I'm here." Uncertainty tinged her voice.

"I trust your trip went well." Hell, he had to say something, but cringed, knowing without a doubt, it had been miles of eating dust in sweltering heat, even by train.

"The trip was long, but not as bad as I might have thought. I'm Rose Parker." She held out a slender hand.

He shook it, letting go quickly. "Is this—" he reached for her bag—"all you have?" He'd expected a woman from New York would arrive with trunks of unnecessary items.

"My other things will ship when I send for them."

He held her gaze. Her other things? Was she not planning on staying if things didn't work out? Maybe she wasn't any more sold on this idea than he was. But then why would she travel all this way? He shook his head slightly. With any luck, she would opt out of her agreement, and he could send her back to New York on the next train.

"I thought it best to travel with just a few things as I wasn't sure of the..." she hesitated, "accommodations." The slight blush across her cheeks was rather amusing. Surely she knew she'd have a room of her own? Or did she think westerners were savages, and she would find herself in his bed as soon as she arrived.

He fought off the image, and while the thought was entertaining, he forced it out of his mind. He turned on his heels, spurs clicking and motioned with a nod for her to follow. "I'll see to a wagon for getting you to the ranch." He was keenly aware of her gaze on him as they walked toward the jail. Best if she waited on him there, given she'd already caught the gaze of every man they'd passed, including the no-goods hanging outside the saloon. He glared a hard warning in their direction and picked up the pace.

****

Rose scurried to keep up with Sheriff McCade, wondering why he hadn't thought of a wagon before now. At least he had met her as planned. The trip was long, and she didn't anticipate there would be further travel once she got off the train. She should have known he might not live right in the town of Cheyenne. He had said something about a ranch. Well at least he wasn't whisking her off to the preacher and right into his bed. Unless he planned to bypass the preacher part. She shivered.

He opened the jailhouse door, set her bag on a chair, and turned to face her. "There's water in the pitcher and no prisoners right now. I'll be back."

"I'll be fine." Her pulse raced. This all felt like a terrible dream, but at least it wasn't the nightmare she had left behind.

He hesitated, then headed across the dusty road toward the livery without a backward glance. He didn't say much, and while she usually wasn't at a loss for words, the whole thing was overwhelming enough to keep her well-rehearsed lines at bay.

She moseyed to the door and took the opportunity to examine him while he wasn't looking. He was quite handsome, with his deep gray eyes and tall muscular build. Dark hair touched his collar, and his close-cut beard revealed the hint of a dimple in his chin. He wore a holstered gun strapped low around his narrow hips, but he was far from the gruff, unkempt sheriff of her imagination.

She brushed the dust from her dress, contemplating her situation. She'd somehow escaped the evils of New York, but now wondered of becoming an instant bride. Max Ferguson, a lawyer and her cousin Muriel's husband, had assured her that this was the best way for her to hide given the circumstances. At the time she had agreed. But now, after arriving in Cheyenne she wondered if trading her chastity for safety would indeed be worth it.

She peered at the buildings along the main road. Many looked new or freshly painted, like the bank down the way, but others were in need of repair. There was a mercantile, post office, hotel, and even a barbershop. The large number of merchants surprised her. Cheyenne wasn't a modern town by any means, but it offered more than she would've thought.

The sheriff shook his head at the old mare offered to him and pulled a buggy, not a wagon, by hand toward the jail. The dark brown quarter horse tied just outside the jail was probably his. She walked outside onto the porch, taking a closer look at the large animal. Near seventeen hands and gelded as were most good riding horses. *Well, at least her knowledge of horses would be of some use to her in a place like this.*

The sheriff let go of the buggy, his gray eyes piercing and clear. "You need to wait inside." His stern tone caught her off guard.

"I was just—"

"Wait inside." His deep voice lowered an octave.

"I beg your pardon? I was just admiring the town." This might not be the city of New York, but she would not be disrespected.

He stepped around the buggy, narrowing his brows. "Miss Parker, look behind me."

The dangerously calm edge to his voice struck unknown fear inside her, but she turned her gaze toward the saloon. Several men stared at them—at her, their leers leaving no doubt as to their intentions. She was accustomed to men taking second glances at her, even along the streets of New York, but this was something entirely different. Still, he didn't need to boss her as though she was his. She wasn't. Not yet, anyway. She turned back to the sheriff and shrugged as though being ogled by unkempt men of the plains was nothing to worry about.

His jaw tensed, and he stepped even closer, blocking her with his body. So close she could smell leather and the surprising aroma of actual soap. "Those are cowboys, miners, men from the railroad and God knows who else. And they're all watching you. Now, step back inside before things get interesting."

Rose obeyed at last but couldn't resist a final challenge. "How am I to live here, if I cannot be seen in town?"

He glared at her before turning back to work on the buggy hitch. "That's why I'm taking you to the ranch. Cheyenne isn't safe for any lady, much less one dressed like you." He untied the horse, and his tone was that of annoyance.

Rose huffed and peered down at her gown, one of her best. "I dressed very appropriately for the trip."

He removed the saddle from the horse and sat it in the back of the buggy, turning to face her. "But not for walking the streets of Cheyenne. It's rare for men like these to see a woman, much less one from New York in a fancy dress."

Heat shot to her cheeks as his gaze scanned her breasts, and she shrunk back from the doorway. She hadn't fled all this distance only to find herself in a much worse situation. She took another step back into the relative darkness of the jail. Would she ever feel safe enough, again? Maybe Cheyenne wasn't the best plan after all.

The sheriff turned his full attention to the less-than-easy task of hitching the horse to the buggy. The animal didn't seem to want to be controlled, and there was some part of her that could understand as much.

"Colonel, easy boy." His voice was tender, but firm, and the horse settled into place, and somehow her own pulse lessened for the moment. Oh Lord, what was she even doing here? But there had been little by the way of options for her.

"He isn't used to being hitched like that." It was a statement, not a question. She knew horses, and this one didn't like the idea of the buggy.

"He's just ornery. Ready?" The sheriff didn't even look at her as he spoke.

"Of course." She walked to the buggy, and gathered her dress, finding the step higher than she had expected. When she hesitated, the sheriff grabbed her by the waist and plopped her inside before she could quite realize what was happening. His strong hands on her waist sent shivers up her spine and she flushed at the sensation. "Thank you," she said, willing her voice to remain steady.

He retrieved her bag in silence and tossed it in the back beside the saddle. Then he climbed in and snapped the reins, heading them out of town to Lord knew where. Maybe it was best. Rose peeked at him from the corner of her eye, almost afraid of further direct eye contact. But if she were to be his bride, and she wasn't sure of that yet, she needed to be able to talk to him. She gathered her courage. "Cheyenne is bigger than I anticipated," she said, hoping to get him talking. Max had said he was the best lawman he'd ever known and insisted she would be safe with him.

He nodded but didn't even glance her way. The heat of his nearness played across the skin of her arm and side, spreading warmth through her center. Or was that simply the heat of the summer in Cheyenne?

She tried again, wanting to know more of him that Max hadn't been able to tell her. "I mean it's really more settled than what I read about."

He only shrugged.

All right, if he wasn't going to say anything perhaps a question would do, though she waited a minute. "How long have you been sheriff?"

"Nine, ten years." He finally glanced at her, then back to the sandy road ahead.

"That's a long time to be sheriff from what I have read, what with outlaws and Indians." She steadied her hands, wondering whether their trembling was caused by her current situation or the one she had left behind.

"You read about lawmen?" He cocked an eyebrow her direction, callused hands remaining on the reins.

Just like a man. Mention his job and he was ready to chat. Maybe things weren't so different in Cheyenne after all. "I read a great deal about living in the West. One of my favorite books was called *Settling the West*. Have you read it?"

His chuckle caught her off guard. "My father wrote it."

"John McCade." She studied the name as it crossed her lips. "I didn't think of the connection, but it's a wonderful book on building prosperous cities in the West."

"He wrote a number of books, mostly about law." A nerve in his jaw ticked, and his gray eyes hardened. "Before he died."

"I'm sorry." She knew what it was like to lose a father, but she could also tell he wouldn't welcome her compassion.

"It's fine." Obviously it wasn't. Well, at least she knew more about him than she had.

She turned her attention to the surroundings, tired of trying to force him to talk. Now that they were outside of town, the rolling hills held tall green grasses, and the mountains in the distance rose to breathtaking heights against the clear blue sky. The Big Horn Mountains she guessed. She'd never seen a sight so lovely in New York. She lost herself in the peacefulness around her, forcing her mind to go completely blank so that it wouldn't wander back to the last few weeks. The easy rhythm of the buggy and the roll of the wheels against the hard-packed dirt road lulled her into a trance until his words, sharp and unexpected, jostled her back to reality.

"Why did you come here?"

Her mouth dropped open, and no words would come, her breath taken with the impact of his words. Was he seriously asking her reasons when he had met her at the train as planned? As far as he should be concerned, she was an ordered bride and she wouldn't be telling anything more than that. She gulped and forced her words. "I...I responded to your advertisement."

He shook his head, and a bitter half-laugh escaped him. "New York must be full of men suited to be a husband, especially for a woman such as yourself."

She forced herself to meet his gaze. She might one day tell him her reasons, but it wouldn't be today. "My father talked of the West, telling stories of his travels with Lewis and Clark. I suppose I have his same sense of adventure." In truth, her sense of adventure was limited, but she'd had little choice. She had weighed her options, made her decisions, and was now following through.

"Your father traveled with Lewis and Clark?" A note of interest echoed in his tone.

"As a very young man. He drew maps." She had always been proud of her father's accomplishments, and he seemed equally impressed.

"Why not adventure without opting for marriage?"

She would have preferred to talk about her father's travels, but the sheriff seemed adamant about getting an answer, so she turned it around. "Why then, did you send for a bride?"

He pulled up on the reins, and the buggy jerked to a sudden halt, sending Rose scrambling for a hold. She glared at him in shock. *What on earth?*

He shook his head, his gray eyes dark. "Miss Parker, I think it's only fair to tell you. I didn't send for you."

"What?" Panic gripped her and her heart dropped, the pain in her chest as physical as if she had been thrown from the buggy. What could that mean? This had all been planned for her protection, and he didn't know or understand anything about it given his questions. Something had gone very wrong.

"Dodge, my mother, sent for you without my knowledge." He spoke softly as if choosing his words carefully.

His mother? Rose's heart thudded against her ribs, and she closed her fists to keep her hands from shaking even more. "I don't understand…" She gazed out

21

across the vast prairie before them, unable to put any of it together. Perspiration collected on her brow, and she was aware it wasn't from the heat of Cheyenne but the fear that pulsed through her.

He fiddled with the reins in his calloused hands, drawing her attention. "I knew nothing about you until about an hour before your train came in."

How was this even happening? Rose fought back tears that she wasn't sure were from disappointment or perhaps—relief. So, she was suddenly free from a marriage she hadn't really wanted, but this changed everything.

"I can assure you, you'll be safe until I can arrange for your return home."

Home? Terror flooded through her at the word. No, she couldn't go back there. Even if Cheyenne was a dangerous place and even if he didn't want her. She'd have to do something, go somewhere. Anywhere would be better than home. She swallowed hard, the bile rising in her throat. "Then would you be so kind as to return to town, where I can inquire about a hotel room?" She could not turn back now, and with any luck Max would let her know soon that her marriage, that wasn't—had been annulled. Maybe it was best that she would not be married right away. At least she wouldn't be breaking any laws.

"Not safe." His voice was stern.

His comment almost made her laugh of all things. If he had only known what she had been through. The last few weeks of her life had been enough to teach her all she ever wanted to know about being—not safe.

"There won't be another train for a few weeks, and the ranch is guarded. No harm will come to you there."

He whistled and Colonel pulled the buggy forward again.

No Harm. She said the words over and over in her head until they didn't sound like words anymore. Max's well-laid plans were falling apart—and with them her life. She fought to find her courage again. Miles passed and she only stared dazed—shocked. What would she do? Once again her choices were limited.

"The ranch is just ahead." He slowed the buggy as they topped a ridge, startling her back from her thoughts.

Rose forgot her troubles for a moment, breathless at the view of such a huge ranch. The house was painted white and had several levels. There were a number of barns with fencing and corrals. The land rolled into green fields sprinkled with cattle in every direction. Horses grazed in pastures beyond the house and bunkhouses stood further away. A small river broke up the vast amount of green land with a deep sapphire blue.

"You live here alone?" She couldn't see how one man needed such a large home in a place like Cheyenne.

"With my mother and two brothers," he explained, loosening his grip on the reins. "My youngest brother, Evan, is away herding cattle to market, and Wyatt's in Denver taking a prisoner for trial. But Dawson lives in a cabin thirty minutes hard ridin' from here."

"And your mother is here now?" She was very interested in meeting the woman who had sent for her in his stead, and she had to wonder just who knew what about her.

"She'll be here tomorrow." He hopped out and

went to her side of the buggy. He helped her down, letting go of her the moment her feet touched the ground. Without even looking at her, he grabbed her bag and led the way to the house.

She followed him inside to the parlor, still feeling as if she couldn't focus on any one thing. Her pulse raced and her mind whirled around what she should do, but the inside of the home was beautiful and modern to her surprise. Expensive furniture seemed out of place for a ranch so far west. There were paintings on the walls, flowers in vases, and even strips of fancy rugs along the polished wooden floors. A real home, not a filthy cabin in the middle of nowhere as she had feared.

"You can take a room upstairs." He turned and started up without another word.

She gathered her dress and held tightly to the railing, relieved she'd have her own room for the time being. At least he wasn't taking her to his bed, but then again the thought of him sending her back to New York was even more frightening. She entered the room as he plopped her bag down with a thud, right on the bed.

"I'll fetch some hot water. There's a tub in the water closet across the hall, drains outside." He shoved his hands into the pocket of his trousers and rocked back on his heels, looking at the ceiling, out the window—anywhere but at her.

"I would appreciate it." Her face flushed with heat, but she had been looking forward to washing up, the train having offered little in that respect. Perhaps the hot water would calm her racing heart and provide the courage she had lost once more.

The spurs of his heavy boots clanked each step as he retreated down the stairs without so much as another word. She sat on the bed, looking around and exhaling softly. Sheriff Sawyer McCade was treating her as a fine houseguest, yet it was difficult to feel welcome when he'd apparently been tricked into having her in his care.

She'd been prepared to become an instant wife once more, but her fast-made plans, now destroyed, left only mounting fear. Sniffling, she blinked back tears and stood to unpack her things. Well, she had conquered the worst of her demons by leaving New York behind her, and while she might know very little about living in a western town, she did know a thing or two about men. The sheriff was honorable, of that she was sure. And if he wanted her at the ranch for her protection, she would stay and there might just be the slightest chance if she played her cards right, she would be successful in changing the stubborn sheriff's mind.

Chapter Two

Mei Ling turned to Sawyer, speaking in her usual broken English. "I see bride arrive. I prepare nice meal."

Sawyer stopped cold. The cherry wood table in the dining room was set for two and with the fancy Sunday dishes. "She is not my bride."

"In China, arrange marriage work fine."

"This is not an arranged marriage. This is Dodge up to her usual antics, and you right along with her." He wanted to curse out loud. Long time friend to Dodge, Mei Ling had always felt free to speak her mind. After all, she'd done as much to raise the McCade boys as their own mother.

"Dinner on table half hour. Wear clean shirt." Mei Ling scurried back toward the kitchen, speaking to herself in her native Chinese tongue.

Sawyer slammed through the back door. As if the situation wasn't bad enough, Mei Ling was in on everything as well. He shouldn't have doubted it for a minute, she and Dodge being thick as thieves. How would he get through dinner, given he was still all stirred up by thoughts of Miss Parker upstairs bathing in the hot water he'd added to the tub? Worse still was the shock on her face when he told her the truth that he hadn't sent for her.

Groaning, he wished for drunken cowboys or a

gang of outlaws to shoot up Cheyenne, so he'd be called away to play sheriff. Dealing with the likes of outlaws had to be easier than dealing with Miss Parker and the way she looked in that dress. Well, he'd get through dinner and the next few weeks and then send Miss Parker back east. The sooner she was gone and out of his mind, the sooner he could work without distraction.

He stomped out a bit of the frustration and then made his way back inside to clean up for dinner. A freshly pressed white shirt lay stiffly across his bed. Mei Ling again. He rolled his eyes but snatched up the starched garment, shucking his more comfortable one in favor of being presentable. He walked to the small mirror and ran a comb through his dark hair and headed to the dining room, wishing like hell he were somewhere else—anywhere else.

The house smelled of fried chicken, roasted potatoes, and fresh baked bread, but it wasn't likely he'd be eating, given the knot in his stomach. He eyed the serving dishes again. This was a farce. The door behind him creaked, and he turned thinking it once again Mei Ling, but it was Miss Parker who met his gaze, and he damn near lost his breath.

"It smells wonderful." Rose inhaled deeply, her chest rising enticingly with the action.

Sawyer forced the air from his lungs, then back in. She had bathed and changed into a blue dress the same color as her eyes. Her light hair was tied with a matching ribbon that flowed down her back and he could darn well smell her lemon verbena perfume from where he stood. She walked to the far side of the dining room to view a set of framed photographs, hanging near the fancy wooden hutch. His father had taken them long ago, and while he hadn't paid that much attention to them of late, her interest was cause enough for him to step closer. At least he told himself it was her interest in the pictures.

"These are really beautiful." The sincerity in her voice touched him unexpectedly. He reminded himself she wasn't staying, nor did he want her to.

"My father took most of those for his books."

She traced a finger along the ridge in one picture. "This is the land this ranch is built on isn't it?"

She was observant, he'd give her that. The land looked nothing like the picture anymore. "Father saw its potential. He owned a lot of land, but this was his favorite plot."

"I watched from the train for all those miles. It's so beautiful and untouched out here." She turned to face him, folding her hands together.

"Uh, Miss Parker…would you—" He motioned to the table, thinking the terrain wasn't the only thing beautiful. *Son of a bitch.* He was usually good with women. Well, he was good at some things with women, but talking wasn't one of them. He watched her for a moment, wondering of her complete change in demeanor, not as upset as he'd left her.

"Please call me Rose."

He cleared his throat. "Uh. Rose…" Saying her given name was asking for trouble, but she was waiting and he needed dinner behind him. "Would you like to sit?" *Holy hell!* He plopped down and grabbed his fork. When she didn't sit, he glanced up and scolded himself for his lack of manners. At the same time, he was reluctant to make her too comfortable, after all she wasn't staying. Nevertheless, he rose to appease her.

"Uh…allow me." He pulled her chair back, and she held the skirt of her dress so she could sit. Scooting her in, he was consumed by her scent once more—not to mention the view of round, creamy breasts pushed high by her corset. He forced his eyes away, shaking his head and finding his seat again.

"Thank you." She placed her napkin in her lap.

Sawyer stabbed at the chicken and shoved a bite in his mouth. When he saw she wasn't eating, he finished chewing the food he hadn't even tasted, swallowing hard. Now what? He watched as she picked up her own fork, her arms held daintily at the edge of the table. Ah, shit! Removing his elbows from the table, he picked up his napkin and tucked it across his lap, trying to recall table manners long since put away. She was waiting on him to say a prayer no doubt, but enough was enough. He might help her with her chair, but he wasn't praying. He snatched up his fork and continued eating.

"I met Mei Ling a little while ago when you were outside. How long has she worked for you?" She finally picked up her fork and knife, placing them correctly but not digging into her food yet.

He wiped his mouth. Is that how she saw it? A natural mistake, he supposed. "She isn't hired. She and my mother are long-time friends."

"Oh. Does she have a family?" She took a tiny bite of her chicken and chewed, using her linen napkin to wipe her mouth.

"Her husband died in a railroad accident years ago. She helped raise me and my brothers. *We're* her family." Not that he intended to get into *that* story tonight.

When he didn't continue, she spoke again. "This is quite good compared to the food on board the train."

"Mei Ling cooks, all but Sundays. Dodge cooks then." He sipped his coffee, wishing he had something stronger to wash down his discomfort. Rotgut whiskey might do the trick.

"So when will I get to meet Mrs. McCade?" She sipped her water and her tone went up an octave. "Perhaps I should meet the woman who…sent for me."

Sawyer cringed. Was that a challenge? The details of Dodge's current location would be better left alone, but Rose's sarcasm deserved an honest answer. "Dodge is…visiting a friend."

She peered at him with her intense blue eyes, and he wondered if she was going to press the issue, but she merely took a bite of the roasted potatoes and changed the subject. "So, as sheriff, are you in town most days?"

"Yep." That wasn't a lie, exactly. Cheyenne never slept, and even if he did have a day on the ranch, he was often called into town for problems.

"What does a sheriff do all day long?"

"Keep the saloon quiet. Arrest those that are out of order, keep things safe, head off trouble early." He shrugged. Surely he'd never eaten a more difficult meal—or had a harder time keeping his eyes on his plate. She had the fairest skin, ivory and flawless, unlike the few women in Cheyenne who carried the deep tanned skin from hard work outdoors.

"There must be more than that."

Shit, this was growing old. "Keep drunks off the street and whores in the brothel." Whores. Why did he have to say that? He stabbed at the meat on his plate once more. He needed a moment. He needed air.

She went back to her food with a simple nod.

He finished eating, but the silence was as nerve-wracking as all her questions had been. While he had no intentions of marrying her, he didn't have to be rude. "I know a lawman from New York. Max Ferguson. Met him around a year ago."

The color drained from her face, and she went as pale as she had earlier. She nearly choked on her food, grabbing her napkin as she coughed. "Oh. Mr. Ferguson. He bought horses from my father, I believe. I don't know much about him though."

So she knew Max Ferguson and given how she was dressed, he had no doubts she came from money. Real money. While that mattered little to him, it said a lot about who she was and how well she'd cope living in Cheyenne. Still, the mention of Max seemed to startle her somehow, and he wondered why. He knew the look she carried well. She was hiding something.

"Horses?" he asked, wondering what she might give away.

She seemed to struggle to gather her composure. "My father raised Arabians. It was more of a hobby before he died."

"Arabians." So she did know horses. He'd suspected as much given the way she'd watched Colonel earlier. "That's an expensive hobby." If true, it meant she'd been born to wealth, and something didn't add up. Why would a rich woman of her beauty need to leave the luxury of New York behind for a place like Cheyenne?

She flushed red, her tone curt. "Actually, Chestnut Arabians. My father took great care of the horses and yes, they were expensive."

31

For a moment he wanted to grin. She was just as beautiful flustered as calm. Yeah, she definitely had a story, and there was something captivating in her feisty, quick temper.

"I'm sorry," he offered.

She met his gaze, eyes suspicious, but then relaxed against her chair back. "Apology accepted."

"Good. I thought you were about to send a dagger my way."

"I wouldn't do that." She glared at him again, and a smile slowly emerged.

Against his better judgment, he smiled in response, though the effort was difficult. If he wanted to know her story, he had to play his part, but he saw through to her vulnerability. She was scared and something inside him didn't like it.

"So the sheriff can smile?"

"I smile." *When I can breathe.*

"Well, you should do it more often."

Mei Ling marched in and set a small plate of round cakes on the table. "Moon cake of China." She bowed and exited quickly.

Sawyer wanted to growl, but was grateful Mei Ling's entrance had pulled them both from the moment.

Rose picked up a small fork, tasting the cake. "This is nice, not so sweet but certainly far from chocolate mousse." She took another bite, sighing and closing her eyes for a moment.

So she liked fine chocolate desserts. It figured, but Sawyer couldn't take his eyes off the way she placed the fork in her mouth, closing her eyes with a sigh of satisfaction. What would those rosy lips look like enveloping—never mind. He shifted in his seat. He had no business thinking thoughts like that about a lady, especially one he wasn't interested in. He was ready for escape. and if those renegades would ramble in to town real soon, he'd be a happy man.

"Uhmm, these are wonderful. You don't care for moon cakes?" She asked, licking her lips.

"Sometimes." He'd been treated to the cakes most of his life, but watching her eat was far more interesting.

"Would it be all right if I took a look around the ranch?" she asked. "Perhaps you could show me?"

Sawyer thought about it. Well, there was no time like the present, and the sooner he got her settled for the evening, the less he had to deal with her. He stood, tossing his napkin down. When she scurried to stand, he sat. With her standing, he was up again as manners would call for, but she sat as he stood once more. She let out a hesitant giggle.

He held his hand up to stop her from standing again. "Wait." He found the humor in the situation in spite of his frustration, and this time allowed a real grin to escape. "Would you like to see the ranch?" He pulled out her chair.

"Thank you." She stood, still wearing a heated blush along with her smile.

"The sun will be setting soon." He turned and led the way, seeking the relief of fresh air.

"It's such a large ranch and the house is beautiful," she said once outside.

"We added to the house a few years ago. Made some changes, like the bathtub." The picture of her bathing rose to the forefront of his mind once again and with it, his—interest. *Shit.*

"It was nice to get a real bath." She caught up to him.

I'm sure the hell it was. As much as he tried to push the mental picture of her bathing from his mind he couldn't. He pointed to the smaller barns as they strolled and focused on telling her about what she was seeing. "Those are for winter hay reserves."

"I've read the winters can be brutal."

"Is there anything you haven't read?" When she only gave him a knowing smile he continued, fighting to keep his mind fixed to the task. "We had two blizzards last year, but that doesn't happen often."

"I read a few things to prepare for the trip, but I also worked for the newspaper."

"You worked?" He shoved his hands in the pockets of his trousers and followed her gaze to the horses in the corral. If she came from money, and apparently she did, then why would she have need to work?

"I wrote women's articles for a small paper in the city." Pride tinged her voice.

When she said no more, he pointed out the bunkhouses, and as he might have suspected, a few of the hands were outside having a smoke and looking his way. He led her toward the barn. At least inside they wouldn't be on display. He didn't need to be the brunt of bunkhouse gossip any more then he needed his brother's teasing, though both would surely come. What in the hell had Dodge been thinking?

"We've had this barn for about six years." He walked to Colonel's stall and patted the horse on the side of the neck.

"So Colonel, after your father?" She gave the horse a slight scratch to the chin, and Colonel dipped his head as if she was offering a bit of food.

He nodded. Her perceptiveness would be to her advantage, having ventured so far alone. "Most of our horses stay here, in the corral outside."

She took a full turn around the barn, looking at everything and stopping to pet a few horses. She seemed very comfortable with the animals. A smile played around her pink lips, and Sawyer leaned against Colonel's stall, finding her entertainment rather amusing.

"So how many cattle do you have on the ranch?"

"Two to three thousand head." He wasn't sure as Evan handled running the ranch for the most part, but his estimate was close.

"The New York papers often reported the falling prices of the cattle market."

"The market rises and falls, but we do all right." What the hell hadn't this woman read? Now he understood Dodge's meaning behind ordering an educated woman. He found himself caught up in the conversation in spite of himself.

She wandered to a stall closer to him and rubbed the horse inside. "Why did you become sheriff?"

That was a loaded question. He enjoyed the law, liked keeping order, but there was more. More he wasn't about to discuss right now. "My father lectured me and Wyatt out of the books he wrote. It seemed to come natural. Father was a lawyer, though he was more interested in the writing of laws and mapping the land with pictures for the railroad."

"All your brothers didn't study law with him?"

Sawyer shrugged. "Dawson was never interested, much to my father's chagrin, and Evan was too young at the time."

"Well, it's admirable work. The crime in New York requires a surprising number of lawmen. So much crime." She turned back to the horse, smothering a yawn. "I suppose the trip was more wearying than I thought."

"It's gettin' dark anyway." The sooner he got her back inside and away from him, he'd be able to take the deep breath he'd been needing since she'd arrived.

Outside the barn, the sun dipped behind the mountains to the west, leaving the deep blue sky of the darkening prairie in its wake. He followed her up the porch steps. At the top, she turned to face him.

"Thank you for the tour. The ranch is really beautiful."

"If there's anything you need..." He aimed for courtesy, unsure of his ability to offer anything else and unsettled by his urges to offer far more. He'd leave Dodge to deal with her tomorrow and escape back to town.

Her gaze captured his and vulnerability shone in her eyes. As brave as she was trying to be, she was lost. She'd been covering it well, but it was late and she was tired. "Miss Parker, I still feel out of sorts as I know you do."

"Rose," she corrected.

"Rose. I want to reassure you." He took a step closer. "I mean I hadn't planned on a marriage, not that you aren't—well, you are very..." *Hell!* She was beautiful. Damn beautiful. And it had taken a lot of courage for her to travel so far to an uncertain future. "Well, a lady like you. I didn't want you to think my hesitation was due to...you."

"A lady like me? You keep saying that." She folded her arms around herself.

"A lady raised in the big city with money, beauty. New York must have offered you a husband and an easier life than Wyoming."

She held his gaze. "Not everyone seeks an easy life, Sheriff McCade."

"But women like you don't become ordered brides." He'd meet her where she was leading.

"You don't know me. Perhaps I am not like other women." Her fists clenched and her body stiffened. Her quick posturing made him want to chuckle, but he'd rather get to the bottom of her story. She was still dodging the question no doubt.

"I'm a lawman, remember, and I read people very well. I know when I'm only hearing part of a story."

Her blue eyes narrowed, and that too-enticing flush lit her cheeks to a bright pink. She darted past him to look out across the ranch and then spoke. "I came here looking for a new life. Accepting a husband is a means to survival for any woman in the West. But getting here and finding out you didn't send for me—" She swung around. "Well that's certainly a relief. I thought I was going to step off the train in Cheyenne, be whisked to the judge and right into your bed. Frankly, that idea was rather frightening."

Was she trying to be funny? It wasn't that the thought hadn't crossed his mind. Bedding her would be more than interesting, but he didn't need a wife. Not right now. "Then why are you here?"

"I wanted to see the West and find adventure like I told you. So why not start here? Did you read the papers I sent?" She shook her head realizing he hadn't.

"I suppose your mother got those."

He supposed so, too.

"I filled in my application." She took a deep breath, "And I realized I had led an incredibly normal life. An only child, raised by my father, schooled in the proper etiquette, sent to university, and spoiled to the point I hadn't lived for myself. I am here to create a new life—my life. If you do not wish to marry, I will find my own way, which is probably best anyway." She stared out across the horizon, blinking back tears.

"You can't stay here alone, not in Cheyenne. I'll get your fare paid and send you home."

She snapped around and glared at him. "I will not be returning home, regardless of a marriage. You have no idea what I am capable of, and I think that makes me somewhat of a—thorn in your side?"

Sawyer wasn't sure which was more annoying, her presence and will to stay or the thoughts she made him think. She wasn't a thorn, but damned if he'd be able to sleep with her in the same house for any length of time.

When he only nodded, a knowing smile spread across her face. "Good."

As furious as he was, he couldn't take his eyes off the sway of her hips as she spun around and went inside. She couldn't possibly think she would be staying in Cheyenne as an unescorted woman. Well, he had no intention of marrying her either, and one way or the other he'd see her on a train back to New York if it was the last thing he did.

Chapter Three

"Call me Dodge. I've never been good at being Mrs. McCade." Dodge smiled at Rose as they prepared the Sunday evening meal together.

The first few days on the ranch were more pleasant by having Dodge and Mei Ling to talk with. And helping prepare a few of the meals made her feel useful, or at least kept her mind from whirling around her situation.

"Where did you get the name Dodge?" Rose asked, her hands embedded in the bowl of thick dough. She enjoyed the conversations with Dodge, who acted much younger than her age. She was a very attractive woman, tall and slender with light hair and high cheekbones. Her blue eyes were bright and danced when she talked.

Dodge stirred a pot of simmering stew and added chopped vegetables. "I was raised by my grandfather, from a young girl. He was a shopkeeper and needed my help, but of course I was off doing what I wanted most of the time. He said I was good at *dodging* chores. Somehow, over the years, the name just stuck. I learned a great deal from him."

Dodge turned to grab the plate of chopped onions and continued. "He taught me a woman does have the right to think for herself and the business skills that have benefitted me my entire life. I suppose that is why John was so interesting to me. He was excellent at

39

business, and I fell for his aspirations to build a new country."

Rose thought about that. A woman did have the right to think for herself, and that is just what she had done in leaving New York—well, not entirely. She didn't know what she was going to do now, but if Sawyer didn't come around, she would find her own way just as she told him she would.

"What happened to Colonel McCade, if I am not imposing?" Rose asked, continuing to knead the dough.

Dodge began without the least hesitation. "He headed up a lot of the development of the lands where railroads were to be built. We moved here when the boys were young, before Dawson and Evan were born, even before there was a real town."

Rose listened, trying to imagine Sawyer as a youngster and Dodge with four young boys.

"John was shot out on a scouting tour with officials. We don't know the full details, or who the man was, only that John's men killed him. Sawyer was with them, and he will not speak of it, never really has."

"I'm sorry, I am sure it was hard to raise your sons on your own." Rose shaped the dough into a round ball, pressing firmly.

Dodge shrugged. "Sawyer was seventeen and the other boys right behind him, all but Evan, who was only ten. They took it hard, especially Wyatt. He is so much like John to this day, the same temperament. They butted heads a lot, but when John died they all struggled in one way or another. One day I finally sat them down and reminded them how their father had made them men from the day they were born. They were all named from the last names of soldiers John admired—ones he thought good men. I told them to cry all they wanted that day, and then they were never to cry about it again. Frankly, I was tired of grieving myself."

"I suppose that is how I ended up here. After losing my father, I needed something new." Rose hesitated. "My father always spoiled me and when he died, I realized this *was* the rest of my life. I wanted something different. As I told you, I've never had to cook or work for anything and something's not right about that." It wasn't the full truth, but it was some of it. Her father had spoiled her, but he had also pushed her to make the highest marks in school and university and to excel in showing his horses, that was until his health began to fail.

"You are doing fine with that bread. You'll be cooking all we make around here in no time. There is also nothing wrong with your reasons for seeking something new. I still want to apologize again for not being truthful in my scheming along with Max to keep you hidden. I suppose I thought it would be a good idea for Sawyer to think you were a mail-order-bride I had sent for in his name. He's a good man who needs the right kind of woman. Perhaps someone like you." Dodge's clear blue eyes offered her nothing more than the freedom to choose her own path, though it was evident she was hopeful she was the woman for Sawyer.

She had accepted the apology, though it settled her nerves little. Max was the one who had assured her over and over that the plan to become a bride was a better way of hiding. A marriage offered her a name change and protection until her ill fated marriage could be annulled, though it was unlikely that would happen any time soon. But she hadn't known of Dodge's involvement and neither Max nor Dodge had planned on Sawyer's lack of participation in the well laid plans.

"Well, learning to bake bread is one thing, but Sawyer isn't very happy with me I suppose." She wondered how much was too much to tell regarding the conversations she and Sawyer had shared. He was just downright angry with her if she had to guess.

"Sawyer can be a hard man to read sometimes." Dodge washed her hands at the sink pump, glancing back at her.

"I mean to find my life here, and he is adamant I return to New York." And she would honestly die before she returned there—ever.

Dodge leaned on the counter, wiping her hands on a cloth. "I know you are scared, perhaps even lonesome, but as I told you, you are welcome here as long as you like—with or without Sawyer's interest."

Rose stopped kneading. "I think he'll not rest until he has sent me back, though I have put my foot down about the train."

"Did he say that?"

"He just keeps saying that a woman like me cannot live in Cheyenne alone."

Dodge gave her a knowing smile. "Don't give up so easily on Sawyer. I've seen him look at you and his mind is whirling."

"But I think I might have angered him." Rose was nervous about what she had said to him on the porch her first evening and knew that her refusal to return home infuriated him. "He was so annoyed with me, but given he didn't expect me, I told him I must surely be a thorn in his side and when he agreed I simply said—*good*."

"The best way to get to a man is to keep him keenly aware of your presence. If Sawyer cannot see what I already see in you, then he doesn't deserve you at all. And regardless if you wish to marry or not, you have a place here, which is the least I can do and honestly I have enjoyed your company immensely." Dodge gave her a genuine smile.

Rose placed the readied bread dough in a dish to bake. Perhaps Sawyer was paying attention. She'd seen him all but looking for her each time he had arrived home in the evenings. But, if he didn't come around, she'd find her own way no matter the sheriff's intentions. What other choice did she have?

****

Sawyer sat in his office, where he had been most of the morning. It hadn't gone past him that the saloon remained rowdy in spite of his warnings to a group of miners stirring up trouble. He'd walked through every few hours to keep things in check, but didn't like the knowing glances that came from one particular table of poker players. He couldn't place the men, but they were likely as no-good as the miners who'd started the trouble in the first place. Regardless, the distraction was something of a good thing, given it was all he could do to keep Rose Parker from his mind.

He'd seen her standing in the window of her room the last two evenings when he'd arrived home later than expected. He wasn't sure what he thought about that. Was she waiting on him, or did she just happen to be looking out over the ranch from her vantage point of the upper house? She was adamant she wasn't going back to New York, and their bickering over the matter had ended with him stomping off to the barn more than once. She was downright annoying and having her at the ranch caused far too many sleepless nights picturing her in her bed one floor above.

While that picture was tempting, it was the things that she wasn't telling that kept him from sleeping. He was good at analyzing people and their motivations, a definite asset being sheriff, and he had come to the conclusion she was running. Maybe not like an outlaw, but from something or someone in New York. No matter, he'd get to the bottom of it, sooner or later.

He would be back at the ranch for the evening meal in a few hours. Sunday supper was the one meal each week that Dodge insisted her sons attend. Since not all his brothers would be home, he'd likely avoid unmerciful teasing at his situation if he were lucky. He turned back to his work, sorting through papers on his desk, but finally tossed them aside, his mind still whirling across thoughts of Rose.

A commotion outside pulled him from his thoughts. The saloon. He strode to the office door and saw men fighting as suspected. He touched the gun strapped to his hip to make sure and ran. Two men crashed through the swinging half doors to the ground just as he got there. One of the men got up and ran back inside, while the other took off across the street.

He pushed through the double doors with caution. Men fought all over in packs of two and three. Jacob Sanders, the saloon owner, stood perched on top of the bar shouting and swinging his shotgun in the air. If any of the fighting men had sense, they would know Jacob didn't wait too long before he started firing.

Sawyer grabbed the first two cowboys to separate them and took a hit to the jaw. His head snapped back, but he regained his footing, sending the man to the floor with a right hook of his own. The other swung and Sawyer ducked to avoid the blow, tackling the dirty miner to the floor. He punched hard, and the man stayed down, hands pressed to his bleeding nose. Sawyer tasted blood but got back up to fight. Using his gun would prove futile, only getting himself or someone else shot and besides this was just another Cheyenne brawl he could handle—if Jacob would behave.

He made it to the next pack of brawlers, slinging one aside and taking a hit to the cheek from another. He wobbled, and the man rushed forward, taking him down hard. Air gushed from his lungs as he smacked to the hard wooden floor. He struggled for position, rolling around on the floor until he made a direct hit with a knee to the man's groin. The miner choked and curled into a ball, giving up the fight.

"Damn, I'll bet that hurt. Now stay down." He hated fighting dirty, but sometimes it was called for. Better doubled over with a hit to the male parts than a bullet when it came down to it.

Sawyer was back up and into another group brawling near the door, scrambling to pull them apart. He took a left fist hard to his right brow and belted around to take out the man who'd tossed it, coming face to face with Wyatt. Both men froze for a moment, then each grabbed another man and continued the fight. He should have known a hit like that could only come from Wyatt. His younger brother was built for fighting, with thick arms and a solid body. Well at least the odds were

45

more even now. He cursed at the sting of his brow, and warm blood dripped down the side of his face. He slung a man out of the way then hollered to Wyatt, who fought behind him. "What are you doing back so soon?"

"Court was quick." Wyatt rubbed his knuckles when his sparring partner held his hands up in defeat.

Sawyer wasn't surprised. The outlaw Wyatt had turned in was guilty no doubt. Little by little, the fighting ended as men tuckered out—or got knocked out instead, and thankfully Jacob had not started firing the shotgun. The last time there had been a big brawl, the old man shot half his roof away, trying to get it stopped.

"Put the gun away, Jacob." Wyatt tied the last man, who wrestled against the ropes. His brother shook his head and sent a left fist into the man's belly. The cowboy buckled, finding his spot alongside the others.

Jacob climbed down from the bar, glaring at the prisoners. "Damn miners. Should have shot them in the ass is what I should've done. Fools."

Wyatt dusted his hands together and inspected his busted knuckles. "Looks like I got back just in time."

"It's been quiet until now." Sawyer touched his bloody brow, curing under his breath. *Shit.*

"You're gonna need to see the doc for that." Wyatt tapped his own brow and folded his arms.

"If you hadn't tossed such a damn hard punch," Sawyer scolded. *Holy Hell!*

"I didn't know it was you." Wyatt took a step back, guarded.

Sawyer jerked the bandana from his neck and placed it against his wound. "Get 'em locked up, will ya'?"

Wyatt turned to the four men on the floor. "Up." The men reluctantly obeyed, moving in single file toward the jail.

Sawyer watched his brother for a minute, then followed. Inside the jailhouse he tossed his hat aside and grabbed the log book to enter the names of the troublemakers.

Wyatt returned from the back, rolling up his sleeves. "They're locked up. Anyone we should be looking for?"

"Not if they're who they say they are." Sawyer glanced up. As a bounty hunter, Wyatt made a living bringing men in, but it wasn't money that fed his brother. As with himself, it was the fierce need to fill something that would never be sated. Something that would make the past right again, though if it came right down to it, they both knew nothing could do that.

Wyatt stuck his head out the front door of the office and yelled across the street to Lang, at the livery. "Hey, Lang, send the doc." He gazed back at Sawyer. "So anything else interesting happen while I was gone?"

Sawyer thought about it, not sure he wanted to explain Rose Parker. "You wouldn't believe it if I told you."

"You said it was quiet." Wyatt plopped on one of the wooden chairs, rocking it back off the front legs, stretching his elbows across the back.

"Is anything ever really quiet with Dodge?"

"What'd she do now?" Wyatt raised an eyebrow that ended in a frown.

"She left me to pick up a mail-order-bride that she

sent for, for me. Of course Dodge was off frolicking with Brett as usual, and I had nowhere to take the woman besides the ranch." Sawyer put the bandana back on his brow. Getting it said didn't lessen the knot in his stomach that had been there since Rose arrived. The woman was annoying and headstrong and wasn't about to leave Cheyenne, and all he could do was wonder what the hell to do with her. Not that his brother would be of any help.

"She did what?" Wyatt caught Sawyer's glare and stifled his laughter.

"Glad you find it amusing," Sawyer hissed, pressing harder at his wound.

"You gonna marry her?" Wyatt didn't let things drop, slamming his chair legs to the floor and folding his arms with curiosity.

"No. I'm not marrying her. I didn't send for her!" Sawyer scowled, narrowing his eyes.

"Well, is she pretty? It's not such a bad idea. Women come here all the time to be brides." Wyatt acted as if it were nothing at all, but he should know better.

"Don't ask me that. Yes, she is pretty, but this whole thing wasn't my idea." Sawyer was growing tired of the conversation and was grateful when Doc Tess trotted inside the jail carrying her bag.

"Afternoon Doc." Wyatt stood, removing his hat and setting it aside. Sawyer watched his brother's gaze follow the physician across the room. His younger brother had been smitten with the physician for years now.

Doc Tess all but ignored Wyatt, pulling the cloth away from Sawyer's wound. "What happened?"

"Fight at the saloon." Sawyer leaned his head back as she assessed the damage.

"It'll need a stitch or two. Wyatt, I'll need some water." She reached into her bag, not looking at his brother.

"Goes with the territory." Sawyer met her concerned gaze. It wasn't the first time she had sewn him up. His body was full of scars from his battles as sheriff and hard work on the ranch.

Wyatt returned with a small bowl of water, which Tess used to clean the cut. She added antiseptic to a cloth and glanced at Sawyer, who nodded. He closed his eyes and sucked in a deep breath, groaning when she placed the cloth to the open wound. *Holy Hell!*

"Oh, be a man, brother." Wyatt leaned closer pearing at the wound he had no interest in. It was the doc his brother wanted to be near if he were guessing right.

Sawyer opened his eyes. "Your fault, sending random damn punches."

"You hit your brother?" Tess glared at Wyatt, obviously shocked at the idea.

"No, not on purpose. The whole saloon was fighting, and I was taking out the next man. Turned out to be Sawyer." Wyatt shrugged.

"You men. So rough all the time. Let's get this stitched." Tess pulled a threaded needle from a small bottle of alcohol.

Sawyer took a deep breath as she held the wound closed and began. The stitches weren't quite as bad as the antiseptic had been. He closed his eyes, and in no time it was over.

"There, you should heal fine. Just keep it clean."

She placed a small dressing over the sutured cut.

"You want the first prisoner?" Sawyer nodded to Wyatt who headed to the back once more.

Tess looked at him. "How many are hurt?"

"One's got a good cut to the head; the other young man's likely got a broken arm." He touched his left wrist to explain.

Wyatt returned tugging along one of the men. He tried to jerk free, but Wyatt grabbed him and slung him into the chair with little effort and a sarcastic grin.

"We expect you to behave like a gentleman." Sawyer warned, and the man settled in his chair with a cold glare at Wyatt.

"Where are you hurt?" Tess asked, taking a step forward.

The man pulled his hat back with his tied hands, showing a cut to his forehead. "Well now, a real lady doctor?"

"Keep your mouth shut." Wyatt kicked his shin, causing him to yelp.

Tess scowled at Wyatt but addressed the prisoner. "It's not bad, we'll just clean it up a little."

As Tess went about her work, Sawyer studied his brother, who never took his eyes from the doc. Wyatt was smitten with her, but he wasn't sure of the reason Tess held back from his advances. At first he guessed the recent loss of her husband, but even after a long period of mourning, she'd never given into Wyatt's interest.

When Tess was done, Wyatt tugged the man along by his ropes toward the back and returned with the younger man. This one sat down in the chair quietly. Sawyer studied him with interest, though he didn't make eye contact.

"Let's take a look." Tess bent down to remove the man's right hand from his left wrist. He winced as she traced along his forearm and across the protruding bump near his hand.

"You have a broken arm. I'll need to set it." She dug in her bag, retrieving splints and wraps, laying them aside.

She then rolled up the young man's sleeve and glanced at Wyatt. "Hold his arm, but be nice."

Wyatt raised his eyebrows in defense. "I'm always nice, if they are."

"He needs to hold your arm like this." She placed Wyatt's hands on the man's shoulder and forearm.

"It's gonna hurt bad isn't it?" The young man began to panic, trying to tug his arm away.

"Only for a second and you need to keep the splint on for six weeks." She took hold of his wrist.

"Wait." The young man tried to back out of the plan.

"Hey! Look over there!" Tess shouted, nodding to the window. All three men glanced that direction. Tess jerked hard, setting the bone with a loud crack. The young man yelped, tossing his head back in pain, but remained sitting.

"All done." She reached for the splints with a smile, wrapping them in place with a dressing and tying it off near his elbow. "How's that?" She smiled at the young man, who only nodded, still trying to regain his composure.

After a moment he stood on his own. "Thank you, ma'am. I will see to paying you when I can get some work."

Tess turned from him to Sawyer and back. "There's no charge, but I do want to check this arm in about two weeks. Just come by the office in the afternoon."

The young man nodded, his brown eyes defeated.

"Come on." Wyatt led him to the back once more.

"Sawyer, he isn't more than a boy. You can't keep him a prisoner." Tess said, her concern over the young gentleman apparent.

"He's evidently a pick pocket who tried to make off with the money from one of the miners, but he didn't have anything on him. Not so sure he's guilty. Said he was looking for work when he got caught up in the fight." Sawyer stood again. As far as he knew, the boy wasn't a thief but had just found himself in the wrong place at the wrong time and Tess' willingness to bypass her fees wasn't a surprise.

"You seen him before?" Wyatt asked as he returned, shutting the door to the cells behind him.

"No. He can't be more than fifteen," Sawyer answered. "We'll put him to work on the ranch, knock some sense into him."

"He's thin and pale. Feed him first and he can have some laudanum at night if he can't sleep." Tess set a bottle of medication on his desk, adding a small spoon, then grabbing her bag.

Wyatt followed her to the door, plopping his hat back on his head. "Doc, you, ahh…want to come to the ranch for supper tonight?"

"I've got patients, but thank your mother." She walked out the door without looking back.

Wyatt waited a moment and hit the door frame with his palm. "She's so damn difficult."

"She's had a loss, give her some time." Sawyer closed his desk drawer. "Try not to pester her so much."

"He's been dead for over a year, and I don't pester her. I'm just—persistent." Wyatt defended, cursing under his breath.

Hudson Collier, the night deputy, rushed into the office and hung his hat on the rack, greeting them, late as usual. "Boys. Hear we got a few on board."

"Yeah. Let 'em sleep it off, give 'em a warning and run them out of town. Hold the younger man with the broken arm, though. He may need pain medication to sleep." Sawyer pushed the medication on the table toward him, heading to the door.

"See you boys in the morning. Sorry I missed the fun." Hudson chuckled and found his way to the desk.

"The saloon's quiet, but keep an eye on Jacob," Sawyer added, grabbing his hat and heading out the door. Hudson could handle things for now without a doubt. He'd ridden for bounties with Wyatt often enough as the two had been friends since their youth. He was a good man, a bit younger than Wyatt and full of smarts.

Outside, Wyatt spoke as they mounted their horses. "You really taking that boy to the ranch? You know Evan hates it when you bring home strays."

Sawyer thought on it. Evan ran the ranch and managed the hiring and firing of the hands. He hated Sawyer's habit of bringing home men he thought had simply run a streak of bad luck.

"If I turn him loose, he just does the same thing somewhere else. He'll eventually end up on the wrong end of a gun." Sawyer slowed Colonel. "If we give him a job, maybe we change the course of his life. Besides, I don't think stealing is his line of work. He hadn't a penny on him and described the knife the others took from him."

"Always crusading for a cause, like Father." Wyatt shook his head but smiled as they rode along.

A slight jolt of pain edged through Sawyer's chest as it always did with the mention of his father. Their father had always tried to find the good in men, and somehow, Sawyer did the same when he could. Maybe they all did in their own way.

"So, what are you going to do with the bride?" Wyatt changed the subject, his lip curling into a grin.

"Take Dodge down a notch for starters. Enough is enough, and she's always playing where she needn't be." He cursed to himself and urged Colonel to a trot.

"She must have your wedding planned by now." Wyatt chuckled.

Sawyer scowled, not finding humor in the comment.

"It could be worse; you said the lady was pretty." His brother added, urging his horse to catch up.

How could things possibly be worse, but he nodded? The whole thing was ridiculous as far as he was concerned.

But Wyatt didn't let things go. "That has to be hard. Dodge orders you a bride, and she gets you a pretty one, and if I know you, that means some kind of beautiful." Wyatt raised his eyebrows, blue eyes in question.

"We are not having this conversation." Sawyer spat, gripping tighter to the reins.

"Well, what's her name?" Wyatt gave an inquisitive glance.

"Miss Parker to you."

His brother held his hands up. "All right, I know you're apt to kick my ass if I keep on."

"Her name is Rose Parker, from New York."

Wyatt's laughter echoed around them. "Damn. New York City? You are in trouble big brother." He hit the reins of his horse, dodging the swift kick Sawyer sent his way. "Hey, I'm kidding, come on Sawyer."

Sawyer cursed under his breath as Wyatt rode ahead, still laughing. He didn't have time for nonsense with the ranch just over the next ridge. He had to get his mind set for sitting at dinner once more with Rose Parker, and this time with an audience. Damn it to hell, how was he to do that when he could hardly breathe with her in the same room? He slowed Colonel. He could not halt the inevitable, but he also couldn't help peering up at the window of her room, wondering just what she had been up to all day.

Chapter Four

Sawyer dismounted behind Wyatt, noticing that Evan and the men were already home from the market. Damn, he wasn't going to have any luck at all. With Wyatt and Evan home early and Dawson sure to show for the Sunday evening meal, he wouldn't have a prayer. He gritted his teeth and led Colonel into the barn for his brush down. Rose wasn't at the window, and he cursed himself for having even glanced in that direction yet again.

"What'd you name that horse anyway?" Sawyer tossed the question at Wyatt as he brushed Colonel inside the barn.

Wyatt turned his horse out into the corral from inside. "No name makes it easier. Can't keep one alive long enough to name him, bad luck." Wyatt shrugged and followed Sawyer to the water pump outside the barn once he'd turned Colonel out.

"Thought you'd be a few more days." Wyatt called as Evan scurried up to the pump beside them.

Evan's light hair curled around his ears due to the humidity, and he carried at least a month's beard on his usually clean-shaven face. "Got back a little while ago."

"Did you make the purchase of the cattle from Kansas?" Sawyer asked, shaking his brother's outstretched hand.

"Yep. It may be a couple of months." Evan shifted

to a whisper, pointing over his shoulder. "So who is she and what's she doing here?"

Sawyer's jaw clenched as he followed Evan's gaze to where Rose was helping Mei Ling hang the wash. At least she was making herself useful, but he didn't need his womanizing younger brother making a play for Rose right under his nose.

Wyatt butted in as usual. "Dodge ordered our older brother here an original mail-order-bride." He laughed, but squinted as if expecting a right hook from Sawyer.

Evan's mouth dropped open. Looking at her again, he shook his head. "What the heck are you waiting on brother? She's rather—"

"That's enough from both of you." Sawyer washed his hands at the pump, cursing under his breath.

Wyatt exchanged glances with Evan, both men stifling laughter.

Evan winked at Wyatt and stepped closer to Sawyer. "I'll take her if you aren't interested." He was quick to scurry out of the range of Sawyer's fist.

"You'd both be wise to keep it down at dinner," Sawyer yelled after them as they raced toward the house. He headed inside, praying to a God he usually ignored that dinner would go well. Reaching the porch, he noticed a lone rider coming in. Dawson. Just as he suspected, this night would be complete with all three brothers home. At least Dawson would behave, something he couldn't predict with Wyatt or Evan.

Dawson rode close to the porch and dismounted. "What happened to your head?"

Sawyer touched the dressing to his brow. "Saloon brawl."

Dawson smiled, pulling back his long, brown hair

from his face, his deep blue eyes shining and serious as usual.

"How was your trip?"

"I got back a few days ago. The Cheyenne aren't able to leave the reservation to hunt, and the promised rations provide little. The cavalry doesn't need much reason for abuse or neglect." Dawson tied off his horse with a shrug.

Sawyer understood well that the government promised the Indians a lot of things that never happened, and his brother's interest in helping the Cheyenne was admirable, but dangerous. At times he worried, as did the family. That Dawson was back from Dakota Territory once more would be a relief for Dodge if nothing else.

"Got a new horse back at the cabin, from Rapid City." Dawson followed Sawyer up the front porch stairs.

"From the Hagen's?" Sawyer asked. Samuel and Will Hagen's large ranch near Rapid City, was known for the mustangs they bred with larger horses to increase their size. The result was a bigger horse with a wild spirit and most were fast as hell. Just like Dawson liked them.

"Yep. This is one Samuel raised, large for half mustang, sixteen hands or so. Painted and spirited." Dawson peered up as Dodge came to the doorway, folding her arms.

"You boys wash up for dinner." She smiled at Dawson, but avoided eye contact with Sawyer, just as she seemed to magically disappear when he had been home the last few days.

Dawson kissed his mother's cheek. "Dodge."

"I'm glad to see you're back. You missed two Sunday dinners, so you'll owe us two visits more this month." She scolded Dawson, her worry and relief evident.

"Yes, ma'am." He went on inside.

Dodge turned to Sawyer. "Well, I hope you have taken a little time to get to know Rose. Isn't she lovely?"

Sawyer took her arm before she could duck back inside, leaving him to mull over the comment as she'd planned. "I got her here, fixed her bath, and we ate dinner, but just because I haven't put her back on the train doesn't mean I'm marrying her. So, any little ideas that you and Mei Ling are stirring up need to be halted. Do I make myself clear?"

"Crystal." She patted his hand, glaring at him before returning inside.

Sawyer threw his head back in frustration, jerking the hat from his head and followed her inside to his fate.

****

Rose helped Dodge set the last of the plates around the dining room table. Dinner was served family style, and the dishes she and Dodge had spent the day putting together loaded down the buffet. She was quite nervous at the prospect that the entire family was attending.

"So much food?" she asked Dodge as the older woman scooted platters around to make room for one more.

"Feeding four grown men, let's just say it takes a feast. I enjoy cooking for my boys."

"So all four are home every Sunday?" The last few days she'd worked alongside Dodge and Mei Ling to learn a bit of the routines, but the planned meal with everyone in attendance was frightening.

"Dawson just came in, and Evan's back from business in Kansas. Wyatt's arrived in from Denver earlier today. They're all here." Dodge put the last of the food on the table, then headed back to the kitchen.

The dining room door popped open, and a large man with blond curls and the darkest green eyes she had ever seen stood before her.

"Hello," Rose said, figuring him one of the brothers. She had seen him outside earlier, and without a doubt he'd noticed her. No use hiding the heat that rushed to her cheeks now. All cleaned up, he wore no hat, and his face was shaven from the thick beard she noticed before.

"Hi, yourself. I'm Evan." He smiled, taking her hand and bringing it to his lips.

Rose held her hand steady for the tender kiss. Well, at least he had manners. "I'm Rose." How else was she to describe herself at this time? She contemplated further conversation, but Sawyer lunged into the room, pushing through the door.

His eyes flashed at the sight of his brother still holding Rose's hand. "I see you've met my brother, *Evan*."

"We were just saying hello." Evan let go of her hand with a nod and backed away.

Sawyer pulled out his chair and sat as Dodge returned with a large bowl of steaming mashed potatoes, plopping it onto the middle of the table.

Rose watched Sawyer as he sat, glaring at his brother. Maybe Dodge was right, and he was interested in her.

Evan pulled out the chair beside Sawyer for her and then sat beside her without assisting her. "Can't wait to dig into this. It smells great, Dodge. Had enough trail food to last me a while."

Rose sat and let her gaze scan Sawyer once more. He looked away as quickly as she caught it.

"I'm glad you're home." Dodge glanced at Evan. "Brett said you made the purchase of the cattle and brought in another thousand."

"Got a good price and that should let us set the market next spring. A lot of the heifers are expecting." Evan took a sip of his water and reached for the plate of biscuits, only to receive a smack on the hand from Dodge. He dropped the biscuit with a frown of puzzlement.

Two men walked in from the kitchen discussing something between themselves, but both dropped the conversation as they eyed her.

Rose studied each, assuming Dawson the one wearing a feather in his long brown hair. Dodge had described them both very well, stating Wyatt was tall with dark hair, and Dawson resembled an Indian most of the time, given his wardrobe. She noticed Wyatt looked a lot like Sawyer. His dark hair was only a bit shorter than Sawyer's, and his beard was full, but neatly trimmed. He nodded and sat down across from her.

"Sorry, I didn't realize we had company." Dawson pulled out his chair and sat next to Wyatt, eyeing her.

Dodge took it upon herself to make the introductions, nodding to each of her sons. "Miss Rose Parker, these are my sons, Wyatt, Dawson, and Evan. Rose will be staying at the ranch for a while. She's all the way from New York."

Dawson gave the hint of a smile, and Rose nodded back politely. He was handsome with blue eyes similar to Wyatt's and his skin was bronzed from the sun.

"Welcome to Cheyenne," Wyatt said, tilting back his chair and resting his elbows on the table.

"Thank you." Rose tried to relax with the introductions over.

"Sawyer, would you say grace." Dodge bowed her head as all four of her sons stared at her, in what Rose thought looked like disbelief.

Sawyer's gray eyes narrowed, and she pondered the reason for the bandage along his brow. Being so close to him again, her pulse raced, but the look of shock on his face made her wonder what was going on. It was apparent Wyatt across from her and Evan beside her were trying their best to hide their laughter. Dawson watched Sawyer, then bowed his head elbowing Wyatt.

Sawyer never bowed his head but began to speak. "Ah, Lord...we thank you for this food...we give thanks..." He hesitated as if at a loss for words, but then Evan let his laughter slip, and Wyatt put both his praying hands up to cover his face, shaking in laughter without making a sound. Through squinted eyes, Rose watched Sawyer grip the edge of the table with both hands.

"*And thank you lord for bringing my dear sweet brothers home safely once more.*" Sawyer accentuated his words.

Evan and Wyatt stopped laughing abruptly.

"A-men." Sawyer glared at each of his brothers, his gaze stopping on Dodge.

Rose wasn't sure what to think. It was apparent that Sawyer was being sarcastic and that his brothers were taunting him, due to her presence and the prayer. She felt a bit sorry for him and was suddenly aware again of her own nerves.

Dodge picked up the conversation, grabbing the bowl of mashed potatoes to begin passing them. "So Wyatt, the trial in Denver must have gone fast."

Wyatt took the potatoes from Dawson. "He was convicted. He'll be sent back east for sentencing."

Evan stabbed two pieces of sliced beef with his fork. "They gonna hang him?"

"Probably. He had little alibi."

Sawyer took the potatoes from Wyatt then lifted a heaping spoonful to his plate. He handed the spoon to Rose and held the bowl for her. She met his gaze, but he only looked back at Wyatt to her disappointment. He was an impossible man to read, all except the part where he either stayed annoyed with her or ignored her.

"The circuit judge wired he'd be spared the hanging if he'd give up the names of the other men involved." Sawyer added, handing the potatoes on to Evan.

Wyatt shook his head. "He's not going to tell. I think he's more afraid of them than he is of dying. The Ashburn Brothers are ruthless, even to their own men."

"I read in the paper the Ashburns took a train outside of Council Bluffs a few weeks back. They seem to be leaving a trail of death behind them, even lawmen. How'd you get one of their men?" Dawson asked.

"Grabbed him before he had a chance to do much," Sawyer explained and took a sip of his coffee.

Rose hadn't started eating yet. She was too caught up watching the men around her. They ate ravenously, with little concern for manners. All but Sawyer, who seemed determined to act like a gentleman.

"What happened to your brow Sawyer?" Dodge was simply sitting back, watching her sons as well.

"Wyatt nearly took me out in a saloon brawl." Sawyer smiled slyly at his brother.

Dodge glared at Wyatt. "You hit your brother?"

"Not like he is saying. Everyone was fighting, and the next punch I threw got him." Wyatt smiled as if innocent with a shrug that matched.

Rose found his grin contagious. He was just as handsome a man as Sawyer. Actually, she thought all four of Dodge's sons were very handsome, tall, muscular. Each somehow unique.

"Did Tess stitch you?" Dodge pressed.

"Yeah. By the way, Evan, there was a young man involved in the brawl, not his doing. His arm is broken, and he'll be mending for a while. I'm bringing him to work the ranch." Sawyer sipped his coffee again, pushing his plate away.

"Sawyer, you bring all kinds out here and the last two took off with horses." Evan pointed his fork at Sawyer as he talked through a cheek full of food.

"He's hungry and doesn't have any family. He wasn't the problem at the saloon. He was looking for work, and the miners tried to take what little money he had. When he tried to stop them, the fighting started. If he's any trouble, I'll take care of it," Sawyer explained.

"His name is Billy. Says he knows cattle." Wyatt added fuel to the fire.

"They all do." Evan rolled his eyes and shoved in another mouthful of beef.

"Well, if he's hungry, I think you should give it the effort once he heals." Dodge uttered the final word on the matter, then turned to Rose. "So Rose, how are things these days in New York?"

Rose wiped her mouth with the linen napkin from her lap, glancing around. "Well, it is a very busy place with lots of growth the last few years. So many new buildings and companies I can hardly keep up." She hoped that was enough of an answer. Telling anymore might lead her to slip about her situation. While Dodge was aware that she had arrived as a mail-order-bride, she wasn't aware of her reasons for leaving New York, and it wasn't likely Max had told her anymore than she already knew.

"I loved New York when I was there, a long time ago," Dodge said. "You know Sawyer was there only about a year ago. He was invited to speak at a law convention."

"Really, what did you speak about?" Rose asked, glad of the chance for open conversation with the sheriff, even if everyone was watching. That had to be how he knew Max Ferguson and it might help her to know their connection.

"On controlling outlaws in the smaller cities west. Ways to keep a town free from trouble." He spoke in short, clipped sentences and barely glanced her way, preferring to contemplate the depths of his coffee cup.

"Come on Sawyer," said Wyatt. "What my brother is not telling is that he was asked to speak because he was the first and only sheriff to round up the Fuller Gang—alive. They killed more than twelve lawmen and no telling how many innocent people in towns all over Kansas, Texas, and Wyoming." Wyatt beamed at his brother. "It was quite amazing, so don't let him play down what that was really about."

"How did you capture them?" It wasn't an idle question but she was truly curious.

Sawyer shrugged. "Every law man I knew at the time headed out to find those men, wanting the bounty. But men like that can't be found. They find you, so I waited. We all waited, and they eventually came to town. We were sneaky, grabbed one at a time. Got their leader first, and if you get the leader, the men fight amongst themselves and fall apart. One by one they were jailed. It really wasn't something special, just well planned with a lot of luck."

Rose thought it sounded smart and at least he was talking—and looking at her. For a moment she forgot the others in the room lost in the deep gray eyes of the sheriff. "So is that how you do things every time with other outlaws?"

Sawyer shook his head. "Outlaws—men like that aren't all the same. You have to know who you're dealing with and how they think, work, and play."

She nodded. He really was a handsome man, but she still had a bit of nerves about his lack of interest. "You make it sound almost simple."

"It's never simple." He finally pulled his plate closer and stirred the food around with his fork.

Evan piped in, taking away the conversation. "Dawson how was your trip?"

Dawson sighed. "Same thing every time. The Cheyenne are in trouble if they leave the reservation to hunt, and the government sends only empty promises or spoiled food. Tensions are stirring up the soldiers as usual."

Rose examined Dawson as he talked. She'd been curious about the fringed leather shirt and colorful beaded necklace he wore, thinking he must have made them both. His facial features were similar to Sawyer and Wyatt's, but he was clean-shaven and had intense blue eyes, a lot like Dodge's.

"So you help Indians?" Rose asked, wanting to stay in the conversation.

He wiped his mouth and placed a serious gaze on her. "I translate, act as a negotiator between the government and the Cheyenne. But sometimes, it feels like I get little accomplished."

"Are you ever afraid? I was warned about Indians by the men on the train." Rose thought her question innocent enough, but the instant change in Dawson's dark eyes alarmed her.

Wyatt exchanged glances with Evan, who sighed, and then rested his chin on his folded hands, fixing his gaze on the table. The sudden silence was puzzling, and Rose scanned from one face to the next, finding that Sawyer was the only one who didn't seem troubled.

Finally Dawson spoke, breaking the quiet. "All Indians are not as bad as some may lead you to think. Attacks you might have read about in the New York papers portray them all as heartless savages, but that would be the renegade bands of dog soldiers more times than not. I represent the tribes of Cheyenne trying to maintain their way of life and keep the lands that belong to them. And, no, I've never been afraid." He went back to his food after a long glance at Sawyer.

"I see," Rose replied. She had obviously said the wrong thing, though she hadn't meant for that to be the case.

"Dawson lives in a cabin north of here. He doesn't care much for civilized living." It was Dodge who spoke, clearly trying to ease the tension.

"I like my cabin and being in the woods alone, which is where I need to be heading." Dawson tossed his napkin down.

Rose watched as he kissed his mother and left the table, unable to shake a vague sense of guilt. When he was gone, she set her gaze on Dodge. "I hope I didn't say something in error."

Evan answered, "You have to watch what you say around him about the damn—sorry, about the Cheyenne."

"You said nothing wrong," Dodge reassured her. "Dawson has found his calling in helping the Indians, and he takes it very personally. It's fine."

Rose was surprised when Sawyer added his thoughts. "Dawson serves a good purpose, but I'm afraid the government doesn't see it the same."

"I'll speak to him." Wyatt left the table after a quick nod.

Evan shoved a spoonful of beans in his mouth and changed the subject. "Sawyer, you going out with us tomorrow? You too Dodge?"

Sawyer nodded and finally took a bite of potatoes. "Wyatt's got the jail."

"Wyatt hates branding day," Evan explained, seeming to notice Rose's confused expression.

"I'll ride out with the mid-day meal with Mei Ling," Dodge added, sipping coffee.

"What is branding day?" Rose asked. Well, she knew what branding encompassed, but not a day for the event.

Dodge answered with a hint of a smile. "The men will be branding the new cattle. It can be a long hot day, but you are welcome to come along."

"I think I might enjoy a day out." Rose sipped her mint tea. It was clear her pronouncement had stirred Sawyer's attention to the conversation.

His head snapped up. "You'd have to ride a horse—all day."

"I am actually very good at that." She raised her eyebrows in a challenge he wouldn't miss as she turned back to Evan. "So how many cattle do you have to brand?" Out of the corner of her eye, she saw Sawyer shake his head. Well, at least she now had his attention.

Evan talked through his chewing once more. "All the new ones we brought in earlier today. Brett's cattle get a different brand, but we all work together. Sawyer, you know we got the cattle past Benton's side of the river this time, but we've got another couple thousand head to bring in soon, and it's getting ugly. His men are holding up the river and popping off warning caps, scattering the cattle. It's all we can do to hold them in and Brett's a little more than tense."

"Brett needs to keep his temper down, and you need to keep from spouting off in town," Sawyer warned.

Rose watched the exchange wondering exactly what was going on. Sawyer's face reddened, and he shoved his plate away once more.

"I haven't even been to town lately." Evan tossed his fork down glaring at his bother.

"I'll handle Benton when the time comes. You said it might be a few weeks before the cattle arrive in Kansas." Sawyer's tone warned further, and the tension in his voice was frightening.

Evan shook his head. "Maybe, but Benton's a

problem."

"I've got Benton. You just get the cattle to the ranch when it's time."

Rose watched as Sawyer clenched his fists, the look on his face changing to something of full anger. While his frustration seemed to be aimed at his brother, it was the mention of Marcus Benton that caused his eyes to narrow. She could only wonder of this man named Benton, given the quiet that fell over the room. As much as she wanted to ask who the man was and why the mere mention of his name turned Sawyer's gray eyes cold, she held back. What had she gotten herself into? She had to wonder if being in Wyoming was really any safer than home.

Chapter Five

Sawyer lay awake listening to a light rain tap against the eaves of the house. It didn't sound heavy enough to hinder branding the cattle, but he needed sleep to be his best. It was after midnight, and he'd yet to close his eyes. Groaning, he faced the fact that it wasn't the weather keeping him awake. The mention of Marcus Benton had once again stirred his mind to pull together the pieces of a long and confusing story. A puzzle he'd been working on for years.

As if that wasn't enough to keep him awake, thoughts of Rose curled up in bed certainly was. She had no business on the range, hanging around while a thousand head of cattle got branded. And without a doubt he'd have to keep her out of trouble. Well, if she wanted a day of branding, he'd see to it that she learned all about it—firsthand. Maybe a day playing with cattle in the heat of Wyoming would send her scurrying back to New York—not likely. She'd been more than clear on her aspirations not to return there.

It made him uneasy that she seemed to be settling right in at the ranch, with Dodge acting as if she were some welcomed boarder. He'd lost patience with Rose all together. So if she was staying, maybe he needed to see about digging a little further into the reason she was here in the first place. She hadn't come to Cheyenne to marry, she was here as an escape. It was only a matter of time. Women weren't able to keep secrets from his experience, and she would slip up sooner or later.

Why was she so willing to be a bride and so determined to stay in Wyoming, even if not married? What could have been so bad in New York to make a rich, beautiful young woman leave it all behind—in a hurry? Women of her status didn't up and walk away from their worldly comforts, yet she had. He fluffed his pillow and slammed back down again, kicking the heavier covers from his legs. Damn, he needed to sleep, but every time he closed his eyes all he could see was Rose.

****

Upstairs, Rose lay in bed listening to the rain, wondering if it was reason enough for the branding to be canceled. The look of surprise on Sawyer's face had quickly turned to annoyance when she'd asserted how well she rode a horse. Without a doubt she needed to prove the point to the unbelieving sheriff. She had ridden horses before she had even walked, thanks to her father's love of the animals. But her aged father was gone now.

She sat up in the bed, tugging on the quilt to bring it closer. It was her father's quilt, and she missed him dearly. Having grown up without a mother, he had been her rock, the most kind and loving man she had ever known. The quilt somehow still smelled of him and was the only thing she now had to make her feel close. Papa had often wrapped it around them both as he read to her from the time she was a child.

She longed for the happiness that daily life before her father's death had offered. She dreamed often of the days they'd spent riding horses outside the city and the evenings when she'd sat with him by the evening fire, reading to him after his vision failed. She'd felt safe with her father, always. Now, that feeling was far away, and somehow she was just surviving day to day, hour to hour. The well-laid plans for her safety seemed to be evaporating, and she wondered if she'd ever find peace and comfort again.

Light rain continued to tap against the window, and she pulled the covers back, getting out of bed. Walking over, she peered outside, unable to see much across the darkened prairie. The barn was visible, and the bunk houses held the glow of a dimmed lantern, but it remained dark—especially inside her heart. She burst into silent tears, those were the worst kind—the ones cried alone. She'd remained strong in New York, even when she had been a laughing stock, shunned and humiliated. How could she have known? Not even Muriel, her cousin and only friend, had suspected. She didn't understand how it had all even happened and then to barely escape with her life...she shivered. Nothing would ever be the same again.

Well, in spite of being young and naïve to all that had taken place, it had pushed her to grow up fast. And whether or not sheriff Sawyer McCade wanted her, she would prove she could take care of herself, one way or the other. What would the sheriff think if she did strike out on her own? What would he think if he knew for the time being she was still married, not that it had been a real marriage? Maybe it was best he hadn't taken right to her, though once she had the annulment, another marriage would assure that her father's remaining assets were once again her own.

She lay down on the bed again, thinking of Sawyer.

He'd disappeared outside after dinner and hadn't returned until long after dark. She could easily love him, but if he were interested, he'd not let on very much, in spite of what Dodge thought. Somewhere inside the handsome sheriff, there was a peaceful calm, not that a man like him would ever admit to having a softer side. Even at dinner, her pulse had raced at his presence. The marriage of convenience she sought would be worth nothing if he wasn't interested, regardless of her father's assets. She pulled Papa's quilt closer in spite of the heat and closed her eyes. Eventually she gave in to the darkness of the night, still weeping her silent empty tears.

****

Sawyer woke with a start, not realizing he'd slept. He no longer heard the rain, but Evan's heavy boots clomped toward the kitchen. He rose and washed his face and dressed, then made his way to the kitchen to catch his brother.

"Morning." Evan yawned, handing him a streaming cup of black coffee.

He took the tin mug. "At least the rain stopped."

"Oh, playing in the mud just makes it fun." Evan chugged his coffee and set it aside.

"I'll ride, you play in the mud." Sawyer put down his own mug and finished buttoning his shirt. He reached for his holster, hanging on the back of one of the kitchen chairs. Hell, he usually kept it with him, but Rose had distracted him out of his routine. He cursed silently, having been so annoyed with her pronouncement that she would ride along for the branding. He'd spent a few hours tidying the barn the evening before, just to avoid further contact with her.

"You taking Colonel?" Evan led the way outside, though the back door.

"Yeah, he needs a good workout." The horse wasn't the only one. Thinking about Rose all night had him stirred up. The mental picture he'd had of her bathing was one thing, but the idea of her lying in her bed—well, that was entirely something else. While he rarely visited the local brothel, the thought had crossed his mind. Maybe working off a bit of steam would help him sleep, but he doubted it would do anything but fuel the fire that was beginning to burn every time he thought of her. He shook his head to clear his thoughts and followed his brother to the barn, cursing himself for thinking any of it.

Moments later, he led Colonel from the stall as Evan saddled his horse outside the barn.

"Good morning." A female voice greeted his brother.

Sawyer jerked his gaze up in time to watch Evan turn a full circle as Rose pranced past him to enter the barn. "Good...morning, Miss...Parker," Evan answered in a slur of words.

Sawyer froze in his tracks. Holy son of a—he gulped for a breath of air.

Rose moseyed closer with an all too confident smile. "Good morning, Sheriff."

Sawyer had to think to breathe. Her brown riding trousers left no mystery about her womanly curves, and his mind was quick to picture just how she might look without them. Heat rushed to his face and he couldn't pry his gaze off her for a second. "Morning." He turned quickly and lifted the saddle onto Colonel, cursing the reaction of his body which betrayed him at the sight of her.

"Which horse should I take?" She scanned the barn and stopped before him.

What in the hell, she was riding out this early? He'd thought she might ride one of the horses along with Dodge and Mei Ling who would bring the wagon. Well, if that was how she wanted things. "Take your pick." He waved his hand to the other stalls and went back to tightening the saddle on Colonel.

Rose glanced around the stalls and after eyeing the saddles turned back to him, obviously confused. "Could you help me? These saddles aren't like the English saddles I'm used to."

She sounded sure of herself, but Sawyer wasn't playing that game. If she wanted to ride out on the range, she could damn well saddle her own horse, although he might not mind watching, since she was dressed so—*appropriately*. He wasn't going to make it easy for her but given the strain in his trousers, he wished the train would plow right up to the ranch to return her home. That or he'd like to drag her to the loft to take care of business.

Since neither was an option, he stomped past her swearing under his breath. "The saddles are right over there. The smaller ones are a bit lighter." He gestured with his thumb and tugged Colonel outside. Climbing up and settling in the saddle, he exchanged glances with Evan, who tilted his hat back and raised his brows.

"Enough." Sawyer stopped him before he could say what they both were thinking.

Evan leaned across the saddle horn for a better view inside the barn and shook his head.

Sawyer was inclined to kick his brother but kept

his own gaze inside the barn as well. Rose, never looked at either of them, but found a saddle and struggled to carry it across to where the closest horse waited in a stall.

"You gonna help her?" Evan eyed him with curiosity and turned his attention back to the barn.

"Nope and neither are you," he whispered sternly, taking another look himself.

Ten minutes later, Rose led the horse she had chosen outside the barn where Sawyer and Evan still waited. Sawyer pulled his pocket watch from his vest, glanced at it and met her gaze.

She mounted the horse with ease. "It's been a while since I saddled a horse, but I ride very well." She hit the reins not giving him a chance to say anything. He started to call after her, but turned to Evan, who let go with a loud bout of cackling laughter.

"Laugh it up brother." Sawyer scowled.

"Better go after her. Looks like you have a full day ahead of you, Sheriff." Evan turned his horse the opposite direction of Rose and continued laughing into the distance.

Sawyer snarled and gave Colonel a swift kick, heading after Rose. The morning sun had not yet topped the eastern hills, but in the little light, he had no trouble seeing that she did ride well, especially in those damn pants. Her rump rose and fell as a properly trained rider, leaving thoughts of her riding a few other things playing in his mind. Son of a bitch! How was he supposed to work around her like that all day?

As he brought Colonel alongside her, she shot him a puzzled glance and slowed her horse.

"I told you I ride very well." She gave him a crisp

77

nod before he could say anything.

Yep, she rode well, damn well enough that he had to concentrate to speak. "Oh, you ride just fine. But the cattle—they're the other direction." He pointed east, waited a second, and laughed at her expense.

Rose gritted her teeth and turned her horse to follow him. "Well, at least I finally know that you can laugh."

Damn, she was some kind of beautiful, and good-natured. Very few women had ever caused his breath to hitch. Well, there had been only one other—Catherine. While he wanted no part of Rose on a permanent basis, something about her intrigued him enough to keep his interest piqued. He and Catherine had been like oil and water, bickering and never finding common ground except as lovers. He took Colonel to a bit of a gallop. Maybe harder riding would get his mind off the deadly combination of both women in the same thought.

Arriving at the top of the ridge east of the ranch, he waited for Rose to catch up. He looked on as her expression changed from that of determination to surprise at all before them. Below, near the river, men on horseback brought in herds of cattle that stretched as far as where the deep blue summer sky met the tall green grasses of the ground in the distance.

"So all these cattle have to be branded in a single day?" She seemed surprised, her eyes wide with wonder.

"Every last one." Sawyer was anxious to get started, but he wasn't sure what she should be doing.

"It's so vast, but already warm." She wiped her long sleeve across her brow.

He nodded. "That's why we like to start early. It'll

be miserable by the afternoon."

Rose shifted the fancy hat that had been hanging around her neck to her head and gave him a slight smile.

"Stick close, but don't get into the middle of the herd. We'll swing wide and sweep to bring in cattle from the west, just—" He hesitated glancing at her in warning. "Be careful, spooked cattle can knock you from your horse."

"I am certainly capable of staying on my horse, but I will heed your advice." She cocked an eyebrow in challenge.

Sawyer met her gaze with his own raised brows and took Colonel off at a swift gallop. He didn't look back. If she thought she could handle it, he'd leave her to it. Making it to the cattle below, he swung wide, herding them toward the east with little effort. Turning back for a few strays, he caught sight of Rose.

She urged her horse to a gallop toward a small number of cattle that weren't moving along. He turned Colonel and watched her in the distance, rounding the horse once more to head up the cattle before him. There was no doubt she had no idea what she was doing, but watching her was rather entertaining. He had to laugh as she herded the cattle in circles, confusing them and her horse. Once his cattle were trotting at a decent pace, he circled back to help her. *Well, help her a little.*

Rose peered up as he arrived but kept her determination on the task.

"Cut them to the left," Sawyer yelled. "Keep your horse going forward." He watched as she tried to follow orders, clear concentration on her face. She turned her horse again, trying to get the right angle on the startled cattle.

"Don't turn your horse. Meet them straight on, angle right, then left," he advised. He could have done today without her and enjoyed himself, but then again—he caught himself simply watching her hips bounce along in the saddle and her long legs gripping tight to stay on the horse. He cursed his distracting thoughts but found himself more captivated by the fact she was actually trying to learn what he was teaching her.

Rose circled back, keeping her horse right and then left as directed. All but two of the cows headed to join the others. She looked back at Sawyer, beaming at her accomplishment.

"You let two get away." He pointed his gloved finger, critical of her skill.

"You go on." She hit the reins again to circle behind the two cows.

Sawyer left for the herd, thinking the strays would keep her busy for a while, but he wasn't sure about leaving her behind. It was harder to round up two cows than an entire herd at times, and it wasn't like she knew the horse she was on very well, even if she did seem comfortable in the saddle.

He continued on, driving behind the large number of cattle he'd headed east. Arriving to the round-up, he dismounted. Evan and Brett were dividing cattle as they were headed in, Brett with the logbook and pencil in hand. It took a team to get the cattle corralled, sending in two to six at a time to be branded. Several men were branding at two different fires, and the already branded cattle were directed from the corral to the southern pastures.

"Sawyer." Brett nodded in greeting.

"You boys still got a lot of cattle sprinkled across the west." Sawyer sipped from his canteen and hung it back on Colonel's saddle, turning to lean against the corral opposite Brett.

Evan's lips curled into a smile, his light shirt damp with sweat. "What'd you do with your help?"

"She's rounding up strays." Sawyer shot a warning look at his brother.

"Heard you got yourself a handful of woman." Brett pushed a cow further along, glancing up from his clipboard.

Sawyer studied him for a second. "You know as well as I do what Dodge is capable of."

Brett spat a large plug of tobacco from his mouth, seemingly in a hurry. "I know that right well, speak of the devil."

Dodge made her way over, carrying a basket. "Brett, I saw that. It's a nasty, filthy habit. Boys." Dodge leaned to kiss Brett on the cheek anyway.

"Dodge." Evan pulled a branded yearling across the corral to set her out.

"What have you done with Rose?" Dodge inquired of Sawyer.

He could see it coming and pushed his hat back a bit and smoothed his dark beard. "She...well, she's rounding up a few strays. I'm sure she'll be here in a bit."

"Sawyer McCade...if that woman is harmed in any way—never mind the Indians, rustlers, or other bandits. And she doesn't even know our horses." Dodge stopped at Evan's snicker behind her.

"She's fine on a horse, Dodge, but it would be

worth making sure she doesn't lose her direction." Evan cackled, avoiding the swift kick Sawyer sent his direction.

It didn't go past Sawyer that Brett was stifling his own laughter. There was no telling what Evan had told him. He fisted his hands and glanced at Dodge once more and turned to mount Colonel. He'd deal with Evan and Brett later on, and as much as he didn't want to think it—Dodge was right, though the dangers she mentioned were rare on McCade lands. He'd still never forgive himself if he'd left Rose to her own and something did happen. Cursing he urged Colonel to a gallop back the direction he'd come from.

Chapter Six

Rose caught sight of Sawyer riding toward her in the distance. She'd been working to get a few cattle across a small stream when one got stuck in the mud. She hadn't known the mud was so deep, but the cow didn't seem to be able to pull herself free.

"I'm afraid she got stuck when I tried to get her herded. Shoo…come on. Go! Go!" She yelled at the cow, pacing her horse nearby, but not close enough to trap her horse.

"You're never going to get her out like that." Sawyer gave her a half grin but waited, stopping Colonel.

"Well, what would you suggest?" She felt sorry for the cow, which was a rather large calf and the hint of a smile on Sawyer's face didn't help matters. He had probably wished this on her.

Sawyer looked at the struggling calf that bayed over and over. He pulled his lasso free and held it up with a smile, tossing it toward her after a slight nod.

It was all Rose could do to catch the rope and stay on her horse. Did he really expect her to rope the cow and drag it out? She couldn't believe it, but his continued grin told her he wasn't kidding. She glared in protest. Well, she didn't know a thing about how to lasso a cow, but she could tie a rope. She dismounted her horse and began walking in the thick mud toward the cow. Thankful she had the good sense to wear her only pair of boots, she stopped as she began getting deeper, wondering if she dared go any further.

The calf was stuck knee deep and distressed over it. The last thing she wanted was for Sawyer to have to rescue her and the cow. He'd probably lasso her and drag her out given the chance. She took another step and realized she'd simply have to try to toss the rope over the calf's head. If she went any further, she'd sink too deep to get out. She grabbed the rope by the loop end and tossed it, but it landed nowhere near the calf. She took a deep breath and pulled the filthy rope back to try again.

"I tell you what, while you get her tied, I'm gonna round up the rest of the strays." Sawyer turned Colonel, never looking back.

Rose let her mouth drop open and clenched her fist not believing he had left her again. "Oh, fiddlesticks!" She was beginning to think her boots were stuck and the more she moved, the more she seemed to sink. The calf struggled for a minute and then stilled. She sighed and sent the rope sailing toward the calf again and again without moving herself closer.

"Oh, darn it!" She clenched the rope in anger and pulled it back toward her once more. Maybe she should have stayed back at the ranch after all.

Giving the rope one last toss, it caught along the cow's horns. Surprised, she froze, but when the cow's head dipped, the rope nearly slid off.

"No! Don't...no...no!" Rose tugged on the rope, angling it to keep it from coming off, and to her amazement, it tightened. She gave it a tug, and the cow's head bent. Now all she had to do was hang onto the rope and get out of the muck she was nearly knee deep in now. She pulled up on each foot, thick chunks of black mud sticking to her boots. As she got one foot down she fell, her entire left hip in mud. She scampered up as quickly as she could from the mucky mess but didn't let go of that darn rope.

"As soon as I get out of this, I'll show him I did it." She stomped hard once on solid earth. Mud slung from her boots and her pants as she walked. She shook her head, still hanging onto the rope and took a look at Sawyer galloping his horse with a large number of cattle pacing before him.

He was so sure in the saddle, the outline of his muscular thighs hanging onto the horse. His broad shoulders tightened and her heart skipped a beat, but then she remembered he had left her and she still had to get the calf out of the mud.

She allowed the rope length to walk to her waiting horse. Climbing into the saddle, she wrapped the rope around the horn. Turning the horse, she urged him away from the calf to pull it free of the mud. The calf resisted, sinking further in its struggle. Somehow it wasn't working, and the horse didn't seem to know what to do, not to mention her saddle was pulling to the side from the weight of the calf on the rope. She tugged harder at the reins, the horse bucking, and without warning, the saddle slipped and she fell from the horse.

She braced for the earth below, landing hard on her backside. The wind left her lungs, and she grunted on impact. She gulped a quick breath of air, grabbing her backside. Oh God, she knew she must've broken something, and if she hadn't seen Sawyer out of the corner of her eye, she might have cried. She turned and the cow was finally free of the mud, dragging the rope along.

Letting go of her aching behind, she stood and grabbed the rope trying to hang on, but the calf ran. She yelped and let go of the rope, clenching her fists. Rope burns. She opened her palms and cringed at the blistered skin. She should have known to wear gloves, but she had never imagined she'd be doing what she had. Now she fought hard to keep tears at bay. Sawyer was dismounting behind her and she couldn't let him know her hands were burned and she couldn't let him know her pride and rear end ached even worse.

He ran to catch the rope still tied to the cow, wrestled the yearling closer and set it free. Pulling in the rope, he turned back to Rose. "Are you hurt?"

"I am just fine." She lied. Her backside pained and she was sure she'd be purple by afternoon.

He took a few steps toward her, but stopped short. "You hit hard, maybe I should take a look."

"You will do no such thing. I am just fine." She turned back to her horse, warmth spreading across her cheeks. Did he honestly think she'd let him have a look?

"No. Really. You fell hard? You did well until you tied her to the horse, it's better to back the horse up instead of urge him forward. Rose, are you hurt?"

She stopped to look at him. He'd said her name so softly, she thought he might truly be concerned. "I've been thrown before." She whispered as she adjusted the saddle, pulling tightly to secure it and trying not to grimace with her blistered hands. She mounted the horse again, aware he watched her.

"Thrown before?" He mounted Colonel and rode

closer.

"Is that so hard to believe? I rode for showing Papa's prize horses since a very young age, and if you ride long enough, it's bound to happen. Besides I didn't fall, the saddle shifted."

"Well, you hit hard. Let's head back, it's nearly lunch time." He took Colonel to a slow canter, peering into the sky.

Rose took a quick peek at her raw hands once more and struggled to find a comfortable grip on the reins. She would need to add gloves to the list of things she wanted to buy when she went to town, that and likely another pair of riding pants, given the stains the ones she wore would now carry.

Arriving where the cattle were merging, she lost track of Sawyer, ambling along on her own horse. A number of dusty cowboys pushed cattle toward the branding area, but past there she spotted the chuck wagon as they called it. She rode closer. Mei Ling was cooking over a fire, the hint of a meaty stew lingering in the air, along with the smell of earth and cattle. She dismounted and tied her horse to the wagon. It was so hot her blouse was sticking to her, and she used her sleeve once again to wipe her face, grateful she'd thought of wearing her hat that she pushed back.

"Miss Parker returns." Mei Ling glanced up with a smile. She was a beautiful woman, with her bronze colored skin and her deep almond shaped eyes. She had wondered the friendship Mei Ling and Dodge seemed to share, almost as if they were sisters, even down to the occasional bickering and fussing over how things should be done from cooking to cleaning.

"Please, you must call me Rose." Rose stepped

closer looking into the large pot of stew.

Mei Ling nodded in respect and continued with her work, humming quietly.

"I can see Sawyer has had you pulling cattle out of the mud." Dodge came from behind the chuck wagon, carrying a basket of bread loaves.

"Nothing a little soap and water won't cure." Rose looked down. She was a mess, given the fall in the mud. At least she had gotten the cow out and proven to Sawyer she could, even if her backside still ached.

"The men will be along shortly, would you like to help us serve?" Dodge set the bread basket down and reached for a pile of stacked bowls.

"Of course." Rose followed her to the back of the wagon.

"Fill the cups with water from the barrel and set a cup alongside each bowl. It's an army of men who'll be eating."

Men from both ranches began coming by a few at a time for a quick meal of stew, bread, and cool water.

"Ladies." A tall cowboy with a matt of thick gray hair and mustache to match nodded his head.

"Brett, I'd like for you to meet Miss Rose Parker. She'll be staying with us for a time, seeking the adventure of the West." Dodge made the introduction as if Rose were an old family friend.

Brett nodded again. "You'll find more than adventure out here."

"I think I already have. It's a pleasure to meet you." Rose handed him a cup of water. He was a handsome man, and she'd seen the knowing glance he'd exchanged with Dodge. So this was the Brett she'd heard Dodge and Sawyer both mention.

Evan joined them, tilting his hat back and using his bandana to wipe the sweat from his brow. "Mei Ling, hope you got the stew going strong."

"You eat too much." Mei Ling stirred the pot but filled a larger bowl to heaping.

"My youngest son happens to be the one built like a wall, all due to Mei Ling feeding him so well," Dodge explained to Rose but gave Evan a side hug.

"I'm the favorite all around." Evan dug into his bowl of stew with a chuckle.

"He's not the favorite, but he is damned spoiled." Sawyer grabbed a bowl and eyed Rose, bracing against the hard shove Evan gave him as he passed by. "He's really a whiny baby."

Rose laughed at the playful exchange. What was it like to have siblings and brothers at that? Muriel had been the closest thing she'd had to knowing what it would be like to have a sister. Sawyer and his brothers constantly picked at each other, but there was a hint of caring in the jests of fun.

Evan gave Sawyer a smirk. "I'm not whiny, I just have high expectations like someone else I know."

Sawyer raised an eyebrow at his brother but turned his attention back to Rose. "You're limping?"

"I'm fine." She nodded, but could say nothing more with his face so close to hers. Her heart thudded against her ribcage, and for a half second, she wished he *would* kiss her. But he simply took his stew and turned to sit nearby, leaving her alone with her racing pulse and aching backside.

Men continued coming up for their meal a few at a time. Most seemed surprised by her presence. Some of the men spoke, while others only smiled and went about their business. She felt quite the spectacle, and each time she glanced Sawyer's direction, he was watching her, though he'd quickly find something else to focus on. She wasn't sure what to make of his actions. He was obviously keeping track of her in spite of most often being annoyed with her.

When they had finished eating, she assisted Dodge and Mei Ling with cleaning up, the cool water providing a bit of relief for her burning hands.

Suddenly, Sawyer grabbed her by the arm, startling her. "Come on, we're going branding."

"Wait, I need to help finish—" She needed to help Dodge and Mei Ling with the clean up.

"They got it. Let's go." He tugged her along to where Brett, Evan, and a few other men were branding one cow at a time. One man had the long branding iron and was pushing it hard to the resisting cattle. Some bucked and kicked for a second and were then released.

Rose wrinkled her nose to the smell of burnt hair and flesh.

"Not much to your liking?" Sawyer urged her closer to watch.

"It must be painful. Is there not a better way?"

"No, there isn't another way. We can't put silly collars on them like ladies in New York with their fancy dogs." He reached a gloved hand for the iron, taking it from the man who held it with a nod.

The next cow was put into place, and Sawyer shoved the iron into her hands. She stifled a screech at the pain but would not give him the satisfaction of knowing her hands were burned.

"I can't do this." She tried to hand the iron back to him, her hands stinging at the effort.

"Go ahead, you're holding up progress." He nodded toward the waiting men.

Rose hesitated for a moment. He'd planned for her to have a hard day, and this was part of it. He might be a cowboy sheriff, with experience of the ranch behind him, but she could do anything if she tried hard enough. The iron was heavy and very warm, adding to the pain of her rope blistered hands, but she held it tight. Smirking back at him, she focused on the task. She held the metal rod, took a deep breath, and pressed it firmly to the cow's rump. It surprised her that it only took a second to make a brand, which left an *M* with an overlapping *C* singed into the cow's flesh.

"There." She handed the iron to Sawyer, smiling spryly and trotted away in triumph.

"Got yourself some kind of feisty right there, Sheriff." Brett chuckled along with Evan, but turned back to his work.

Rose didn't turn but heard Sawyer's curse. In spite of her injured pride, she was elated at her small victory and continued back to her horse.

****

By dusk, the cattle had been branded, and Dodge and Mei Ling had taken the wagon back to the ranch after the evening meal. Sawyer had seen Rose riding toward the ranch following another group of hands, but he'd gotten distracted and lost track of her. He'd thought she might have waited on him, but then he had all but ignored her for the afternoon and evening.

"Heading in...haven't seen Wyatt today, likely means things were busy in town." He rode toward Evan who was tallying numbers, leaning on the corral fencing.

"You and I both know he's avoiding hard work." Evan didn't look up from the tablet he held.

"Yep." Sawyer shrugged. It was true, Wyatt hated cattle branding and generally anything to do with the ranching business. He usually managed the jail or found a reason to be out of town for a bounty, and it was no surprise he hadn't shown.

Sawyer urged Colonel toward home, taking his time and enjoying the cooler night air. Arriving at the ranch, he dismounted and led the tuckered horse by the reins into the barn. Rose was still inside, and he watched her for a moment. Even mud-covered and messy-haired, she was still entertaining for the eyes as she went about unsaddling her horse.

"So you made it back." He led Colonel into his stall, feeling a bit guilty he had made her day harder.

"I actually have a good sense of direction, but I had no idea where the cattle drive was being held." She glanced at him briefly and went back to the saddle she'd been working on.

Actually, he thought she'd done well even in the mud and with the fall she had taken. He'd learned something about her determination which wasn't a surprise given her reluctance to get back on the train to New York. He removed Colonel's saddle and turned the horse out to the corral after a quick brush down.

Suddenly Rose yelped.

"What happened?" Sawyer darted his gaze her way, slinging the saddle on its mount.

She kept her hands fisted, avoiding eye contact. "Nothing—"

He trotted closer, giving her a cautious look and grabbing her wrists before she could resist, suspecting injury.

Trying to free herself from his grasp, she gripped her fists tight, glaring at him.

"Open." Sawyer held her wrists firmly, holding her stubborn gaze.

She clenched her fists tight for a moment. Her blue eyes held a hint of anger, but then she slowly opened her hands. He lightened his grip and studied her palms. Both held dark red rope burns with torn blistered skin.

"Rope burns." He shook his head. "I should have given you gloves." He led her to the workbench behind them. Not letting go of her, he opened one of the cupboard cabinets and grabbed a round tin, opening it and dipping his fingers inside.

"I'm fine." Rose tried to tug free of his grip once more.

He slid his hand from her wrist to hold her open palm and tenderly rubbed in the ointment. He watched as she bit her bottom lip and shivered. He loosened his grip, worried he'd hurt her, but realized she watched his face intently. He lingered, rubbing in the ointment longer than needed. Touching her like this turned his body to a furnace, and he hadn't expected that. Against his better judgment, he drew her nearer with each swirling round of his fingertips.

She resisted, digging in her boots.

"Hold still." He peered down at what he was doing and then repeated the massage of her other hand meeting her gaze, the ointment silky and warm and— damn she was beautiful, up close.

She stopped resisting but held her stubborn frown.

"This'll help. Put it on a couple of times a day. You'll be good as new." He was surprised at his own reaction in touching her. Somehow she'd stirred up a lot of feelings he hadn't felt in a long time. "Might help that backside of yours too."

Her mouth dropped opened and her face blushed to the angry boil he liked. "You are so...rude!"

Sawyer shook his head. "I'm not rude, just offering my help." He smiled sincerely but held her tighter, not allowing her to pull away. If he were to medicate her backside, they would both be in a heap of trouble. He glanced at her again, and she was trying to stifle her smile. Was that an invite? All right then. He'd have his kiss, the one he'd been thinking of since she'd gotten off the train a few weeks ago. He pulled her closer and leaned toward her.

"What are you doing?" Her words faded to a breathless whisper the closer she got.

"I'm about to kiss you...Rose Parker." His lips touched hers, tender and soft. He thought for sure she would pull away and perhaps even slap him, but a soft sigh escaped her and her body relaxed into his. He wrapped his hands around her and pulled her against him, deepening the kiss, needing to taste her and wanting a hell of a lot more than that. He parted her lips, and his tongue touched hers in a soft tender dance. She tasted of mint, just as sweet as he'd thought she might. He let his hands wander down her sides, touching her hips, touching the damn pants he'd admired all day. Sweet, damn sweet.

"Billy, you get the horses put away, and we'll see about you taking a shift as soon as the doc says you're healed."

Evan. *Shit.* Sawyer should have figured one of his brothers would ruin the moment.

Rose pulled from him with one lasting gaze, her face flushed pink, and she slipped from his grip and the barn, not looking back.

Sawyer cursed under his breath and glared at Evan who only gave him a knowing grin and headed outside to the corral. Well at least he had the decency not to embarrass Rose by spouting off and making light of the situation.

Sawyer turned and glanced outside the barn where Rose had disappeared. He shook his head unsure how he felt about any of it. He should have never let his guard down with the woman, but now it was too late and without a doubt he knew it. He had kissed her because she hadn't resisted when he tugged her closer. He had kissed her because he hadn't thought about anything else for weeks. And finally he had kissed her because—he just plain damn wanted to.

Chapter Seven

Sawyer shuffled through the wanted posters that had arrived with the morning stage. He read the reports and studied each picture, committing faces to memory. He rose from his chair and stretched, then wandered outside the office to pin the posters on the wooden notice board. As he turned, he caught a glimpse of a woman walking into the mercantile and stopped in his tracks. Rose. She must have ridden into town on horseback, and she was in those darn riding pants, minus the mud, once again. If that didn't cause a major disturbance in town, he didn't know what would.

He stomped toward the mercantile to handle the situation, gritting his teeth and swearing a few choice words. Trying to keep Rose at a distance was becoming difficult and worse was his own darn interest being the problem. He couldn't keep a thought of her out of his mind. He shook his head. Inside, Dodge was looking over the books with Burt Lester who managed the mercantile.

"Hi, Sheriff. Your mother is swindling me out of more profit." Burt rolled his eyes waiting as Dodge figured and jotted down numbers.

"You shouldn't trust her, not for one second." Sawyer narrowed his eyes, folding his arms.

Dodge paid them little attention and continued with the books. "I swindle no one. Your numbers are right on track, Burt, but it's summer. You don't need the piles of feed you ordered, least not until fall. You'll end up selling it for less the price just to get rid of it."

"I think I found just what I needed Mr. Lester." Rose arrived at the counter and laid down a pair of gloves, a writing tablet, some candles and pink satin ribbon. She acted as if she hadn't seen Sawyer and reached into her purse for the coins.

Sawyer simply watched her, speechless for the moment. "Rose, I'm just about ready." Dodge turned to Sawyer. "We're having lunch, and I'm showing Rose further around town. Want to join us?"

"Uh…no. I'm meeting Marcus Benton." Sawyer wasn't looking forward to it, but he needed to see exactly what Benton was thinking about the river and the cattle making the crossing where his men stayed on guard. He eyed Rose who had yet to talk to him since they'd shared the interrupted kiss just a few days ago.

"You got Marcus to come to town?" Concern laced Dodge's voice.

"If he shows." Benton's men usually handled his business dealings, and it was odd he would be in town unless it was for a visit to the bank. He'd sent a rider out with the request days ago, and earlier that morning, one of Benton's hands had come by with the message he would arrive by afternoon.

"Don't aggravate things further," Dodge warned, coming around the counter.

"I've got this Dodge." Sawyer gazed from her to Rose and back, shoving his hands in his trouser pockets.

"I know you've got it but be careful anyway," Dodge scolded.

"Perhaps lunch another day then, Sheriff McCade?" Rose finally glanced at him but followed Dodge outside after only a slight smile.

He followed, watching Rose from behind, certainly a sight worth seeing. She was petite, but full of womanly curves and still seemed to have no idea how inviting she really was. The thought brought him back to the real reason for having followed her to the mercantile. He was going to suggest she not wear those damn pants to town. It just wasn't safe.

Two men stepped outside the saloon, apparently for the express purpose of watching Rose in her riding gear. A hint of possessiveness bolted through him, and he crossed the street. That did it.

"You boys got something of interest here?" His tone was sharp as he tilted his hat back and folded his arms.

One man nodded toward Rose, who was walking with Dodge through the hustle and bustle of town.

The man whistled and then commented, "That's some kind of woman right there, Sheriff."

Sawyer wanted to put a stop to them both, but Jacob walked outside the saloon.

"She is off limits boys." Jacob never took his gaze from Sawyer, and the two men returned inside the saloon, one still trying to ogle a look at Rose.

Sawyer knew Jacob well, and he also knew he and Lang from the livery gossiped more than a quilting circle. Lang was already aware of the situation between Sawyer and Rose, and Jacob's sly grin said he knew too.

"You and Lang been chatting?"

"Ain't no secret, you following her around town

like a hound got the scent." Jacob gave a hearty, toothless laugh.

Sawyer hadn't thought his interest in Rose so obvious. She had only been in town a couple of times since arriving in Cheyenne. Damn busybodies, but there was no point in arguing further. "Keep these drunks off the street." He headed toward the office, leaving Jacob with an icy glare of warning.

As he passed the barbershop, he caught sight of Wyatt and shook his head. The man spent more time primping than working. Stepping inside he kicked his brother's boot, causing Harry, the barber to jerk the razor away from Wyatt's face.

"What's that for?" His brother never opened his eyes.

"Hold still deputy, or you'll lose your nose." Harry scowled.

"For slacking." Sawyer plopped down in a chair. "You primp like a girl."

"Yep, but I look good. Got a new shirt to boot. Did Benton show?" Wyatt tugged up the front of the light brown, dressy buttoned shirt.

"Probably later this afternoon." Sawyer shook his head. Wyatt had been known to order fancy shirts and trousers out of Chicago now and then. It made no sense to him, given the work they both did.

"Evan's all stirred up." Wyatt's eyes remained closed.

"Evan needs to watch his mouth, and you need to keep a low profile. Evan irritates the man, but he hates the likes of you." Of course, it was no secret that Marcus Benton cared little for all the McCade brothers, but he had some kind of deep seated hatred for Wyatt. It worried Sawyer. Hell, everything about the man kept him on edge. Of late, he couldn't help but feel there was more trouble brewing besides the obvious—and he'd been waiting a long time for what was coming.

"I'll keep that in mind." Wyatt used a towel to clean the remaining shaving cream from his face, then handed Harry a coin along with the cloth.

Sawyer recognized Wyatt's tone and was well aware of his brother's short fuse. Wyatt was a hard man. Driven at times. He rarely carried on business dealings without escalation, but he thought things through, and could out-think even the best outlaws.

"I'm asking you to keep your mouth shut." Sawyer stepped out on the porch with a stern warning. Wyatt tended to think he could take on the world and at times needed to be grounded, made to realize he wasn't invincible.

Wyatt followed. "I'll play nice if he does."

Sawyer turned to glare at his brother, but Wyatt was looking across town, his interest elsewhere.

"Damn, brother, why can't you jump right into that?" Wyatt nodded to Rose waiting outside the jail, her back to them.

Sawyer smacked a fist into Wyatt's right shoulder, hard enough to knock him back a few steps.

"Hey, I'm just saying. Look at her, Sawyer. I don't have any idea what's holding you back. That right there is downright breathtaking." Wyatt rubbed his shoulder. "Jackass."

"Handle the men at the saloon." A whole flock of men were hanging outside, as if Rose were some kind of main attraction at a tented circus.

Wyatt shook his head and strolled that direction.

Sawyer glared another warning toward the saloon and made his way across the street, to face Rose. "You need to head back to the ranch if you and Dodge are done with lunch."

"Dodge went back to the mercantile for a while. I brought you and Wyatt sandwiches." She gave him a hint of a smile, but it was apparent she had no idea what a spectacle she currently had become.

He lowered his voice. "I'm going to have Wyatt ride with you back to the ranch. You can't trust these men, as I've told you."

Rose followed him into the office. "I don't need an escort. I'll keep my distance."

"Wyatt's going to take you back to the ranch and that is that." He looked up as his brother's form darkened the doorway.

"What am I doing?" Wyatt asked, tossing his hat to a nearby chair, clomping inside.

"You need to get her back to the ranch. She shouldn't ride alone." Sawyer upped his tone a bit. Getting Rose to the house safely was a ploy to get Wyatt out of town before Marcus Benton arrived and his brother damn well knew it.

"Sawyer, it's broad daylight. and those men are too drunk to follow her," his brother protested, staring out the window. "Besides. Benton just rode in."

"Damn it," Sawyer hissed. "Rose, just…over there and keep quiet. Wyatt, watch yourself." Damn it, this was all he needed with Rose inside and his brother already on the defense. Rose sat, obviously startled at his tone, but at least following his direction for once. Her blue eyes were wide with wonder, and he had to force his gaze away.

He turned as Benton and two men entered the office. Wyatt moved in behind him.

"Sheriff." Benton waited. He glared at Wyatt with a snide smirk and back to Sawyer.

"Benton." Sawyer stuck out his hand.

The man ignored the gesture, walking closer. "You got me here, *McCade*. I assume our discussion is about my men guarding the river."

"Have a seat, gentlemen." Sawyer nodded to the chairs, cursing under his breath at the man's clear avoidance of his gesture.

"We won't be here long enough to sit." Benton's stern voice echoed in the office.

Sawyer never wavered. "Always down to business. All right. Several ranches are bringing in cattle from Kansas in a few weeks. I'm asking that you allow them to cross the river on your property as usual, minus the gunfire." Even if Benton agreed, he wasn't to be trusted. He was indirectly responsible for crime from Wyoming territory through the Dakotas and as far as San Francisco.

"It's exactly as you said. *My property*." Benton tilted his hat back, glaring.

"The river is not yours, it belongs to the Wyoming Territory and cattle have always crossed there." Sawyer never raised his voice, but this wasn't about the river alone and Benton knew that too.

"Did Brett Morgan put you up to this?" Benton asked, narrowing his dark eyes.

"I am asking you man to man, but I am telling you as the sheriff of Cheyenne." While that didn't make one bit of difference to the man Sawyer said it anyway.

"Morgan is the least of my worries, but that

younger brother of yours, his spouting off won't be tolerated much longer." Benton folded his arms across his chest.

Wyatt moved closer, glaring at Benton, who took his own step forward. Sawyer placed himself between them. "My father respected you as a man of integrity. I am asking you to allow the cattle to pass." Sawyer waited to see if the mention of his father would work on Benton's conscience—if the man had one. If what he suspected was true and it was, he'd been biding his time for a long while, but time was running short and so was his patience.

Benton only nodded. "Your father was a good man."

"My father was a great man." Sawyer countered. Benton's comment wasn't sincere. The two had once been friends, turned enemies over land disputes and— Dodge. He wasn't sure how much Wyatt knew, but Benton had loved Dodge before she married their father. Sawyer didn't know all the details either, but Benton's hatred stemmed from that and the fact that Brett had somehow won Dodge's heart over the years. And there was no doubt there was plenty more swept under that rug.

Benton only glared.

"The cattle can't be taken another route. There's no other water. The men will be bringing the cattle through with the law if that's your only compromise." Sawyer gritted his teeth and balled his fists.

"Then men will die, starting with that mouthy brother of yours." Benton turned to leave, his men moving out the door before him.

Wyatt pushed closer. "You know, I'm going to

enjoy dragging your ass in, when I collect the bounty on you and your mile long list of counts. I've already taken in two of your best men. How's that setting with you?"

Benton turned abruptly, glaring at Wyatt.

"That's right. You won't be able to hide behind your money and connections for much longer. You are digging yourself in deeper every day, and God help you if you lay a hand on my brother." Wyatt's dark blue eyes were full of rage, his fists clenched.

Sawyer wedged himself in between his brother and Marcus Benton. Wyatt was about to blow and that was the last thing he needed.

Benton only smirked "No, Bounty Hunter—God help *you*." He joined his men outside.

Wyatt fought to pull free, but Sawyer held him until Benton was out of sight. "That's enough!" Sawyer strained to keep Wyatt in place. If he didn't make things clear, Wyatt would follow Benton outside and get himself shot.

Sawyer pushed him hard against the wall, holding him there. He hated manhandling Wyatt, but there'd been times like this where he'd had no other choice. "That's enough!"

"I'll kill that bastard before this is all over, I swear to God, I'll slit his throat," Wyatt spoke through gritted teeth.

"He'll kill you if you aren't careful."

Wyatt pulled free, holding his brother's gaze.

Sawyer glanced at Rose who sat still, her eyes wide in fright. She couldn't have any idea what was truly going on. She opened her mouth to speak, but he held his hand up, turning back to Wyatt. "This isn't just about the crossing and you know that."

"I'll bring him in one day, or I'll bring him down." Wyatt stomped past him and outside.

Sawyer took a deep breath. Wyatt was hard to handle when he let his temper go. Actually, he could feel his own anger escalating inside at just being near Marcus Benton. As much as he could taste revenge, he had to make sure. He turned back to Rose. "I'm sorry you had to see all this."

Dodge trotted quickly through the open door, her expression that of concern. "I suppose Wyatt and Marcus got heated once again."

"If it isn't bad enough that Evan is running his mouth all over town, I got Wyatt who can't control his temper." How was he supposed to act as sheriff, when he couldn't keep his brothers in check, never mind himself, where Marcus Benton was involved?

Dodge glanced at Rose and back. "You know Wyatt will find his way. He always does. And the cattle?"

"We'll get the cattle across." He wasn't so sure it would be without blood loss.

"I'll talk to Evan and Wyatt. Rose, I'm heading to the ranch, are you ready?" Dodge touched her arm.

"I'll meet you at your buggy in a moment." Rose said it never taking her eyes from Sawyer.

Dodge nodded and glanced at him once more before she turned to go.

"There's more than the river then?" Rose spoke softly after a moment of silence.

"Brett and Benton have had an ongoing feud for years, and each one keeps adding to the pot. It's something new that Benton won't let the herds cross the river. Why don't you go ahead with Dodge. I'll catch up in a bit." He hoped to head her back to the ranch before she could ask anything more or remain the town attraction. He couldn't very well explain it all right now, but his gut was telling him it wouldn't be long— not anymore.

She nodded as she walked past him, placing her hand in his and squeezing, meeting his gaze. Damn she was some kind of beautiful, her blue eyes sincere and concerned. He turned her hand in his and peered down at their joined fingers. She let go and left the jail, saying no more. He turned and watched her walk all the way to where Dodge waited at her buggy. He'd still forgotten to tell her about her damn riding pants. *Holy, holy hell.*

He'd barely recovered from her touch when Hudson arrived for his shift. Sawyer filled in the deputy on the happenings and made his way outside. Taking Colonel to a full run once he was outside of town, he caught up with the ladies, and Wyatt was just ahead. So, even in spite of his anger, Wyatt had made sure to escort them home. He urged Colonel faster to catch up to his brother.

"Hudson came in early for a change." He tried to gain his brothers attention.

"I'll get there early tomorrow to relieve him." Wyatt never glanced his way, obviously still peeved.

Thunder cracked in the distance, threatening rain. Well that would just add to his mood.

"Mei Ling said the rain was coming in." Dodge held her hat on her head, catching up to them, Rose just behind on her own mount.

Sawyer gazed at the darkening sky. "It's on the way." He met glances with Rose for a moment. It

106

surprised him she had reached out to him so easily, given she hadn't talked to him since that kiss. He had seen her in the window of her room, watching as he'd come home each evening, and had somehow started looking forward to that view. But now her touch. Somehow, it had stirred a place in his heart he thought he'd long since put away. It had been a long time since a woman's simple touch was able to calm him—and he liked it. A lot.

****

Large drops of rain hit the dry soil, stirring up puffs of dust as they arrived at the ranch. Wyatt dismounted and grabbed the reins to Dodge's horse and waited as she climbed down and vanished inside the house.

Rose was quick to scamper off her horse near Sawyer, who reached for the reins in her hand.

She shook her head. "I'll take her. We're getting to be good friends." She shielded her face from the rain and led the horse along toward the barn, Sawyer following with Colonel.

"She's a good trail horse, not much for work anymore." Sawyer removed his hat and shook it, water slinging to the barn floor.

"That's why I picked her, seems no one rides her much and she has the gentlest spirit. Dodge calls her Sadie." Rose began to remove the saddle, the raindrops having left large spots of water across her shirt and trousers and her hair dripping.

"Nope, I'll get that. Let me see your hands." Sawyer worked his way closer for a view.

"All better." She held up her palms for his inspection. "Besides, I don't think they were hurt as much as my pride." Frankly she had been embarrassed as she knew how to ride a horse, just not how to get a cow from the mud.

"I tried to help you with your pride." His lips curled into a smile. "You ride well."

"But not because you wanted me to," she challenged, eyeing him.

"You needed a real taste of the West, a day out on the trail chasing cattle and I think you got it." He started with Colonel, turning his back to her.

"And I think you got a little taste of something else as well." She continued working on the horse as if it were nothing. Just the thought of that kiss caused heat to rise to her cheeks and then make a thorough path through her belly and lower.

Sawyer snapped around to look at her, but said nothing.

She slung the saddle across the fencing beside the stall and turned to walk out of the barn. Even if he might not admit it, his interest in her was evident. She might not know about life in Cheyenne and though she wasn't experienced with men in the real sense, she'd known the art of flirting for years. Without a doubt he watched her until she entered the house, and she had to fight not to look back.

Inside, she climbed the stairs to her room, let her hair down, and dried it with a towel. Thunder rolled, shaking the house, and heavier rain began pounding across the roof. She changed her clothing for dinner and brushed through her hair, leaving it down to dry. Laughter came from outside, and she went to the window and pulled back the curtains.

The rain poured in droves, creating large spouts of showering water running from the eaves of the barn. At first she couldn't believe her eyes. She blinked, thinking she was seeing things, and then had to giggle, covering her mouth.

Evan and some of the hands were washing in the downpour of water from the barn spouts. As she watched, most, including Evan, stripped off their clothes and bathed off in the pouring streams. There were probably six or seven men bathing, some scrubbing hard, while others horsed around, slinging soap and even mud at each other. She started to close the curtain, but as she did, Wyatt and then Sawyer came from the barn, both as naked as the day they were born.

She froze, closing the curtain a bit more, lest Sawyer see her ogling. She'd never seen a grown man undressed in spite of being married, and now there was a ranch full of them. But at seeing Sawyer—her cheeks heated, and she couldn't pull her gaze from the view outside the rain slicked glass.

His body was muscular, with broad shoulders and a sculpted chest that was covered with a scattering of dark hair. His upper body and arms were muscular and tanned, though his lower half was lighter. She watched as he lathered his hair and body with a soapy rag, allowing the water to pour over him and then standing under one of the spouts of water to rinse. A small trail of dark hair led down the center of his chest to his sculpted belly. He had thick powerful thighs and narrow hips that led to his—he turned. She squeezed her eyes shut and dropped the curtain.

"It's quite the spectacle isn't it?" Dodge asked from the doorway.

Rose's face flamed, She'd been caught spying on the bathing men. Embarrassed she opened her mouth to say something but the words failed her.

"The men around here do that any time it rains, so you might as well get used to it. Their father started it when they were very young, and it's a tradition any time there is a downpour." Dodge walked over to the window and gazed out.

"I heard the laughter and didn't know what they were doing." What could she even say?

Dodge pulled the curtain back further. "You know the funny thing is they couldn't care less who is watching. My boys have never been shy. Evan especially would prefer never to wear clothing. In the heat of the summer, he'll bathe right in the middle of the barn, so a word of warning. Living in a house full of men, it was bound to happen sooner or later. Enjoy." Dodge let go of the curtain and patted her arm as if watching a ranch full of bathing men were nothing at all.

Rose could not believe her comment. *Enjoy?* As the older woman left the room, she turned back to the window. And, with Dodge's permission of sorts, curiosity had the better of her, and she made the smallest opening in the curtain and angled it until all she could see was Sawyer.

Chapter Eight

Sawyer sat on the porch after dinner, looking out across the darkened ranch. He and Rose were the only ones home and had enjoyed their meal along with Mei Ling. Rose and Mei Ling had spent the entire dinner discussing Chinese tradition. He'd not been interested in the stories he'd heard all his life, but he'd watched Rose's response to all she heard. Her expression and chatter were captivating to say the least, though his mind remained focused on the river crossing.

Wyatt was on edge, and while Evan had been warned, there had been a couple of close calls in town with Benton's men. Things were so tense now, that it seemed both sides were ready to blow, and he'd yet to figure the best course of action. His wire for assistance from the cavalry had been denied due to Indian issues in the Dakota Territory. Marcus Benton had kept a low profile since their meeting, and while the night was peaceful, it hardly meant things were quiet. The man was unpredictable and had a lot of hands working for him, and when and if he said the word, there could be an all-out battle on the river or in town, neither of which Sawyer wanted to face for the time being.

He was in deep thought when the door opened. Rose. The evening was warm, but the wind blew a slight breeze across the porch. Thunder rumbled in the distance, threatening yet another summer storm before the night was over. He watched as she walked to the edge of the porch and leaned across the railing, the crimson floral gown she'd worn to dinner swaying lightly in the wind. She took a deep breath, her breasts heaving full.

"God it's so beautiful here." She spoke to herself, unaware he was sitting nearby.

He said nothing, only watched her. She'd let her hair down, and it hung across her shoulders and down her back. When she'd first arrived, he had avoided her, but since they'd kissed, he hadn't had one single night in his bed without thinking about the many ways he'd like to have her.

"A lot of things here are beautiful," he whispered, but some part of him meant for her to hear it.

She darted around, gripping her hand to her chest, her eyes wide. "You startled me. What are you doing?"

He shrugged. "Thinking." While he had frightened her, she was so quick to respond there was still no doubt in his mind she was on the run—overly cautious.

"About the cattle crossing the river?"

"Among other things." He stood and moved to the edge of the porch alongside her.

"Watch in the distance, at the skyline." He pointed, and Rose turned to peer at the distant sky. "The heat brings on the lightning, and it will turn almost pink." He waited, basking in the sweetness of her perfume. The brilliance of lightning hit the darkness, swirling oranges and pinks around the darkened clouds miles from the ranch.

"You can see so far away. In New York, you can't see farther than the city block you are on." Her voice trailed off.

"So...why did you leave New York?"

Rose glowered his way. "I've told you before."

"I don't think so." Sawyer folded his arms.

She said nothing more, looking away from him and across the ranch again.

"I can look at a renegade, watch how he behaves, listen to what he says, and figure a story." He wanted to know the story she wasn't telling. If she were in some kind of trouble, he'd help her if he could, but he had to gain her trust first. She was guarded and had been since she had arrived.

Suddenly she escalated to the feisty temper that always intrigued him. "Well then, if you must know. I held up a train in New York, took all the gold off a ship in the harbor, and I am responsible for robbing two banks. And now I am hiding out among you and your family for safety—a bandit right under the sheriff's nose."

Sawyer frowned, then let out a roar of laughter. He had to hand it to her, she was tough as nails and full of spitfire when riled, but she was avoiding the question.

"It's nice when you let down your guard and laugh." She smirked.

"So you keep telling me."

She went quiet for so long he thought she wasn't going to answer him. When she finally spoke her voice was crisp and mild. "I have a story, same as you, but there's nothing much to tell, in spite of what you may think."

"So you're running?" How could he get her to trust him? He would only do right by her and he didn't figure her a criminal of any kind.

"I'm not running." Panic threaded through her

voice and she took a deep breath. "Why is it so wrong of me to seek something new Sawyer?" She turned to go back in the house, but there was something about the way his given name rolled off her lips. He'd frustrated her, but he didn't want to run her back in the house. He grabbed her wrist, turning her. "I'm sorry, don't go."

She tried to pull free, meeting his gaze. "You're hurting me." She pushed at his hand, and he lightened his grip as he pulled her closer. He hadn't meant to be rough or hurt her, but he wasn't done yet. He'd been waiting for another kiss long enough. He cursed to himself, in spite of it all and tugged her even closer. Without a thought he placed his lips to hers, ever so gently.

He'd known what he was doing, until she sighed and his body went rigid with need. He raised his hand from her back and placed it along her cheek. He nipped at her lips and swirled his tongue along hers, tasting her. He pulled from the kiss and fixed on her half-open eyes for a moment, giving her a second to recover, trying to catch his own breath. Damn he wanted her something fierce. He wanted her fully beneath him, naked and writhing in passion.

Rose drew in a quick nervous breath and let it out, She opened her mouth to speak what he thought might be protest, but wasn't. "I should…go…back inside."

Sawyer gazed into her eyes, waiting, wanting. Damn and he'd have her too, eventually. And one way or another he'd find out the story she wasn't telling and no matter what it was he'd protect her from whatever God forsaken thing was plaguing her. "I'll figure you out Rose Parker…sooner or later."

And then the protest came. "You did that on

purpose, mocking me." She shoved against his chest with both hands, pushing him away and turning to go into the house. The heavy door slammed behind her.

"Rose...Rose...I didn't mean...damn it." He shook his head in disgust. He'd a mind to go after her, but he didn't think it would do any good. He'd been sincere, but it hadn't come out like that. He'd have to wait and let her tell him her story when she was ready and then when the time was right, he'd show her a few other things related to his burning thoughts.

****

Sawyer watched Dodge ride into town from his vantage point across from the mercantile. She had her bag on the back of her horse, hinting to the whole town she'd not been in her own bed last night. It wasn't anything new, but sometimes he wondered why the hell she didn't just marry Brett. She'd planned well enough for him to take a wife in sending for Rose, but she never saw fit to make an honest man out of Brett. He laughed at that backward thought. Dodge never did anything according to etiquette, save her business dealings. And those could be questionable.

As she rode closer, he trotted across the street to meet up with her outside the mercantile. While she'd been at Brett's for the night, she hadn't ridden into town from the direction of his ranch.

"Did you accomplish much by going to Marcus Benton's?" Sawyer took the reins of her horse, brow's narrowed.

"I've just come in from Brett's." She dismounted, grabbing for her bag and holding it up as proof.

He shook his head letting her know he didn't agree with her. "Brett came through here just a while ago."

115

"Well, I hardly need a chaperone with the two of you." She scowled at him as she stepped up to the porch.

"You know, Marcus Benton wouldn't stop at hurting you to get to Brett." Benton's continued interest in his mother didn't mean she was safe from the likes of the man in his book.

"I'm not afraid of him." She turned to go inside.

Sawyer stepped in front of her. "He's capable of a lot more than you are giving him credit for. The river is one thing, but you and I both know this is far from over."

"Yes, and he'll not stop short of killing you boys as well. I simply let him know the consequences of such action." She hissed through her teeth, lowering her voice.

"He'll have to follow the law or be dealt with, that's how it works, but I don't need you in the middle of it all."

"He's not convincible for now anyway, the bastard that he is." She tugged her bag over her shoulder and waited.

"You stay away from him, or I'll jail you to keep you out of trouble." He'd done as much before when she'd stirred up a bit too much trouble a few years ago, with the bright idea that she might just run for mayor. She'd pretty much started a riot among the men in town, and he'd jailed her for her own safety, but she had sworn she would do it again, and he hadn't any doubt that the issue would surface again.

"I'm not afraid of you either." She smirked and pranced past him into the mercantile. He turned back to the street to head to the jail. He'd have to keep a closer eye on her, but he needed to keep an even closer eye on the things happening at Benton's ranch.

****

Rose spent part of the morning shopping and contemplating a telegram to Max or Muriel. Max had warned her not to send anything under any circumstances, but if she were careful or sent word— she sighed. She missed her chats with Muriel. It saddened her that she might never see her again, but it couldn't be helped. Max had gone to great lengths, risking his own livelihood to see her safely out of New York and any contact might make things worse for them and her.

Passing the newspaper office, she noticed the *Help Wanted: Editor/Typesetter* sign just inside the window. She passed by, but then stopped. She needed a job and this was one she could do. While Sawyer hadn't pushed any further about sending her home, he was only interested in figuring out her past. His latest interest in her had seemed promising, though he was so caught up in all the things related to Marcus Benton, he'd been distracted from his attention of her. Maybe it was time she found her own way. After all, he wouldn't let go of trying to find out her reasons, and for now she may as well take those secrets to her grave.

A marriage was obviously not going to happen, but she needed make sure she didn't continue to attract attention around town. Max had sent her as an ordered bride, but he probably had no idea how things had turned out, and a telegram just wasn't wise for now. She studied the sign once more. Writing was her specialty, and she had worked for a paper before, though she knew little about setting type. No matter, she was a fast learner. Taking a deep breath and opening the door, she put on her best smile and made her way inside.

Mr. McDonald came out from the back, holding a large stack of paper in his arms. "Miss Parker, what brings you to the paper today?" He set the pile on the counter, smiling as he shoved his tiny glasses to a better position on his nose.

"Good afternoon Mr. McDonald. I thought I might inquire about your sign, the one about needing an editor and print setter." She chose her words carefully.

"Well, who is interested?"

"I ask for myself. I worked for a newspaper in New York and did a bit of writing and editing," she explained, clutching her purse tighter.

"But typesetting and working the press. Miss Parker, that's very hard work." He spoke nervously, shaking his head.

"I've seen type set, and I know how a press works. I've written numerous articles. I believe I can do this Mr. McDonald." Rose hoped she sounded convincing.

He frowned. "Miss Parker, I...I...understand your interest, but this is probably not...not an appropriate job for...well, for a woman such as yourself."

Rose ignored his stuttering which she had noticed before and tried again. "Has anyone else applied?"

He shuffled the papers before him. "Well...no...not exactly."

"Then what have you to lose in letting me try? I can start as soon as you like." Rose raised her eyebrows and grabbed the stack of papers he'd been trying to shuffle since she had walked in. She stacked them and set them back on the table.

The old man, clearly flustered, thought for a long moment. "I don't know, perhaps I...I...could let you try a few weeks."

"Thank you Mr. McDonald. I won't let you down." Rose jumped up and down and then let go of a giggle of happiness.

He hesitated. "The job comes with a room. The one above the post office. But I suppose you won't be needing that."

"I'll take it. The McCades have been more than accommodating, but it's time I found my own place. I'm sure it will be perfect." A job and a place to live all in one day? Things were looking up.

"I'll show you the room and...an...and you can start at the paper in a few weeks, once you are settled, if you are sure." He swallowed hard, making it through the sentence without a bobble. The poor man had probably never hired a woman—or even dreamed of it.

Rose grinned her satisfaction. "Thank you Mr. McDonald. I am very sure." She knew Dodge wouldn't approve of her being on her own in Cheyenne anymore than Sawyer, but she would be proud of her finding productive work as a woman. She was all but sure that Sawyer would probably have a fit. She went into the mercantile, then made her way to the counter, where Dodge sat working at a small desk.

"Working hard today?" She leaned on the counter.

"Of course." Dodge stood, sorting receipts and setting them aside.

"It's a lovely day, not so hot."

"Mei Ling is our weather expert and says there will be continued drought now." Dodge studied her. "What are you up to? I see it in your eyes."

119

"Well..." She thought carefully. "I will be writing for the paper for Mr. McDonald, along with a few other tasks."

"Ah, a job. I knew you were an entrepreneur the first time I met you." Dodge nodded her approval.

Now for the tough part. "And, I will be taking a room in town. It comes with the job, but I'd rather keep that a secret until I have all the details. It will be a few weeks before I move."

"I suppose there is a certain sheriff who could give you trouble about being in town on your own. Your secret is safe with me, but you don't have to leave the ranch. I've enjoyed having you there." A hint of sadness touched her blue eyes as Dodge took her hand.

"I still have to convince Mr. McDonald I am capable of the task, but I think it's best I find my own way, though you have all been more than generous." She was saddened too. She would miss Dodge and Mei Ling's company.

A commotion came from outside, followed by a familiar voice shouting. Rose turned toward the door, wondering what on earth was happening.

"Evan." Dodge ran for the door, and Rose followed her outside.

On the street in front of the saloon, two men held Evan as another threw punches to his face and belly. Evan buckled but righted himself after each blow, blood dripping from his nose and mouth, as he struggled to free himself.

Rose instantly recognized the men she had seen with Marcus Benton. The larger man had dark hair and evil green eyes. He was laughing after each fist he threw. The other was wearing a dark hat and struggling to hold Evan in place.

"Oh, my Lord." Dodge started forward, but Rose grabbed her arm, stopping her.

"They'll hurt you." She gripped Dodge tighter.

Evan freed a fist, dragging the man with the dark hat along and popping green eyes right in the jaw. Rose caught herself jumping with each fist that landed with a swift smack.

"You son of a bitch!" Green eyes drew back a fist once more.

Out of nowhere, Sawyer ran in to stop the blow, wrestling green eyes to the ground. Both men rolled, punching and kicking in a haze of dust. Rose couldn't believe her eyes and stifled a scream at the display.

"We're damn sick of you running your mouth McCade!" The man with the dark hat, rounded on Evan and swung, hitting him mid abdomen.

Evan doubled over holding his belly. "You wanted…a fight…you…got one!"

Sawyer struggled to free himself from being pinned by the larger man he'd tackled. He rolled to avoid a hit and then pounded a forearm across the man's brow, knocking him back.

Rose couldn't take her eyes from Sawyer, fearing the worst, but he was graceful in each move, often avoiding the fist coming at him and finally kicking green eyes from him and leaping to his feet. The man was nearly twice the weight of Sawyer and came at him quickly pulling a large knife from his boot and roaring in laughter so evil that Rose covered her mouth.

Dodge held tighter to her, and she wasn't sure if it was out of fear or support.

"Oh my God." Rose clung to Dodge just as tightly.

Why had Sawyer not simply pulled his gun from the holster? Wouldn't that put a stop to everything? He was the sheriff, but something inside her didn't want to see him hurt.

When green eyes lunged for him, Sawyer grabbed him by the wrist, jerking him down to his knees. In only a second, he was behind the man, placing the knife to his neck, using the man's own hand. Rose had never seen anything like it. The men she'd known from New York wouldn't last a minute in such fighting. She had never seen such skill and bravery.

"It ends here!" Sawyer shouted, the knife still held steady to green eyes thick neck. The fighting stopped, and Evan dropped to his knees panting and spitting blood to the dirt.

"That's it, all of you." Sawyer glared at each man in turn.

Hudson dashed onto the scene, hand on his holstered revolver. He wore only his suspendered trousers and boots, and no shirt, given the fact he slept most days and worked nights. He froze, glancing at Sawyer, waiting for direction.

"That's right, Sheriff, your brother here—you'd be wise to teach him some manners. We're right tired of his mouth!" Dark hat took a step back.

"Get the hell out of town. I don't want to see you back here." Sawyer's voice was devoid of emotion and dangerously calm.

"Do what he says." Green eyes had his hands in the air, a small trickle of blood dripping down his unshaven neck.

Rose froze as Sawyer slowly removed the knife from the man's throat and allowed him up, shoving him forward. Green eyes only scowled and scampered to join his friend.

Evan crawled to his feet heading after them, though he couldn't keep his balance.

Sawyer grabbed him. "Damn it, you've done enough. It's over."

"No it's not! Those bastards started this, and I aim to finish it." Evan shoved Sawyer backward, his size to his advantage against his older brother.

Rose sucked in a breath of air at their exchange, but it was Dodge who gasped when Sawyer punched Evan in the mouth. Evan's head popped back, and he staggered.

"Sawyer no!" Dodge tore from Rose's grasp, running toward her sons. Rose followed, unsure of how close to get, but picking up Sawyer's hat and stopping just short of the men.

"You're drunk." Sawyer grabbed the front of Evan's shirt.

Rose stared as Sawyer dragged Evan across the street with his arm behind his back. Was he arresting his brother? She followed as did Dodge both entering the jail office behind Sawyer.

"They run their damn mouths, and you're locking me up." Evan yelled so loud his voice echoed inside.

Rose stopped just inside the door, hoping to stay out of the way, but uncertain about leaving Dodge. She could smell the alcohol from Evan's breath which lingered stale in the jail office.

"I've warned you to keep your mouth shut." Sawyer slammed the gate closed after shoving Evan inside the cell, the ringing of the metal causing Rose and Dodge to jump.

"You can't arrest me and not them!" Evan grabbed the bars, shaking them so loudly that Rose squinted.

"I've told you to stop stirring up talk in the saloon," Sawyer shouted back. "You're damn lucky no one pulled a gun."

"They're spouting off at the river, shooting near anyone who crosses, why don't you arrest Benton for starters." Evan slammed his hands on the bars again. "The bastard's causing trouble all over the place and you just let it happen...*Sheriff*. What's the damn hold he has on you anyway?"

Sawyer reached through the bars, grabbed Evan's shirt, and hauled him closer. "This isn't a joke Evan. I've asked you to stay out of the saloon regardless what they start. I'll handle Benton; you just see to it you run the cattle, the men, and yourself." Sawyer gave him a shove backward.

"You can't leave me in here," he yelled.

"Sleep it off, Evan." Sawyer cursed under his breath and shut the door to the back, leaving Evan in silence behind it.

Rose dared not say anything. She'd never seen such a fight and was still shaking. Something in her told her she needed to leave, but another part of her wanted to reach out and touch Sawyer's bruised cheek. She could see the disappointment, hurt, and worry in his darkened gray eyes.

"He'll need Doc Tess to take a look at him." Dodge took a step closer, folding her arms and waiting for Sawyer to respond.

"He can sleep it off first. It's the middle of the week. What's he doing in the saloon anyway?" Sawyer wiped the blood from his lip with the back of his hand, still panting to catch his breath.

Dodge gave a heavy sigh, sorrow in her eyes and lowered her voice to more of a whisper. "Sawyer, it's July—fourteenth."

Sawyer went pale as a ghost right before their eyes, "I've got work to do." He walked past Rose and grabbed his hat from her hands. He never even glanced at her as he stomped from the jail.

Dodge waited only a moment and returned to her natural tone to explain. "It's the anniversary of John's death." She placed her hands on her hips shaking her head as she spoke. "We treat it like the full moon around here. Everyone loses themselves all over again. I try to keep things normal and not even remind them, but it's no use. Wyatt disappears for days at a time. Evan drinks. Sawyer finds work he didn't know he had. The only one who deals well with it is Dawson, who prays to some unknown Cheyenne god."

Rose's heart twisted in pain for Sawyer. "The first anniversary of my father's death was incredibly hard."

"It's been fifteen years, and it doesn't seem to get any better for any of them. Come on, we'll get Doc Tess. Sawyer will likely be gone for a while." Dodge led the way toward the clinic with Rose following.

Rose wondered where Sawyer had gone. She didn't know if the hurt in his eyes was from what had happened with his brother or from remembering his father, though she suspected the latter. Somehow his sadness seemed to echo her own, and if she could have, she might have simply taken him in her arms and held him for a very long time.

Chapter Nine

From the top of the tree line on the ridge, Sawyer waited gazing at the river below. Marcus Benton's men were on guard as they had been for weeks. Funny that they were there to keep ranchers with herds from crossing, yet remained unaware of the band of Sioux watching them from the trees on the other side of the ridge. He'd kept his distance when spotting the braves who were likely only hunting given the number of wild game tied to their horses and their lack of face paint.

He turned his horse toward home given Benton's men remained quiet. As he reached the bottom of the ridge, he rode along the edge of the trail, thinking about his brothers. The river was an endless open sore and now with Evan's recent fight, there wasn't a doubt things wouldn't go well when the herds were brought in. With no cavalry help, it would require him to recruit the other ranchers and hands as sworn in deputies, but then things could easily go awry regardless.

Wyatt was right. It was only a matter of time before someone called Benton's bluff and caught him in all the illegal things he was funding. He never did his own dirty work, and Sawyer had to wonder at the allegiance he gained from his men. It was odd. Some of those men had to know he was crooked and why they stayed made no sense. The two men Wyatt had apprehended recently had worked for Benton at one time and would likely hang for murder in his place, and he knew for a fact they weren't the first men to fall in such a way.

Well, he'd worry about that another day and pushed the thoughts from his head, which opened his mind to the one person who seemed to live there now—Rose. He'd been so preoccupied with the river issues, he hadn't had much time to talk to her, but she'd seemed to keep busy on the ranch helping to prepare the meals and taking care of the wash with Mei Ling. He'd arrived home so late the last week, he hadn't had dinner with the family, and he had to admit he missed her—a little. Hell, he missed her a lot. Her conversations were intriguing and she was definitely educated enough to comment on most any subject.

As he headed his horse along the trail toward town, a movement to the south caught his attention. Grabbing a scope from his saddlebag, he spotted a saddled horse with no rider. The animal appeared to be bleeding and he cautiously turned Colonel in its direction, remembering the Indians. Dismounting, he walked a ways before getting to the nervous mustang, who rocked its head and snorted in warning. It was a beautiful animal, a brown and white paint with blue eyes. Had it not been for the saddle, he would have assumed it belonged to the Indians he'd just seen.

He walked closer grabbing the reins of the frightened animal. "It's all right. That's it...where's your rider?" He continued to move slow and sure, taking a look at the horse's injuries, which oozed streaks of blood along one hindquarter. There were deep scrapes from flank to hip. This horse had taken a fall, and there had to be an injured rider close by.

He tied the limping horse beside Colonel. Pulling his revolver, he began the search on foot. Topping the largest boulders just near the tree line, he took a moment to look around. There was a scattering of items along where the horse must have fallen across slip rocks in the distance. Jumping from the boulders, he made his way over finding saddlebags, a bedroll, a loose bag of clothing, a broken looking glass and a loaded revolver. Careful not to slide down the rocks himself, he grabbed the last item, a hard brown leather case. He slid down keeping his balance along the loose-slated rocks.

Once at the bottom, he piled the things on the ground and glanced around again. An injured rider couldn't have gotten far and even if so, wouldn't have left his things. Surely not the revolver. There were lined tracks along the earth, but no boot prints that led away from the upturned earth. He walked that direction with caution. Glancing further, he spotted the silhouette of a figure lying against a small fallen tree. As he got closer, he realized the rider wasn't a man, but a boy. His eyes were closed and his breathing rapid.

Sawyer moved closer and bent down, touching the boy's arm lightly. "Hey."

The boy stirred, moaning and curling tighter.

"Hey, wake up." Sawyer touched him again, getting a loud moan as he opened his eyes. It was clear he struggled to focus and grunted with each breath, holding his side.

"What happened to you?" Sawyer gently tugged the boy's hand away from his side, taking a look.

"My horse...fell." Grimacing in pain, he focused on Sawyer.

"Let's take a look." Sawyer opened his bloody shirt. He was scraped badly with a large purple bruise leading from his chest down to his belly.

"You likely got broken ribs, what about your shoulder?" He touched it lightly, the boy giving a yelp. It looked broken or at least out of place. "Easy, let's get you fixed up." Sawyer removed his own belt.

The boy closed his eyes, giving in to exhaustion and trying to curl on his side once more.

"Hey. No sleeping." Sawyer spoke loud. It was three miles to town, and it wasn't likely this youngster could sit a horse, but he had to keep him talking to keep him alive.

"What's your name?"

The boy opened his eyes again. His mouth opened but he said nothing for a long moment, something of recognition coming across his face. Gripping his side with a groan, he spoke. "You're…him."

Sawyer pulled the belt around the injured arm binding it to his side to keep it from moving. "I'm who?"

"You're…Sawyer McCade." He yelped loudly as Sawyer tightened the belt.

"Easy. And how do you know that?"

"Because…" The boy winced, throwing his head back in pain. "Ahhhhh. Because…I'm…your son."

Sawyer rocked back on his knees, tilting his hat up. *What the hell?*

The boy opened tear-filled eyes again and locked gazes with Sawyer. He looked more frightened now than when Sawyer had found him.

"I'm Zane Carver…my mother…" He fought to get the words out, "…was Catherine."

Sawyer exhaled every trace of air in his lungs. Catherine? Catherine's son? His son? How could that be? His mind whirled, and for a moment he thought he might pass out cold. He studied Zane again. Zane. His own middle name. Only Catherine would have known—he met gazes with the boy once more, and in that instant he knew. He just knew. He was looking into his own face, his own gray eyes. The face of his son.

"Catherine?"

Zane's chin quivered. "She died last year...I don't...want anything. I...just didn't have...anywhere...else to go."

Sawyer sucked in the breath he'd yet to take. Catherine was dead? He couldn't take it all in or make any sense of it. Catherine was gone, and this was his son. How in the hell had this happened? Well, he knew how it had happened, but why was he just now finding out he was a father?

"It hurts so bad." Zane clutched his side, falling further back against the tree and closing his eyes, his entire frame shivering.

"You stay awake. I've gotta get the horses." He patted Zane's dirty face to keep him alert. Damn if this kid wasn't his spitting image. How had he not seen that? "Are your legs hurt?"

"No sir." Zane glanced around. "My horse?"

"I have your horse. When did you fall?"

"Morning, I...think." He cried with the effort of speaking again.

"I'll be right back." Sawyer stood, so weak in the legs he wasn't sure he could even walk.

"Don't...go." Zane gave into panic, reaching out to him.

"I'll be right back. You stay awake." He went for Zane's things and ran toward the horses his mind whirling the details as he secured what he could to Zane's horse. He and Catherine should never have—too late. He had a son. A son who needed his help, and in no time he returned, bending down and offering the canteen to the pain ridden boy. "Take some water."

Zane sipped little and turned his head, unable to take more than a small swallow.

"If I get you on the horse, can you ride?" Sawyer knew it wasn't likely.

"I'll…try."

"Easy." He grabbed Zane by the right arm and belt, pulling him up.

Zane grimaced, crying as Sawyer got him to his feet. He could barely hold his own weight. Getting him up was one thing, but onto Colonel would be another.

"It's gonna hurt, but we gotta get you up." He tugged Zane's right hand to the saddle horn and his left foot into the stirrup. "Now hold on and pull." He shoved him up onto Colonel, but it was all he could do to keep him there. A wagon would have been better, but there wasn't time for that.

"Ahhhhh…I can't." Zane tried to let go, succumbing to tears.

"Hang on. Falling off will hurt worse." Sawyer held him steady, allowing him to catch his breath.

"I'm…trying."

"It's only a few miles. We'll talk, so you can stay awake." He had plenty of questions, but he wasn't sure he was ready for the answers.

"How old are you anyway?"

"Almost fourteen…my birthday…is August

131

twenty-second." Zane didn't open his eyes but continued as Sawyer pulled the horses along calculating things in his mind that figured correctly. "She never told me of you, but…I read about you…in the papers. I can't ride…I need…to lay…down."

"Yes you can. It's just a little ways, and we're gonna move a little faster." Sawyer held to Zane's knee keeping him in place and urging Colonel to a faster trot. Zane's injured horse managed to keep up, tied to Colonel's other side.

Colonel took a dip in a shallow ditch, and Zane grimaced grabbing his side.

"Steady. I'm gonna get you to the doc." Sawyer braced him, grabbing his arm for a moment, never having felt someone shake so hard.

"I…hurt…so bad. I was…doing good…until today."

"Did you ride all the way from Mankato alone?" Mankato was where he'd gone to see Catherine for the last time, and even though they had agreed to part, how could she have kept a son from him?

"It took…more than…a month and a half." Zane close his eyes and swayed.

"Hey, stay awake!" Sawyer slapped his leg lightly a few times. If Zane had come from Mankato, that had to be more than eight hundred miles. Zane opened his eyes again. Sawyer watched his hand grip the saddle horn trying to stay on Colonel. A hand that looked much like his own, only smaller. If he hadn't come along Zane would've died. He still might. He shook his head and gripped Zane's knee tighter. Some part of him wasn't willing to let the boy go, no matter the cost. Something deep inside him had surfaced and had he the power he would have traded places with—his son.

Zane remained quiet, but he did manage to hold himself on Colonel for the remainder of the ride. The sun was beginning to fall from the blistering sky, offering a bit of relief from the heat, though Zane still shivered. Sawyer led both horses into town, entering from behind the buildings to make the quicker path to the clinic. As soon as he turned the corner at the livery, Wyatt came running from outside the sheriff's office.

"What the hell?" He grabbed the reins to the injured horse, tugging them free from where they were tied to Colonel's saddle.

Sawyer stopped outside the clinic as Lang from the livery came out of nowhere and bolted up the stairs of the clinic. "I'll fetch the doc."

"I found him past the ridge at the river, took a spill on the horse." Sawyer dropped Colonel's reins and nodded for Wyatt to help him.

Zane cried as they lifted him from the horse and carried him into the clinic. Doc Tess met them at the door.

"Get him on the table. What happened?" Tess trotted into the exam room and immediately began washing her hands vigorously in the nearby basin.

"He must've rolled his horse sometime this morning. I got him here as quickly as I could," Sawyer explained, his mind still whirling on the details about Zane.

"Alone? Where was he headed?" Wyatt asked as they got Zane on the table.

Zane shrieked in pain but lay back against the pillow with Sawyer's assistance.

"He's got a bad bruise across his chest, likely

broken ribs and the shoulder is injured." Sawyer wasn't sure how to explain who Zane was for the moment. He wasn't even sure it had sunk if for *him* yet, but nothing mattered save keeping Zane alive. His heart raced, and his mind whirled as he gazed at his son. He wouldn't lose him, not like this, he wouldn't.

"Wyatt get that blanket over there and get his boots and trousers off." Tess changed her tone as she bent to make eye contact with Zane offering a smile. "It's going to be all right. I'm Doctor Tess. I'm going to loosen the belt to your arm so I can take a look. I know you are hurting, but I will be as gentle as I can. Tell me your name." She began with the belt.

Zane settled a little, his breath still short. "Zane."

"Now I want you to relax and let me move your arm." Tess tugged gently at the buckle while keeping Zane's arm steady.

Zane tensed and yelped.

"It's all right. Relax. I'm going to take the belt away. Here we go." She steadied his shoulder and pulled the belt swiftly from around his arm and slowly laid his arm on the table.

Tears escaped Zane's eyes, disappearing into his light brown hair at his temples, but he didn't make a sound as she began cutting his shirt away and examining his injuries.

Wyatt made easy work of tossing Zane's boots aside and tugging his trousers off, leaving him in long underwear.

Sawyer kept a hand on Zane's arm, not wanting to let go. It didn't go past him that Tess froze for a moment at the sight on the bruises on his ribs and upper belly.

"I'll get you something for the pain once I see what all you have going on." She ran her hands over and around his skull and touched some of the bruises to his face. She then took her stethoscope and placed it to various locations along his chest causing Zane to wince when she listened over the injured left side of his ribcage.

Sawyer waited quietly at a loss for words, but studying Zane. He was muscular and tanned from the sun, no less due to his recent travels. That the boy had made such a trip alone likely said a lot about his character. Brave. And he could see that now as he lay on the table trying not to cry and quickly wiping any tears that did escape.

Zane focused on Tess for a moment. "I never…saw…a lady…doctor."

Tess smiled. "Well, I'm all you've got right now."

"No…my mother…said…women should be…anything they…want." Zane explained, wiping his wet face once more.

Sawyer wanted to smile in spite of his concern. Catherine was as feisty as they came. She was fond of pushing the rights of women. But if Zane continued talking of his mother, he'd have to share the story.

"Is most of your pain here?" Tess placed her hands to the bruising on his belly.

Zane grabbed her hand to stop her from touching him, groaning in short raspy breaths. "Please…don't hurt…me."

"Let the doctor work." Sawyer pulled his hand away, keeping a grasp of it.

"I'm going to do this as gently as I can, now tell me where it hurts the worst." Tess began to assess his injuries, pressing gently in various areas just under his ribs.

Zane tensed. "Ahhhhhh! Noooo!"

"I'll get you some laudanum for pain. It will be just a small pinch to your leg." Tess spoke calmly, but something in her face told Sawyer things were worse than he thought. She turned to the medicine cabinet and used a glass syringe to draw up the medicine. She lifted the blanket and gazed at Zane. "Ready?" With his slight nod, she stuck his thigh with the needle and slowly pushed in the medication.

Tess glanced from Sawyer to Wyatt, nodding and leading them into the hallway. "His shoulder is dislocated, and he has four broken ribs, but he's going to need surgery. I suspect he has some bleeding in his abdomen. We need to hurry. He's so young, are you sure he was alone? No family?"

Sawyer nodded. He turned away from them both, sucking in a breath. *What the hell?* Turning back, he met gazes with Tess and then Wyatt. "He's...my son."

"What?" Wyatt frowned in question, shaking his head.

Tess' mouth dropped open. "Your son?"

"I didn't know until I found him. He was riding this way to find me and rolled his horse on slip rocks." Sawyer struggled to explain. Hell, he barely had time to rationalize it himself.

"Your son? Sawyer?" Wyatt's deep blue eyes questioned further.

Sawyer jerked off his hat and ran a hand through his dark hair, wiping sweat from his brow. "Catherine. How does a woman keep a secret like that?"

"Sawyer." Tess spoke, unsure. "He needs surgery

now. I've stopped bleeding like this before, in Boston a number of times, but he isn't good, and I don't know...if he'll even survive."

"You have to try." Sawyer was quick to respond. Losing his son now wasn't an option he wanted to face. He'd seen her save men from death numerous times. Tess held his gaze for a long moment before turning to Wyatt. "Wyatt, I need you to go to the mercantile for Dodge. Sawyer, he needs to know he's going to have surgery. Do you want me to tell him?"

Sawyer shook his head. "I'll do it." Zane was his son, his responsibility, regardless the circumstances. A son. Damn it to hell that Catherine had kept this boy from him. He turned and went back in the exam room, wondering what words to choose.

Tess followed, gathering supplies from the clinic cabinets.

"Zane?" Sawyer spoke softly, his gut clenching tight at the whole situation.

Zane struggled to open his drowsy gray eyes.

Sawyer hesitated, not knowing how to explain. The sudden impact that Zane might actually die was enough to bring him to his knees. He fought the nausea and bile rising in his throat. He was at a loss for words, but it was Zane who spoke first.

"You...aren't mad...I came—" His words were slurred due to the medication. "I don't...want anything...just wanted to know...who you were." He winced, losing his breath to the pain.

Sawyer grabbed his hand. It shook within his own. "Easy." The horse must have fallen right on top of him given the bruises. "I'm not mad." He didn't really know what he felt, but it wasn't anger.

Zane continued. "I thought you might not...want me here."

Dodge raced into the room, followed by Rose. It was apparent that they both knew the story. It wasn't often Sawyer had seen a look of shock on Dodge's face, and he purposely avoided glancing at Rose. When he finally did catch her gaze, all he wanted to do was pull her close and lose himself in the warmth of her body.

Zane squeezed Sawyer's hand, dragging his gaze from Rose. "I didn't mean for this...to happen." Tears ran down his cheeks once more.

Sawyer looked up at Tess who nodded it was time and then back to Zane. "It's all right...I'm glad you came. We can talk about things later, but the doc needs to do surgery."

"No!" Zane glanced away from Sawyer toward Tess, and tried to get up, but the pain was too much and he fell back to the table.

"Zane, you are bleeding inside," Tess explained. "This is Dodge. She is going to help me. We'll give you chloroform, and you won't feel anything. When you wake up, you won't hurt like you do right now. You will only be sore."

Zane shook his head in complete panic. "No, I just need to...rest for a while and...I'll be fine."

"It'll be all right. It will," Sawyer assured him, a stab of dread bolting through him at Zane's fear.

"No, what if I...I don't wake up?" He looked at Sawyer pleading, his chin quivering.

Sawyer lightened his touch and spoke calmly. "Zane. It'll be all right. Doc Tess is the best there is."

"I'm...afraid." He kept his focus on Sawyer.

Sawyer shook his head. "You're not going

138

anywhere. You and I have a lot to talk about."

Sawyer glanced up as Dodge moved into place at Zane's head, reaching for the chloroform and pouring a small amount on a cloth. She remained quiet, studying Zane and likely knowing the situation wasn't good.

Zane's drowsy eyes closed and then opened again. "You'll...stay?"

Tess nodded at Sawyer.

"I'll be right here." Sawyer gripped his son's hand tighter.

Tess motioned to Dodge, who placed the cloth over Zane's mouth and nose. He struggled for a moment trying to turn his head, but Sawyer spoke. "It's all right. We're going to talk when you're all done." He held tight until Zane's shaking hand let go, pleading silently in spite of his own failings as a man, God would have mercy on his son.

Chapter Ten

"Sawyer, hold your hand on his hip and under his arm here. I need to get his shoulder back in place first. Rose steady his legs." Tess took Zane's left arm and moved his shoulder around, feeling for the catch and pulling his arm straight out beside her.

Sawyer held Zane's body as she instructed, still unable to comprehend what was taking place. Rose placed her arms across Zane's legs to add her weight in keeping them there. She glanced at him, and all he could do was look away. He couldn't handle the raw emotions he had now about his son, much less the ones he was feeling for her. Everything seemed to be spinning out of control. How had a simple ride to spy on Benton led him to finding a son? Even in spite of all that had happened, why had Catherine not let him know? He kept playing the past over in his mind, fighting to concentrate. And then there was Rose, so beautiful and...what the hell must she be thinking?

"Don't let me pull him off this table, give me counter pressure." Tess directed them sternly, as Dodge dropped another drop of chloroform to the cloth over Zane's face.

Sawyer shook his head clear so he could follow directions. He had a son, and now his son might die. He didn't like it that Zane had been so fearful of the surgery. Somehow he'd wanted to protect him, even take his place, but he couldn't.

Tess counted and jerked hard, and Zane's shoulder popped back in place with a loud crack. She moved the arm again to make sure it was adjusted, giving a nod of approval.

Rose cringed, turning her head at the loud sound of the bones, but steadied her position. Dodge held Zane's head, keeping a count of his breathing using a pocket watch. Sawyer was amazed she hadn't said as much as a word to him. She'd likely been as shocked as he with the news of a grandson.

"We'll put it in a sling later on." Tess placed Zane's arm to his side. "Rose, can you assist?"

Rose shrugged. "Yes, but I haven't much experience I'm afraid, only with horses."

"That'll do. I need someone washing and sterilizing instruments, boiling water." Tess continued counting instruments and laying them aside.

"I'll start the water." Rose glanced at Sawyer once, her blue eyes concerned and left for the kitchen.

Sawyer stood watching Tess and Dodge who seemed to know what the other was thinking. Few words exchanged between them on the order of things. Dodge often helped Tess, but he hadn't realized how skilled she was with all she did.

"Dodge?" Tess waited scalpel in hand, preparing to start the surgery.

"His breathing is thirty-six and one hundred-forty for his heartbeat." Dodge glanced up from her pocket watch.

Tess made a cut in the middle of Zane's abdomen just under his ribcage. Blood gathered at the incision, spilling off Zane and onto the table. She used cloths that Dodge handed her to soak up blood as she got deeper into Zane's abdomen, working rapidly.

"Sawyer, sit down." Dodge spoke to him, finally.

Sawyer decided while he had promised to stay with Zane, he needed air. Actually, he needed a double whiskey to take the edge off—and he wasn't normally a drinking man. He couldn't think one clear thought. "I'll be back." He walked toward the door as Rose came back in with the rolling pot of hot water. He took it from her and sat it on the counter behind him, turning back to her.

"I'll stay and help all I can." She laid down the armload of cloths trapped under her elbow.

Sawyer nodded. Words were of no use to him right now, but the urge to wrap his arms around her was almost overwhelming, and he didn't understand that any more than he did his son lying near death on the table.

"I've gotta get some air." He walked out, passing Wyatt and Dawson who waited in the office.

"Sawyer?" Dawson's dark blue eyes showed his concern.

Sawyer made his way outside saying nothing, wanting a moment alone so he could think. He left the door open and sat in one of the chairs on the porch. He leaned forward, resting his elbows on his knees and holding his head in his hands. Some part of him wanted to run, but his shaking legs wouldn't have allowed it.

"Why wouldn't she tell him something like that?" Dawson whispered the question to Wyatt.

Wyatt's answer was typical. "Women are damn strange creatures. She didn't like him being a law man."

Hearing his brothers discuss his past mattered little

given Zane's situation. For a moment he thought he might be sick, but he gulped back the nausea once more.

"I should go see about getting his horse to Evan. He can care for the wounds better than Lang." Dawson headed out the door with Wyatt following.

Sawyer leaned back, gazing out across town to avoid eye contact with his brothers. Dawson touched his shoulder as he walked by, heading to the livery.

"Sawyer?" Wyatt stood in the doorway.

"Why didn't she tell me...he's damn near grown...if he survives?" It was a rhetorical question that had no answers.

Wyatt sat in the chair beside him. "He looks strong...Doc can do miracles at times."

They sat in silence for a long while. The sun was setting. It would be dark soon. A son, damn...he had a son. He glanced up as Dawson trotted back across the street toward them. He handed a folded brown envelope to Sawyer. "I was packing up his things to take back to the ranch with the horse. You probably need to take a look."

Sawyer took the envelope and pulled out multiple newspaper clippings. There were various articles, all about him. The sheriff who caught this renegade or that gang. The sheriff in Wyoming who had nabbed a bandit in the act. There was newsprint about Wyatt as a bounty hunter as well. The last thing was a simple folded piece of yellow writing paper. He eyed it with caution, glancing back at Dawson.

"You'll wanna read that." Dawson nodded, folding his arms.

Sawyer opened it carefully. It was written in black

cursive ink, and before he even started reading, he knew Catherine's handwriting. His hands shook as he held the thin paper, running his fingers along it. Knowing she was gone and even though he knew they would never have made things work, somewhere in the back of his mind he might have still thought they'd one day try. He began reading.

My dearest Zane,

When you read this letter, I will no longer be with you. For that I am truly sorry, but as I have often told you, life is not to be taken for granted.

Please do not grieve as your whole life is still ahead of you. You are so brave and strong for me, but I want you to put my passing behind you. You have so many gifts my beautiful son.

Life can be hard and sometimes full of regrets, and I have often felt my one failure in life was keeping you from your father. When you were born, I thought it was the right thing to do, but as you grew, I knew it was a mistake. His name is Sawyer McCade, and last I heard he was still in Cheyenne. If you think at some point you would like to meet him, you have my blessing. Remember though, he will not know about you and getting to know someone takes time. You are a lot like him. You have his eyes, his calm manner, and his deep compassion for others. I know that if he knew of you, he would be very proud.

The homestead will be yours, and I have arranged for Mr. Spain at the bank to make sure that your name is on the account. You do as you see fit with the homestead. I know that Angus will take care of you so do as he says, he's a very good man. Don't forget to practice and play your music as it seems to be the heart of you. And please be careful with guns and on that horse of yours. And don't forget to say your prayers. I love you, son of my heart, forever and ever and always.

Mama

Sawyer folded the paper again. So how had Catherine died? How had she kept a son from him for this long? He would have been there, done the right thing, regardless of their differences.

"What's it say?" Wyatt asked, thumbing through the newspaper clippings.

Sawyer handed the letter to him. Hell, he held no secrets from his brothers, save one.

Wyatt took a few minutes to read it and stuck the articles and letter back inside the envelope, handing it all back to Sawyer. "What're you going to do?"

Sawyer took a deep breath and stood. "I don't know. I need to go back inside."

Dawson stepped from the porch and headed toward the livery again. "I'll get his horse to Evan, and I'll be back toward morning."

Sawyer turned toward the door. Something in him wanted to laugh—first a mail-order-bride and now a son. Hell, an instant family and all he'd ever wanted, yet it felt as if the world was crashing down.

"I'll take care of things in town, just stay with him." Wyatt gripped his shoulder.

He nodded and walked back inside and into the room where Tess continued with Zane. He made it to the chair, knowing he needed to sit. Catching a glimpse of Tess' hand deep inside Zane's abdomen caused his stomach to roll. He wasn't usually squeamish about such things but found himself unnerved simply because it was his son.

Tess worked as she explained. "He had a couple of small vessels that were bleeding, but I've got them sutured. Dodge?"

Dodge counted for a few more seconds her head nodding. "Eighteen breathing. One hundred heart."

"The only issue now is the amount of blood he's lost, which isn't as much as I thought to begin with. He's going to be very weak for a while." Tess only glanced up for a second.

"He'll survive then?" Sawyer questioned, his heart pounding hard against his chest.

"It looks good, but the first forty-eight hours can be critical. Infection and the fact that he was in such a state of shock. Time and rest will tell." Tess never looked up, but it was apparent her face had relaxed with that prognosis, giving him a glimmer of hope.

Dodge added another drop of chloroform to the cloth on Zane's face, and Rose continued to clean instruments and drop them into the sterilizing water. She glanced at him, but things were too intense for him to hold her there.

Sawyer focused on his son, pale and unmoving. While he wanted to be angry at Catherine, he wanted Zane to be all right. He'd cursed himself many times for not going back to change Catherine's mind about a marriage. Now he sat looking at every reason why he should have. Nope, it never would have worked. They had both been miserable and heading two different directions. But he still could have been a father, couldn't he?

Tess finished the last stitch with a "that's it." She bandaged Zane's abdomen and wiped the sweat from her brow. A moment more and she had Zane's arm in a sling supporting his shoulder. "I sure don't know what I would do without you." She smiled at Dodge. "Thank you as well Rose."

Rose glanced over her shoulder from the counter where she laid down the last scalpel she had cleaned. "You two are amazing at what you do."

"We make a good team with you included." Dodge pulled the chloroform away from Zane's face and covered him with another blanket. She focused on him for a long moment, then brushed strands of light brown hair from his forehead. "He's you made all over again. He has your father's eyes." She turned to face Sawyer.

He nodded.

"He should rouse from the chloroform in a little while. When he wakes, we have to get him to drink. He may still need blood, Sawyer, but we'll wait for now." Tess explained.

Dodge eyed him. "You didn't know?"

"You know I didn't. She should have told me," Sawyer whispered sternly.

"A woman's reasons…." Dodge shook her head.

Sawyer gazed from her to Rose and back. "I'm not sure I can explain something I don't even understand myself." He jerked himself to standing and walked to the window to look outside, wondering what in the hell he *was* going to do.

"Do you need me to stay?" Dodge asked, moving closer to him.

"I'll be all right." He wasn't so sure but turned back around to look at his mother.

"I'll bring you some breakfast and a change of clothing in the morning. If his condition changes, send Wyatt to the ranch." Dodge walked closer and hugged him around the middle and turned to go.

He pulled a chair closer to where Zane still lay, watching his sleeping son. Rose continued working nearby, cleaning instruments, the clicking of metal, filling the room.

"His pulse and breathing are good. He's a strong boy." Tess removed the stethoscope from her ears as she spoke, but Sawyer caught the edge of worry in her voice, in spite of what appeared to be relief on her face.

"He should've woken by now?"

"I've always thought the body responds when it can, when it heals or rests enough. We have to give him a bit of time. Shock and fatigue can add to the delay. He really is doing very well. I'll get us some coffee." She turned for the kitchen.

Rose dried her hands on a small towel and moved slowly toward him. She glanced at him but said nothing.

What was he to say to her? "I didn't know about him. I—"

"You were wonderful with him."

"What?" He snapped his head up to meet her gaze. Had he heard her right?

"You were good with him. He was so frightened he was shaking, so scared and you coaxed him to relax, gave him the comfort he needed." She set the cloth aside and didn't stop moving toward him until she had wrapped her arms around his middle, hugging him tightly.

The hug from Dodge had been that of support and encouragement, but Rose's embrace had a far different effect. Her physical warmth enveloped him, and he closed his eyes trying to inhale a breath that nearly strangled him. Shit, he wasn't about to cry. Nope anything but that. He used a sleeve to wipe the pending tears and wrapped his arms around her so tightly he thought she might break. Though he was the one who was broken.

After what seemed a long time, she loosened her grip and turned to go, offering a smile, her blue eyes bright but worried. He watched until she was gone and listened for the door to open and close again. She would be riding home with Dodge. Maybe he should have asked her to stay, since her embrace had touched a part of him he thought his body no longer held. He wasn't sure what had just exchanged between them and the fact he could still smell her flowery perfume had his head spinning if it hadn't been already.

He turned and touched Zane's hand. He was a good size for a boy of thirteen. Strange the connection he already felt for his son. He and Catherine had caused each other so much pain when it didn't really have to be that way. And he'd already given Rose such a hard time, though she had not let it deter her in the least. If anything, today had shown him how short life could be. This boy he was touching and the woman who had just touched him deserved all he had to offer for a lifetime and of that he was sure. He gulped a deep breath, the world before him clear for the first time in years. And when he saw Rose again, he'd make things right. If she would let him.

****

Sawyer jerked his head from the table, where he'd slept. Disoriented for only a moment, he glanced at Zane, whose hand had moved within his own. He was sure of it. The night had lingered in silence, as Zane hadn't recovered from the effects of the chloroform, even hours after surgery. Tess remained attentive to his care, but her concern had been more than evident.

"His fingers moved." Sawyer stood and whispered squeezing his son's hand, "Zane?"

Tess jumped from the chair where she had been reading a medical book. "Are you sure?"

Zane moaned, and his eyelids flickered open.

"Zane...it's Doc Tess." She touched his face with her palm.

Zane pulled his hand away from Sawyer's and tried to touch his abdomen, grimacing. His brows furrowed into a frown.

"The operation is over...don't try to move." Tess placed a stethoscope to his chest.

Sawyer grabbed Zane's hand once more. "I know it hurts but don't touch right now."

Zane focused drowsy eyes on Sawyer. "You...really stayed."

"I told you I'd be here." He touched a tuft of Zane's hair, pushing it away from his forehead.

"I thought you might...be mad, not...want me here." Zane's eyes filled with tears.

"I'm not mad. You rest, we can talk later," Sawyer whispered. His mind was full of unanswered questions, but Zane needed rest. He had a son; this was his son. Some part of his chest swelled with pride, though he wished he could have taken the pain away.

Wyatt entered, removing his hat and waiting just inside the door.

Sawyer met glances with him. "He just came to."

Wyatt nodded, gazing at Tess.

"Do you think you could take a little water?" Tess

held a cup and spoon toward Zane who made a sour face. "Let's try a bit."

Sawyer lifted Zane's head, and she placed the spoon to his lips several times, and he took the water sip by sip.

"No...more...thank you." His eyes closed again, and Sawyer rested his head back on the pillow.

Tess giggled, causing Sawyer and Wyatt to glance at her in question. "I'm not sure he is related to either of you. He's more polite than the both of you on a good day." She gave Wyatt a smirk.

"We're law men." Wyatt took offense.

"That doesn't mean you can't have manners." She sent him a raised brow.

"Well the next time I put drunken outlaws in the jail, I'll say please." Wyatt folded his arms, eyes narrowing.

Sawyer ignored them, looking back at Zane. He did have so many questions, and he was sure the boy had his own. But for now he needed rest in order to recover.

"My...horse?" Zane glanced toward the window.

"The horse is fine," Sawyer answered, still grasping his hand.

"He...doesn't like...anyone..." Zane's voice faded with the effort. "But...me."

"He'll be all right. Just skinned up a bit," Sawyer reassured.

Tess leaned closer. "Zane, I can get you something for the pain, but only a little. It took you a while to wake so not too much."

"It's...not...like...before, but I'm...dizzy." He blinked several times and closed his eyes.

Tess touched his brow again, glancing at Sawyer.

"It's the effects of the chloroform."

Zane opened his eyes again, studying Wyatt. "You're Wyatt. I read…about…you."

"We didn't know we were so famous." Wyatt beamed with pride and touched Zane's foot through the blankets.

"We found all the articles with your things," Sawyer added and then nearly cringed. Perhaps that should have waited.

"You read…the letter then?" Zane's voice was soft.

Sawyer nodded.

"Then…you believe…me."

Sawyer gave the hint of a smile, shaking his head. "I didn't need the letter to know."

"I figured out…who…" Tears filled Zane's eyes. "You were and started…requesting newspapers…to read about you."

"We really didn't know that much had been written." Sawyer had known from time to time his name made the headlines in Cheyenne or Denver, but hadn't thought about all over the West. The pile of clippings Zane had was rather impressive.

"She…never told…" Zane touched his stomach, struggling for a moment. "Me about you."

Tess shook her head at Sawyer, who took Zane's hand from his abdomen once more. "Just rest. Take the pain medicine, and we'll talk later."

Zane nodded, closing his eyes.

"Rest." Sawyer pulled the covers back so that Tess could give the pain injection. Zane frowned with the stick but kept his eyes closed and in no time slept. Eventually Wyatt went back to the jail, and Tess busied herself around the clinic. Sawyer watched Zane sleep for hours. He was still amazed at the resemblance to himself. They had the same facial features with high cheek bones and the large set gray eyes of his father. His throat tightened, and he blinked back emotions he had never juggled before. His father would adore this boy as a grandson.

He touched Zane's hair. The light brown locks were soft and fine, like Catherine's. Some part of him wanted to weep over her death, and another part of him wanted to curse her for robbing him of so many years with his son. He let his hand stop to rest along the boy's cheek. He had no idea what Zane's plans were, but he'd make sure they got to know one another. If the loss of his own father at a young age had taught him anything, it was to value time.

Once Zane recovered, he'd value all the time they could have together, and somewhere in the midst of his rambling thoughts he hoped that picture included Rose.

Chapter Eleven

Sawyer stepped into the clinic after spending a few hours in the office catching up on paperwork and reading the latest reports from back east. Wyatt had let him know the afternoon train was delayed, held up by outlaws just outside Council Bluffs. There was also a wire from Washington raising the bounty on the Ashburn brothers. No doubt they had something to do with the robbery. Several passengers, the conductor, and an armed guard had lost their lives.

Zane had been moved to one of the upper rooms at Doc Tess' clinic to recover and seemed to grow stronger by the day. He slept a lot due to the pain medication, and while Tess insisted that was best, Sawyer had enjoyed the small conversations he had shared with his son.

Sawyer stopped, catching Tess in the exam room as he headed to the stairs.

"He's awake. Dodge is with him." She moseyed closer, smiling. "You look tired. Get some rest; he really is doing well. In fact I've never seen someone with a surgery do so well, even with all my experiences."

Sawyer nodded. Tess had often talked of her meticulous training as a surgeon in Boston after she had completed her course of study at the Philadelphia College for Women. He also knew it was her physician uncle who had made her the surgeon she was, even if the hospital administrators back east were reluctant to employ women as doctors. He supposed that was how she had found her way west, well that and the fact that her husband sought the venture before he died. He'd never doubted her skills with Zane, and yes, he was tired. Very tired. Making his way up the stairs, he heard Dodge and Zane talking and stood outside the doorway to listen.

"Well, you are an amazing boy to have made that long journey alone. I think we're all surprised, but happy you're here," Dodge explained matter of fact.

"I collected articles on Sawyer, and some…talked about Wyatt, but I never thought…about more family or a grandmother. Do I call…you that?" Zane's voice sounded stronger, but he was still winded by any exertion.

"Dodge will be just fine, thank you," Dodge answered quickly.

"Yes, ma'am, but…to be respectful…"

"My sons all call me Dodge as does everyone else, and you can do the same. It's respect enough."

Sawyer stifled laughter at Dodge's assertive tone. He'd have to teach Zane the finer art of riling Dodge by calling her "Grandmother" in public when needed.

"Dodge." Zane's voice softened. "I didn't come here to…cause problems. I even thought…Sawyer might have a family…and maybe not want me around. I just wanted to meet him so I would know who he was."

Sawyer leaned against the wall outside the room. It wasn't Zane's fault things had happened as they had, but he kept trying to push the point, making it clear to everyone he expected little. How could the boy understand things he'd never understood himself? He'd been young when he and Catherine had been together, and he had been angry over losing his father and hell bent on revenge. And Catherine had wanted no part of the man he had become. He was full of spitfire at the time and ready to take down the earth. When he'd secured the spot as a deputy in Gillette, she turned down his proposal intending to stay on in Mankato to be near her mother, and he'd left for the job. It was the last time he'd talked to her, a heated argument that should've never happened, but one that had enlightened them both that they weren't meant for a marriage. It might have been different if he'd know she was— pregnant. Nope, it had been for the best, but he never would have wished her death or the pain it was causing his son.

"Zane, you are welcome here. I knew your mother, Catherine, very well." There was a hint of sadness in Dodge's voice.

"You did?" Zane's sounded surprised.

"She was a lovely woman, and I enjoyed our many conversations."

"I would ask about my father, but she would just change the subject. She never knew I figured out a few years ago that Sawyer was him. She had a picture of him she kept hidden, and I found it. And one day I was looking at a paper and there he was. But then she got sick..." His voice faded.

"You did right by coming here," Dodge reassured him.

Sawyer took a deep breath and turned into the room. "Look at you, sitting up. How're ya feeling?"

"Great, if I don't move or breathe." Zane hinted at

a smile.

Sawyer laughed, as did Dodge. Zane was wide awake, his gray eyes bright. Well, that was certainly improvement.

Sawyer sat down on the edge of the bed, glancing at Dodge. "Did he eat?"

"He drank a little water."

"My stomach doesn't feel right." He continued, changing the subject. "I have money in my saddle bags to pay Doc Tess."

Sawyer shook his head. "You needn't worry about the money. Let's worry about getting you to eat."

Zane held his stomach. "I'm afraid I won't keep it down."

"You don't have to eat a lot, maybe just sip some broth." Sawyer winked at him and changed the subject. "I rode out to the ranch. Evan says your horse is doing well, but he's quite spirited."

Zane's eyes lit up. "I didn't know about slip rocks...he's probably mad."

"Oh, horses never hold a grudge. I'll get some broth warmed up for you." Dodge left, humming to herself.

Sawyer turned back to Zane. "You came a long way for slip rocks to be your only trouble. The day I found you, Indians were in the area. You're damn lucky."

"I saw those Indians, but....turned the other direction...to avoid them." Zane met his gaze and adjusted in bed.

Sawyer studied his son's serious expression. "I would've come for you if you'd sent word."

"I don't know why she never told you or me. I

asked about you my whole life." Zane still seemed to have the need to explain things.

Sawyer got up and walked to the window looking outside. He shoved his hands in his trouser pockets, thinking on the right words, facing his son again. "I don't know, Zane, sometimes things between a man and a woman can be complicated. She didn't want any part of moving further west, and she was afraid of me being a law man. She was—" Sawyer stopped. *Damn.* Catherine had been a very strong-willed, complicated woman, and he'd been hell-bent on becoming a sheriff one day. There was simply nothing more to it.

"She was relentless." Zane finished his sentence for him, smiling. "It was her way or no way, and she was darn hard to live with. I lived with her twelve years, remember?"

Sawyer was shocked at Zane's summing up his mother. He moved closer to the bed. "If I had known about you, things might've been different between us."

Zane shook his head. "Maybe, but I didn't come here because I want some kind of explanation."

"You keep saying you don't want anything, but I do—want something—from you Zane." Sawyer stopped, choosing the right words. "I want the chance to get to know you. I want you to stay here. Call this home."

Zane studied him for a moment, a glisten to his young eyes. "I'd like…that."

"Who from Mankato might be looking for you?" Surely the boy had been watched after when his mother passed.

"Mr. Mason. Angus Mason. He taught me to hunt and fish, since I was young. He watched out for us. He helped me sell the homestead. I couldn't stay there anymore, but the money is in the bank in Mankato." Zane grabbed his belly to adjust his position.

"He knows you came all that way alone?"

Zane nodded. "He said every boy needs a journey to remember. I need to telegram him that I made it, barely."

"I'll send word," Sawyer said. "If you'll drink the broth, we might get you home sooner."

"Then I can see Shadow?"

Sawyer smiled. "Where'd you get that horse anyway?"

"There's a horse ranch in Rapid City. I saved up for nearly two years," Zane explained.

"You got him from the Hagen Ranch?" Sawyer's attention peaked.

"You know Samuel Hagen?" Zane's brows went up in question and surprise.

"Dawson's gotten a couple of horses from them, knows them very well." Sawyer glanced up as Dodge eased into the room, holding a small tray with steaming broth.

Zane beamed. "Samuel Hagen brought Shadow to me on the train. He said he deserved special delivering. I think he knew I wouldn't be able to make that trip, and he was surprised when I had earned enough money, but he ended up handing me half back telling me I had done the work of a man and I deserved it."

Sawyer wasn't surprised in the least. "Sam's a good man."

Dodge sat on the side of the bed and lifted the spoon of broth to Zane's lips. "Here, try a bit."

Zane sipped once and then twice more. "It's good."

"You need to get your strength, and this will help." Dodge dipped into the bowl again and again.

"I didn't know I was so hungry." Zane sipped the last of the broth in no time.

"I'd offer you more, but that's enough for now. Sawyer, I'm headed to Brett's, and Rose will be by with sandwiches later." She sat the bowl aside, pulling the covers up to Zane's chin. "You rest."

Zane smiled at her. "Yes, ma'am."

Sawyer had barely had time to think about Rose— that wasn't true. Somehow she'd remained on his mind no matter his thoughts, and if he had to confess, he was missing her—a lot. He'd look forward to her visit and he was hungry, but he wasn't sure it was for the sandwiches alone.

****

Sawyer sat beside Zane's bed as Tess examined him. He'd made good progress over the last week. He was moving around a lot better, his pale face now offered a bit of color, and he was finally eating.

"How are you feeling altogether?" Doc Tess took the stethoscope from her ears. "Better." Zane's lip curled into a smile.

Tess sorted through a small box of supplies. "I heard your day was busy, Sawyer. Wyatt said you brought in two wanted men from the saloon."

"Wyatt brought 'em in. Likely to cause a disturbance, given their buddies are still hanging around." Sawyer leaned back in the chair. Wyatt had taken the men in the saloon with ease due to their drunken state, but the others still there weren't happy about things.

Tess turned back to Zane. "It's time to change your

dressing."

"Will it hurt?" He placed a hand over his abdomen.

"That's why I gave you the pain injection earlier." She laid the wrappings on the cloth by the bed and sat next to him. "I won't be touching, just taking off the old dressing and putting a new one. Nothing will hurt if you relax."

Zane didn't seem convinced, his brows furrowing.

"I won't let it stick." She used a small pair of scissors to cut the wrappings away and tugged them from around his body.

Zane's face held panic, and Sawyer moved closer as Tess completed the task.

"It looks really good, you are healing nicely." She smiled at him as she tenderly applied an ointment to the dressing and placed it over his incision. "Tomorrow I think we need to see about you walking around the room a couple of times to get your strength back."

"Then I can see my horse?" Zane's frown turned to wide hopeful eyes.

"You have to let it heal. You mustn't lift anything at all for several months and *no* riding a horse." Tess scolded but she held a slight grin, tousling his hair.

"I know." Zane held himself up for her to begin wrapping the outer dressings around his middle.

"You'll feel better each day. By the time all the bruises are faded, we'll talk about how much longer before you ride." Tess patted the pillow, and Zane leaned back again holding his belly with a groan.

"Not sure you're ready for the horse yet." Sawyer sat back down, crossing a leg over his knee.

Zane only nodded in agreement.

"You're a good patient. Most grown man would

not do as well as you have. I'll check on you in a little while." Tess picked up the old dressings and headed downstairs.

"So you arrested those men...did they fight?" Zane adjusted his pillow but kept a hand to his belly.

Sawyer kicked his leg back down and leaned forward placing his elbows on his knees. "Nah, Wyatt had 'em before they knew it."

Zane's gaze rested on him. "I read that newsprint where you went to New York. That's sure something. The lawmen in Mankato were talking about you, but I couldn't say anything about who you were."

Sawyer had been summoned to New York after reporting the capture of the entire Fuller gang. Rumor or statistics had it that lawmen in the rougher territories lasted an average of a few years before either they were killed or gave it up. He and Wyatt had done well, but they'd never let their guard down, constantly conscious of happenings and of those around them. "The laws are stricter and law men are getting smarter. It takes all of us, looking out for each other."

"Well, that was some speech, to turn the heads of the lawmen where I'm from."

"How is it you know the lawmen in Mankato so well?" Sawyer asked sending a curious gaze.

"I worked for Mr. Horns in the law office so I could learn what you did." He wiggled his feet which were sticking out from under the blankets.

"So you're interested in law?"

"Some, but I needed the money to buy Shadow." Zane twisted for comfort once more.

"I can tell you have a lot of your mother in you. She worked hard to save for what she wanted, as I recall." And while the boy looked a lot like him, he had a number of his mother's expressions.

"She always said I had a lot of you in me, even though she never said who you were." Zane lifted his eyes, studying Sawyer intently, popping his knuckles and resting his hands on his outstretched thighs.

"I'm glad you're here Zane, I'm just sorry I didn't know you before now." Sawyer wanted to say so much more. How did he tell Zane he'd always longed for a son, someone to share what he and his father had once shared.

The light knock at the door drew their attention. Rose. Sawyer swallowed hard, his breath escaping him. "Rose?"

Rose held a basket of food. "Hi, I hope I'm not intruding. I brought sandwiches."

Sawyer swallowed all but his tongue, standing to take the basket from her and setting it aside. She looked radiant. Her cream colored blouse was tucked into her skirt and her corset, pushed her breasts tight against the fabric, skimming this thoughts across ideas he knew better than to think.

She glanced at Zane. "Well, you are looking much better than when I saw you last."

Zane glanced at Sawyer but gave her the hint of a smile. "Thank you, ma'am."

Sawyer fumbled for words, his mouth dry as cotton. "Uh, Zane, this is Rose…Miss Parker. She and I are—she's a family friend." He cringed wishing he could crawl out the window. What were he and Rose anyway? *Holy Hell!*

"It's a pleasure." Zane greeted with a nod and thankfully asked nothing more.

"Likewise." Rose came a bit closer to the bed. "Dodge said you are doing very well. How are you feeling?"

"The doc said I can try getting up to walk tomorrow." He rested further back in the bedding closing his eyes and then opening them again, the recent dose of pain medication taking effect.

Rose gazed at Sawyer and back to him. "Well, that would be wonderful. I am sure you are tired of being in bed all this time."

Zane opened his eyes nodding in agreement. Sawyer couldn't help but wonder what he might be thinking, not that he was explaining further right now. Hell he could barely breathe, but the sight of Rose was refreshing, given the last few days in his idling tired mind. His heart pounded against his chest, and as much as he appreciated her visit, she'd likely put herself at risk by being in town alone once more. "I know you didn't ride into town alone."

"I was careful and dressed accordingly." She touched her long brown skirt and raised her eyebrows. "I used Dodge's buggy. I'll make you a plate."

He really wished he could grab and consume her instead of the sandwich, but that would have to wait.

Rose set his plate on the dresser adding a sandwich and carrot slices and poured a small amount of broth into a cup for Zane. "And broth for you Zane, unless you'd like a sandwich." She turned with the cup, but Zane was asleep, and she set it aside, glancing at Sawyer.

He motioned toward the door, following her out into the hallway. "He falls asleep easy with the pain medication."

Rose turned to face him, folding her arms. "I'm glad he is better. He really looks so like you it's amazing."

Sawyer wasn't sure how to answer. "I didn't know about him until now. His mother and I—it never worked out. There isn't much more than that." He ran his hands through his hair. Actually, there were a lot of things, but with Catherine gone the only things that mattered now were Zane—and this beautiful woman before him.

He took a step closer. "I thank you for the meal, but you need to head to the ranch before it gets dark. I'll be home in a few days to get him settled."

She nodded. "Dodge has readied the room next to yours."

Sawyer wanted to touch her…hell, more than that. He wanted to grab her and kiss her hard—all of her. He might have tried to keep her at bay when she first arrived, but now he didn't like being away from the ranch at all. He had been preoccupied with Zane's care but rarely had she left his thoughts. He'd spent hours while Zane slept, wondering about her and remembering the softness of her lips against his own. Hell, he'd like to have a taste of those again right now. He scanned their rosy plump—damn.

"I'll be in town tomorrow. I have a meeting at the bank," she informed him and adjusted the small bag on her shoulder, avoiding his gaze.

"Banking?"

"I need to set up an account for my expenses." She wasn't telling him everything. She was fidgeting her fingers along the small purse hanging from her shoulder and while she did look at him, she was too quick with her explanation.

He studied her for a moment. Something wasn't right. "You don't have to pay to stay here…you don't need money."

She took a step back avoiding eye contact, but then met his gaze. "I know I am welcome, even Dodge keeps pleading, but I think it's best if I find my own way."

"You're leaving then?" He'd ignored her and been mean-spirited at times. But truthfully, he just wasn't done with her, but maybe she was done with him. He might have to work harder at wooing her than he'd done at pushing her away. She couldn't leave now, now that he knew what he wanted.

"I'm moving to the room over the post office. Mr. McDonald has hired me to write for the paper. I start in a few days, though it will take a bit to get my home in order." Rose's satisfaction was evident, but she still fidgeted her hand along her purse.

She was leaving the ranch for a room and a job—in Cheyenne? No, he wouldn't allow that. It wasn't safe, not even a little. "Oh, no, that's not happening, you are staying on the ranch."

Rose held her ground, mouth dropping open. "You have no right. The paper here leaves a lot to be desired in the way of proper writing and I am…needed. The room was an added benefit."

Sawyer couldn't believe her stubbornness. It was one thing she had refused the train home, but living in town was plain foolish. "You can't stay here alone—it isn't safe, or do I need to remind you of that on a daily basis?"

"If you didn't know, Sheriff, there are a number of ladies in town of the same status as myself. Miss

Dowell, the seamstress, and Melody Purvis at the post office—even Doctor Tess. She folded her arms in defense. "They are all unmarried women doing just fine, and I will as well."

"You cannot think living on your own in Cheyenne is anything like living in New York City." That was it. Sawyer grabbed her by the elbow to keep her from backing up again. "Just today, Wyatt pulled in three men wanted for the murder of a woman on a wagon train—do I need to describe how she died?"

Rose turned away as Tess came to the lower stairs.

Tess glared at him. "Sawyer...I'm not sure what is going on here, but you lower your voice and let that boy rest."

"Sorry Doctor, I was just leaving." Rose turned back to him. "I would be happy to come and sit with Zane while you work evenings."

Sawyer wanted to curse as he watched her trot down the stairs, smile at Tess, and leave the office. *Son of a bitch!* He shoved his hands in his pockets and turned back down the hallway to keep from saying his curses out loud.

Tess climbed the stairs and went into Zane's room. "She will do just fine. Give her a little credit, she is very capable."

He followed her inside, striving to keep his voice at a stern whisper. "She has no idea what she's doing."

Tess pulled the covers higher up around Zane and turned back to Sawyer. "Neither did I when I got here."

"Tess, you didn't come here alone." Tess rarely spoke of the husband who had died last year related to influenza.

Tess gazed at him, the sadness in her eyes making

him regret his words. "No, but I was left alone to figure it all out, and she will too." She busied herself with tidying the room, but he'd seen the tears that rimmed her eyes. The ones she didn't let fall.

Sawyer tried again, though arguing with another woman would only add to his frustration, and he hadn't meant to upset her. He shrugged and moved to the window to look outside. "She really has no idea what she is in for."

"Then perhaps you should change her plans. Isn't that why she is here in the first place?" She had her back to him.

Sawyer turned, eyes narrowed, gripping his fists. "If I didn't know any better, I would highly suspect you knew all about Rose before she ever got here. Dodge can't keep a secret, at least not from the likes of you or Mei Ling."

Tess whipped around to face him, stifling her voice to a jaunt whisper as well. "If you're asking if I knew about this, the answer is no, but if you aren't going to change her plans with a marriage, then you can't stop her from trying."

"Just like Wyatt keeps trying to change yours?" Now he was being mean.

Tess glared at him. "Wyatt hasn't changed my plans because I'm not sure Wyatt is meant for one woman."

While his brother tried to keep things discreet, he was in the brothel quite regular, and there was no doubt that Tess knew it. "Perhaps the promise of a good woman would change a man like Wyatt."

"I know you're tired. It's fine for you to use the next room for some sleep if you like." She made her exit, avoiding his comment.

Sawyer turned back to Zane who stirred in his sleep. Tess had avoided commenting further and that had been on purpose if he were guessing. While she avoided Wyatt's advances, he'd seen her watching his brother. and it was no secret to him that she kept up with his coming and goings. Still, Tess on her own as a physician was one thing, but Rose had no idea what it meant to live by herself in a place like Cheyenne.

He took one more glance at Zane and walked to the next room and dropped across the bed on his belly, not bothering with the blankets. Even as aggravated as he was, he didn't need to will himself to sleep. Fatigue had overtaken him days ago, and closing his eyes, he gave into it, with thoughts of Rose whirling through his mind.

Chapter Twelve

Rose glanced around her new home, admiring all she'd accomplished the first few days in town. She'd had a bed, a table, and two chairs delivered, along with a sofa and sitting room chair. Her limited funds had been well spent, though the anonymous telegram to New York would mean more money in the bank very soon. Max would understand her message, but she'd been afraid to attempt any other contact. Leaving the safety of the ranch was a concern, but the bigger concern was her lack of a marriage.

She shivered. Hiding was better done with an alias, and a marriage would mean her life would finally come back to some kind of order, eventually. She sat on her new couch for a moment, avoiding tears. Sawyer had figured her out all too well and even now, he knew she was hiding things. And she was, but until she heard from Max, she could trust no one. Getting her stipends to the bank every month was one thing, but until she had an official marriage, annulling the one she left behind, she was stuck.

She glanced at the window across the room and dabbed at her eyes. She'd measured for curtains and sewn them herself, but there were the burnt muffins still in the pan in the small sink. She'd have to work on cooking and baking, but that would come. Still, the dusty old room now looked livable compared to when

Mr. McDonald had first shown it to her, though it was still a far cry from what she was used to in New York or the ranch for that matter.

She didn't want to be late for her first day on the job and got up, straightening her skirt. She had made it this far, and the job would also keep her mind from things. The Cheyenne residents deserved a paper that included stories from around the country rather than only local events.

She was still amazed she had managed to pull it all together. A new home, a new job, and even a new life of sorts. Now she simply had to prove to herself and Sawyer that she could make it just fine on her own.

Sawyer. A shiver went through her. She'd said little when she left the ranch, but he'd carried her bag to the waiting horse she'd purchased from Evan. Actually, Evan had refused payment for Sadie, claiming the horse was too old to sell.

Still, she'd expected Sawyer to put his foot down about her leaving, though she would have done as she pleased anyway. The look in his darkened gray eyes hadn't been anger, but more like regret if she were guessing right. And while he would probably deny it, he made a pass by her home each evening when he left the clinic for home. It made her feel a bit safer, though she would rather not admit it to him.

Finishing her breakfast, she checked her satchel again, inspecting the dictionary and thesaurus she had ordered from Denver. Tucking them back inside with her tablet and a few ideas for articles, she clipped the brackets together to close the bag. She smiled, and in a flash she was down the stairs and on the streets of Cheyenne. On her own. She smiled as she passed Ms.

Dowell at the dress shop and continued on her way. All was well until she turned the corner past the now silent saloon, when she hit a wall.

"Oh!" She bobbled trying to keep her footing and dropped her satchel but found herself face to face with Sawyer. The Wall.

He steadied her and bent to grab her satchel. "Where's the fire *Miss Reporter*?"

"No fire, just getting to work on time." She tugged her satchel from his grip and slung it over her shoulder. "So how is Zane doing?"

"Doc Tess says he can go home this afternoon."

"Well, that's wonderful news. I'll go see him before the afternoon to wish him well." She'd miss the time she spent playing chess with Zane while Sawyer worked.

"He's more worried about seeing his horse than the ranch or anything else." His smile was genuine.

"Maybe the horse will be good for him." Gazing into his deep gray eyes was more overwhelming by the minute, and she needed to get to work. Being this close to him always made her keenly aware she was indeed a woman. Thoughts of the close embrace they had shared after Zane's surgery still played through her mind time and again. She wasn't sure what had compelled her to hold him that night, but he'd been so broken and she had wanted to fix things for him, let him know everything would be all right and now they were—at least for him and Zane.

And standing before him right now, she needed a quick exit. Her heart was pounding, and it wasn't due to her new job. How was it Sawyer had such power over her? "I should be heading to work."

"You have yourself a nice day at the paper." He smiled, his tone sarcastic.

"I plan to." She nodded and walked past him, glancing back once to see him tip his hat. The smirk on his face was enough to make her all the more determined. He was mocking her again. Well, she would make her way in spite of him if it was the last thing she ever did. Now if she could just lessen her pulse a bit.

****

After finishing his rounds through town, Sawyer headed back to his office.

"Prisoners are still sleepin'." Hudson grabbed his duster, tossing it over his shoulder and placing his hat on his head. "I'll be back in tonight."

"The cavalry will be here for the two in the first cell today." Sawyer hung his hat and ran a hand through his dark hair.

"What about the other one?" Hudson asked, stopping at the door.

"Not sure. He'll likely be picked up by the federal marshal when he comes through," Sawyer answered shaking his head. They would all be served justice, most likely all three meeting a rope. But they had chosen their paths and this was the job.

"Hey, tell Zane good-bye for me. I'll see him at the ranch sometime." Hudson headed out, lifting his chin toward the morning sun.

Sawyer nodded. He had spent the evening before playing a few hands of poker with Zane, who seemed to have a good bit of skill in the area. He was humorous and when he smiled, there was a hint of Catherine. Sawyer still couldn't believe she'd kept Zane from him,

173

but things were starting to feel more comfortable for both of them, and he looked forward to getting his son home.

He had just poured his morning coffee when Wyatt strolled in on a whirlwind of dust and obvious frustration. "What's wrong with you?"

Wyatt tossed his hat aside, and stomped across the room to pour his own coffee, being loud about it all. "Doc."

"She turned you down again?" Sawyer studied his brother closely.

"She saw me at the saloon a few nights ago. I tried to explain it was business." Wyatt slammed the metal tin of coffee back on the small stove and cursed at burning his hand.

Sawyer narrowed his eyes at his brother. "Business?" He chuckled under his breath. "Your endeavors at the saloon aren't related to work."

"What would you know about it?" Wyatt glared at him.

"Jail business then?" Sawyer grabbed his mug of coffee and backed away. Wyatt could be fierce when angered but riling him was worth a bucket of fun.

"No." Wyatt searched his vest.

"Ranch business then?" Sawyer kept on, as he sat at the desk and leaned back in the old chair.

Wyatt pulled a cigar from his vest and glared. "Shut the hell up."

"You know, if you stayed out of there for any length of time, Tess might find you interesting enough to try." Sawyer sipped his coffee and set it back down carefully.

"Damn it! A man has needs, and I've waited over a

year for her to come around. Why don't you worry about handling your *mail-order-bride* that has moved to town to stir things up?" His brother smirked, raising a dark brow.

Sawyer eyed his brother again. He'd not get into that discussion. He probably should've tried to stop Rose from moving to town, but he'd come to the conclusion it was best to let her try and fail on her own. And maybe he'd be just lucky enough to catch her when she fell.

"Well, Doc is enough to drive anyone crazy, but it looks like we got bigger fish to fry." Wyatt stepped to the doorway again.

Sawyer joined him. Five men on horseback were dismounting outside the saloon, and there was no doubt they were up to no good. "Recognize them?"

"Nope." Wyatt squinted.

"If you don't know them, chances are they don't know you." Sawyer grabbed his revolver and checked the bullets out of habit. Fully loaded, as always. The men, up to no good, likely knew he was the sheriff of Cheyenne as was usually the case, and even while Wyatt had a reputation as a bounty hunter, they'd likely not think him present in a town like Cheyenne.

"I'll be in the saloon." Wyatt glanced at him. "Unless you want to question them first?"

"From the looks of them, that's not a good idea." Sawyer slammed the revolver back at his hip and grabbed his hat. Unknown men riding into town wasn't unusual. Most were from local mines or the railroad and were usually harmless, only in town to spend their hard-earned money on drink and women. These men were carrying rifles, and all of them had gun belts, and it was obvious they'd been on the trail for a while. Given the recent train hold-up, idle groups of no-goods were suspect.

"I'll go in the back." Wyatt nodded and left the jail, heading the opposite direction.

Sawyer continued his watch as the men dismounted, again all trail-worn, save one. He wore a dress coat and top hat much like the men from back east, likely their leader. Sawyer could tell when men were trouble long before ever speaking with them, and the hair on the back of his neck was already standing up.

Thinking through the plan in his head, Sawyer made his way from the back of the jail toward the post office for a better vantage point. So much for the latest reports from back east with neither he or Wyatt knowing these men. He made his way between the post office and the mercantile and went inside the post office to give Wyatt time and watch the saloon, as the men watered and tied their horses to the hitching post of the saloon.

Melody Purvis sat poised behind the counter, holding a small pistol. "Sheriff, I knew it was bad when they rode in here."

Sawyer eyed the weapon. "Put it away; it's not likely they are headed in here."

Melody shoved the pistol in her bosom with a nod. Maybe the single ladies of Cheyenne were more capable than he thought. He turned back to view the men out the window as they headed inside the saloon, laughing and jostling each other as they entered. Wyatt would already be in place inside in case of trouble. And with any luck, these men would have their drinks and move along.

Sawyer turned back to Melody. "Mrs. Purvis, why don't you make your way to the bank and have Herschel lock it up. You find another place to stay for a while, just in case."

"All right, but please be careful, Sheriff." She locked the small desk drawer with the key around her neck and disappeared out the back.

He doubted the men would head to the bank, and he needed Melody somewhere safe. Now in the deserted post office, he checked his revolver was in place once more. Just as he leaned against the doorway out of sight, a single shot rang out. He dashed for the saloon, taking cover where he could. That shot hadn't come from a revolver which meant it hadn't been Wyatt's weapon.

He dove onto the saloon porch and scooted to one of the lower windows, as several men ran outside and people on the street headed indoors. Inside, a man held a gun to Wyatt's temple, and another held a gun on Jacob, who stood by the bar. A stillness fell over the men who remained seated. What in the hell had happened?

He cursed under his breath, a trickle of blood running down his brother's temple. He'd been pistol whipped no doubts. The streets had cleared at the sound of gunfire, so he was on his own. Even if someone thought to find Hudson, there wasn't time.

He peered inside again. The man in the fancy jacket was walking back and forth in front of Wyatt lecturing in an—Irish brogue? *Son of a bitch. Pat McDuffy*. There had been a telegram over a month ago that described McDuffy as a well-dressed man who

177

ratcheted up a cheating game of cards, usually taking everyone's money along with a few lives if the game didn't go well. That they already had the upper hand on Wyatt told him just how dangerous they were.

Sawyer took a few deep breaths to clear his head. *Take the leader and the men usually fall apart.* He repeated his own now famous words. Well, there was no time like the present. He jumped up and slammed through the swinging doors and fired once through the ceiling to get everyone's attention. The distraction allowed him to point his revolver at McDuffy's mid section. While it had been bold and chancy, he'd needed shock to get to the position he now held.

"The famous Sawyer McCade. I think we haven't been properly introduced." The man never flinched or looked at his men."Allow me to introduce myself—"

"I know who you are McDuffy." Sawyer held his voice sure and his revolver steady.

"Very good, sir, but it seems you're outnumbered, Sheriff, and now your revolver is short by one shot." The Irishman looked at the hole in the roof and back to Sawyer.

"I got four rounds."

"Why, Sheriff McCade, why weren't you fully loaded?" The jaunty man chortled as did his men.

Sawyer hadn't miscounted. He had five full rounds remaining, but never hesitated in his response, meeting the man's gaze. "Just planning on shooting you twice."

McDuffy hesitated and then laughed even louder. "Come now, Sheriff, one word and my men simply end this starting with your brother."

Sawyer didn't move. So they knew who Wyatt was as well, and they had come here looking for trouble as suspected. Rather boldly too. He chanced a glance at Wyatt, who looked up with a long blink of his eyes. So in spite of being hit, Wyatt had enough sense to help and likely another gun in his boot, given the blink.

"Boss, he has a gun on you." One of the men spoke in a harsh whisper.

McDuffy only turned and glared at the man.

In that split second, Sawyer fired at the man holding the gun on Wyatt, then dropped to one knee, shooting the one with a gun on Jacob. At the same time, Wyatt rolled away, pulled a pistol from his boot and took out the man behind Duffy. The fourth man ran quickly for the saloon's double swinging doors, only to back up, dropping his weapon and raising his hands. Hudson entered, a rifle to the man's chest.

McDuffy turned to face Sawyer, as if his entry was no issue at all.

"It appears, *sir*, you aren't outnumbered, but you are out manned." Sawyer was back on his feet and moved closer. "On your knees. Now!"

McDuffy slowly bent his rotund body to his knees, never taking his eyes from Sawyer, cursing under his breath.

Sawyer kicked him hard, sending him face down on the wooden floor. He held the gun to his head grabbing a fist full of the man's dark hair. "Look around, all but one are dead...I hope it was worth it. You know anything about the train robbery at Council Bluffs?" Sawyer moved aside as Hudson came to tie the Irishman, who never answered. "Big mistake coming to my town."

Sawyer turned and glanced around the saloon, catching his breath. Some of the men inside still sat frozen, others had already made their exit. Three of McDuffy's men lay dead, and Hudson was now pushing the ringleader and the last of his men out the saloon. He turned back to Wyatt who sat on the floor, holding his head. "Wyatt?"

"I'm good." Wyatt gazed up at him, blinking and shaking his head.

"Nope. Jacob send for the doc." Sawyer glanced over his shoulder at the old man surprised that he'd not blasted the shotgun and gotten them all killed.

"I'll get her, but now there is a hole in my roof again." The man scampered outside.

Sawyer shook his head. Jacob would make him pay for the repairs on the shabby roof, regardless he'd blow most of it away in the past.

"Help me up, brother." Wyatt held up a hand, and Sawyer pulled him to his feet. He wobbled until he gained his stance and looked down at the man he'd killed. "Can't even see straight, how the hell did I do that?"

Sawyer grabbed him, pulling him toward a chair. "Sit."

Wyatt sat reluctantly with a groan, holding his head. "I should've had eyes in the back of my head. Two of them were on me before I knew it."

Sawyer let out a deep breath. "We're lucky to be alive." His hands shook. Funny, he could hold his nerves in any situation until it was done. He gripped his fists tight. While it had seemed easy, it hadn't been. Any number of things could have gone wrong, and there was always the feeling that one day their luck might run dry.

Tess ran in carrying her bag, her face pale and

searching. "Wyatt?" She ran to him assessing the deep gash to his scalp.

Wyatt opened his eyes, trying to focus on her. "I'm fine."

Tess held his face with both hands. "Wyatt, look at me, what do you see?"

Wyatt squinted and then chuckled. "There's two of you, that's damn sweet."

"It's not funny Wyatt, you have a severe concussion if you are seeing double." She held his eyelids open, looking closer. She then took a cloth from her bag and placed it in his hand and helped him hold it to the wound. "Keep your eyes closed if you feel dizzy. I'll stitch you at the clinic."

Sawyer got behind Wyatt and steadied him as he stood.

"I got it." Wyatt shrugged from his hold and idly stepped forward.

Sawyer grabbed hold of him again, "You can't even stand up. Cooperate will ya?" He tugged Wyatt all the way to the clinic, where Tess took over once he had his brother laying on the examination table.

He turned toward the stairs, thinking of Zane. No doubt he'd be disappointed in the delay getting home, or worried with the gunfire he'd probably heard. He climbed the stairs one by one and froze half way up. Rose stood in the hallway at the top of the stairs.

"I worried Zane might be upset, but he didn't know anything. He's sleeping." Her voice was soft, and her blue eyes glistened.

Sawyer swallowed hard. She'd done that for him? For Zane? He removed his hat and climbed the remainder of the stairs never taking his eyes from her.

Her face was ghost white. He didn't like that he'd caused her to worry, but something about her thinking of Zane, tugged at his heart. "Thank you." He stopped before her.

Rose hesitated. "Wyatt?"

"He's got a cut to the head. Tess is with him." Sawyer nodded behind him to the stairs. Damned if he could understand what he was feeling, and then a single tear slipped down her cheek. Had she been *that* worried for him? Something inside him melted at the thought. She took a step toward him and another and he met her, taking her in his arms and holding her against his body.

She burst into tears and hung onto him so tightly he could feel her shake. And he held her, taking in the sweet smell of her hair, running his hands along her back. After a few minutes, she pulled from him, looking up as if to explain her behavior, but he didn't give her the chance. Without any hesitation he placed his lips softly to hers, bringing his hand up to cup her cheek. God, she tasted sweet, sweeter because there didn't seem to be anything between them. And while he never wanted to let her go, he pulled away and gazed into her eyes, using his thumb to wipe another tear from her face, trying to read her.

"I'm sorry," she whispered. "I thought if anything happened to you…" Her voice cracked, and she wiped a few more tears, tugging from his arms.

"I'm all right." Her tears caused him physical pain, right through his chest and he fought to take a deep breath. That she had been concerned enough to check on Zane was one thing, but that she'd worried about him—he pulled her closer thinking maybe he'd never let her go again.

Chapter Thirteen

Sawyer walked inside the clinic, taking a look at his pocketwatch and shoving it back into his vest pocket. Tess was in the office sorting through the papers on her desk.

"Hi Sawyer, Rose is upstairs with Zane. He's fine to go if he rests, and you can take Wyatt with you. Neither needs to be on a horse, Zane indefinitely and Wyatt for at least a few days." Tess exaggerated the horse part, glancing toward Wyatt in the room behind her.

"I can ride." Wyatt clomped into the hallway, tucking in his shirt.

Sawyer shook his head. "I'll make sure about Zane, but there isn't much I can do with this one."

"I'm good, just seeing one of you today." Wyatt smiled, but then touched the small dressing on his head. "I'll help you with Zane in a little while. Let me check in with Hudson first."

"You are not planning on working?" Tess scolded, placing her hand on her rounded hips.

"He needs to get Zane home. I can wear a headache here as good as at the ranch." Wyatt kissed her cheek before she knew what he was up to and walked outside, leaving her with her hand on her check and speechless.

Tess glanced at Sawyer and turned back to the exam room, saying nothing more.

Sawyer raised his eyebrows and shook his head. Figuring those two took great effort and he had no energy for that at the moment. He trotted upstairs figuring Zane was biting at the bit to head home. All he'd talked of was his horse non-stop, though he still had a long way to go in healing. He found Zane in a chair, and Rose giving him a much-needed haircut.

Zane fidgeted. "Don't cut it too short."

"Oh, you won't even notice." Rose glanced up, noticing Sawyer in the doorway.

"Afternoon." Sawyer leaned against the doorframe.

"Careful or she will come at you with the scissors." Zane pulled at the hair on the back of his head, checking the length.

"I think he looks more mature. What do you think?" Rose raised her light brows and held the scissors high.

"I think I will be incriminated no matter how I answer." Sawyer had to grin.

"Did you get the buggy?" Zane asked.

"Yep."

"I can't wait to see Shadow. He's probably forgotten me." Zane beamed with delight.

Sawyer thought about it. He'd seen the horse give Evan a bit of trouble, but the animal calmed for the most part with Dawson, who had been feeding him. "Evan says he's hard to handle, but Dawson thinks he's looking for you."

"He's fine when I'm around," Zane reassured, with a nod.

Sawyer sat on the bed, and Rose went back to trimming Zane's hair.

"Well, you still aren't moving real good. You

needn't think this trip to the ranch is going to be easy." Sawyer warned, though he couldn't help but join in Zane's excitement.

Rose finished, laying the scissors aside. "All done and I need to get back to the paper. My mid day break is about over."

"Thank you." Zane continued to tug at his shorter hair.

Rose grabbed her bag, and Sawyer followed her out into the hallway. He'd spent the night in the room next to Zane again, thinking on her tears of concern and wondering that she might have feelings for him, in spite of it all.

"It's good he can go home." Rose gave him the edge of a smile across her lips.

"I think he'll miss the chess games." Sawyer shoved his hands in his pockets and leaned against the wall. Small talk, both cautious if not nervous, tip-toeing around their words.

"He's a tough opponent."

"So the job is going well?" Sawyer asked, having seen her at the press, laboring for the most part.

There was that fiery blush of her cheeks, defensive on cue. "It is going very well, and thanks to you I feel incredibly safe."

Sawyer shot her a raised brow.

"Your deputy follows me all over town."

Damn it, he'd told Hudson to follow from a distance. Hudson was a good man and usually did that sort of thing effortlessly. If Rose had spotted him more than once, then it was obvious she was paying very close attention to the things happening around her. One more reason for him to think she was running.

"He's just making sure you get safely home each evening." If he couldn't watch out for her, someone had to. He folded his arms.

"Well, it isn't necessary." She dropped her tone a bit and brushed back a stray strand of hair. It occurred to him that he would've liked to have done that.

"Look, he does the same thing for other ladies in town. It's his job." Sawyer pulled his hands from his pockets holding them up to protest the innocence of his actions. "Given yesterday's events, I thought it best." He wanted to touch her again as he had, but she turned toward the stairs.

She seemingly gave up and grabbed the rail. "It's fine. I'm going to be late."

He couldn't help but watch until she was gone, feeling as though they kept going one step forward and one step back. He'd tell Hudson to be more discreet, but he wouldn't tell him to back off. With Zane going home, he wouldn't be in town as much to keep an eye on Rose himself. He turned to go into Zane's room, contemplating the next few days.

"So are you ready?" He was ready, all but the part of leaving Rose in town alone. He and Zane had gotten to know each other within the confines of the clinic, but now he could take his son home to see where he really came from and what he'd one day inherit.

Zane smiled, but it faded. "I want to see Shadow, but I know—well, I mean, I don't want to be any trouble and I know I have been already."

"Zane, the ranch is your home if you want it to be. Cheyenne. All of it." Sawyer shook his head, meeting his son with a direct gaze.

"I know everyone keeps saying that." Zane looked

away.

Sawyer couldn't figure it. Zane had talked of nothing but seeing Shadow. "You and I need to be able to talk about things, if we are going to get to know each other. Something's wrong?"

Zane's eyes glistened and he was hesitant for a moment but then continued. "There's just a lot of difference in knowing you have nowhere else to go and having a home."

"Zane, look at me." Sawyer lowered his voice and put a hand on Zane's shoulder. "You are a McCade. The ranch is your home now, later, whenever you want it to be. No one is going to take that from you." He'd already missed a lifetime with his son, but if Zane didn't want to stay, he wasn't sure what he would do.

"But I'm not *McCade*. I'm Zane Carver. People will talk, they always do, and I don't want them saying things—things to hurt you or Dodge."

Sawyer thought on his words and nodded. Now it made sense. "I think I know what you are talking about. Let them talk. We won't be hurt, and you won't be either, and you are a McCade regardless."

"It isn't much fun being called the names I've been called…bastard." Zane whispered the curse.

Sawyer inhaled a deep breath. How the hell did he deal with this one? It was his fault his son had suffered that word. "You know Zane, people who call names like that usually have something to hide themselves. You don't owe anyone an explanation of who you are or how you came to be here."

"I'm used to it, but maybe you and Dodge—"

Sawyer helped him up carefully "If you haven't figured it out yet, Dodge can handle herself pretty well.

187

I've got my end under control…let's worry about things more important. Besides I'm the sheriff—and they are all scared of me." He smiled, watching Zane give in to his own slight grin.

Moments later, Sawyer stepped out onto the porch, holding Zane by his good arm, the conversation forgotten. Zane scanned across town. "Cheyenne is a busy place. I can't remember when I got here what it looked like."

Sawyer let go of him once they were standing on the road. "Well, you could hardly stand by the time I got you to the clinic."

"Mark my words, Cheyenne will be big one of these days." Wyatt trotted up, tilted his hat back exposing the bandage just in his hairline.

Zane placed his good hand along his belly. "It feels good to get fresh air, but the stairs are hard to do."

"Easy, it's still a long way home." Sawyer and Wyatt helped him into the buggy with great effort and stifled groans from Zane.

"I'm…all right, but this isn't much of a man's ride home." Zane struggled to find a comfortable position in the buggy.

Wyatt ruffled Zane's hair. "Hey, no being a tough guy for the ladies just yet."

"The same goes for you though I know that thick skull of yours will keep you from behaving." Sawyer scolded Wyatt and joined Zane in the buggy. He whistled, urging the horse ahead, leaving Wyatt behind to cover the jail.

"It looks like Mankato on some of the back streets," Zane said as they pulled though town.

"We've got most of what the more modern cities

have, just smaller." Sawyer eyed the saloon as they rode by, and Zane leaned over slightly to see inside. "Don't get any ideas."

"Just lookin'."

"Let's keep it that way." Sawyer had to smile.

Zane remained quiet most of the ride, and Sawyer had to wonder if it he was nervous about going to the ranch. He'd left a lot behind in Mankato and then traveled such a long way. Regardless whether he stayed on in Cheyenne, he'd likely always think his home was Mankato.

Sawyer took the buggy to the top of the ridge where the view of the McCade lands was clear. He slowed the buggy and glanced at Zane.

"Evan was telling me how big the ranch was." Zane's eyes widened and he leaned forward.

"Welcome home, Zane." Moments later, Sawyer brought the buggy to a stop near the house and looked on as Zane scanned the barn and corrals, likely looking for his horse.

Dodge and Mei Ling hurried down the stairs from the porch to meet them.

"Zane, it's wonderful to finally have you home." Dodge hurried to his side of the buggy along with Mei Ling. "Zane this is Mei Ling, my dearest friend."

Zane nodded as Sawyer helped him down. "It's a pleasure, ma'am."

"Zane." Mei Ling bowed. "You are much like father and grandfather."

Zane offered her a slight bow and another smile.

Dodge took back the conversation. "If you think Doc Tess was tough, I am in charge at this ranch and you are going right to bed."

"You should be frightened." Sawyer warned with a chuckle when Zane gaze sought him for help.

Evan trotted out of the house, taking the stairs two at a time, his large boots clunking along. "About time you quit lying around the clinic."

"I'm going to see to your bedding." Dodge made her exit, touching Zane's hand, her blue eyes wide with excitement.

Mei Ling nodded once more to Zane following her.

"I'm right tired of that clinic anyway." Zane shook his head, glancing at Evan.

"Ah, you'll mend soon enough, and then I'll have you out taking a shift watching the cattle," Evan teased, shoving his hands in the front pockets of his trousers.

Zane's gray eyes lit up. "I'd like that."

"Let's get you inside for now," Sawyer said, the fatigue on Zane's face apparent.

A horse neighed from the corral outside the barn. Zane turned quickly, shucking Sawyer's grip and walking that direction without any hesitation.

"Zane. You can see the horse later." Sawyer scolded, but Evan placed a hand on his shoulder.

"Let him see the horse."

Zane took slow steps toward Shadow, who was prancing and stomping in the corral. The wounds along the horse's side had healed to large scabs, and he snorted as he ran around the corral, bucking a time or two. When Zane lifted the rope to open the gate and stepped inside, Sawyer took a step forward, shaking his head.

"Wait, it's all right." Evan stopped him again.

Sawyer's heart was in his throat, but he held his position and didn't call out to Zane.

Shadow snorted, kicking up dirt as Zane drifted to the center of the corral. With his arm still in a sling, ribs broken, and not yet healed from surgery, it was all Sawyer could do to remain still.

"Sawyer." Dodge gave an urgent whisper from the porch.

"It's fine Dodge." Dawson trotted down the stairs and stood alongside Sawyer and Evan, folding his arms to watch as well.

Zane stood in the center of the corral and held out his right hand, palm up, never saying a word. The horse continued to display for a moment longer and then suddenly calmed.

"I'll be damned," Evan said. "What the hell's he doing?"

"He's talking to the horse with hand signals," Dawson answered.

Sawyer's breath caught as Shadow slowly paced toward Zane. He'd just gotten his injured son home, and this horse could be more than unpredictable. Shadow stopped before Zane and snorted. Then the horse took one more step and leaned his head over Zane's good shoulder.

Zane spoke softly, rubbing the painted horse. "Good boy Shadow. I've missed ya, boy." He continued to stroke the animal along the neck, the horse calmer than he'd been since arriving to the ranch. After some time, Zane stepped back to the gate. Shadow followed him and waited as he exited the corral. Then Zane turned and looked at Sawyer and smiled.

Sawyer had never witnessed anything like it. The spirited horse instantly tamed was one thing, but the genuine smile on his son's face was something quite amazing. Zane walked closer, holding his belly. "He's good, but I think I need to lie down for a minute."

Sawyer took him by the arm, leading him to the house and up the stairs to the porch. Zane shook from fatigue as he led him down the hallway to his room, but took in the sights of the house as they made their way.

"This'll be yours. It used to be my room, but I'll be right next door." Sawyer could remember himself in the room at Zane's same age. A quick memory of his father talking to him in the very same place he himself was standing made the moment more surreal.

Zane looked around and turned to the dresser where his things had been placed. He touched his bag and then the clothing in a neatly organized pile.

"Dodge got you a few changes of clothing from the mercantile. I brought your other things here, everything I found from where you fell." Sawyer cringed as Zane ran his hand across the hard leather case. The fiddle inside had been smashed beyond repair. He hadn't tossed it but wondered now if he should have.

Zane pulled up the buckles to open the broken case and glanced inside.

"It was your mother's?" Sawyer didn't have to ask.

Zane nodded and touched the broken neck and crushed body of the fine instrument.

"You play too, don't you?" Sawyer asked, though he somehow already knew that too.

"Since I was three. It was religion." The edge of sadness in his son's voice shot pain through his own heart.

Sawyer took a deep breath, wishing like hell to ease the pain for his son. "I think it's beyond repair, but we can see about it."

"It's all right. I can save for another, when I am well or maybe use some of the money from the homestead." Zane didn't look up but continued touching the contents of the busted violin and bow.

Sawyer nodded. He'd listened for hours as Catherine had played, and it was probably the same with Zane if he guessed. "Let's get you to bed."

He tugged Zane along and got him settled, covering him with a light blanket. Turning, he dimmed the lantern and replaced the glass dome, the task taking a moment. "Do you think you can eat in a while?"

When Zane didn't answer, he swung around, finding him fast asleep. He smiled and headed to the dining room to join his brothers and Dodge, who were already at the table beginning the meal.

"I've never seen anything like it." Evan shoved a biscuit in his mouth and chewed, glancing at Wyatt.

"It was amazing he didn't get hurt." Dodge, using her fork and knife properly took a bite of the roasted pork.

"The Cheyenne have been training horses like that for hundreds of years. They spend several days alone with the animal. The man and the horse respect each other that way." Dawson made it sound simple.

Evan rolled his eyes, digging into his food.

Sawyer hadn't believed it either, but so far this son of his was full of surprises, and now Zane was home. His son was home.

"Well, at least he is better." Dodge wiped her mouth. "We all need to do what we can to make him welcome and help him heal."

"So he is going to stay from now on isn't he?" Evan asked, looking at Sawyer. "He's a good kid."

Sawyer hesitated for a moment, but he thought so. "He knows this is his home if he wants it to be." He changed the subject. "Wyatt, Denver telegrammed we have to get the last prisoner there for the circuit judge by Monday."

Wyatt sipped his coffee and sat the mug down. "I thought they were coming here, with the judge."

"Change in plans." Sawyer picked up his fork and glanced at the empty chair where Rose once sat, and his gut tightened. The sky was darkening, and she would be alone, and he wasn't there to protect her.

"I've got work in Laramie next week. Gotta pick up the bounty on that Miller bandit I hauled in a month ago from Casper." Wyatt leaned back in his chair.

Sawyer shrugged. "I suppose I can take him. Dodge, can you look after Zane for a few days? I'll be back by Wednesday or Thursday."

"Of course, the mercantile will be fine with Burt. I was planning to stay here for a few weeks to see to him anyway. It will be nice to have a young man in the house again." She beamed.

"Evan, with Wyatt and I both gone, you need to delay the cattle." Sawyer knew he was opening a can of worms, but it was a good excuse to keep the heated cattle situation at bay and delay the inevitable.

"The gods must be listening. Brett came by today and rains have kept the herd from making it to Kansas, so we'll be a few more weeks." The sarcasm in Evan's voice was evident.

"That gives me time to take care of a few things, so I'll thank the gods." Sawyer took a bite of pork, making himself eat. The delay was a good thing in his opinion, though it hardly solved the problem. He had his hands full with Zane, never mind dealing with the likes of Marcus Benton and then to top it all off, there was still Rose to worry about. Thinking of her in town, while he was on the ranch, had him on edge. Hell, it had him coming out of his skin. He couldn't sit still, and he knew sleep wouldn't come this night.

He managed the rest of the meal without drama from Evan and was thankful for that. Excusing himself, he went back to check on Zane, finding him still asleep. He wanted Zane to think of this ranch as home and to feel he belonged, but he supposed everything would take time.

"Do you know how many hours I've watched you boys sleep?" Dodge stepped up behind him.

"I've missed a lot of things with him."

"You both have a lifetime ahead of you." Dodge hooked her arms through his, hanging onto his elbow.

"I would've made things right," he offered.

"Sawyer, you and Catherine—I never understood it, but what's done is done. If I were you, I'd start thinking about a beautiful lady sleeping in town who might already have a heart for you."

"It isn't that easy." And it wasn't or was it?

"You can hide your heart Sawyer McCade. I am your mother. Your mind hasn't stopped whirling since she got here. I suggest you get on with it." She kissed his cheek and turned to climb the stairs to her room.

Sawyer sucked in a deep breath. She was right. He hadn't had Rose off his mind more than five minutes since she'd arrived in Cheyenne. He'd lost sleep with her under the same roof, but now with her in town, it wouldn't be any better. Damn, the thoughts of pulling her in his arms and against his body were so easy to relive in his mind. She had been warm and tender, and her tears had nearly brought him to his knees. In spite of wishing she'd never arrived, he now couldn't imagine not having her around. In fact, he had even let it cross his mind to make things permanent with her, and though the thought of marriage was overwhelming, letting her slip from his grasp would be far worse.

Chapter Fourteen

After two hours setting type, Rose was relieved to pull down the top roller of the printing press. She'd learned a lot in a short time, though it was nothing like a big New York paper. Actually, the *Cheyenne Weekly* was an extra long sheet of newsprint that might also have a story or print on the backside. She'd talked Mr. McDonald into subscribing to papers from some of the larger cities near Cheyenne, but he seemed set on reporting just the things that had taken place in town.

She struggled to roll the press, adding a new sheet of news print each time, but the ink smeared more times than not, and when it did print clear, the newsprint seemed to wrinkle.

"Oh! Darn it!" She raised the lever and pulled the paper up, tossing it aside. It seemed for each page she printed, there was another that didn't turn out. The old press was not in the best shape considering the rust and wear, and it creaked as she worked.

"An honest day's work for an honest day's pay?" Sawyer wandered in, his spurs clinking along the wooden floor.

Just his presence made her breath catch, though she didn't stop working. She hadn't seen him for a couple of days, but she'd been so busy and he'd had to care for Zane. And given she was so tired after work each day, she went home for a quiet meal and rest, though she knew that Deputy Collier still watched her.

"Oh, and what would you know about that?" She scowled but her tone was teasing, until the press stopped again.

"I know about a hard day's work." He moved closer to take a look at the press. Spotting the problem, he walked around beside her. She backed up a step, but her apron caught, the press not allowing her escape.

He leaned in, not taking his eyes from hers getting closer and closer, face-to-face. She braced herself. He was going to kiss her again, wasn't he? She wanted to run. No—she didn't. She waited. Would he do that in broad daylight? He leaned ever closer and grabbed the front of her smock. Catching the handle of the roller by placing his calloused hand over hers, he rolled it backward. The tight grip on her loosened, and the stained apron fell from the press, and he never took those handsome gray eyes from her own.

Rose could hardly breathe, but then he raised the tail of her smock to show her. It was torn and covered in purple ink where it had been caught in the rollers.

"Having a good week on the presses?" He smiled, and stepped back, taking with him the kiss she knew without a doubt she had wanted.

"As a matter of fact I am. This is...is just part of the job," she defended, placing her hands on her hips.

He nodded as if he agreed with her, but the slight smirk didn't go past her.

He was making light of her again, and she didn't like it. Maybe the next time he had a big outlaw capture, she would write the best story ever written about him and just show him how good she really was, but she had still wanted that kiss. His heated breath so close to her own had stirred feelings inside her she wasn't sure she had ever felt before—save his prior kisses.

"What are you doing here anyway?" She couldn't work with him watching her—distracting her.

He adjusted his hat and studied her for a moment. "I'm going to Denver for a few days. I'll be back by Wednesday. I wanted to invite you to the ranch for Zane's birthday next Friday. Six. It's a surprise."

"Oh, of course. How is he?" She had missed time with Zane, who had occupied her evenings with chess and short chats.

"He's better each day." As he answered, he reached out to touch her chin. Rose moved her head to avoid him, and he stopped short of touching her. "You've got ink on your cheek." He put his thumb under her eye and rubbed the stain away.

Rose fought the sigh that wanted to escape given his touch. She could still feel his lips from before, and the warm embrace he'd given her when she worried he and Wyatt might be killed. And now his simple touch caused things within her to warm to a glow she didn't understand. He was so close, looking at her intently and it caused a moment of panic. So she was going to get his kiss after all and while something told her to run, something entirely different told her to stay.

He leaned into her, so close she was overly aware of the pounding of her own heart. He smelled of leather and soap. She closed her eyes, and the slightest warmth of his lips played across hers, ever so softly. A tingle of heat shot through her center and she lost her breath, dropping her hands to her sides.

"Miss Parker, I was hoping for a shipment today."

Mr. McDonald sauntered in from the back.

Sawyer jerked away, walking across to look at a stack of books on the counter, leaving Rose to face Mr. McDonald and to somehow try to recover from his touch. How was she to do that with her knees weak and her breath short?

"Oh, Sheriff, it's good to…to…see you today. How is that son of yours?" Mr. McDonald asked, his stuttering something she was growing accustomed to.

"He's doing much better," Sawyer answered, pretending to read one of the newsprints he'd scrambled to pick up.

Rose took deep breaths to calm her pulse and hoped she looked as if she were printing as usual. How much had her boss seen?

"Do you have need of a paper today sir?" Mr. McDonald picked up one of the dry prints and handed it to him.

Sawyer took the paper, eyeing it as though deeply interested, setting aside the wet one he'd been holding.

"Miss Parker, I'll be in the back for a while. I placed the order for more paper from Chicago. It should have been here by now, but they telegrammed they had not gotten the order. It's always something." The old man made his exit, leaving her alone with Sawyer once more.

Sawyer held a knowing grin, and he only shook his head, tossing the newsprint aside.

She looked back at the press but couldn't hide her own as she cranked the handle once more. She was still breathless with her heart nearly pounding out of her chest.

"I'm just gonna go. I didn't come here to get you

fired, at least not the first week." He turned toward the door and glanced back at her. "You, uh…you still have ink on your cheek." He smiled at her once more and left, leaving her to her press, not that she remembered where she was with the task.

****

The evening sun sat low in the sky to the west, though the heat of the afternoon played thick. Sawyer gazed into the sky and wiped the sweat from his brow as he rode up to the ranch, scanning the window where Rose no longer waited. He brought Colonel to a stop. "What're you doing out here?" He dismounted, just outside the house. Zane was on the porch in one of the chairs, his feet propped on a stool. His arm was free of the sling, allowing him to wear a buttoned shirt for the first time in weeks.

"Doc Tess told me to get some fresh air." Zane's lip curled into a smile.

"Doc was here?" He'd hoped to hear the report on his son's progress, but then he'd worked later than he had expected.

"She's still inside with Dodge and Mei Ling."

Sawyer trotted up the stairs to the porch and leaned against the railing. "So how does the arm feel?"

"I don't need the sling anymore, but it's sore and stiff. Doc Tess said to move it while I am sitting, and I'll get my strength back." He moved his shoulder, brows narrowing into a frown.

"Did you walk out here by yourself?"

Zane put his feet down and scooted forward in the chair. "Yes, sir. I went to the barn to see Shadow too. Doc Tess said it was all right."

Dodge led Tess out onto the porch, both women

201

chattering until spying him.

"Ladies." Sawyer removed his hat and glanced at Tess.

Tess made her way over to Zane. "How do you feel moving around and sitting out here?"

"Better than all day in bed." Zane was resting at the chair's edge.

"Well, you follow directions and don't even think about riding that horse of yours." Tess rubbed the top of his head and turned back to Sawyer and Dodge.

"He can be up, walking around the house several times a day, but Zane..." Tess looked back at him. "No lifting anything for now, not even a book or heavy blanket. Any lifting could cause you to bleed again. I'll take your sutures out in a few more days. Just bring him to town. He's healing remarkably well." Tess smiled at Sawyer and headed down the stairs to her buggy.

Dodge turned to look at Zane, folding her arms. "Well, mister, you have all the rules."

"I can't do much more than the rules anyway." Zane shrugged a bit and then rubbed his shoulder.

"Dinner will be ready soon. Sawyer, why don't you wash up and help Zane back to bed? I'll bring your dinner in shortly." Dodge moseyed back inside.

Sawyer leaned forward and outstretched his hand.

Zane shook his head. "I can do it. I'm good once I am up." He stood, steadying himself for a moment.

"It's good to see you move around so easily." Sawyer fought the urge to take hold of his arm and allowed him to walk on his own. He was doing very well, stronger and even a bit of color to his cheeks.

"It's good to be up." Zane moved gingerly beside him, along the porch. "Shadow is healing too. He's real good."

"Evan says he's less agitated since you came to the ranch." Sawyer had been to the barn to take a look at the animal several times, though the horse only snorted at him for the most part. He held the door, and Zane went into the house before him, leading the way. "I'll be leaving town tomorrow. Wyatt has business elsewhere, and I have a prisoner to get to Denver."

Zane glanced over his shoulder, brows furrowing into a slight frown. "How long will you be gone?"

"I should be back by Wednesday. I won't be long," Sawyer reassured him. "I'm going to go wash up for dinner. You rest."

"Can I ask you something?" Zane settled back in the bed, holding his belly.

Sawyer turned from the door and leaned against the frame.

"Do you think when I am better, I could ride along with you to Denver sometime? Maybe watch the judge and court? I got to see court a little in Mankato." Zane kicked from his boots, letting them clunk to the wooden floor.

Sawyer nodded and held his gaze for a moment longer, finding it intriguing he seemed to have a true interest in law. It occurred to him that his father would be proud, very proud, of such a grandson. "We can do that."

Zane smiled and closed his eyes. Sawyer watched him a moment more, then found his way to the dining room where Wyatt and Evan had just sat to the meal. He took his chair, but as he sat Dodge entered from the kitchen, followed by Brett.

Sawyer met Brett's gaze, idling over what had

brought the rancher to dinner and figuring Dodge up to something given the less than innocent look that plagued her bright blue eyes.

"Brett." Evan leaned forward in greeting, shaking Brett's hand across the table.

"Gentlemen." Brett sat, jerking his hat off and setting it aside, his thick matt of gray hair flattened to his head.

"Boys, I asked Brett to join us tonight because I want to talk to all of you." Dodge placed her elbows on the table and glanced at each of them in turn.

Sawyer took a deep breath and focused on his mother. Without a doubt she was going to discuss Marcus Benton and how they needed to handle getting the cattle home. Well, that was all he needed, having his mother in the mix, and if he were guessing right, Brett was none too fond of the idea either, given he scowled and folded his arms.

Sawyer caught the exchange of glances between Wyatt and Evan, but focused on Dodge once more. His brothers, like him, knew if she'd pulled Brett in, she wanted serious discussion.

Mei Ling brought in the beginnings of dinner, a plate of roast beef with gravy and another full plate of roasted potatoes and shucked ears of corn.

"More to come." She returned a moment later with a plate of steaming cornmeal muffins slathered in butter and honey.

"Thank you Mei Ling, please join us." Dodge waited as Mei Ling sat in the chair that Wyatt pulled out for her.

Dodge rarely kept anything from Mei Ling. She knew as much about the situation as any of them.

"I'll just get right to the point." Dodge rested her gaze on Brett.

Evan groaned, rolling his eyes and received a swift kick underneath the table from Wyatt.

Dodge thumped his ear leaving him rubbing it. "You'll listen whether you like it or not. I have some things to say about the cattle crossing."

Brett sat stoic, and Sawyer had the slight urge to grin. Dodge had probably promised him a good meal but hadn't enlightened him about the discussion she was going to have. She was good at being deceptive when she wanted, but she usually had everyone's best interest at heart.

"The cattle are delayed to give us a bit of time to think about the action we need to take." She continued, in spite of Evan's continued displays of folding his arms, adjusting in his chair, and all but cursing.

"Action we take? We're crossing the river." He spouted.

Sawyer began eating, thinking he'd listen and plan his own action. He'd been watching Benton's men at the river here and there over the last few weeks. No matter who came near, they shot in warning, but most were still allowed to cross. It wasn't likely it would be so easy for them when the time came, and that was just what Marcus Benton was waiting for.

Dodge held up a hand and glared Evan's way. "The first thing that is going to happen is you are going to stop stirring things up with the men in the bunk house, and when you are in town with Benton's men."

"I didn't start that fight," Evan insisted, glaring at her and then Sawyer.

Dodge raised her voice a notch, slapping her hands

on the table. "You lead the hands on this ranch, and you need to be the example." She then turned to Brett. "And the same goes for you with your men."

Brett postured where he sat, but his gaze never changed. He knew Dodge, and he knew her well. Leaving the table wasn't an option, though Sawyer had no doubts he'd likely still do what he wanted to do as well.

"You two lead all these men. You both need to order the men to stay on the ranches. The more they are in town, the worse things will become." Dodge usually planned things very orderly, and Sawyer's guess was she had been thinking on things for a time now. Much like him.

"The men have a right to their leave," Evan argued, unfolding his arms again and gripping the table with both hands.

"Yes they do, so you are going to offer them a bit more pay to play this game." She glanced at Brett and raised her eyebrows.

"I can keep the men from town without paying them," Brett grumbled in his low deep voice.

"Yes, but when you pay a man, he feels obligated." Dodge sent a charged rebuttal.

"It doesn't change that much; they still have to cross on Benton's property regardless of who is mouthing off in town." Wyatt added his two bits worth to the conversation but seemed to be the only one of them besides Sawyer who was eating.

"Benton isn't budging, and there won't be any cavalry coming this way." Sawyer hadn't let them all know that.

"I suppose the cavalry isn't up to dealing with

cattle tensions when the Indians are stirred up." Brett glanced at him with a nod.

"I'm not losing two thousand head of cattle to thirst, and Benton's men shoot at anyone near the river." Evan sat forward with a frown.

Wyatt tossed down his fork in disgust. "We can't arrest them for warning fire alone, and the damn cavalry is worthless as we all know."

Sawyer shook his head and looked around the table. He'd been thinking on it for days now, and he had a few things he could pull to keep Benton in check, but he wasn't sure the timing was right. As he thought what to say, the door to the dining room opened.

Dodge glanced up. "Zane?"

"I…thought I might sit with you for dinner." He sounded uncertain as he gazed shyly around the room.

Sawyer kicked out the chair beside him, and Zane sat cautiously as he turned back to the conversation. "Benton isn't bluffing. He'll order his men to shoot when he's ready."

"Then he'll get back what he dishes out," Evan shouted, slamming a fist on the table and gulping down a hunk of beef.

Sawyer raised his own voice. "You need to cut that fight in you right now. I'm the law, and I'll handle Benton."

Zane's eyes widened at his father's tone, but he remained quiet.

"I run this ranch, and we are getting our cattle through, regardless of the law!" Evan ranted, glaring eyes of green stone at him.

"There you go, Evan. Are you going to take the first bullet? Benton's already tired of you running your mouth," Sawyer shouted back. The more he talked of Benton, the more he tensed. What had been lying dormant for years was beginning to stir deep inside him.

Evan leaned forward in his chair. "Well at least I'm not sitting still."

Sawyer's control snapped. "I *am* the law! What would you have me do?"

"More than just sit idle and chat kindly with Benton. He wants to capture the market and nothing more!" Evan shook his head. "I'm done with this conversation." He slammed his chair back as he stood.

Sawyer scrambled up, his own chair tossed back. He had to keep Evan under control, or the whole damn thing would end up in a serious loss of lives.

"Sit!" Dodge shouted, pointing to the table. "Both of you!"

Evan grabbed his chair and slung it back in place, plopping down and glaring at Sawyer.

"The cattle will cross, Evan, but Benton has no interest in the cattle market." Sawyer sat back down, his pulse pounding the headache that was beginning. Marcus Benton was more interested in selling the bootleg whiskey. "We'll arrest Benton and his men if it goes too far, but we'll accomplish nothing fighting amongst ourselves."

"Just like that?" Evan mocked, still gripping the table.

"Yes!" Sawyer slammed a fist on the table and forks clinked. He hated losing his temper, but Evan always pushed him, too young to think he might well lose his own life. He still thought he could take on the world, and it was probably a good thing he hadn't become a lawman. He might have already met his fate. *Holy hell!*

"Likely it won't be Benton you will have to take. It'll be his men. He doesn't do his own fightin' or killin'." Brett finally went to his food, forking a piece of meat and chewing slowly.

"He'll be held accountable for his men, just as you both will." There, Sawyer had said what he needed to, not that Brett needed the reminder.

Evan held his glare but said no more.

Mei Ling, who had gotten up when the heated conversation began, returned with dessert for each person. She set the first plate in front of Zane.

When Zane didn't reach for his fork right away, Sawyer encouraged him. "Eat." He picked up his own fork. It wasn't an uncommon event for the McCade family to have a heated discussion at dinner, and it might be wise for Zane to get used to the way they hashed things out around the table.

Zane picked up his fork and took a bite of the warm blackberry pie.

Dodge did the same but didn't taste the steaming dessert. "Well, my only request is to keep the hands on both ranches. No more brawls in town. Marcus Benton likes his money too much to hang for a bunch of cattle."

Brett pointed his fork at them. "Boys, I think we've been swindled. I was actually brought here tonight to say hello to you, young man." He glanced toward Zane with a smile gleaming out from under the thick white mustache.

"Zane, this is Brett, a friend of the family for years." Dodge placed a small bite of pie in her mouth with a smile at both.

"Sir." Zane replied and nodded.

"I saw that horse of yours. It's an impressive animal." He gave Zane a wink.

"Thank you, sir. He's *really* impressive when he rolls right over you." Zane's cheeks glowed with his grin.

Brett laughed as did the others, all but Sawyer who didn't care to relive what that picture had been like. There had only been a handful of times in his life that he'd been really afraid and finding Zane, so near to death had nearly been his undoing. "Don't encourage him, he's still got some healing to do."

"Ah, he's gonna be riding before long at all. Can't let him stay puny forever," Wyatt teased, still bearing a scab where he'd been pistol whipped.

"Did you eat your dinner?" Sawyer asked nodding toward the pie Zane had barely touched.

"Some." Zane shrugged.

"You're a regular mother hen Sawyer." Wyatt winked at Zane. "He'll eat when he's ready."

Sawyer only glared at his brother.

"It's nice to spend an evening with you fine folks, but I'll need to be heading out." Brett got up, nodding and leaving the room.

"I'll walk you out." Dodge followed him outside, trading glances with her sons once more on the way.

Sawyer finished his dessert, joining the idle chat at the table when Dodge returned. He still couldn't knock the feeling inside him that things were gathering momentum. Marcus Benton's men were shooting, but it was innocent enough for right now.

He wished he could think he was right on that notion, but where Benton was concerned, there was only foul play and whether or not he was ready, things were coming soon.

Chapter Fifteen

Sawyer sat on the front porch railing, watching Evan teach Zane the finer art of playing poker. He wasn't sure who was teaching whom. He'd been delayed getting back from Denver due to rain, but had returned late the night before, not wanting to miss Zane's birthday. When he had found Zane injured, he'd said his birthday was August twenty-second, though the boy hadn't mentioned anything about it of late. Maybe he'd forgotten with his injuries and all that had happened.

Evan threw his cards down in disgust. "You can't bluff anyone if you don't play it for all it's worth. If your hand is that good, then act as if it's a tough call, only raise a bit and keep the game going."

Zane raked over the small pile of money on the little table before them, shoving the coins in his trouser pockets.

"So what did you have?" Evan leaned to take a look.

Zane quickly shuffled the cards with his eyebrows raised high. "You didn't pay to see."

Evan growled, folding his arms, spurs clanking across the wooden boards of the porch as he stretched out his legs.

"I think he got you." Sawyer chuckled at the exchange.

"It's all about reading faces." Zane quoted Evan's own advice in mockery, talking with a deeper voice to act as if he were Evan.

"There is still an art to the game." Evan shook his head.

"Yep and I just used it to take all your money." Zane shuffled the deck, eyeing his uncle.

"Deal 'em again." Evan pushed his hat back, determined.

"Evan, I'm afraid I'm taking him from the game." Sawyer needed a reason to get Zane off the ranch for an hour, so that Dodge and Mei Ling could ready things for the party.

"I'll win my money back another day...wise ass." Evan laughed and tossed Zane the one coin he had left.

"Where are we going?" Zane caught the coin and turned to follow Sawyer toward the barn, shoving his winnings in the front pocket of his trousers.

Sawyer only motioned him to follow with a nod of the shoulder. Inside the barn, he opened the stall where Colonel waited, saddled a while ago by Billy.

"Well?" Sawyer gestured toward Shadow's stall.

Zane walked over to the stall peering at the horse and then he glanced at his father.

"Aren't you coming?" Sawyer led Colonel outside the stall and then the barn.

"You're gonna let me ride?" Zane's face lit up as he took Shadow by the reins and followed, the horse saddled and waiting.

"Yep, but if he cuts up we're trading horses, got it?" Sawyer mounted up, hoping like hell the horse behaved. It was true the animal really liked no one but Zane, and he wasn't in the mood for a complicated ride.

Zane struggled to get his foot in the stirrup and pull up into the saddle, it taking some effort.

"Just do everything slowly," Sawyer warned, wondering if this were such a good idea. The boy was healing, but things still weren't so easy for him.

"Feels good to be back up here." Zane smiled cautiously, patting the horse.

Sawyer took Colonel to a slow canter leading the way, keeping an eye on Shadow. They rode east in silence, to where herds of cattle could be seen for miles. Sawyer took glimpses of Zane enjoying the ride and the scenery. It gave him a bit of the picture of the long ride his son had made to arrive to Cheyenne in search of him. He was an amazing boy, and he couldn't be more proud.

After following the river for half an hour, Sawyer stopped Colonel and dismounted. "Can you get down? We'll water them here."

Zane managed, looking around and patting his painted horse. "I didn't realize the river was so wide here."

"Yeah, it's wide but not so deep. Sit and rest for a minute." Sawyer pointed toward large boulders piled just at the edge of the water. He took the reins to both horses and led them to the river.

"Is this where the cattle will cross?" Zane bent to pick up a stone and tossed it toward the river, the slate skipping several times.

"Further south." Sawyer tightened Shadow's saddle just to make sure, amazed the horse allowed it.

"So, there will really be shooting?" Zane leaned forward with his hands on his knees, gray eyes serious.

"The feud between Brett and Marcus Benton goes

way back. It's more than about crossing cattle." Sawyer glanced his way and turned back to the horses. Hell explaining this topic wasn't going to be easy.

Zane studied him. "What did they feud over?"

Sawyer had to laugh, why not? The answer was plain and simple. "Dodge."

Zane frowned. "Dodge?"

"When my father died, I believe Benton thought he'd marry Dodge and own this ranch and the land for his railroad purposes. Dodge was smarter than that, though she kept his company for a while until she figured out the truth about him. Funny thing is, she kept his company when she was younger as well and chose my father instead." Watching Zane brought back the memory of his father who had often brought him, Wyatt, and Dawson to the river to teach them their studies. He could picture the colonel, tall and proud, holding his hat in his hands pacing as he lectured them. A jolt of pain bolted through him. He missed the man more than words could ever say and probably always would.

"I thought Brett and Dodge were courting—" Zane pulled him from his thoughts, and he grabbed Colonel's reins along with Shadow's.

"Brett and Dodge are good for each other." Sawyer raised his eyebrows and turned back to the horses. Hell he wouldn't be explaining Dodge's relationship any further than that, though it was no secret to most they had been carrying on for years. Zane would have to figure out that one for himself.

"When the cattle cross, you'll arrest Benton and his men then?"

Sawyer shrugged and turned back to him. "It

depends. Benton doesn't fear the law—me or anyone. He's done a lot of law breaking out here, bad business deals, crime. We'll do our best to keep it under control, but Brett and Evan have to keep their men in check." He fully expected Benton to create a scene of havoc. Deadly havoc, but there was no reason to cause Zane worry, even if he himself wasn't sleeping nights.

"I could help," Zane offered, standing.

"Oh, no. You are far too young for the likes of this." Sawyer shook his head. The last thing he needed was to worry about Zane when it all came down—and it was coming.

"But I shoot really well, rifle or revolver." Zane shoved his hands in his pocket, kicking the toe of a boot in the edge of the river, stirring up mud.

"You shoot very well?" Sawyer narrowed his brows and tied both horses to a low hanging branch. "Come here." He pulled the revolver from his hip.

Zane followed. "Angus took me hunting and taught me to ride and shoot, said I was good as any grown man."

"Is that right?" Sawyer wasn't sure he agreed, but he'd find out. He paced off sixteen feet and tugged Zane behind him, thinking about what he'd said. "The tree straight ahead, right on the scar. See it?"

"Yes, sir." Zane narrowed his eyes.

Sawyer cocked the revolver and fired, repeating it three times. Each bullet hit right near the bad spot on the tree, no more than half an inch away from dead center.

Sawyer pulled Zane into the spot where he'd been standing and handed him the revolver. He wanted to be the one to teach his son about shooting, riding, ranching, law, and even ladies. Well, he might need to figure out the part about ladies before he shared that with his son. He'd basically failed at that so far.

Zane glanced at him with caution, hesitating.

"Go ahead, the gun has a kick." He stepped behind Zane, tilting his hat back.

The boy held the revolver and cocked it with little effort, took a deep breath, and held it steady squinting one eye. He fired. The scar on the tree splintered dead center of Sawyer's three marks.

Sawyer's mouth dropped open. He couldn't believe it. It had to be beginner's luck. Boys Zane's age couldn't do that with a heavy revolver, and especially one they hadn't practiced with. He pushed the gun back toward Zane.

"Again, aim for the small dark circle of bark just below there." He folded his arms and waited in doubt.

Zane cocked the revolver, aimedm and fired again. The bad spot on the tree shattered with a thud of the bullet.

"Unbelievable. Who taught you?" Sawyer put a hand on Zane's shoulder, turning him. Most grown men couldn't shoot that well.

"Mr. Mason, the one you wired. He's really old, but said in his younger days, he was a gunslinger. He took me hunting and fishing since I was small, even though Mama hated guns." He handed the revolver carefully back to Sawyer.

"I guess that explains you owning that revolver I found with your things." Sawyer had wondered about the gun but had let the boy keep it, though he'd given him specific orders he wasn't to carry it at all for now.

"I used it to shoot rabbits while I was traveling to

find you. Kept myself fed." Pride tinged his young face.

"I'm going to have some fun with you and my brothers when you are well. For now, just remember, shooting a target is one thing, but taking a man's life in haste is another, that's why I suggested you keep your gun put away for now." Sawyer strolled back to the horses with Zane following. There was apparently a lot more to this son of his than he had known.

"They all shoot well? I know Wyatt does, but Dawson and Evan too?" Zane walked rapidly, trying to keep up.

Sawyer nodded. "Very well, but I have a feeling you can give them a run."

"So you won't need me at the crossing?"

"No. That rule is still set." Sawyer had to grin as he reached Colonel and glanced back at Zane.

Zane untied Shadow's reins, the horse nudging his shoulder. "Mama hated guns. She hated worse I knew how to play poker, but Angus taught me that too."

"Well, you'll keep Evan busy with taking his money it seems." Sawyer chuckled.

Zane's grin was almost contagious. "Do you play when there's a big game at the saloon? Evan said there are a couple of good games a year."

"Not often, but I can hardly keep Wyatt or Evan out of the saloon when Jacob puts up a big pot. I usually have to keep an eye on things and playing doesn't let me do that, but don't you get any ideas, you are too young for the likes of that." He waited as Zane mounted Shadow, holding the horse steady for him.

"We need to head back, we've got a party to go to." While he wanted it to be a surprise, he didn't know how Zane would react to being blindsided.

"Party?" Zane adjusted in the saddle.

"It's August twenty-second." Sawyer mounted up and turned Colonel to face Zane.

Zane's brows tightened into a slight frown. "I guess the fall knocked all the sense out of me."

"Fourteen." Sawyer smiled, but his gut clenched at the lost time with his son.

Zane clucked his tongue, and Shadow moved forward. "Still not old enough to help the family defend the river."

Sawyer laughed loudly, turning Colonel to follow. "You *are* like your mother. Pushy."

"I told you she was relentless. I gave up most times to keep peace, except about Shadow." Zane patted the horse.

"I'm sure that wasn't easy." Catherine was so headstrong there were times he'd backed down and given in to what she wanted as well. Somehow that determination was the part that kept him smitten with her, and if he had to guess, that same feisty, determined demeanor was what had attracted him to Rose as well. The thought of Rose gave his heart a jolt. She'd said she would be there at the party tonight, but having not seen her the last few days while in Denver had given him pause at how much he really did miss her. Denver had also given him more time to think about the fact that he did want to try and earn her love, the right way.

"I hid him for a month before she found out." Zane allowed him to catch up, glancing back.

"She wasn't happy?"

"She was madder than a wet cat." The boy giggled.

Sawyer nodded and laughed. He'd seen that a time or two himself.

"You laugh because you know." Zane's smile faded and he looked away.

Sawyer took a deep breath and swallowed hard. "Zane...I did care for her, a great deal; we just didn't find a place where we could be together. I was young and full of fight, and she was right not to want that."

Zane glanced at him after a moment. "Sawyer?"

"Huh?"

"Do you believe in God?"

Sawyer took a moment of riding to think on it. He believed in God, but he also believed a man had to look out for himself. "I believe in God. Why do you ask?"

"You're a lawman, and you've had to...kill men." Zane said it hesitantly but kept eye contact, awaiting an answer.

"There's a church on the far side of town; it doubles as the school during the week. Dodge and Mei Ling go from time to time. You could go if you want to. As for the men I've killed, most had it coming, and I think God knows that." He hadn't stepped foot in a church in years. It wasn't that he didn't believe in God, but something happened to a man when he took the life of another, right or wrong.

Zane nodded and remained silent.

Sawyer let out another deep breath and rode alongside his son, grateful when the ranch came into view. He had no idea what Zane might be thinking given all he'd been through, and some part of him was hoping he'd answered him well enough.

He helped Zane dismount just outside the barn, worrying the ride might have been too much as he had a harder time this go around and he was pale.

"You sit for a minute. If I take you in looking like

you've been riding, Dodge and Tess will have my hide." He took both horses inside and removed their saddles.

Zane sat on one of the stools. "The doc will kill *me* if she finds out."

"We'll tell her we didn't go far, and only if she asks." Sawyer figured to get a good scolding from Tess either way.

Giving Zane a moment to rest, he walked to the barn door once again and noticed the doc's buggy, but not Rose's horse, Sadie. He'd thought all day about her coming to the birthday party. She might have ridden with Tess if he were guessing.

Zane got up and walked to where he stood. "Who all is here?"

"You'll see, just act surprised."

"Kind of nervous." Zane hesitated when he stepped forward toward the house.

"Nah, come on." Sawyer gave him a smile.

Inside, Zane followed Sawyer, who tossed his hat aside on the chair in the parlor, leading the way through to the dining room door.

"Happy Birthday!" Dodge was holding a cake, the room erupting in cheer.

Zane froze, his cheeks going pink with everyone singing *For He's A Jolly Good Fellow,* but he finally broke into a smile.

Sawyer glanced at Rose. So she had ridden in with Tess. She held his gaze for a long moment before the festivities took her attention. He continued to watch her as she sang, thinking her beauty was unmatched. Yep, he was sinking and fast but somehow, he didn't care anymore. Hell, he couldn't even sing, given his racing pulse and loss of the words.

"Everyone take a seat." Dodge directed, setting the cake at the center of the table.

Rose walked around Evan and took her usual chair next to Sawyer. It had been vacant for too long. He met her gaze once more, and she smiled.

Evan sat and leaned forward, stretching a long arm toward the cake.

Dodge was quick with her pop of his hand, Evan retracting as fast as he'd tried. "Just a taste!"

"It is not your cake." Dodge raised her brows.

"Master Zane, special for you tonight." Mei Ling entered the dining room and sat a platter of fried chicken before him with a bow.

"I haven't had fried chicken in a long time." Zane thanked her with a return bow and sat down, glancing around the room.

Dodge picked up the plate of bread and passed it along to Brett. "What are you smiling at?"

"Dodge and her family. All is well."

"Thank you for humoring me. I know you don't care for a crowd." She patted his cheek.

Sawyer met glances with Brett who actually smiled. How Dodge had gotten him here for the birthday he wasn't sure, but the exchange wasn't surprising. Dodge was happiest when everyone was in the house together.

"Zane." Doc Tess looked his way. "I know you went riding and that had best be the last time your father allows that for a while longer." She glared at them both.

"We went slow Doc, and it won't happen again until we get the okay from you." Sawyer was quick with his answer and faster to sip his coffee.

"It's good to see him moving around. Slacker can't lie in the bed all his life." Evan grabbed the potatoes, plopping a heaping spoonful on his plate.

Zane grinned and held his plate up for Evan to do the same for him.

Sawyer was all too aware of Rose beside him, but with the crowd, it wasn't like he could speak his mind. His chest pounded, and his hunger seemed to abate. She'd worn one of her fancy gowns, pink with satin lace, and her breasts were pushed high by her corset. When her gaze caught his, he nearly choked on his own saliva. "I'm glad you made it." It felt like small talk, but he wanted her to know that he was grateful she had come for Zane—for him.

"I wanted to be here," she answered, putting her napkin in her lap, and her blue eyes pierced right though him or so it seemed. He held her gaze, wishing to hold her.

Dodge brought the room to quiet. "We have a tradition in this family, Zane. When it's your birthday, you have to let everyone know what you're thankful for and what you hope for in the new year."

Sawyer groaned along with his brothers and glanced at Rose who only giggled. He gave into a smile, shaking his head. Dodge and her traditions would be the death of them all, and now Zane was her next victim. He gazed at his son.

Zane glanced around the room but took on the challenge clearing his voice. "I didn't know what to expect...coming here. I just wanted to find Sawyer."

Sawyer swallowed the lump in his throat, focusing on his son.

Zane continued, "I didn't know I was going to find him, or him find me. I owe all of you some kind of thanks for your care and kindness. I think you are expecting me to say something profound..." He scanned the room once more. "A wish for the new year. I really don't have anything I need. I found it here, with all of you. Finding my father and an entire family...friends." Zane's eyes glistened, and while his mouth was open, he seemed to have no more words.

Sawyer picked up. "Zane...I know it's been hard on you physically with your injuries and I know you are still unsure of some things about being here, but...never wonder or think you don't belong here, because you do."

Dodge handed a box to Zane. "Welcome home and happy birthday. I have waited a lifetime for a grandson, given all my boys lack of settling down to wed. So if I spoil you here and there, then you will just have to put up with it."

Zane grinned and took the lid off and looked inside. He lifted the books to thumb through them. "Author John McCade?"

"You have his eyes, just like your father, but I think you need to read up on these until we can get you back to school." Dodge eyed Sawyer.

He nodded. Once Zane was well, school would be good for him, but he had a mind to teach him as he had been taught by his own father.

"Thank you." Zane put the books back in the box, setting it aside.

Brett sent a large knife in a leather case down the table to Zane. "A man should have a good hunting knife in these parts, made that one myself."

Zane reached for it and ran his hand over the roughened horn handle. "Bone handle?"

"Elk Antler."

Zane edged his thumb across the blade and whistled nodding to Brett. "Thank you, sir."

Evan leaned across the table and slapped a dark hat on Zane's head. "You haven't had a hat since you got here. Can't ride that damn horse of yours in the heat without it. I'll be expecting you out with the herds come spring."

"I'll look forward to that and taking your money in poker." Zane took the hat off and examined it with a nod of approval as the entire room erupted in laughter.

"He's all the way from Mankato, but the brat knows his game." Evan shook his head.

"Zane, Rose and I went in together to get this for you." Doc Tess handed him a big package wrapped in brown paper and tied with cord.

Zane tore into it carefully, tugging a heavy brown leather coat free.

"I've yet to live my first winter here, but I understand a good coat is a must." Rose smiled, her eyes bright.

"I appreciate this, the one I have is too small." Zane folded it again, looking completely overwhelmed.

Mei Ling, sitting beside him handed him a small satin bag. "This gift from China. Jade, full of luck."

Zane removed the small green stone on a red ribbon from the box. "I've read about the jade in China."

Mei Ling bowed her head, and Zane returned the gesture and thanked her in Chinese. "*Xie Xie*. Thank you."

Wyatt leaned forward and handed Zane a new scope. "Next time you can take a closer look at where you are riding."

"I won't miss those slip rocks again." Zane shook his head, admiring the scope. "I've never gotten so many gifts at one time. I thank you all."

"One more." Sawyer had waited last for his own gift for his son. He got up and walked out into the hallway and returned with a case and sat it before Zane, who looked at it and back up to him.

"Go ahead." Sawyer encouraged him to open it.

Zane pulled one buckle at a time, laying the lid open. He slowly touched the wood and then the bow of the brand new violin. "I've...never seen a finer one."

It had been expensive, but he wanted Zane to have it. "Let's just say I got a good deal on it in Denver."

Wyatt chuckled. "That means he made a deal with a judge or a lawyer, or swindled a trade for someone to get off scot free from their sentence."

"Or he took it from a down and out renegade and that will be the next man working on the ranch." Evan smirked at his older brother.

Sawyer ignored them and watched Zane touch the instrument, running his hand down the fine wood.

"Zane, I left your gift in the barn. It'll need food and water on a regular basis." Dawson tossed his napkin on the table, leaning back and folding his arms. "A pup I got when I was with the Cheyenne last week, part wolf."

"A dog? It's all right?" he asked looking from Dawson to Sawyer.

"It is if you take care of it and teach him to herd and not eat the cattle." Sawyer shrugged, eyeing his brother.

"Zane, why don't you play for us?" Rose encouraged, clasping her hands and resting her chin on them.

Sawyer met gazes with her and for the life of him couldn't pull his attention away from her. As far as he was concerned, she lit up the entire room and had they not been surrounded by the family, he thought he might simply lean to kiss her.

Zane scanned around the room and picked up the violin, testing its weight and running his thumb across the strings.

Sawyer forced his attention back to his son. "I had them tune it in Denver…it might need a bit more since the ride."

"It's fine." Zane picked up the bow and stood, pushing his chair back. He put the violin in his left hand and steadied it carefully across his injured shoulder. The room hushed as he ran the bow across the strings, eliciting a long vibrato and then moving his fingers rapidly across the strings, closing his eyes.

"Chopin," Rose whispered.

Sawyer looked at her briefly, and back. He'd figured Zane to play well since Catherine had taught him, but everyone around the table seemed surprised at his abilities. Watching him play was amazing—just as much so as when he'd once watched Catherine. It occurred to him that he had somehow put Catherine to rest, now that he and Zane were getting to know each other. There was just so much he would never understand, but the best place for that was behind him where he could think about the future with Zane and perhaps—Rose. He watched her as she enjoyed the music, closing her eyes. She was a real beauty of the likes he was sure he'd never seen.

Zane pushed and pulled the bow rapidly and then the song slowed, with long draws along low and high notes, loud and soft mingling to shape the sounds. He was dropping his elbow on the arm holding the violin, likely due to fatigue of his newly healed shoulder. Dawson reached to support Zane's arm at the elbow, and he continued to play, only a brief second of the music stopping. The song went on a moment more, and when he pulled the bow for the last drawn out note, the room remained silent.

Zane looked up meeting gazes with Sawyer. The room had erupted in clapping, with everyone praising Zane, who quickly laid the instrument back in its case and hurried from the room, the front door of the house slamming behind him.

"Sawyer?" Dodge stood glancing at him.

Sawyer held up a hand to have Dodge wait. "His mother taught him to play. Just...enjoy your cake." Sawyer trotted outside after Zane, who had likely gone to the barn. He hadn't meant for the gift to be upsetting and cursed himself for not thinking it might, and he had seen his son's tears.

"Zane?" He opened the barn door and stepped inside.

Zane stood at Shadow's stall and quickly wiped his eyes with his sleeve, turning away, obviously not wanting his father to see him cry.

Sawyer moved closer. "I'm sorry. I thought the violin was a good idea."

"It was," Zane whispered and sniffled.

Sawyer cursed silently to himself and took a few

more steps toward Zane, who rubbed Shadow's jaw. "I haven't played since she died."

"She would want you to play."

"I know." Zane's voice cracked, tears spilling down his cheeks.

Sawyer hesitated for a moment but stepped even closer, putting a hand on Zane's shoulder. Zane erupted into tears, bringing his hands to his face and trying to pull away, but Sawyer hugged him all the tighter.

"I miss her." Zane wiped his eyes again with his sleeve.

"I know you do. I'm sorry, son."

The puppy Dawson left in a crate whimpered from across the barn, and Zane turned in that direction. He walked over and lifted the furry gray pup. It whined and Zane settled him in the crook of his arm like a baby, rubbing his belly.

"When my father died, I felt like the life had been sucked right out of me. I won't tell you it ever goes away, but it does get better, Zane." Sawyer wasn't sure his words were right, as the pain of his own loss wasn't much better, but the day would come soon enough, when he got his revenge.

Zane nodded. "I didn't mean to leave the party. It was fun, but—" He let the pup chew on his finger, and a slight grin curled across his lips.

"I think everyone understands. You don't have to go back in right now. It's gonna be all right Zane. It may not feel like it, but it is. You stay here and play with the pup for a while. I'll come back in a bit." Sawyer turned and headed outside, finding Rose and Tess standing near the porch. Tess was talking to Wyatt at the foot of the stairs, while Rose waited at the buggy.

He watched her for a moment and trotted over. "Thank you for coming tonight…and for the coat."

"Is he all right?" Rose asked about Zane, her concern apparent.

"He's fine. I think." He wanted to say more than he thought he could or even should. Taking a step closer and making sure that Wyatt was still taking up Tess' time, he turned back to her. "Rose. Uh, things between us, I mean." He stopped, trying to gain his thoughts. "We started out wrong. I started things out wrong, and I wanted to see if I could have dinner this week with you at the hotel, where we can talk."

She studied him for a long time. When she said nothing, he continued. Damn it but her eyes were so beautiful in the darkness where her pupils were wide and black. "I've not been real fair to you, and I'd like the chance to start over." His palms were more than sweaty as he gripped them. *Holy hell.*

"Let's see. No interrogations, no cows in the mud, no ink on my face. Just dinner and conversation?" She held the grin that had struck her face, folding her arms.

"Just dinner and conversation."

"Then I accept your invitation, Sheriff." And with that she leaned up to kiss his cheek.

Sawyer froze, unable to utter a sound. He'd been thinking of dinner with her for days, wanting to talk to her if nothing else. Wanting to really talk to her, not about the hidden story he knew was still there—but about the story of Rose.

Chapter Sixteen

"I've been getting papers from some of the larger cities back east, and Mr. McDonald is giving in to the idea that we can expand the topics we cover in the new *Cheyenne Tribune*. Of course he is worried about recuperating the costs." Rose sipped her wine, sitting across the table from Sawyer, inside the hotel. "But, we are already up to two pages front and back, which means we charge two cents now, and he has actually made a little profit."

Sawyer pushed his empty plate aside, his gaze holding hers. "Two cents is hard to come by for some. You might check here at the hotel and other businesses to see if they can sell them for you. There are a few small towns around here that might do the same."

"I could ask Mr. McDonald about that. At least he has allowed me to write an article or two, though printing takes most of my time." She didn't mind the printing, but she really wanted to research, conduct interviews, and write.

Sawyer reached across the table and lifted her hand turning it palm up and running his thumb across the tips of her purple stained fingers. His knowing grin made her clasp her fist closed, though her heart pounded against her chest at his touch.

She tugged her hand back, folding both in her lap. "It's part of the job."

"So you haven't gotten tangled up anymore?" His gray eyes sparkled with humor.

"That's not funny, and it hasn't happened again." Of course that reminded her of his quick kiss, the one that had heated her body and caught her off guard. She couldn't get over the intensity of his eyes, which seemed to consume her now that he *was* interested and wouldn't be interrogating her about her past. At least he had promised.

She'd been nervous, pacing while waiting on him to escort her to the hotel a short time ago. Still, as they had finished their meal and she began talking of her work, he'd leaned back in his chair and simply listened to all she had to tell him about the paper. It surprised her.

"This was really nice, Sawyer." She lifted her wine glass and sipped.

"I've, uh, taken the liberty to order dessert, too." He'd spent his hard earned wages on making sure the evening was perfect, down to her favorite dinner and dessert.

Rose set her glass back in place and gazed at him again, giving him her best smile. "Well, then I must wonder what the occasion might be."

He remained serious and waited a long moment before he answered. "I told you I haven't really been very fair to you, maybe not so nice either."

She listened as he struggled to explain himself. It was clearly hard for him as he sat forward, shook his head, and seemed to fidget with the edge of his plate. Well, maybe he deserved a bit of discomfort. At least a little, but she also remembered she hadn't been entirely truthful about her own situation, not that she would be telling anything more of that this night.

He went on after taking a deep breath "I just wanted to start over if that's possible. After Zane arrived—things about life being short and missed opportunities hit me, and all I could think about was…you." His gray eyes were wide and intense.

Rose froze for a moment, letting his words sink in. What was he saying? Did he really think of her in such a way? And if he did what did that mean? "I think that is the way I felt when I lost my father, that there was so much more that might have been said."

The waiter arrived with dessert, setting a small dish in front of her and another before Sawyer. Rose stared in awe at the smooth dark chocolate. "Chocolate mousse? In Cheyenne?"

"I had the recipe sent from Max Ferguson in New York. It's taken Douglas a few practice runs to get the mousse to cook just right in his oven." He chuckled, obviously pleased with his effort to surprise her. Yet, the mention of Max caught her off guard and she swallowed hard.

"So thoughtful." She picked up the fancy silver spoon and dipped into the swirled chocolate froth, taking a bite and closing her eyes. She moaned, savoring the deep, rich cocoa, trying not to think too hard on his contact with Max.

Sawyer shifted in his chair.

"Aren't you going to try it?" she asked.

He nodded, and reached for his own spoon and tasted. "It's good, though I've been trying a bite of different batches all week."

"You went to so much trouble, Sheriff." Without a doubt she was smitten with the man before her. He'd dressed in dark trousers and a starched white shirt without his vest. He even had a ribbon tied and closing his collar. And without his hat and his thick long hair tucked behind his ears, she could hardly breathe. A man like Sawyer probably had no idea just how handsome he really was, and she felt the heat to her cheeks at her thoughts. Regardless, her situation didn't mean she could let her guard down not even with the sheriff.

"Not too much."

She smiled and took another bite of the mousse and glanced at him again. She had been aware of how he'd watched her all evening, and something was different about him. She couldn't put her finger on it, but his continuous gaze held something more than simple interest. If she didn't know better, he was acting as a man in love. The thought caused her heart to surge, in spite of all the warning bells that seemed to ring inside her head.

"Dodge said something about the cattle being delayed?" She thought quickly to keep from feeling as if she were on the spot.

He nodded. "The rains kept the cattle from getting to Kansas. It's a chore to keep Evan and Brett out of trouble, but it's a good thing for now."

"So, Mr. Benton?" She really didn't understand what had transpired between Sawyer and Marcus Benton, but if nothing else it was seeded by a deep hatred on both counts. "I've seen him in town on and off the last few days. He's been to the paper to talk to Mr. McDonald. He isn't very talkative, but he nods when I say hello. He always has those two gruff-looking men with him." She shivered.

"He and Brett don't mix well. You stay away from

him. He's a dangerous man." He sat forward, his eyes dark and his tone stern.

Rose wondered if she had started on the wrong thing. "Everyone in town seems so fearful of him."

He sighed heavily and his eyes narrowed as he spoke. "The men you mentioned—the ones with Benton and most anyone else he has a relationship with—they aren't to be trusted. He leaves a long line of indirect crime behind him. Evil crime."

"Why not arrest him if you know these things." She questioned, and still wondered on the entire feud. At least she thought of it as a feud between ranches and of things that had happened a long time ago from what Dodge had shared with her. None of it seemed to make any sense to her. Why would allowing cattle to cross on his part of the river be such a problem for Mr. Benton? But given Sawyer's alarm over the conversation there had to be more.

"Nothing tracks to him clearly enough to arrest him or bring him in." He changed the subject and seemingly relaxed against his chair again. "So, I saw you got a large shipment from New York this week."

"Yes, my clothing and a few things I needed. My friend Muriel shipped everything." She said it before she realized and resisted the urged to cover her mouth with her hand. She'd slipped. *Oh, dear God!*

"Muriel?"

Careful. If Sawyer knew Muriel was Max's wife, he'd smell a mystery and start digging. "She and I grew up together. She is married, expecting her first child." She missed Muriel but had been so happy to read the news in the letter hidden among her shipment, probably without Max's knowledge. Her friend had also assured her that things were still fine in New York, but that hardly settled her mind here.

"You wanted adventure, but you left such a good friend?"

Rose jerked her gaze directly to his serious gray eyes. "You said no interrogations."

He gave her a slight grin and chuckled. "I'll walk you home."

He stood and held a hand out, assisting her up and motioning her ahead.

Rose walked outside the hotel followed by Sawyer, who offered his elbow. She hesitated and then placed her hand gently at the bend of his muscular arm with a smile. So he did have manners, and she was all too aware of her own racing heart. "It's a nice evening, finally a bit cooler." Small talk seemed best, and the night air was clear and crisp, perfect for the walk they were taking.

"Just a change of weather. Heat's not gone yet." He glanced at her, taking her breath.

She relished in touching him again, and the muscles in his bicep moved as he took his steps alongside her. He walked proudly with her attached to his arm, not avoiding the random glances of those that passed who were likely aware he was sheriff. Staring up at him as they walked, she thought about his intentions toward her and his words at dinner. There was no doubt in her mind he was sincere, but there were so many things. She needed a marriage, the reason she'd come here, and while it hadn't been an option at first, it seemed perhaps time had changed things.

"Sawyer?"

"Huh?" He glanced at her again, but continued

with the relaxed pace.

She watched him for a moment. "What is it you want out of this life?"

He turned giving her a set of wrinkled eyebrows.

Rose rephrased the question. "Well, I mean, you are sheriff and seemingly have no need to prove yourself. Everyone in town has a certain respect of you, but is that all? Well, you have Zane now and of course your brothers and Dodge. But what does a man like you dream about, long for in life?" All she had ever wanted was the love of a true husband and perhaps a family.

Sawyer gave a little shrug. It took another row of buildings for him to finally say something. "Never really promised myself much more than being the best lawman I could be."

Rose nodded and added a second hand to the one holding to his arm, wrapping her fingers around each other. "And your future plans?"

"You have any easy questions?" He chuckled and shook his head.

"Well, I was just—"

He interrupted her. "I don't have any kind of agenda for life, leastwise, never thought about things like that till now."

She stopped at the bottom of the stairs to her home and turned to him, letting go of his arm reluctantly. It had been a nice evening. Maybe the nicest since she'd arrived in Cheyenne. And his candid answers left her flushed and hopeful.

"I'll see you tomorrow. I'll be in town most of the day." He kicked at the dirt and then focused on her.

Rose could have simply melted into those deep gray eyes. Gathering her nerves, she finally asked what she'd wanted to the entire evening. Maybe she did know, but she wanted to hear it. "So why did you ask me to dinner?"

"I—" He stopped.

"There must be a reason." She did know the fine art of flirting and she'd been at it all evening.

"We agreed to no cows in the mud or interrogations." He stepped closer, and she could smell the clean scent of lye soap and leather.

She backed up, the railing of the stairs to her back. He was getting closer and closer. "What are you—"

He didn't give her the chance to finish, his face close to hers as he whispered. "Kissing you goodnight, with your permission."

"Oh." His breath mingled with her own, and her heart pounded so hard inside her chest she could hardly speak.

"Is that a yes?"

She nodded and Sawyer's lips touched hers ever so gently. A surge of warmth flowed all the way through her. She might not have stayed upright had he not slid his hands around her and pulled her close to his body. She shivered at his tenderness. His hands caressed her back and his soft tongue teased to the point she sighed out loud, not even knowing she was going to do it.

Suddenly, he ended the kiss, pulling his face from hers. Rose's eyes remained closed as he held her face but then she opened them. "So no questions this time?"

"Nope." His voice was but a whisper as he held her body against his own.

"But you must have some reason for such a kiss." There was something happening between them, something she'd never felt before. Love? Maybe this was love. Her heart pounded, her knees felt weak and if she thought much more on it, she would just as soon melt into this man's arms forever.

He kissed her quick and deep, pulling and tugging until she all but moaned again, "Is that reason enough?"

His hands continued touching her body, sending a warmth in her low belly and places he hadn't touched. Rose sucked in a quick breath of air. She'd never felt such passion. It wasn't proper for a man—much less the sheriff—to kiss her on the streets in town. What if someone saw them? His gray eyes sparkled, and he gave her a slight smile as he nodded at the stairs behind her. She turned and climbed them one at a time, lips tingling as she looked back at him once more before entering her home. When she had shut the door, she leaned against it. She'd dreamed of what a really passionate kiss from Sawyer McCade would be like, but she had never imagined it would take her breath and—her heart.

****

Sawyer waited until Rose climbed the stairs and disappeared inside. He laughed to himself. If she were smart, she'd know to run, not walk away from him in the future. He took a deep breath and exhaled. Dodge had been right. Since Rose had moved to town, he'd paid more attention. Not knowing what she was up to made him damn near crazy. He had fallen right into dangerous territory, and it wasn't a band of renegades keeping him on edge. Just a woman he couldn't get out of his mind.

He glanced at her closed door once more, then crossed the street toward the saloon, taking a deep breath and giving his body a bit of time to cool down.

He wanted her and he'd have her too, when the time was right. But her questions had stirred up more than the physical. He wasn't sure what he wanted. He'd never thought much past the day to day—until Rose.

Hell, he should have fallen right to his knees and asked her to become the wife he had always wanted. He cursed and stomped through the saloon's open doors, dropping his thoughts. Of course Wyatt was belly up to the bar, talking to Jacob.

"How was dinner?" Wyatt tossed down a shot of whiskey.

Sawyer glared and ordered. "Whiskey."

Jacob slapped down the small glass, pouring it full. "Sheriff's drinking tonight and all gussied up. Must be rough to want a woman so bad." The old man cackled out loud and refilled Wyatt's glass.

"Dinner was fine, but it was just dinner." Sawyer tossed his whiskey down and slammed the glass back down on the bar, swallowing the burning liquid with a growl. While he rarely drank, he needed something to calm the fire in him.

Wyatt sipped his whiskey and sat his glass down. "We got two in the back playing cards. They were rowdy until I came in."

Sawyer gazed over Wyatt's shoulder. "You know 'em?"

"No. But I overhead them talking about being with the outlaws that just hit Fort Morgan and the bank in Sterling." Wyatt kept his voice low.

"The reports didn't claim the same group of men in both places." He'd read them a couple of times.

"You know as well as I do what get's written isn't always truth." Wyatt's tone said he knew something.

240

The man spent a great deal of time studying outlaws and their practices. When he brought in a man or gang for a bounty, it was because he knew all there was to know.

"Enlighten me." Sawyer turned and placed his elbows on the bar, resting his weight closer to his brother.

Wyatt lit his skinny cigar and took a long draw, blowing smoke away from Sawyer and checking to make sure Jacob was out of earshot. "The man on the left, in the brown hat is Jed Davis. He runs with the Ashburn brothers, and they can't be far if he's here."

"So the question is what they are doing here?"

Wyatt tossed his whiskey down in a gulp. "That would be the question."

"Either have a bounty?" Sawyer eyed the mirror on the wall behind the bar and scooted a step from Wyatt where he could watch the men without their knowing.

"Nope." Wyatt watched them too.

"Put Hudson on 'em."

"I've got it. You go home to Zane." Wyatt nodded for him to go ahead.

"I'll be in early." Sawyer made his exit and headed back to the jail. There was no way to tell if the Ashburns would show, but it was rare that bands of outlaws didn't hook back up at some point on the trail. The streets of Cheyenne remained quiet, only a lone horseman riding toward the hotel. Sawyer crossed the street and used his key to enter the office.

He lit the lantern on his desk, casting a yellow glow across the entire front room. Opening the desk drawer, he fumbled through the files. There were reports from Washington on the activities of the

Ashburn brothers, but there had been nothing of late. He picked up a newsprint out of Omaha, looking close at the sketches of Frank and J.J. Ashburn. The drawing of each brother wasn't clear, but it gave him a general idea. He'd read enough about them to know that it was Frank, the eldest brother, who carried the smarts and called the shots. J.J., the younger brother, wasn't so smart but could be unpredictable.

Well, there was nothing to do about any of it right now. He dimmed the lantern, leaving it lit. Wyatt and Hudson would likely be in and out during the night. He left the paper face up on the desk to remind them. Best they all be prepared. He stepped outside again and locked the door, peering across town. The air was crisp given how hot the day had been, but it left him with an air of concern.

Things were still quiet as he mounted up, yet as he rode Colonel back through town, the hair on his arms stood up. Something wasn't right. He could feel it. He turned Colonel abruptly, riding back by the post office, glancing above to where Rose lived. Her room was dark. She was probably asleep, and he was being overprotective. He urged Colonel on, wishing he had a reason to knock at her door to kiss her once more. And the truth was he'd like a lot more than that from her.

If he didn't get another taste of her soon, he'd be tempted to retreat to the brothel to work off some steam. But Rose was a lady and he had no doubts worth the wait and he had no interest in the ladies at the brothel to begin with. While his physical need was strong, she also touched some part of him he'd thought lost. For the first time since Catherine, he'd found a woman consuming his mind, body, and his heart. And so he would wait as long as it tool for the woman he was coming to love.

"Son of a bitch." He cursed to himself. Kissing Rose was meant to show her just how he felt, but he hadn't figured it to send him over the edge. Having more than that from her might simply jolt him into a frenzy of need he hadn't felt in a long time. Thoughts of Rose naked, lying beneath him or riding high above him were enough to make him growl. He shook his head and took Colonel to a full gallop, not to run it out of the horse, but to run it out of himself.

It was good and dark by the time he made it to the ranch and entered the barn with Colonel just behind him. He removed the saddle and had begun brushing down the horse for the night, when he heard a woman giggle. He shook his head looking toward the loft. "Evan?"

It took a moment but finally Evan spoke. "What the hell, Sawyer, can't you just move on and let things be?" Evan was buttoning his trousers, standing at the edge of the loft, looking down. Behind him, Eliza from the brothel, stood and adjusted her corset, grinning with the best of her efforts.

"Hi, Sawyer," she said it in her sweetest voice.

"Eliza." Sawyer didn't smile, though her scantily clad body was something to behold. He didn't need Zane asking questions. If Evan had to do this sort of thing, the least he could do was go to town.

Evan and Eliza climbed down from the loft. Evan helped her with the last of the ladder and settled her to the dirt floor of the barn, where she kissed him and turned back to Sawyer.

"I suppose I should head back to town, seeing the

sheriff has caught us. See you boys. You know, Sheriff, if you ever come to the brothel." She gave Sawyer a knowing smile, slung her purse over her shoulder, and blew Evan one more kiss.

Sawyer eyed his brother. "She must be short of funds if she came all the way out here to see to you."

"What do you care what she's paid?" Evan adjusted his shirt, brushing hay from his sleeves.

Sawyer just shook his head, lugging the heavy saddle to its mount and slamming it down.

Evan followed, raising his voice. "You know I don't have to defend myself or her. I had a need; she had a need. That's how it works."

"Just keep it in town. I'd rather not explain this to Zane." Sawyer glared at him, but continued his work.

Evan laughed. "You are the one who told me to stay out of town. Damn Sawyer, he's fourteen, I believe he's probably figured out a thing or two by now."

"He probably has, but that doesn't mean we turn the barn into a brothel." Sawyer walked past him.

"When's the last time you—"

Oh, hell no, his brother wasn't going to take the conversation there. Sawyer shoved him back. "I'm asking you to behave for the sake of my son, and as for myself, it isn't any of your concern."

"What the hell's with you anyway?" Evan dusted himself off again.

"Just mind your manners. We've got some men in town, possibly connected to the Ashburn brothers." Sawyer changed the subject.

"The Ashburns?"

Sawyer fought to clear his thoughts. "It might mean nothing, but we need to be aware and that means for starters staying out of the loft and out with the cattle where you can keep watch on more than the cattle."

Evan raised his hands in surrender. "I've got the cattle, you just watch yourself. You and Wyatt both. I hear they are fond of killing men wearing badges."

Sawyer stopped short and eyed his brother. "We are guarded, paying attention." As the youngest of his brothers, Evan had always been a spoiled pain in the ass, but there were times like now that he found a kind word. Sawyer nodded and followed him out of the barn and back toward the house where Evan went on inside.

Sawyer turned on the porch and eyed the surroundings, unable to shake the uneasiness. He was used to being aware of everything most all the time, but there were very few times in his life when he'd known for sure all wasn't well. And this was one of those times. He glanced into the darkness, the moon lighting a slight glow across the prairie. Shadows danced and played with his mind, shaping into dark riders, jousting his thoughts. Nodding to the darkness, he turned to go inside. As his brother Wyatt was fond of saying, *"quiet didn't mean things were still."*

Chapter Seventeen

Sawyer flipped the paper in his hand. He'd found it interesting to read the small section that Mr. McDonald allowed Rose to write each week. She'd said it had been a challenge to convince him to allow her the topics she was writing, but much to the elder man's surprise, sales were up. Mostly on account of the women of Cheyenne, not that there were many of those. He'd seen Rose making rounds, interviewing people, and her writing was very good, though reading about the trends in skin care products out of Boston wasn't quite something he'd define as interesting.

"Brother of mine." Wyatt stormed in, allowing the door to slam against the wall. Zane followed him inside, going to great efforts to close the door carefully behind him, with a glance at his father.

"I thought you were worn out from your trip." Sawyer stood and set the paper aside, then sat on the side of the desk.

"Ahh, I'll get plenty of sleep one day when I am dead." Wyatt chuckled and went for coffee.

"Doc's gotta take my stitches out." Zane held a hand to his middle.

"Your father forgot, as he's a little *pre-occupied* in town these days." Wyatt turned sipping his coffee.

Sawyer ignored his sarcasm. He'd reminded himself a day or so ago about Zane's appointment, but things had been busy. "What time do you see the doc?"

"She said whenever I got here." Zane sat but never took his hand from his belly. Wyatt sat his coffee down and grabbed the paper from the desk. "What she doesn't know is he rode Shadow here today."

"The idea was a wagon, not a horse." Sawyer scolded, glancing from Wyatt to Zane, though he'd been the first one to allow the boy on a horse.

Wyatt scanned the paper as he spoke. "When you *neglected* your son's appointment, I, as the doting uncle, had to step in and I don't do wagons."

Zane tried to hide a grin. "I rode slowly, and I didn't lift the saddle. I felt a lot better today than the last time. Leastwise it was easier, so I must be getting better."

"And you'll go slowly back home as well, as soon as you are done this morning." Sawyer walked over and ruffled Zane's light brown hair.

"Women's skin care products of Boston..." Wyatt eyed Sawyer over the top of the paper, a grin on his face. "Interesting reading brother?"

Sawyer threw him a smirk and glanced back at Zane. "Did you eat this morning?" It still concerned him that Zane had such a light appetite, but Tess had assured him it might take some time.

"Dodge made me eat an egg and some cheese." Zane shrugged.

"Oh, and this boy of yours is on my list." Wyatt tossed the paper back to the desk. "That pup was crying last night, so it gets to sleep in his room—on the bed."

"Dodge let you bring the pup inside?" Sawyer couldn't believe it. Dodge had never allowed animals in the house.

"Nope. She brought him in herself. Said she got tired of his whining, but I think she likes him." Zane's gray eyes showed a hint of worry.

"Really?" Sawyer couldn't imagine Dodge or Mei Ling putting up with a puppy inside.

"And here I thought Evan was the spoiled one." Wyatt kicked Zane's boot, and the boy giggled shoving his hands in his pockets.

"Well, make sure you take him out often. Come on, we'll walk to the clinic." Sawyer led the way, thinking Dodge had been more of a stickler with him, Wyatt, and Dawson than she'd ever been with Evan. But he too had noticed her lack of rules when it came to Zane. Maybe becoming a grandmother was good for her.

"So what did you name the pup?" Sawyer hadn't heard him say.

"Sirius." Zane caught up to him with a trot.

Sawyer thought about it for a moment. "After the dog star?"

Zane seemed surprised he figured it out. "Dawson said I should pick a Cheyenne name, but I think it fits. I don't know any Cheyenne names anyway."

"Does he answer to it?" Sawyer opened the clinic door holding it for his son. The office was empty, but the lingering smell of antiseptic and medicines wafted high in the air.

"No. He does what he wants, but I will get him trained." Zane clutched his stomach, growing pale.

"Good morning, Sheriff. Zane, are you ready?" Tess wandered down the hallway from the back to meet them.

"Not sure." Zane hesitated, but followed her into the exam room.

"I'll be very gentle." Tess patted the table. "Just unbutton your shirt and lay back."

Zane slowly unbuttoned his shirt, hopped on the table, and lay back breathing deeply.

"Relax Zane, this really isn't bad. I have to cut each stitch, not you, and pull it through." Tess began, clipping and tugging each suture gently away from the wound. "The healing is really remarkable." The next stitch snagged, and Tess stopped for a moment.

Zane sucked a breath in through his teeth, opening his eyes again and looking at Tess.

"Sorry, sometimes the dried blood makes them stick a bit." She tenderly used her tiny forceps to work it loose and the stitch slid through.

Sawyer touched his arm. "It's almost over." He'd watched Zane get better each day, but seeing him on the table again brought him back to the day he'd watched his son almost die.

When she was done, Tess cleaned the incision site. "This looks really good. You have healed beautifully. Keep a clean bandage on it. Dodge can help you, and I will check you in another week or two."

Zane sat up. "And I know, no lifting or doing man's work."

Tess narrowed her eyes. "Ha. You boys think I am not paying attention. I saw you ride into town with Wyatt a little while ago, young man. I am not happy one bit about that."

Zane's face flushed. "I rode slow. Wyatt said he don't do wagons and I told him but—"

"Dodge is in town today, and you are riding home with her—in the buggy. Your father or Wyatt can bring your horse home later." Tess scolded but added a smile.

"Yes ma'am." Zane tucked his shirt, the color returning to his face.

"If I catch you on that horse again before I tell you it is all right, I'm purposely going to re-do your sutures for fun and practice," Tess threatened, taking Zane into a hug.

"I promise." Zane tugged away and headed out the door.

"Thanks Doc." Sawyer stopped on the porch, watching as Zane went ahead to the jail.

Tess stepped out on the porch. "Sawyer, I know I keep harping on the horse. The wound looks good. He has healed remarkably in a short time, but it was a large incision. If that horse threw him, serious bleeding could start again. You are his father. Keep him off that animal."

He nodded and adjusted his hat. "I'll make sure."

Tess took a step closer gazing at him suspiciously. "On another note, how are things with Rose?"

Sawyer cleared his throat, half tempted to ask her advice, but thought better of it. "I'll make sure he stays off the horse."

"She's good for you, you know." Tess' smile was genuine.

Sawyer hopped from the porch and kicked at the dirt, turning back at her. "You, Dodge, and Mei Ling have too much time on your hands."

"She adores you."

Sawyer gritted his teeth. "We're not having this conversation, but I am sure I will see you at dinner Sunday." Why was it women couldn't leave things like relationships alone to those who were in them? If it wasn't bad enough Dodge continued to push him and

Mei Ling still called Rose his bride, he now had Tess right in the mix. *Holy Hell*!

He looked across the way to the paper office. He'd made a habit out of dropping by more than once each day, but Rose had told him he was being overprotective, so he'd backed off and taken to afternoons when she took a break from the press. Obviously his lack of discretion had alerted Tess. That or Dodge and Mei Ling had enlightened her. He walked on past the clinic and back toward the jail office, cursing under his breath.

Inside, Wyatt was horsing around with Zane. He grabbed the boy and pulled him inside a cell, locking the bars that rattled, and shoving the key in his pocket.

"So this is what it's like to be a renegade?" Zane clenched the iron bars, shaking them.

"No, a renegade usually feels a stretched neck. Don't forget that." Wyatt raised a brow, then let him back out of the cell.

Sawyer listened in amusement as Wyatt explained all the fine details of being a lawman, and Zane asked question after question. It was good that all his brothers had taken to his son, welcoming him into the family without question. While he'd fought with his brothers now and then, they had all remained close, and adding Zane to that made having a son all the more surreal. The McCade line was now secured for future generations through him, and that meant a great deal to them all.

Gunfire blasted from across the street, turning Sawyer from the desk with a start. Wyatt was already at the door, revolver in hand, before he could even grab his hat.

"Where'd it come from?" Sawyer gripped the revolver, scanning across town.

"Looks like the bank. Heading to the post office." Wyatt took off outside, weapon poised.

Sawyer turned to Zane before following his brother. "Don't leave this jail until I come back."

Zane nodded with eyes wide as saucers.

Sawyer scampered outside, catching a glimpse of Wyatt ducking into the post office for cover. People ran from the streets, and shop owners closed doors and window shutters. Cheyenne turned into a ghost town in a matter of seconds. He made a run for it and slammed through the post office door just behind Wyatt. He took a deep breath and met gazes with his brother. Here they were, together once again doing what they had been made to do.

Wyatt eyed him with his usual nod of getting to the business at hand.

Sawyer turned to the men who'd run inside the post office just before them. "Who's in there?"

Visibly shaken, Mr. McDonald from the print shop stuttered to speak. "There were t-t-two men. They didn't ask any qu-questions, and they shot Herschel Barnes when he didn't m-m-m-move fast enough. They said they were holding out for demands."

Melody Purvis stood at the counter, pistol in hand. "I was afraid they might come in here." She tucked the weapon away inside her corset, with Sawyer's frown.

"Is Hershel alive?" Wyatt checked his revolvers, rolling the barrel of one and returning it to his holster.

"I don't know, he-he-he fell and I ran. I thought Miss Parker was behind me, but she must still be in-inside." Mr. McDonald wiped his brow with the back of his shirt sleeve.

Sawyer turned on a dime, a stab of pain scoring through his chest. "You left her in there?"

"I th...thought she was behind me and wh..when I got outside she wasn't. It all ha...happened so fast." Mr. McDonald backed up as Sawyer took a step forward.

"Sawyer." Wyatt caught hold of his arm, stopping him.

The front door of the bank opened, and a man dragged out Herschel Barnes and dumped him on the porch. "Until we get our demands met, one person will die every hour, just like this one." He went back inside, pistol poised. He'd been too quick for Sawyer to make a positive identification.

"How many are inside?" Sawyer turned back to Mr. McDonald. What was he thinking, in leaving *any* woman behind, much less Rose? His gut clenched tight as the frightened picture of her crossed his mind. If whoever was inside laid a hand on her, he'd carve their hearts out with a spoon, and he was certain of that.

"I don't know, Sheriff, p-p-probably t-ten p-people." The old man continued to stutter.

Wyatt peered outside, studying the bank. "What the hell do they want?"

Mr. McDonald only shrugged.

"I'll find out." Sawyer headed toward the door.

"You can't just walk out there." Wyatt blocked his path, shaking his head.

Sawyer met his brother's gaze. "I need to see what demands they have. All of you clear out and take cover on the other side of town." He nodded to the men inside, who had all remained quiet but obviously startled and narrowed his gaze on Mr. McDonald. The old man hesitated only a moment and led the others through the back door of the post office. Melody was quick to follow.

"Cover me. I'm going to see what we got." Sawyer took in a deep breath of air and let it out, still not believing Rose had been inside.

Wyatt pulled both revolvers, narrowing his brows. "You're gonna get your ass shot."

"Probably." Sawyer stomped across the porch and out into the middle of the street in plain sight. There was a chance he'd meet with a bullet, but Wyatt was quick and he'd found it sometimes confused outlaws to have the sheriff walk right out into the open. He hoped this was one of those times, being the man had given them one hour. He eyed the watering trough nearby, thinking if shots were fired he'd duck that direction if he had the chance.

"I'm the sheriff of Cheyenne. Who's in charge here?" Sawyer spoke loud and clear. There wouldn't be much he could do if they simply decided to shoot him dead. It was risky, but he had to know who he was dealing with and he had to get Rose out alive. Nothing else mattered.

From inside the bank, one of the men spoke. "Hear that brother? Sawyer McCade. I'll be damned, we are in Cheyenne." A loud laugh followed. Moments later, the same man exited the bank and stood on the porch, pistol in hand at his side.

Sawyer met his gaze and his pulse surged momentarily. Frank Ashburn. And he'd been talking to his brother J.J. no doubt. *Well,* it had been bound to happen, and he'd let it damn happen right under their noses, but he hadn't expected Rose to be a pawn in the games.

"Why Sheriff McCade. Sir, I've not had the pleasure." Frank spat tobacco off the porch of the bank, his dark eyes gleaming as if he were truly honored.

Sawyer didn't move but held eye contact. From what he knew about the Ashburns, he should already be a dead man, but it seemed Frank Ashburn liked the little game he was playing.

"We, kind of have a little situation here Sheriff McCade. My brother and I, well, we are wanted men, and we are kind of in a hurry, so that don't give you much time, sir." He spoke as if the situation were comical.

"I'm listening."

"We got a lame horse, so we'll be needing two saddled horses, loaded with ammunition, food, and staples for a few weeks. And two extra packhorses. I'll also need the combination to the safe, since this man is likely on the other side of hell." He kicked Herschel Barnes' lifeless body and of all things laughed.

"Anything else?" Sawyer cursed under his breath, glancing inside the bank doorway to look for Rose though he could see nothing. He sucked in a breath, fighting his own inner strength to be patient.

"A couple of bottles of whiskey, the fine kind, not rot gut," Frank added. Laughter echoed inside the bank.

So, the bastard did think he was in charge. "As soon as you release the people inside the bank, Ashburn, I'll meet your demands and you can ride out of town no questions asked."

"I heard about you too sheriff Sawyer McCade, taking the law all serious. You'll get no prisoners until I see the goods."Ashburn waved the pistol agitated.

Sawyer turned around, thinking he might feel the burn of a bullet at any moment, with turning his back while the man was still ranting behind him.

"You hear me McCade. One will die every hour. You listening?" Frank yelled, and it echoed across the town of Cheyenne.

Sawyer stepped back into the post office, where he finally let out a full breath. "Son of a bitch." But all he could see in his mind was Rose.

Wyatt lowered his revolvers. "Frank and J.J Ashburn at our service."

Hudson was inside the post office, waiting with Wyatt. "Ashburns? They'll kill everyone inside, no questions asked."

Sawyer glared at both men. "Then we have to move quickly."

"You're giving into them?" Wyatt held both revolvers, pointed toward the ceiling.

Sawyer met his brother's gaze. He and Wyatt had always lived by a certain code and giving in to outlaws was something they'd never done.

Wyatt shook his head. "Look, I know Rose is in there, but you have to keep your mind, Sawyer."

"I'm not giving into them. Frank is smart, but his brother—no smarts there." Sawyer nodded to Hudson. "Bring the long rifle and send Zane to the livery to keep him out of the way. Have Lang load up horses with all the provisions."

Hudson glanced at Wyatt but was out the back door before Sawyer could say anything more.

"The long rifle? Sawyer, that takes care of one, not both." Wyatt slammed both revolvers into the holsters low on his hips and jerked off his hat. He ran a hand through his short dark hair in frustration.

Sawyer didn't care. He had to get Rose out alive, even if he died in the process.

"And you're dropping your gun belt?" Wyatt shook his head.

"I'm going for Herschel. It might give me a peek inside. I don't think he's alive; he's gut shot." He had to do what he needed to do, in spite of his brother's reservations. Wyatt pulled his revolvers once more, his blue eyes dark.

"Frank!" Sawyer walked to the center of the street again, still anticipating a bullet. "I'm coming to get the banker. He needs a doctor."

"You have forty minutes before you have another to drag along," Frank's voice sounded from inside the bank.

Sawyer hurried to where Herschel lay unmoving. If the Ashburns wanted him dead, he would be. Likely they figured they wouldn't get what they wanted without him alive—for now. He grabbed Herschel by the arms, sneaking a look inside the bank as he did so. A few men lay face-down on the floor in front of the counter, but he couldn't see Rose. J.J. Ashburn sat on the edge of one of the tables, pistol aimed toward the door of the bank, watching him with a big toothless grin.

Sawyer fought the urge to simply bolt right into the bank and take care of the situation. He made his way across the street, dragging Herschel Barnes's limp body along and laying the man on the ground outside the post office.

"No doc needed." He spouted on entering once

more.

"Figured." Wyatt lowered his guns. "Well, it was only a matter of time before someone put the crooked bastard out of his misery anyway."

"I couldn't tell much, but J.J. is watching the door. If we go in the back, we'll get everyone killed. The long rifle is all we got." Sawyer eyed his brother. The bank wasn't set up for rescuing hostages, and their choices were limited.

Wyatt sat back on the table. "These two like the game. They kept everyone on that train for hours with negotiations, then killed the last few before taking off when they got what they wanted."

Sawyer met his gaze. He knew well the danger he was putting in place, and he knew even better the risk to all inside, but there was Rose. No matter how things went, he would get her out—or die trying. "Well, that's not happening today."

Chapter Eighteen

Hudson laid the long rifle across the counter and set a box of bullets beside it. "It's loaded and Lang's getting the horses and other things together. I sent Zane to the livery, though he didn't want to budge since you told him to stay put at the jail."

Sawyer nodded. The last thing he needed was Zane in the middle of all this. The livery was out of view, for the most part. His thoughts went back to Rose. She had to be terrified. And that she was in danger played havoc with his emotions. He'd no doubt kill these men before the day was over, but he had to make sure Rose stayed out of the danger.

"Jacob's inside." Hudson glanced from Sawyer to Wyatt and back.

Sawyer shook his head and slammed a palm against the doorframe. Jacob wasn't afraid of anyone or anything, and that put them all at further risk.

"Damn it," Wyatt cursed. "You can't predict what Jacob might pull. Probably get himself killed."

"Jacob is the least of our worries. Stay here." Sawyer walked back outside to the post office porch. "Frank?"

"Yeah."

"We're getting things together, but with the banker dead, no one else knows the safe combination, not even me. I know someone, but the ride out is twenty minutes from town. I've already sent a rider." He hadn't actually sent a rider, but Frank wouldn't know that.

"I'll give you an extra forty minutes! Not one minute more."

Sawyer stepped back inside and turned to Hudson. "Bring Marcus Benton here. Take Dodge with you. She'll get him to come and if she's with you, you'll be safe. Go, quickly."

Hudson gave Sawyer a hard look and bolted from the post office's rear door. Sawyer hoped he was right. Benton would have the combination but getting it out of him might prove difficult—if he even showed. And if he didn't—

"Benton? Damn it Sawyer! And Dodge?" Wyatt's eyes narrowed. "Benton's not coming, not if he knows we need something from him."

"He's got the combination to the safe, being he's on the bank's council. Dodge'll get him here. You just don't react and make things worse when he shows" Sawyer warned, sitting hard on the edge of the desk.

"Even if he comes, he won't give up the combination." Wyatt slammed his revolvers into their holsters once more.

"He will." One way or the other. Sawyer had been sitting on what he knew for a long time, and Marcus Benton made his blood boil with the urge for revenge he'd tasted for too long. Well, there was no time like the present.

Wyatt took a step closer, glaring his way. "You can't save her alone, unarmed. Then it'll be me trying to get both of you out."

"I'm not going in unarmed. Remember Gillette?" Sawyer held his brother's gaze.

Wyatt's answer was abrupt. "Yes, you took a bullet, remember that? This isn't the same thing. Frank Ashburn will kill you before you ever walk inside."

"We took down four armed men because you are the best shot there is. Frank isn't going to kill me because I will be the only one with the combination to the safe. You get Frank with the long rifle. I'll handle J.J." Sawyer figured the plan would work. Wyatt never missed—ever. And he could take one idiot outlaw alone, getting Rose to safety.

"Just because it worked once...and anyway, shooting Frank over your shoulder is insane at this angle. These men are unpredictable and fear nothing." Wyatt stomped across the room and then spun around again, clearly frustrated.

"Let's see if Ashburn will negotiate for the women." Sawyer turned to the door and took a deep breath before stepping outside once more. He was losing patience with this whole thing, but he had to hold it all together for Rose.

Wyatt shook his head. "Careful, he's liable to get tired of this cat and mouse shit you're pulling."

Sawyer waited on the porch, still unable to view inside the bank. If Ashburn wasn't growing tired of the games, he certainly was, but the distraction would buy a little time—for Rose and the others inside.

"Frank?"

"Sheriff, you're beginning to annoy me." Frank spat from inside and came to the door, holding his pistol guarded.

"I know you have women inside. Why don't you play like a gentleman and let them go." Sawyer held his voice steady and his hand swayed near the revolver at his hip.

After a long moment of nothing, Frank Ashburn bolted through the door, dragging Rose along, her hands tied in front of her. A surge of rage raced through Sawyer as he eyed them both. She met his gaze and in that moment, there was no doubt the Ashburns were dead men. She was pale and her eyes were wide with fear, but Frank Ashburn's hands on her was more than he could bare. He gripped his fists tight in retaliation. *Son of a bitch!*

"How many more are inside Frank, men and women?" Sawyer held his stance still and his gaze on the man he would kill soon enough.

"It don't matter none how many we got. Ain't this the one you're looking for Sheriff? She called your name. Right purty if you ask me, smells real nice." Frank pulled Rose closer to him, sniffing along her neck, his gun pointed directly at Sawyer.

Rose's hands twitched drawing his attention, though they were tied. She held out all five fingers on one hand and two on the other. Seven. Good girl. Five men, two women. Maybe he and Wyatt weren't in this all alone after all.

"I know there is another woman, turn them both loose. Let's do this like men, Frank." He pulled his gaze from Rose. Damn, he couldn't look at her any more. He'd get them both killed, trying to take down Frank Ashburn with his bare hands. He glanced at the bastard, trying to keep the hate from showing in his eyes. *You're a dead man.*

"Play it like men? Sheriff McCade, this is a man's game right here." He grabbed Rose by the back of the neck and shoved her toward the ground. She fell to her knees, and he put the gun to her head with a hysterical laugh.

Rose screamed, but froze, unmoving, eyes shut.

"You're a wanted man Ashburn, as good as dead. I'll let you ride out of here, but if you kill anyone else, this is over." Sawyer kept his voice steady. Frank Ashburn wasn't easy to read, but Rose was far too valuable to be a pawn in his charades.

"Get those horses here, get the safe open, and this one here—" Ashburn jerked Rose to her feet, "—will be going with us." He shoved her back inside the bank with a deep guttural laugh and followed.

Sawyer kicked the porch. "Holy fucking hell!" That the man was rough handling Rose was enough to make him shake with anger, but he couldn't lose control—not now. He turned and went back in the post office, clenching his fist in frustration. If Ashburn thought he was leaving town with Rose, well, he was sadly mistaken.

"Damn it!" Wyatt shook his head.

Sawyer never even glanced at his brother and walked to the large desk, bending forward and placing both hands on it. He was about to come apart at his very seams. "Son of a bitch!" He gripped his hands tight and let go with all that was inside him, lifting and slinging the old oak desk with all his might until it turned over with a crash that nearly burst his own eardrums. Papers and booklets streamed across the floor, and ink splattered the floor and wall. He was out of breath at the effort, his heart beating so rapidly in his chest, he might have done a full day's work. Rose so afraid had nearly ripped the heart from his chest, and this had gone on long enough.

"Well, now that you got that out of your system. How many inside?" Wyatt held his place at the window.

Sawyer sucked in a deep breath and turned toward his brother. "Five men, two women." He was shaking, the tremors in his hands, proof of his deep-seated need to kill the man who had put his hands on Rose. He had to calm himself for this to work out right. He should have known these men would show and now because he had let his guard down, Rose was at risk.

"We could storm in after dark," Wyatt offered. "I could go to the roof and make my way inside."

"They'll all be dead before dark. You know that as well as I do." Sawyer walked to the window, still catching his breath and glancing across the street once more.

Dodge suddenly bolted through the back door into the post office, followed by Hudson and much to his surprise, Marcus Benton.

Sawyer met the man's gaze. Well at least the bastard showed, and he was all but sure he owed that thanks to Dodge.

Benton stepped forward without a word, but given the squint to his dark eyes, they'd be damn lucky to get through the next few minutes.

Sawyer met gazes with him and moved in front of Wyatt. He might have just lost his own mind for a minute, but Wyatt getting out of control would only add fuel to any fire that Marcus Benton might set.

Benton stood quietly, his dark eyes giving the hint as to his annoyed mood. Two of his men remained outside the back door as usual. Bastard couldn't go anywhere without his protection.

"How bad is it?" Dodge eyed the mess from the overturned desk, glancing from Sawyer to Wyatt and back.

It was Wyatt who answered. "They've killed Herschel Barnes. Still got seven inside, including Rose."

"Rose?" Dodge's mouth fell open as she focused on Sawyer.

Benton took a step closer, glaring. "All right, you got me here, McCade."

Hudson settled against the counter, tilting his hat back and remaining silent.

"Ever heard of Frank Ashburn and his brother J.J.?" Sawyer let his arms hang at his sides, not to give away anything more than he needed.

Benton shook his head, but Sawyer saw something in his eyes. He knew them, whether or not he'd admit it. "They're holed up in the bank, have a number of hostages, and want the safe open." Damn, if he didn't hate the man before him. Visions of his father's face flooded his mind, and he pushed them away, needing full focus on the issue at hand.

"And your reason for needing me?" Benton snarled.

"Cut the bullshit. Everyone knows you and Herschel played the money game. You have the combination; you're on the damn council." Wyatt bristled, his tone abrupt.

"Wyatt." Dodge calmed him down, tugging on his shirt.

Benton glared passed Sawyer at Wyatt as he spoke. "You know Eleanor, these sons of yours have no manners or respect. This one here is a bit much like his father for my liking."

Wyatt stepped forward, fists clenched, but Hudson was quick to push him back. "Take a walk."

Sawyer never turned as Hudson kept Wyatt at Bay. If Wyatt lost control, there would be more to worry about than Rose inside the bank.

Sawyer turned to Benton again. "I need the combination to the safe."

"*You* need the combination?" Benton shook his head with a hearty laugh.

"That's about the size of it. Hershel Barnes is dead. I'd like that combination before more people die." Sawyer took a step closer and waited.

"The people inside the bank are of no interest to me, but I know of *your* interest inside that bank McCade. You're the *sheriff*. Handle it.*" Benton turned to go, slow and deliberate.

"How about I handle a few things from the past. Should we start with Harrison Colbert?" Sawyer folded his arms. Neither Wyatt nor Dodge knew what he was talking about. But Benton would. Benton's men had been caught killing Harrison Colbert years before, and Sawyer knew the reasons why.

Wyatt exchanged confused glances with Dodge, pushing past Hudson.

"So...you are truly John McCade's eldest son," Benton hissed but stopped where he was and turned.

"John's finest." Sawyer didn't bat an eye.

Benton focused on him for a long moment then turned to the counter. He picked up a pencil and began to scribble across one of the papers. He gave Sawyer the paper along with an evil smirk. "When this is over, McCade."

"I'll be waiting." Sawyer glared his rebuttal. He'd waited a lot of years and the time had nearly come.

"Eleanor." Marcus Benton tipped his hat toward Dodge and exited the rear of the post office.

"Dodge!" She spat, but turned to face her sons again.

Wyatt folded his arms with a curse. "Son of a bitch, what the hell was that about?"

"Politics." Sawyer wasn't about to share what he knew. As long as he was the only one with the details, he'd be the only one in line for Marcus Benton's wrath.

Wyatt glanced toward the bank and back. "We haven't got much time, whatever the hell you're keeping."

Sawyer ignored his brother, taking a deep breath and letting it out in a puff of his cheeks. "Dodge, go to the livery and tell Lang to bring up the horses and tie them outside the bank. Zane's at the livery. Make sure he stays there, and you stay with him."

"Boys…" Dodge moved closer, and the look in her eyes said it all. Fear. Fear for her sons, the danger ever present.

"We'll be fine," Sawyer interrupted.

Dodge raised her eyebrows. "When you get Rose to safety, I hope you are smart enough to grab hold and hang on tight. You've drug your feet on this long enough."

Sawyer just looked at her, not believing she'd bring that up now. Shit. Leave it to Dodge to call him out, even in a crisis. She was right, though.

"It's all good Dodge." Wyatt gave her a reassuring smile and kissed her cheek.

She nodded, glancing at them both in turn once

again, then left the post office, not looking back even once.

Sawyer turned back to Wyatt and of all things his brother smiled.

"Let's go Gillette."

Sawyer removed his gun belt and unbuttoned his shirt. Finding a roll of thick leather twine behind the counter of the post office, he tied it around one shoulder and across his back to the other, with Wyatt's help. He tied another piece around his knife and revolver and secured them both, one to each side. He buttoned his shirt again and tucked it into his trousers, adjusting his belt to a larger fit. He needed to be able to pull the shirt free quickly. This had worked once before, and it could work again. It had to.

"Get him in the clear, right shoulder. Be careful brother, one wrong move, and you'll be at their mercy or my bullet." Wyatt touched his shoulder, holding his gaze for a moment. His brother's eyes said what neither would speak.

Sawyer nodded and turned away. He had to focus, seeing it happen in his mind one step at a time. Things could go wrong, but he wouldn't lose Rose, even if they went very wrong. Not now and not like this. Damn it, he should have insisted she stay at the ranch once and for all.

"And for God's sake, keep Rose out of that head of yours for now." Wyatt laughed. "After this, you'd best marry her like Dodge said, or she'll probably run like hell back to New York City."

"If this doesn't go well...watch out for her and Zane." Sawyer hadn't forgotten his son in placing his life on the line. If he were killed, where would that leave Zane, but if he didn't try, then he was the same coward as the men he was about to kill.

"You can take care of them yourself. I'm not meant to be a father, at least not yet. It's the wagon thing." Wyatt's smile said more than what his words had meant, and Sawyer gazed at him for a long moment and turned to leave the post office.

It was as it had to be. Wyatt was the better shot with the long rifle, and it was up to him to get Rose and the others out of danger. Damn, if he ever held her in his arms again, he'd never let her go—ever. If she'd have him. He glanced at Hudson. "Cover Wyatt."

Hudson nodded. "Sawyer these men—"

Sawyer held up his hand, stopping Hudson from speaking his mind. Across the street, four horses were tied and waiting. Lang had come through with the animals. He scanned the streets of Cheyenne. A damn ghost town now as he stepped off the porch.

"Hudson, take the roof. If either of the men leave the bank, take them out, no hesitation. Make sure it's a clean shot." Wyatt grabbed the long rifle.

Hudson whispered furiously behind him. "Wyatt, this is mad. Sawyer can't go in there alone."

Wyatt sighted the long rifle, squinting one eye. "Get to the roof."

Sawyer continued at a steady pace, the exchange between his brother and Hudson a quick reminder of what lie before him, though he never took his mind from Rose.

Chapter Nineteen

Sawyer stood at the center of the deserted street, where he'd been now multiple times. If God was taking prayers, he offered one for Rose to survive and one for his son not to end up fatherless a second time in his life.

"I see you have met *some* of my demands, Sheriff." Frank walked to the door of the bank, eyeing the horses and gripping his pistol.

"I have the combination."

"You said it was another man." Frank narrowed his eyes.

"He sent word. I'm all you've got." Sawyer held his hands up, showing he had no weapons, save the ones hidden in his shirt.

"Give me the numbers." The lanky man, took a step forward.

Sawyer paced ahead slowly. "There's a glitch in the safe that I know how to get through. I'm your only way to that money."

"Stop." Frank poised the pistol on him.

Sawyer froze.

Frank cocked and waved the weapon. "Kick out of your boots. Open your shirt and turn around."

Sawyer carefully unbuttoned his shirt, hoping his vest was enough to conceal the hanging weapons. Then he worked his socked feet out of his boots, pissed he wouldn't have them. When his shirt was open, he turned, holding his arms up. He could feel the gun and knife at his sides which remained hidden from the man before him. If Ashburn wanted a closer look, he'd never get Rose out alive, and that was something he wouldn't let happen.

"All right." Frank nodded. "Come on then. Time's a wastin'."

Sawyer moved up the stairs, his narrowed eyes never leaving Frank as he walked slowly into the bank. He was well aware he couldn't look at Rose or he'd lose focus, not that things were real clear anyway. He had to work to get where Wyatt would have the shot. That's all he really knew. His brother would be ready and waiting, long rifle poised. He stopped just inside the door, where he needed to stay. Wyatt would only have a shot with him right in the doorway. He needed to find a way to stall moving further inside.

"You get that safe open." Frank nodded, grabbing Rose by her ties.

Rose struggled to keep her footing, exchanging glances with Sawyer, who forced himself to look away. *Damn it to hell.* She had no idea what was about to happen, and he had no way to warn her. No matter, Frank Ashburn was holding her too close. Wyatt wouldn't get a clear shot, and Rose could be hit. He had to keep calm and avoid any quick movements so Wyatt could pull the trigger when the time was right.

"What are you waiting on, Sheriff?" Frank growled, dragging Rose a bit closer.

Sawyer didn't move. "I'm smart enough to know how you boys work."

"You get to it, Sheriff." The man spat his words so loud Rose closed her eyes and shivered.

"If I open the safe, you'll still kill all of us, so I need you to let the hostages go, at least the women." Sawyer held his position, moving nothing, not even to blink.

"You open that safe now or they all die, starting with this one." Frank put the gun to Rose's head.

Sawyer's breath hitched, and it was all he could do to restrain himself. *Son of a bitch.* Wyatt wouldn't have a shot with the gun on Rose.

"All right, let them all go but her." Sawyer said it boldly.

Rose opened her eyes, and her mouth dropped open. Sawyer had to purposely avoid eye contact with her. She was probably confused, thinking he was insane—or that he didn't care what happened to her. The thought tore at his heart, but he held steady. It was the only chance he had of getting her out alive.

"Come on Frank. I'm a lawman. What guarantee can you give me that these people will live?" Sawyer's heart thudded hard against his chest. The other hostages sat along the counter of the bank on the floor, hands tied, all except Jacob. He was lying on the floor, blood seeping from a blow to the head. Damn it, but the old man had likely put up too much fight, though he was visibly still breathing.

Frank jerked the gun from Rose and lugged her along with him to put the gun almost against Sawyer's chest, yelling. "You are going first if you don't open that safe right damn now!"

Good. Better. If Frank would move just a bit more, he'd give Wyatt the signal, no matter the gun aimed at him. He glanced at Rose trying to warn her to be still, but there was no way. Tears streamed down her cheeks as she gazed at him. In that instant, all Sawyer's being could hardly be contained. Without a doubt, if he lost Rose, he would lose everything.

"All right, Sheriff, that's it," Frank Ashburn hissed, using his gun to point toward the safe. "You open that safe—"

The world seemed to freeze into slow motion as Sawyer gave the signal, a quickly gripped fist, and from across the street, Wyatt pulled the trigger. The deafening shot sounded, and the bullet struck Frank Ashburn right between the eyes. Blood splattered across Rose's face and neck. She screamed and fell backward to the floor. Ashburn staggered and fell near her with a thud. Dead.

Sawyer turned as J.J. raised his pistol and took aim. He rolled quickly to the floor and came up with his own revolver, ripped from the cord at his side and emptied all six rounds into the man. J.J.'s gun fired twice, ricocheting across the room. He focused on Sawyer and laughed and then, staggering, turned his gun toward Rose.

"Nnnnnoooo!" Sawyer pulled his knife, making it to his feet as gunfire exploded. J.J. slammed backward into him, the impact shoving them both to the floor. The crush of the heavier man took his breath, but he pushed until J.J. rolled off him. He scrambled up. What in the hell had just happened? He scanned for Rose and couldn't believe his eyes. *Holy hell!* On the floor before him, Rose held a smoking derringer, her eyes wide with surprise as she stared at the unmoving body of J.J.

"Sawyer?" Wyatt burst inside calling to him, heading to make sure both men were dead.

"We're fine." Sawyer placed his hand gently on

Rose's. "Give me the gun...it's all right." She didn't loosen her grip, shaking so violently she could easily shoot the second chamber if he weren't careful.

"Rose...let me have the gun sweetheart." He tugged gently, and she fell against his chest, clinging to his open shirt and bursting into tears, that dampened his neck.

"Shhh...it's all over." He couldn't believe she'd had a gun. He should have known better than to empty all his rounds, but he'd lost all sense with her in danger. He tugged her tighter and kissed the top of her head, letting her sob and setting the small smoking gun aside, along with his knife. She was fine. She was whole. She was Rose...his Rose. He wrapped both arms around her. "It's over. It's fine now."

Moments later, a hand touched his shoulder and he turned. Dodge.

"See to the situation." She bent to Rose, embracing her.

"No, I'm fine." Rose brushed a sleeve of her gown across her face, cleaning away the splattered blood.

Sawyer helped her stand, letting go reluctantly.

"I knew you'd come." She gazed at him with the hint of a forced smile.

"Who knew the beautiful lady carried a gun?" He touched her cheek to wipe a stray tear away, and in spite of it all pulled her into his arms hugging her tightly. As he held her, he glanced around the bank.

Doc Tess was caring for Jacob. Wyatt and Hudson had covered both dead men with blankets, and the other hostages were leaving the bank, most still in a state of shock. So it was over. The Ashburn brothers had met their end, thanks to his eagle-eyed brother and the amazing woman in his arms.

"Sawyer, you're hit." Wyatt nodded toward him.

Sawyer let go of Rose and lifted his blood-drenched shirt. He hadn't even felt it, but J.J. must have gotten him with the first shot.

"Sawyer?" Rose shoved his shirt higher, inspecting further.

"It's fine, hardly felt it." He pulled the edge of his trousers down to find the spot where a bullet had tagged his upper left hip with an exit wound about two inches from the entry wound. It wasn't bad, but now that he knew about it, he could damn well feel the burn.

Rose took his hand and led him to the nearby table. "Are you in pain?"

"Nahhh. Just a flesh wound," he lied, but didn't let go of her.

"Sit. I told you that you'd get your ass shot." Wyatt pushed him down into one of the chairs as Dodge scrambled to him.

"It's not bad." He couldn't see all the fuss. Dodge traced along his hip, assessing both wounds. Sawyer twisted in the chair to make it easier for her to see and focused on Rose. She was lost, likely in shock if he were guessing. Her eyes large and glassy.

"It looks like it went through," Dodge said as Tess bent to take a look. Tess pressed around the wounds, eliciting a slight growl from Sawyer.

"Just clean it really well and dress it. You'll be fine." Tess returned to care for Jacob who was coming to. The old man groaned and cursed. "Bastards, hope you boys shot 'em dead."

Wyatt chuckled as he helped the old man up. "We got 'em, but thought you had things under control."

The old man cursed Wyatt and stood on his own, holding is head.

Sawyer pulled his shirt off, turning to get a better look as Dodge dug in Tess' bag. The wound couldn't be deep given they were so close together, but the bruising was already evident.

Rose knelt beside him pulling his gaze from his injury. He pushed a strand of loose hair from her face. "Are you all right?"

She nodded and found the slightest smile once again. Even blood spattered with her light hair a mess, she was without a doubt the most beautiful sight he'd ever seen. And she was alive. They were both alive. He gave her hand a squeeze and brought it to his lips kissing her gently. Shit, what Dodge was doing hurt, but he couldn't take his eyes off Rose.

As Dodge finished up with dressing the wound, Zane came bounding inside. With one look at Sawyer, his son's face went pale.

"I'm fine," Sawyer explained, and Zane gave him a relieved nod. He stood and adjusted his trousers and grabbed his shirt. He tossed it over his shoulder, still gripping Rose by the hand. Hell, he'd probably never let her go, ever again.

Wyatt stood close by. "You called it right brother. I missed your head by a fraction. Scared the hell out of me."

Sawyer glanced around the room again. While things hadn't gone perfect, they could have happened much worse. "Telegram the circuit judge. Have Hudson get the photographer for one picture of each and let Henry bury them, unmarked." Grave robbers were notorious for unearthing outlaws.

Wyatt nodded. "Done. I'll meet you at the office."

"Rose, let me take you home and help you clean up." Dodge tugged her from Sawyer.

"I'll check on you later." Sawyer let go of her hand, feeling as if his heart was being ripped away once more. Dodge led her outside as he looked on. He took a deep breath and turned back to Zane.

"Lang said you and Wyatt would make history today." Zane handed him his boots, his eyes wide with wonder.

"I'm not sure this is one for the history books. Come on, let's go to the office. I need a new set of clothes." While it wasn't worthy of major publication, it would make the papers all the way back east, but they were damn lucky to be alive.

Zane followed him to the jail, waiting while he changed his shirt and trousers. It would only be a short time before the sun went down, and he wanted to check on Rose once Dodge had her cleaned up and settled. He had no intention of leaving her alone for tonight or maybe ever.

"I'll need to stay with Wyatt in town and check on Rose. Take your horse and see Dodge home for me." He tucked his shirt, careful of his hip.

Zane nodded, rising from his chair, large gray eyes still showing how frightened he'd been. "Sawyer?"

Sawyer looked up, bending to step into his boots one at a time.

Zane hesitated for a moment. "I've never seen anything like what you did, the long rifle and all. You and Wyatt."

Sawyer pulled on his vest, fidgeting with his pocket watch, to clip it through the button-hole.

277

"I just…" Zane stepped closer, gazing at him intently.

Sawyer tucked the watch into his vest pocket as Zane struggled to choose his words. He stopped and studied his son waiting.

"I'm really, really proud to be your son. If you aren't opposed—I mean if it's not…I mean, could I call you…Pa." Zane's eyes glistened as he focused on Sawyer.

Sawyer gave him a smile. Hell, he wasn't opposed, not in the least. In fact, his throat felt tight with his own emotions as he whispered. "I think I'd like that, son."

Zane smiled.

Sawyer moved closer. "I know it scared you, but this is what I do."

"Lang said you and Wyatt did something similar years ago." The boy's eyes were wide with wonder.

Sawyer nodded. "Wyatt and I have done a lot of things, some I am proud of and others, not so much. Today was just something that had to happen. Why don't you catch up with Dodge?"

"I'll tie Shadow to her buggy like Doc said." Zane turned to go, but then hesitated only a second before he ran back to hug Sawyer briefly and was gone out the door in a flash.

"Pa?" Sawyer spoke the word. He shook his head still not believing he was a father and relishing in what it felt like to be reminded. For the first time in his life, he now knew just how much his father had loved him and just how much he had sacrificed to love all his sons.

He turned back to the office. His pulse was calm now, but he couldn't shake the uneasy feeling. The

Ashburn brothers were dead, but he still had Marcus Benton to think about. There was no doubt he'd need to be looking over his shoulder from now on and even less doubt the cattle issue would become more of a problem than it already was.

Well, he'd handle Benton when the time came, but for now, he needed to see about Rose. He couldn't forget the look in her eyes when Frank Ashburn was shoving her around and had put the gun to her head. Never in his life had he felt such rage to kill a man— not since his father had died. He thought of the colonel, who would have been proud of how he and Wyatt worked together to bring down the men who had met their fate today. He sat at the desk and pulled out the logbook to record the events, at least what he could remember in fine detail. As he was finishing, Wyatt and Hudson returned, stomping their heavy boots inside and laughing.

"I got the pictures, and the bodies are at the church. I'm gonna head out to the saloon. Everyone's all stirred up, drinking rounds paid for by Jacob. He's telling a tall tale already." Hudson adjusted his hat, nodded to Sawyer, and disappeared to his work.

Wyatt tossed his hat aside. "The federal marshal's office telegrammed. They want a statement."

Sawyer stood and touched a hand to his hip. The bullet wound smarted, still burning and sore. "I'll take care of it tomorrow. I sent Zane home with Dodge. I'm going to stay with Rose, she was pretty shaken."

"Uh huh." Wyatt held his gaze.

"It's not like that." Sawyer raised his eyebrows in challenge.

Wyatt chuckled. "I got it here, take all the time you

need. She's probably scared out of her mind anyway."

Sawyer grabbed his hat and stood. "Keep an eye on the bank."

Wyatt tugged a skinny cigar and a match from his vest pocket. He struck the match along the sole of his boot and lit it. "Won't be much more trouble at the bank tonight, Gillette." He took a long draw and blew out a white puff of smoke, his dark blue eyes intense but clear.

Sawyer met his gaze for a long moment. They'd somehow done it again. "Ever wonder when our streak of luck might just run dry?"

"Nope." Wyatt took another puff, shaking his head.

Sawyer had to smile. "I'll be back by early morning."

Wyatt busied himself with the scattered papers on the desk, filing them away.

Sawyer stepped outside and gazed right and then left. Cheyenne was his town once again. He moved slowly toward the post office, glancing at the bank and saloon as he passed. It wasn't the first time he'd had to defend each and it certainly wouldn't be the last, but he'd never let a fight become personal—until Rose. He was damn lucky to still be alive and so was Wyatt for that matter. And Rose. Damn, the strong-headed woman from New York had saved her own life. He'd never wondered or thought of her having a gun, but he might as well have guessed she did. Not many women living alone in Cheyenne were without some kind of weapon. Even Dodge carried a small pistol in her bag.

He climbed the stairs to Rose's home. Funny he hadn't even thought of the fact she lived above the post office where he had been most of the afternoon. He tapped lightly at the door.

"Rose?" He tapped again.

It took a moment, but she came to the door, peering out and then opening it fully. Her eyes still held a hint of fright, wide and scanning behind him, but she was something to behold. Her light hair hung loose around her face, still damp from where she'd bathed. But she was fragile if he were guessing, still fearful.

"I wanted to check on you." He wasn't sure how to begin.

"Come in." She opened the door further and shut it behind him.

"I thought I could stay here. I mean, you...don't need to be alone." He tugged the hat from his head. There was no need for her to be alone, and the truth was he wouldn't be able to sleep with her out of his sight anyway.

"Dodge said you'd be by. She and Zane left a little while ago. I'll get you some coffee." Her voice cracked and she turned toward the small kitchen.

He followed, stopping behind her and whispering, "I don't need coffee."

Before he could say anything more, she turned, falling into his embrace, her tears dampening his shirt. Sawyer wrapped his arms around her and held her as tight as he could while she cried. He touched her hair, running his hands through the long damp strands, holding her to him, his heart pounding against his chest. She smelled of lavender and her petite frame against his own—well that was something of perfection and he cursed himself for not realizing how much he had needed her long before now. He inhaled deeply closing his eyes and resting his cheek on top of her head, thinking he could have held her for hours. She swayed and he tugged her along to the room where her bed was, Rose leaning on him, eyes closed. She was more than exhausted and needed to rest. She gave no protest until he began with the buttons on her dress. She grabbed her dress front, looking up at him but not pulling away.

"You're exhausted," he whispered as he finished with the buttons and pulled her dress over her head, idly looking away. Of course it wasn't proper, but there was nothing wrong with putting her to bed. He laid the dress over the nearby chair and pulled back the covers, still holding her against him, and rushing his thoughts quickly from his mind.

Then, as if she were a child, he lifted her and laid her on the bed. He gently removed her slippers taking in the sight of her in her chemise and bloomers. She was so fragile right now, but his body reacted instantly. He wanted—damn. Right now he was to care for her, not think about what he'd like to do to that beautiful body, with her pert nipples showing dark under the cotton fabric. He shook his head slightly and sucked in a narrow breath. While he struggled with his reaction, she was in no place for where his thoughts were going. He pulled the covers over her and dimmed the lamp.

"I knew you had a tender side," she whispered, her gaze so intent he all but melted.

"I'll be right here." He bent to kiss her cheek, lingering a moment and turned back toward the kitchen.

"Sawyer?"

He turned.

"Lie beside me...hold me for tonight." She tugged the covers back.

"Rose—" Sawyer shook his head. Lying by her all

night would certainly stir things up for him. That part of his body that wanted her most wouldn't yield to relaxing any time soon, but damn if he'd deny her with all she'd been through. He went to the side of the bed and kicked out of his boots and un-tucked his shirt mindful of his wounds but wincing at the pull.

"You're in pain?" she questioned, shaking her head. "It could have been so much worse."

"Yep, but it wasn't. And I'm fine, just sore." He hesitated a moment and lay on top of the covers, close to her. Under the linens with her, hell he couldn't be trusted, not even for a second. He drew her closer and kissed her hair, breathing deeply to inhale the sweet scent of her lavender soap.

"I was so afraid," she said softly.

"You were amazing. Those men were as dangerous as they come." Without a doubt she would have died, had she not pulled the derringer, and there wasn't much doubt he would be a dead man right alongside her.

"I've never fired a gun before or…killed someone." She turned to him, but lowered her eyes. "Dodge told me not to think of that because outlaws are just waiting on their fate."

Was that how she saw it? She hadn't killed the man, he was already pumped full of six rounds of lead. "You did what you had to do. He was already a dead man." He took her hand in his and held it, needing to feel her as much as she needed him to tell her things would be fine.

"Sawyer?" She held their hands up, gazing at their mingled fingers.

"Uhmm." He had closed his eyes, enjoying the feel of her fingers tracing along his. He opened them again.

"You wanted to know about me. My reasons for coming to Cheyenne."

"Rose, it's really not important right now." After all that had happened, she was going to tell him her reasons now? He was intrigued but that could wait for now.

"No, I want to tell you." She turned toward him, still playing her fingers between his. "I was married just after Papa died. I was foolish, but thought Wes loved me. He was one of my father's closest friends and often seemed very fond of me. It was almost expected we would marry. But, it turned out he was far more interested in my father's assets than he was in me."

Sawyer adjusted his position. So, she was married. He had suspected as much and some part of his heart deflated completely.

Rose gazed at him for a long moment, so close he could feel her breath and feel the light beating of her heart. "I wasn't sure, not at first. There was more than just the money and one day, I just knew and sure enough—"

Sawyer narrowed his eyes, and let her continue. What the hell had she lived through, given her careful choice of words?

"Wes was much older than me, and while I believed his intentions were sincere, he never..." She stopped but after a deep breath continued, "He slept in my bed the first few nights and when he never...well, I thought at first he was giving me time to recover from losing my father, but then there were hints of someone else." She let out a large sigh.

Sawyer said nothing. Funny, it didn't seem so important now to know her reasons, but he did want to know more about any man who wouldn't have found his passion in bed with her.

"I met Wes as planned one evening, but I arrived early and walked in on him in an embrace with the wife of the man who owned the bank," she whispered. "It made perfect sense, and I realized I had fallen deeply into their trap, especially when Papa's monies began to drop drastically."

Sawyer rose up, supporting his head in his hand, leaning on one elbow and rolling toward her. "Trap?"

"I had suspected his interest in her long before, but I had never expected him to take Papa's money. But the bank accounts...all the money was gone. It didn't take much to put it all together." She quickly wiped away tears and sniffled. "I threatened to expose them if they didn't return Papa's money to the accounts, and all they did was laugh at me." Her voice went up an octave. "I couldn't believe it."

"So what happened then?" Sawyer juggled the information in his head, trying to make sense of it, but focusing on the slight pulse that beat rapidly along her neck.

Rose took a deep breath and continued, "Well, I might have been naïve to what had happened to Papa's money, but I was not going to sit still. I knew that Wes would have it all, and there were several accounts my father had from the shipping yard,s and I had that money hidden along with the last six horses Papa owned." She gulped a breath.

"The Arabians you spoke of?" Sawyer whispered, squeezing her hand. She was trembling.

She sat up in bed leaning against the headboard, tugging the covers around her. "When he found I had hidden the horses and the shipyard accounts, he threatened to kill me."

Sawyer sat up, adjusting gingerly to protect his hip. Hell, no wonder she had remained so elusive with her story. He tugged her arm from beneath the blanket and held her hand once more in his own.

She glanced down and mingled her fingers within his as if it were the most natural of things to do. "Max Ferguson helped me find a way to leave New York undetected. Only he knows where the money and horses are. I don't think he even told Muriel."

"Max?" Sawyer raised an eyebrow. His lawyer friend had come up in their conversations before, and now some parts of this story were coming together. That explained her reaction to the mention of his name when they had shared dinner.

"Wes had men, bad men, searching for me and had Max not helped me, I believe I would not be here now." She grabbed a handkerchief from the bedside table and blew her nose.

"So you came here, posing as a bride, but it was Dodge who turned the story upside down?" Sawyer finished for her.

She shrugged. "Yes, but I wasn't to marry until Max had the marriage between Wes and I annulled." She glanced at him. "I just got word yesterday that it's done, and I suppose somehow thought I would find peace in that. All it said was, *Annulment final. Must marry. Horses safe. Do not return.*" She burst into tears and used her handkerchief to rapidly wipe her eyes.

"Rose, you just need to rest." Sawyer wrapped his arm around her, and she settled against his chest. Her slightly clad upper body sent a bolt of warmth to his already tight groin, but he held her anyway. He took a deep breath and let it out, playing his fingers through her hair. Son of bitch, he wanted this woman but more than that, he wanted all of her. Her beautiful body, her incredible mind and her tender heart. Holy damn, he'd have her and soon.

"No. Most of the money has been returned to the accounts in my father's name, the horses are well, wherever they are, but of course Wes will always be out there somewhere." She wiped her eyes once more. "And I will always be looking over my shoulder."

"Why would he come this far, if he did know where you were?"

Rose wrapped her arms around herself, underneath the covers, drawing away from him. "Because, if I am dead, all the money will return to him, but...if I should marry, he has no rights to any of it."

Sawyer felt gut punched. So she had arrived with the full purpose of marriage, even if Dodge had been the instigator. And that her marriage was annulled, she was his again—or she would be. "I'm here Rose, and no one, no one at all will ever hurt you again."

She curled closer. "Do you know what the worst part of it all was?" She didn't wait on him to answer, "It wasn't the money, it was seeing him with her, knowing our marriage wasn't what I thought and feeling so violated and undesired."

Sawyer lifted her chin and gazed into her eyes. God, she was the most beautiful woman he'd ever laid eyes on, even in tears. "You have no need to be ashamed. As for feeling *undesired*, I've wanted you since you stepped off that train, and I owe you an apology for making things so hard on you. You are more than desirable. You damn near take my breath away."

Rose just stared at him. Had it not been dark, he might have seen her cheeks glow pink. He placed his lips to hers and kissed her, parting them. He wanted to consume her fully, taste her, every inch of her and he wanted to touch every part of her until she melted into him forever. But he was overstepping the boundaries of the shock she'd been through.

"Rest Rose—" He tucked her back down into the covers, grateful he hadn't been under them with her. He sucked in a deep breath, cooling things down and snuggled in close to her once more. When the time was right, he'd show her how damn desirable she was, but not without the respect and tenderness she deserved. And while there was little chance he would sleep, there was nothing sweeter than holding her in his arms as she slipped into a quiet slumber.

Chapter Twenty

Sawyer woke early, his arm still draped across Rose. A single glance and his body betrayed him once more. The sweet smell of her teased his senses, and he forced his thoughts away. While he didn't think much would be said about his overnight stay, he didn't want to give anyone in town reason to talk. Cheyenne could be full of those who might gossip, and he wouldn't risk her reputation. He sat up and grabbed his shirt from the foot of the bed, stifling a groan as his sore hip protested the movement. He stood and glanced at Rose once more.

That she had shared her story, he still wasn't sure what to make of it. Max might have helped her escape from New York, but that didn't mean she wouldn't be found. If her ex-husband still wanted the money or the horses, he would find her or most likely send someone else to do the job. Men like that, ones seeking money and power, didn't usually walk away. He did feel better that it was Max who had helped her. He was a good man on the right side of the law and nearly as smart a man as Sawyer had ever conversed with. That he was on the other side of the situation meant Rose had left no trail.

Taking in the sight of Rose, curled on her side, hair splayed across her pillow once more, he smiled. He tugged his shirt on and buttoned it and grabbed his boots. Carrying them to the kitchen, he stepped into them as quietly as he could cursing the clanking of his spurs. Looking back toward the doorway to where she slept, he opened the kitchen door and made his way to the streets of Cheyenne.

Inside the jail office, he found Wyatt and Hudson playing poker as they usually did early mornings when things were quiet.

"Morning." He tossed his hat aside, thinking while he wasn't normally a drinking man, he could do with a stiff shot this morning. Anything to knock off the intoxicating smell of Rose that still lingered on his clothing and something that might dull the burn to his hip.

Wyatt raised an eyebrow. "How's Rose?"

"Pretty fragile." Sawyer strolled closer, eyeing his brother's cards from behind. "Full house."

"Shit, Sawyer." Wyatt didn't look up and threw down his cards.

Hudson did the same, standing and turning to Sawyer. "I cleaned and stored the long rifle. I'll be back tonight. You did well yesterday, scared the hell right out of me."

Sawyer slapped the younger man's back as he passed by. Hudson had been around him and Wyatt long enough to know how they worked, but he was younger and for whatever reason more cautious. He and Wyatt had ridden together for years, and there were times it was the younger man's cautious ways that had kept Wyatt out of trouble.

Wyatt forgot the game. "How's your ass?"

"My *hip* is fine." Sawyer pulled out the desk chair and sat, picking up some of the papers from the desk.

"Any more telegrams?"

"Nope. Lang said Benton was in town this morning asking questions. I suppose I know better than to ask about Harrison Colbert." Wyatt stood from the corner table and folded his arms, eyeing him with deep blue eyes that wanted answers.

"Benton keeps his tracks clean. And yes, you know better than to ask." Sawyer glanced back at the papers, a pile of information they had collected over the years on the Ashburn brothers. He cursed under his breath. He should have known they were too close, and he'd almost lost Rose for his lack of making sure.

"I pulled the reports last night, not much there and I put Colonel at the livery—you forgot your son's appointment with Tess and the horse is riled you forgot him too." Wyatt grabbed his hat. "And you my dear big brother are slowly losing your mind over Rose, best you marry her soon."

Enough was enough. Sawyer glared at his smiling brother. "Are you done?" He was in no mood for Wyatt's jests, not after all that had happened. He was smitten, hell he'd just dropped off the edge of the cliff into the raging river below, but he didn't need his brother to tell him he needed to swim.

Wyatt only chuckled and changed the subject, plopping his hat on his head. "Trouble's not over; Evan's got a telegram. The cattle made it to Kansas."

Sawyer shook his head. The previous day had been a nightmare, Benton was furious, and of course the damn cattle were ready. "Tell Zane to stay on the ranch. I don't want him in town for a while. I'll deal with Evan later. I'll need to be here with Rose."

"Uh huh." Wyatt gave him a wise smirk and

stopped at the door.

Sawyer snapped, slamming a fist on the desk. "Go home Wyatt."

"All right, brother. I'm going." Wyatt stepped outside the doorway, his whistled song fading as he made his way across the street to the livery.

Sawyer stood up and scanned the empty jail. No matter things had seemingly ended well, he had no doubt worse was coming. Grabbing his hat, he stood outside the jail. It was a bright morning, the heat climbing with the rising sun, but the hair on his forearms and neck still bristled.

Melanie should have the post office open by now and would likely have word from Washington in relation to the Ashburns. He made his way back across town, thinking once again about Rose as he entered the office. She was likely still upstairs sleeping, and he'd of given his right arm to have stayed there with her.

Melanie was at her desk behind the counter when he entered through the open doorway. The stench of gunpowder was still thick in the air, and it seemed Wyatt or Hudson must have cleaned up the mess from the overturned desk.

Melanie gazed up, her bright amber eyes cheerful. "Good morning, Sheriff, and I do hope this day is a better one."

Sawyer nodded and leaned on the counter, eyeing the stack of telegrams in front of her. "I'm sorry about the mess. Anything for me?"

"Both of these just came through. Oh, and I have needed to clean up the desk for a while now." Melanie grabbed two that were stacked to the left of the main pile. She might carry a gun and gossip a bit more than she should, but she kept her oath of privacy well for the job she had.

Sawyer took the notes and opened the first, tilting his hat back and taking a deep breath and let it out slowly. He wrinkled the thick paper in his fist and opened the next, scanning the neat penmanship that belonged to Melanie. "Son of a..." He didn't finish and crumpled it as well, gritting his teeth. Taking down renegades was a business that never saw fit to end. Washington warned of possible retaliation, from other men connected to the Ashburns.

Melanie never even looked up at his almost curse, but held out a hand and took the crumpled notes and tossed them in the nearby wood burning stove.

"Let me know if anything else comes in."

She smiled serenely. "I do hope Rose is well this morning. I am sure she needed your company for her protection last night."

Sawyer held her gaze. Shit, that was all he needed. He might have known given Melanie living below Rose that she had seen him enter last night or leave this morning.

"Don't worry, Sheriff, your secret is safe with me." She grinned, batting her eyes at him.

He narrowed his gaze in warning. "Just let me know if anymore telegrams arrive."

The last thing he needed was Melanie and her little gossip chain stirring up things for Rose. The young woman was good at keeping business secrets but was often at the center of roaming news. He turned toward the door and walked back outside with a mind to head to the livery. He needed to talk with Lang about Benton's visit.

Cheyenne was busy now, men on horseback filling the main road and most of the businesses open. The smell of fresh baked bread wafted through the air mingling with the stench of mud and animal, reminding him he hadn't eaten since early the day before. His belly growled, but given Melanie's observations, he wasn't sure he could eat anyway. He cursed under his breath.

As he passed the clinic just before getting to the livery, Tess called out from inside, the door propped open. "Oh, Sawyer, I need to take a look at your hip."

Sawyer stopped and glanced inside, meeting gazes with Rose. He hadn't expected her to bounce back so quickly. In fact he thought she was still inside above the post office, moments ago. He gave her a slight smile, and the one she returned melted him inside. She was dressed in one of her fancier gowns, and her hair was neatly up. She hardly looked like the woman that had nearly been killed the day before, and she didn't look at all like the fragile woman he had held most of the night.

"I thought you might stay in and rest." He climbed the steps to the clinic, clomping inside.

"Cheyenne is going to want a story." She held up her small tablet and pencil with pride.

Tess tugged on his shirt, interrupting the moment. "I checked on Jacob earlier. He'll be fine if I can keep him from drinking whiskey for his headache."

Sawyer pulled his shirt from his trousers, shifting so Tess could take a look at his wounds. "He's a right tough old man, reckon if the whiskey hasn't taken him before now, he'll likely survive." He groaned as Tess tugged on his trousers to inspect the wound, but stifled a smile at Rose who turned away, an amusing shade of pink crossing her cheeks.

"It looks really good, leastwise you are all alive and well in spite of all that took place." Tess backed up folding her arms.

"It's not bad." He tucked his shirt again, "With men like we had here yesterday, retaliation is common. Lock your doors at night and don't leave the front door open, even during the day. Doc, don't round on patients outside of town alone for a little while."

"Wyatt's already been by here this morning." She turned to Rose. "I'd love to read your story when you are done."

Rose headed toward the door and walked outside to the stairs. "Oh, of course, Tess. I should be getting back to the paper. Mr. McDonald was a bit under the weather this morning."

Sawyer shook his head. It wasn't a doubt the stuttering coward wasn't at work. He'd likely still have words with the man for leaving Rose behind in the bank. No man of honor would have done such a thing.

"I'll see you later in the week Rose." Tess followed her to the door and stopped, turning to nod for Sawyer to follow her.

"What?"

Tess whispered in a stifled growl, "I've known you for a long time Sawyer McCade. Now go after her and make sure she is all right."

"She's fine." Sawyer made it to the street, glancing back at Tess.

"Go after her, Sheriff." Tess raised her eyebrows.

This was a battle he had no chance to win. First Dodge and then Wyatt and now Tess. He was doomed, but then maybe he wanted to be right where he was. He trotted after Rose, only taking a moment to catch up to her. "I really am surprised you are out today."

"I knew if I didn't, I might never again." Rose continued walking. "I'm just glad it's over."

Sawyer grabbed her by the arm, stopping her. "It's all right to be afraid."

"I know. I just—the story needs to get written." She tried for a smile that wasn't much of one.

Sawyer took her hand and in spite of it all pulled her into his own large frame, wrapping his arms around her.

"Sawyer! We are outside." She scanned the perimeter around them.

"Yep."

"Do you think retaliation is likely?" She relaxed a bit, allowing his embrace.

"Look, I didn't tell you to scare you. Just be aware, pay attention, but it would be best if you stayed at the ranch." He figured his insistence to change the mood and he let her go.

She hesitated. "I have my home and work."

Sawyer nodded. He reckoned she could handle things on her own, but after lying beside her all night, he wasn't sure he wanted to let her stay alone. She was without a doubt the sweetest thing he'd held in a very long time.

"I'll be here until evening." She pulled from him and gestured toward the paper office.

"I'll come by tonight." If she wasn't willing to stay at the ranch, then he'd stay with her, but one way or the other, she wasn't staying by herself.

"I'd like that." Her blue eyes held a hint of relief.

She walked ahead to the office, smiling back at

him once. He held her gaze. He'd look forward to another night near her, but he had business to take care of first and turned toward the livery again. The wide doors were open as usual and he wandered through, searching for Lang.

"Hi Sheriff, how ya feeling?" Lang glanced up briefly from the horse he was shoeing in the corner stall.

"I'm good. Wyatt said Benton came around this morning." Sawyer leaned on the wooden stall taking a look at the horse and then Lang.

"Yeah, he came in here asking all about how things happened." Lang bent the horse's foreleg up and tapped the shoe in place adding nails from the ones he held in between his pressed lips.

"What'd you tell him?" Sawyer waited, but figured Lang knew a thing or two about dealing with Marcus Benton.

"Oh, he asked if it was just two men. He must know someone who was with them or he'd not be in this livery. He's never come in here before without trying to buy a few horses for half what they are worth. Like I'd tell him a thing." Lang cackled, dropped the horse's hoof, and faced Sawyer.

"Men like him don't work alone, watch yourself and keep an eye on things around here." Sawyer tilted his hat back. "Thanks for the horses yesterday, and I'm glad you didn't lose them to the Ashburns." The costs of four horses would've been more than months of his pay as sheriff, though with Lang, he'd made a deal or two for cattle in the past.

Lang shook his head. "Sheriff, you know me better than that. I sent them horses with marked hooves and one of 'em would have been lame in a day or two."

Leave it to Lang, the man might seem like he didn't have his wits about him, but Sawyer wasn't surprised in the least. "Keep your ears open."

Sawyer left the old man to his work and made his way back to the office, waiting on a wagon pulled by two oxen to pass. Dirt stirred from the weight of the wagon, and he studied the couple sitting on the buckboard with young children standing behind them. More settlers heading further west and by the looks of it, traveling heavy if they were planning to cross the mountains. He crossed the street and stepped up to the jail office.

Tipping his hat back, he moved inside and sat at the desk, his plunge into the chair reminding him of the sore hip he'd forgotten. Groaning he rubbed his backside. He'd had worse, but bullets left the pain of a burn, and this one wasn't in the best of locations. He opened the desk drawer to his left and lifted clean sheets of paper, laying them side by side. He'd need one for each of the Ashburn brothers. He dipped the quill and went to his work listing in chronology the events of that day and all who were involved. Using his logbook from the night before, the details came rambling back. It took a few hours to have it all mapped out for officials in Washington. Setting the papers aside to dry, he picked up the stack of articles Wyatt had pulled once more.

His brother would have studied the names on the reports and had any of the names been a connection, Wyatt would have known. His brothers spent hours on night shift reading reports and memorizing outlaws and the information surrounding them.

He scanned the names throughout all the articles over several more hours, pulling file after file, but none of the ones he read seemed to snag any connection to the Ashburn brothers. And nothing connected anyone or anything to Marcus Benton, but there was a connection.

He sat his hat aside on the desktop and ran a hand through his dark hair. He needed time to find a connection and pull together all the details. And with Benton's threat, he needed to do so fast. He smoothed his hands across his face. It had been over seventeen years since his father had been killed in cold blood, and he'd sworn to avenge the man he had idolized. And now it was here, with his letting out the reminder of Harrison Colbert's untimely death. Benton knew all too well how Colbert had died and all the reasons why, which meant he also had a connection to the man who had killed his father. He'd been holding that information for a long time, but now that it was out, it was just a matter of time before Benton would act on it.

He leaned back in the chair and let out a sigh. If it wasn't enough that he'd just put the whole family in the line of Marcus Benton's wrath, the damn cattle were waiting in Kansas. There was no doubt Brett and Evan would meet with resistance at the river, and Benton would see to it. With no help from the cavalry, he and his deputies were it, but no match for the men on the other side of the river, even if he deputized all his brothers and all the hands on both ranches. Benton didn't fear the law and never had. Things were already out of hand, and it hadn't really even begun.

He pulled out the complete files he and Wyatt had maintained for years and sorted piles of pictures and articles. Engaged in the task, hours passed without him knowing, but also without anything surfacing.

Pushing his thoughts aside, he stood, stretching his shoulders and feeling the pull of the dressing to his hip. The sun had long set, and Rose would be home by now.

Rose. He still wasn't over lying beside her all night. He tugged the edge of his collar to his nose. And he could still smell a hint of lavender on his clothing. He closed his eyes. Undressing her had nearly been his undoing, leaving him breathless and hard, but the timing had been wrong for anything more than how things had happened.

While there had been a time he'd love Catherine with all he was, he'd still never thought of marriage, but with Rose, he'd spent most of the night knowing he would make her his wife before it was all said and done. When she'd first arrived he'd been smitten but reluctant to admit it. But now—she was all he'd ever need—ever. He'd made a lot of mistakes with Catherine, but he'd been young, full of spitfire and set on revenge. Of course, he was still set on revenge, though it had remained idle for a time. But there was something about Rose that consumed him, and when the time was right, he'd see about asking her to become his wife. Somehow she had grown right into the middle of his heart, a place that had lain dormant for far too long. But given the heat of his body in just the mental picture of her in only her chemise and drawers, he'd damn well better ask her soon. He shook his head. He wasn't really sure how it had even happened, but that mattered little. He loved her, like he'd never loved before and by God and all the power he claimed, Rose would be his—if she'd have him.

Chapter Twenty-One

Darkness played across Cheyenne as Sawyer took the stairs to Rose's two at a time. Most of the businesses were closed all except the saloon he'd walked through an hour before. There was no trouble, but Wyatt would make rounds with Hudson before too long. He tapped at the door and waited. He had every intention of staying with Rose all night from now on, but with the gossip mongrel living below them, he'd leave even earlier the next morning, and he'd sleep on the couch and that was that.

"Good evening." Rose opened the door, and the fragrance of dinner wafted around him. Beef stew and fresh baked bread if he were guessing right.

"How was the paper?" He stepped inside, jerking off his hat and juggling it in his hands.

"I printed a few things, but I am still working on the article. I'm almost done." She turned toward the table and sat, her slender fingers pushing the pencil across the paper. "There." She blew the lead dust from the tablet, scanning it and offering it to him.

"I'm not much of an editor." Sawyer kicked off his boots, leaving them at the door, and moved to take the tablet. He had read a few of the articles she had written, but this would be the first on outlaws, though she now had first-hand knowledge of the Ashburn brothers.

"Go ahead," she urged with pride.

He flipped the top pages back and scanned the article. "You're telling a lot of details. You think that's a good idea?"

"Writing helps me, it always has." Her eyebrows lifted, but then frowned. "Are there things I shouldn't mention?"

He shrugged. "Depends. Not sure outlaws are likely to be reading your paper anyway."

"Maybe not. It does mention you and Wyatt, but not what you did to save us all. Only that you had to kill them." She shifted in her seat and took the tablet back from him.

Frankly, he didn't care what she wrote. The story was already old news. There wasn't much to hide. She'd given him and Wyatt credit for the Ashburn's take down, but she hadn't mentioned her part in any of it.

He grinned, handing the tablet back to her. "You've left out the part where *the lady pulled a derringer*."

"I thought it best, as you told me he was already…he wouldn't live. I didn't do it out of bravery, but fear…" She set the tablet on the table.

"You had little choice."

She shivered and hugged her arms to herself. "You were so brave, never even looking frightened at all."

Sawyer held her gaze. She'd been the bravest woman he'd ever seen in such a situation. "I've faced off with outlaws before, but I've never known fear until I saw Ashburn's hands on you. There's a lot of things Rose, and I'm not sure I know how to say them." He shook his head trying to think of the right words as he placed his hand on hers that were now folded on the table. "But I don't want another day to go by that you and I are not together."

Rose looked at their hands, but stood, turning away from him, letting go.

Sawyer followed her not sure of her avoidance. He'd not give her a chance to cry over those men again and he didn't want her tears over his admission of love. He turned her and wrapped his arms around her, relishing in her touch and lifting her chin. "I didn't mean to cause you more tears." He wiped her cheek with his thumb, smiling. "We don't have to rush anything, and I know you've had a shock, but when you are feeling better, we can talk about it, if you'll do me the honor of becoming my wife. If that would make you happy, and it's what you want." He sucked in what little breath he could, relieved he'd gotten it all out. "I have no interest in your money and horses, and I am not offering you the marriage of convenience you need. I am offering you all that I have now and for a lifetime." Hell, now he was rambling. But right now, holding her against him he loved her more than he loved anyone or anything. All of her, the mail-order-bride, the spoiled little rich girl, the horseback rider with no direction and most of all the woman—and without a doubt she was a woman.

By the look on her face, he was sure he'd said it all wrong, but then she melted into his body hanging on tightly around him with both arms.

"Yes." She squeezed harder. "Yes, Sawyer, I want to be yours, only yours."

Sawyer scooped her up in his arms and held her softly against his chest. His heart filled to capacity and nearly overflowed. Carrying her into her bedroom, he laid her back on the bed and looked down at her. And yes, this marriage needed to happen rapidly, as rapidly as the response in his trouser. *Holy hell!*

"Stay." She grabbed his hand as he stood above her. Her blue eyes were dark and inviting, but he shook his head.

"I'll be right here Rose, as long as you need me. Get some rest." He smiled, "I'll be fine out here."

"You are too large for my sofa, and I need to fix you a plate of stew," she protested.

"I'll be fine." He let her go of her hand. "Besides…it's not safe for me to be close to you like last night Rose. Trust me on this."

"You make me blush…but your kind words last night…were appreciated." Her cheeks were pink now, but if she could read his mind, she wouldn't have offered him lying in bed next to her again. He sucked in a deep breath.

"I meant those words and the ones I just said to you." And he did with all of his very being. He leaned down and kissed her on the forehead and turned to go, looking back at her once more wanting to memorize the picture of her before him.

****

Rose twisted in her bed. She was dreaming but couldn't pull herself from the nightmare. The Ashburn brothers were riding out of town, taking her with them. The outlaws laughed, and one turned to look at her, pulling the bandana from his face. Suddenly, he was no longer Frank Ashburn. Rose screamed as the face of Wesley Stadiar emerged, his cold dark eyes glistening as an evil grin spread across his face. She screamed and fought, but he held her tight, allowing no escape. He was taking her back to New York to kill her. She screamed, fighting with all she had.

"Rose...hey, Rose."

She startled awake, still fighting with the blankets.

"It's just a dream." Sawyer smoothed her hair, holding her tightly, the warmth of his naked chest enveloping her.

"It was so real." She hugged him tighter, needing to know he was real. "The Ashburn brothers were dragging me along. They took me...then one of them was...Wes."

"No, you were dreaming. It's only after ten, we must've slept hard." He wore only his trousers, his suspenders hanging. He tugged the blanket higher to keep her covered.

Rose gazed at him. Such a hard rough man, but with a tenderness she'd yet to find in any man, save her father. And he wanted her as his wife and she had said yes. She grasped his hand tighter, wanting his comfort once more, not because of being frightened, but because she wanted him near. "Stay Sawyer."

"Rose—" He stood, taking a step back, shaking his head.

She pulled the covers back, scooting to make a place for him. If he was to be her husband, she didn't want to wait any longer to lie in his arms as a wife. She had no doubts his hesitation was only related to respecting her, but if they were planning to marry...Lord but she knew it was wrong. Still she wanted to know what loving Sawyer McCade would be like and to solve all of the mysteries related to what husbands and wives did behind closed doors. "Stay."

He sighed but stepped closer again and sat on the

edge of the bed. "Rose, it isn't a good idea, sweetheart—that desirable word we talked about will get us into a lot of trouble. I can't lie beside you and not..."

She placed her hands along his cheeks and brought his face closer to hers. "Show me how a man loves a woman, Sawyer. Touch me." She parted his lips, tasting him as he'd tasted her with her wanting kisses. She was long past the age most girls married, and as a woman she wanted to feel his body join with hers, yielding to his touch now and always.

Sawyer devoured her mouth, their breath mingling in the exchange. She had never been kissed as he had kissed her. Warmth spread through her entire being when his hands pulled her closer, pressing her breasts to his naked chest, her nightdress the only thing between them. He smelled of leather and tasted of mint. He'd probably made himself some of the mint tea she kept in the cupboard. She closed her eyes and savored the flavor as his tantalizing tongue tracing along her own, but then he leaned back breaking the kiss as suddenly as it had started.

"Rose...you have to be sure. This changes... things..." He spoke in between quick kisses to her lips once more.

"Sawyer, I'm not some young girl making a hasty decision. I've thought of nothing more for weeks now. I don't want to wait to be yours any longer." She wasn't sure of all that happened when a man and woman were together, but she had no doubts she wanted it to be Sawyer who claimed her and made her a woman. She gazed into his eyes, her heart so full she thought it might simply burst in knowing the handsome sheriff did indeed love her after all. His large frame and strong arms would hold her the rest of her life, and that was all she would ever need. And what would her father think about her marrying a cowboy sheriff in the middle of the rugged West? He would likely tell her to follow her heart, and that was just what she was doing.

"I won't have people think badly of you. I don't care what they think of me, but…" He took her hand and brought it to his lips kissing her fingers one at a time. His hand twitched, and she had to wonder if his heart was pounding as strongly as her own.

He grabbed her suddenly by both her shoulders, his chest heaving as he whispered. "Rose, if I make love to you tonight, I swear to God, I'll never be able to get enough of having you."

"Then perhaps we should marry very soon." She met his gaze once more with her whisper. He was so handsome, like nothing she had ever pictured for herself, but everything she had waited on her whole life.

He kissed her again, grabbing her face with both hands. He traced to her neck with one hand, touching her jaw and swirling his tongue inside her mouth, Rose losing herself in the splendor of his passion.

She moaned as heat rushed to her center and she placed her arms around his neck, somehow as desperately as she had the night before, but this time not in fear. This time in—love.

Sawyer tore from the kiss, sliding his hands from her shoulders down her sides, urging her to lie back in the bed. Ever so slowly, he lifted the hem of her night dress holding her gaze until he had exposed her fully. She sucked in a rapid shallow breath when he bent and placed his lips to the skin of her soft belly, kissing her once and again, working his way up. She let a soft sigh escape her, the moist heat of his lips setting fire to the virgin skin of her bare breasts.

Sawyer growled and raised his head. He stood never taking his eyes from her as he dropped his trousers, kicking them free. Lord but he was a handsome man, with his muscular shoulders and knotted belly and the fine down of dark fur across his chest. She'd seen him naked, when the men had showered in the rain, but of course he didn't—well, that part of him hadn't looked so large then. A moment of fear crossed her mind when he lay back down beside her.

"You are some kind of beautiful Rose Parker." He kissed her neck, and his hand traced down her belly.

She giggled of all things, his beard tickling her neck with him nuzzling so closely.

"So I found the spot." He kissed her again while at the same time freeing her of her nightdress and tossing it aside.

Rose let out a breath and clutched his shoulders as he kissed her neck once more. Never had she felt muscles so tight and hard. Funny that she wasn't afraid as she had always thought she might be when this time came.

Sawyer stopped long enough to glance at her. "So…when you were married he never…"

"No," Rose whispered. No man had ever touched her as he had and while she had been kissed, she had never been kissed as Sawyer had taught her.

"Good." He growled, pulling long stands of her hair through his fingers. He lowered his hand to her breasts, running a calloused thumb across her nipple and then dipped his head to take it in his mouth.

Rose closed her eyes not having expected the sensation to spark where he'd yet to touch her. She ran her hands in his long, dark hair and shivered. So personal, so…oh my…it was rather exquisite, but so…she sighed again.

"It's all right." He continued to the other breast, sucking and nipping, pulling and tugging until Rose thought she might go mad.

How could such a hard man, do absolute gentle things that brought fire deep inside her? She bit her bottom lip to stave off the next sigh that seemed to emerge all on its own.

"How's that?" He glanced up and his gray eyes brightened as if he were some little boy asking about a task at school.

She was so unsure of how she was supposed to react, but she didn't want him to stop. *Oh, my Lord, but it was wonderful.* "So very nice."

His grin was made of mischief as he lowered his lips to her breasts once more, tugging at each of her nipples in turn over and over and when his hand spread across her belly and trailed lower, Rose froze, concentrating on breathing alone.

And then he touched her. So intimate and personal. She shuddered. He didn't rush but seemed to be giving her time to adjust to his hand coursing across her. Rose tangled her hands in his hair once more letting the sensation take her. Why did she feel as though it wasn't enough? She pressed her pelvis forward against his hand, wanting the pressure of him.

"Open your legs." His voice was so soft, and she

simply obeyed. Oh, Lord, but…his fingers parted her and she panted to keep her breath as Sawyer moved lower and kissed her belly. His fingers made short work of finding the tiny nub of pleasure that had pulsed with the first touch of his lips to her breasts.

Rose forced herself to relax and let his touch be the only thing. She'd heard women talk of the pleasures a man could bring, but she hadn't believed them—until now. She sighed loudly eliciting a grin from Sawyer who glanced up at her and worked his fingers more fervently against her. Lord but it was so wonderful, tender and overwhelming at the same time.

When he pressed his finger inside her, Rose opened her eyes and placed her hand to his, uncertain.

"I won't hurt you," he whispered, adding a second finger. Her body clenched around him as if of its own will. She kept her hand on his, and each tug of his fingers sent tingles of pleasure through her. Oh, Lord he couldn't continue. She twisted seeking relief from the exquisite torture, her heart pounding against her chest. What was happening to her?

"Relax, let it…" Sawyer encouraged, but his fingers never stopped.

Suddenly she was aware she was building to the point of some kind of release, and it was Sawyer taking her there. *Oh, the sweet torture*. She arched as searing pleasure consumed her where he played, and she clung to him as waves of shear bliss rushed through her entire being. She cried out his name, as his fingers played havoc inside her, and she rode the spasms of relief losing herself to him, her hand still upon his. When it eased she fell back against the pillows, covering her face with her hands. She had never felt anything so pleasurable and hadn't even known her body could do such a thing. So this was the pleasure Muriel had tried to explain to her. This…this was Sheriff Sawyer McCade.

Sawyer tugged her hands away, gazing at her with his gentle smile. "So?"

Heat scorched her cheeks and she was hardly able to catch her breath. "What did you just do to me?"

"Loved you, how a wife is to be loved." He kissed her slowly once more, but she pulled away, still trying to breathe.

Sawyer played his hands across her breasts again and nibbled along her shoulders as she thought to give her time to recover. If this was what happened every time, she wasn't sure she would survive it. So very personal and as she had built, she had wanted to open herself more and more to him. Rose touched her hand to his bearded cheek when he glanced at her again. His deep gray eyes reflected the candle, and without a doubt she knew all she had gone through was worth it because it had brought her to this man.

He held her gaze, and it was as if no words were needed between them. Rose brushed his long hair from his face, and he tenderly crawled between her legs. He held himself above her and spoke in the slightest whisper. "There'll be pain."

She knew the pain would come, but she wanted his claim of her. "I know, but your wounds"

He placed himself against her. "I'll be fine. Look at me."

Rose tensed as he pressed his hips forward, stretching her to accommodate all of him. She sucked in a breath, tensing. *Oh, Lord.* It hurt more than she had

311

thought it would.

"Rose..." He stopped.

"Please...Sawyer." She braced herself and as quickly as she said it, Sawyer filled her full and deep.

She let out a soft cry, in spite of her efforts to relax, digging her nails into his muscled shoulders.

"Shhhhh." He whispered, running his hand along her hip rubbing her tenderly, his body trembling with the effort of his restraint.

She bit her bottom lip as he slid his hand between them and used his fingers to coax the part of her that was still overly sensitive. She took a deep breath as he began to move pushing and pulling from her. Each deep thrust hurt, but after a time, the searing pain abated and the tension from his fingers built her once more.

"Oh...Sawyer..." She was breathless.

Sawyer pulled his fingers away with a moan, ducking his head to nip at her breast again. There was a fine line between the thrusting pain and the pleasure he stirred within her once more. It was almost too much, but as he pressed deeper, the discomfort eased bringing her hints of pleasure again. Surely it couldn't happen more than once. She squeezed her thighs tight around him wanting the sweet relief once more. Sawyer groaned grasping her hip and pressing fervently into her over and over, his breath hard against her neck.

She tensed; tracing her hands down Sawyer's hard back and along his hips, forgetting his injuries. He sucked in a breath and pulled her hand away from his left side, but never stopped moving against her. She had forgotten his injuries but was on the border of shattering again and pressed herself to meet him over and over. It was indeed happening again, her body began clenching tighter. "Saw…yer."

"That's it." His voice was raspy, his large body damp with perspiration and his long hair sweeping across her cheeks as he rode above her.

Rose tossed her head back to the pillow as tendrils of pleasure scored through her, not as intense this time but lasting with each spasm of her body and taking all her breath once more.

"God Rose…" Sawyer gripped his hands into her hair, breathing harder against her neck and his large body shuddered, the rhythm of his thrust hard and deep. His chest heaved, against her breasts as he struggled to regain his breath, the hardness of him still planted deep inside her, the sweat of their bodies mingling. She didn't move when he stopped, not wanting to part from him, now or ever.

Long moments passed before he raised his head and of all things he smiled, sweat glistening across his brow. She could see his vulnerability, somehow his guard down with the bursting of his own body. Was it the same for him? Had he felt the same pleasure as she?

He didn't move from within her. "I'm sorry I hurt you."

"I'm fine," she whispered, still wondering of her body's abilities. Muriel had been right, that it was the most wonderful thing.

"Are you sure, Mrs. McCade, because I have no intentions of not following through on this. I love you Rose, with all I am or ever will be." His eyes glistened, and he kissed her again. His body laying full on hers.

"I'm sure." She kissed his bearded cheek, keeping her hand along his jaw. Some part of her wanted to smile and another part of her wanted to allow happy tears. She was a woman now, Sawyer McCade's woman—soon to be his wife.

"Let's not delay. My reputation might suffer." He grinned, rubbing his palm across her nipples tenderly as he rolled to her side, their bodies parting.

Rose's mouth dropped open. "*Your* reputation?"

He chuckled. "I've no plans to wait on loving you like this again, but there could be a child now, and I won't have the town gossiping with idle chatter."

Rose gulped hard. She hadn't even let that cross her mind she had been so caught up in wanting his touch. "I...would you want children?" She'd never asked.

"Of course." He didn't seem to give it a second thought.

"Yes...but, you have Zane to think of." She worried.

"He and I have a lot of learning each other to do, but I've waited a lifetime for you." Sawyer tugged a loose strand of hair from her face, tucking it behind her ear.

"He adores you. I don't want to take that from him." She spoke softly.

"He *adores* that horse of his, but he asked permission to call me *Pa,* saying he was proud to be my son." There was a sense of pride in his voice as he pulled her across his chest.

"I would also be very proud to be your wife." Rose kissed his forehead and then each cheek in turn and then his chin and lastly his lips.

He opened the eyes he'd closed at her action. "I love you. I have since the first moment you stepped off that train and yes, you are damned desirable." His hands scrolled down her back and across her buttocks.

"I know."

"You know?" He let out a slight chuckle.

Rose snuggled closer, his warm body against hers and she did indeed know. There was no doubt in her mind that no matter where life took her, she would never find the kind of love she'd discovered with Sheriff Sawyer McCade.

Kim Turner

Chapter Twenty-Two

The afternoon sun scorched down across Cheyenne as Sawyer leaned on a post of the hotel porch. He'd been watching from across the street as Rose ran the printing press inside the paper office. While he'd been at it for more than a half an hour, she was so busy she hadn't even noticed him. No matter, he was enjoying the view while he gathered his thoughts. The heat signaled a storm if he were guessing right. Perhaps the coming weather was the reason his nerves were on edge. He cursed under his breath knowing better.

Marcus Benton hadn't been back in town, but his men had been hanging around the mercantile, post office and saloon for the past two days. If he were a guessing man, he would think the man was trying to get a rise out of the McCades before the cattle crossing, but there was a part of him that figured different, and he wasn't a man who gambled on thought. Marcus Benton was up to more than distraction.

He sucked in a deep breath. There would be no help from the federal marshals or district judge, and he and Wyatt still had differing opinions on how to handle the situation, which drew closer every day. He'd slept little the last few nights, letting the unrest plague him, but he'd found relief from the torment of worry in bed with Rose. The sleek warmth of her body was indeed enough to take his mind from his troubles time and again. He trotted across the street, waiting first for two covered wagons to pass. He stole inside the paper office's wide open doors but shut them behind him.

"Oh, I didn't know you were here." Rose glanced up and stopped the press.

"I've been watching you for a half hour, and you know what I think?" He gave her a wink and stepped closer.

She raised her eyebrows in question, a smudge of purple ink across her chin.

"You are working too hard. You haven't had lunch I'll bet and it's after two."

"I did have lunch only a little while ago." She pulled the press up and removed the newsprint she'd just completed.

"Uh-huh." He chuckled and leaned closer to her.

"What are you doing here anyway?" She held her place, not letting go of the press.

Sawyer walked around to her side of the press. "That depends."

"On what?"

"On where Mr. McDonald went." Sawyer narrowed his eyes as he stepped closer. The old man had ridden his buggy rapidly out of town a short time ago.

Rose shrugged. "He wasn't feeling well, and went home. Why?"

Sawyer moved even closer.

"Stop!" Rose let go of the press, holding both her ink covered hands up in front of her.

Sawyer gave her a sly grin, wanting just another taste of her to get him through the afternoon.

"You are bad, Sawyer McCade, and I have ink on

my fingers. It'll stain your shirt." She took a step back, a slight smile curling across her lips.

Sawyer grabbed both of her wrists and began backing her up with a growl. "I've got two more shirts at the jail office."

"Sawyer?" She relented.

He gently lifted her hands above her head, holding both wrists together with one hand and lowering his other hand to the milky flesh of her exposed neckline. He had told her he'd never get enough of her, and it was true. Last night it had taken very little for him to coax her body to pleasure and the mental picture of her writhing beneath him, stirred up his trousers once more.

"Someone might—"

"Might what?" He kissed her lips tenderly, lifting the weight of her breast.

"Might come in and—"

"There is no one here." He kissed her, parting her lips and traced his tongue along hers. His body hardened at the moist heat of her mouth.

Rose pulled from the kiss, her face flushed. "We mustn't, not here."

Sawyer leaned closer. "Is that an invitation?"

"You have been to my bed every night Sawyer McCade, and I would imagine that is just where you will be tonight." She gazed at him with a grin.

"I'll be by tonight." He kissed her again, letting her wrists go with reluctance. Damn but taking her against the wall hard and fast until her legs quivered might have been more than interesting.

The now closed door of the paper office slammed open. Sawyer cursed under his breath. Wyatt. *Son of a bitch.* He let go of Rose.

"We got trouble at the river." Wyatt nodded at Rose, who'd gone quickly back to the press.

Sawyer cursed under his breath. "Give me a minute."

"Time's wasting." Wyatt went back outside without as much as a glance back.

Sawyer turned back to Rose, his gut clenching.

"The river—" Her eyes were wide with fear, and she let go of the press once more to take his hand, in spite of the purple ink he'd carry with him.

He touched his finger to her lips. "The river will be fine."

"Sawyer, it scares me." Her tone went up an octave as she clung tighter.

"I'll be back as soon as I can. We have plans this evening." He smiled until she finally smiled back. He kissed her cheek. "That's my girl."

He took off out the door, heading toward the jail, hoping his heated body would cool quickly. He hated seeing the fear in Rose's eyes. Trouble at the river was nothing new, though a man being shot would up the ante, and he had little trouble guessing who was behind it. Wyatt was already mounted up on his horse by the time he reached the office. Grabbing Colonel's reins, he stepped in the stirrup and settled in the saddle and followed as his brother took the lead out of town.

"What happened?" Sawyer shouted and let up on Colonel's reins urging the horse to catch his brother's mount.

Wyatt shook his head."Not sure."

"Where's Evan?"

"The better question is where's Brett." Wyatt glanced at him.

If things were stirred up at the river, there was no doubt Evan was in the middle of it. He'd already had words with Evan more than once about Benton's men, but his youngest brother had been looking for a fight most of his life, at least ever since—Evan had only been ten years old when their father died, and he'd emerged from the trauma with a large chip on his shoulder that kept him in trouble. Brett, however, was another story. His temper could be fierce, and he'd end up killing Marcus Benton or getting himself killed if things weren't handled.

"And Zane?" Wyatt lifted his eyebrows.

"Zane's likely with them." A bolt of dread plowed through Sawyer. He had allowed the boy to ride out with the hands since he'd healed. He swallowed hard. If Evan had allowed his son in the middle of the dangers at the river, he would kick his brother's ass once and for all.

At the edge of town, Wyatt urged his horse to a full gallop. Colonel rocked his head, stretching his legs, wanting the run. Sawyer clung tight, bending forward to give the horse his stride.

The thirty minute ride out to the river took only half the time and as they topped the ridge, Wyatt cursed out loud. "Son of a bitch!"

Sawyer gritted his teeth, dismounting before his brother. Across the river from Benton's property, twenty or so men fought on the McCade side of the water. Dust flew along with fists and there was Evan right in the middle of it. He scanned for any sign of Brett or Zane, but found none.

"Let's go." Wyatt ran ahead.

"I got it." Sawyer trotted past Wyatt, who followed

with his left hand on his revolver. The last thing he needed was Wyatt jumping right into the charades. He stepped up on a log and lifting his revolver from his side firing into the air three times.

The blast startled the men who froze little by little in spotting him. He glared at Evan, whose mouth dripped blood. His brother turned away.

"Enough!" Sawyer yelled. "It stops now." He eyed the men and stopped his gaze on the young man on the ground who had taken a bullet. He was alive, but unmoving.

"Who shot this man?" Sawyer kept his voice steady and jumped from the log, his gaze on Benton's men.

"If no one can confess to this, all of you from Marcus Benton's ranch will be detained." He did a head count and figured Benton's men at twelve. The grumbles among them let him know that none were keen on the idea. He nodded to Brett's hands. "Get this man to town to the doc."

The hands went to work lifting the unconscious man and getting him to a wagon.

Wyatt stepped closer, eyeing Benton's men alongside him. "It was Johnson." Wyatt's sixth sense was always on target. His brother would have likely made the better sheriff had he been able to tame the temper so much like their father's.

Sawyer nodded for Wyatt to go ahead. His brother pushed through the men and snatched Milford Johnson's pistol from his belt, then sniffed the chamber and nodded. "Powder, still hot."

Sawyer nodded, suspecting as much. Johnson had always been trouble, and a fired weapon did smell of burnt powder.

The pounding of hooves rang across the ridge and Sawyer glanced that direction. Brett stopped his horse, dismounting and running to look at the injured man in the wagon, shaking his head.

"Who pulled the trigger?" He stomped back to the group of men, eyes dark and serious as he narrowed his eyes at Sawyer.

Sawyer nodded toward Wyatt, who was locking the irons on Johnson's wrists. He dumped the hand in front of Sawyer on his knees.

"You can't prove nothin', McCade," Johnson groaned eyeing Brett.

He was guilty, of that Sawyer had no doubt. "Want to tell me what happened?"

Johnson spat a stream of tobacco. "He knew better than to ride through here."

Brett stomped closer and hauled Johnson up by the collar. "He hasn't worked for me long enough to know about the bullshit at this river. His wife is expecting and if he dies, I'll hang you myself."

Sawyer grabbed Brett's arm, and he let go of the larger man. Brett shook free, walking away, taking a deep breath and turning back to face the men before him. "My men mount up and head back out to the herd. Each man will have his pay docked for not following orders."

Not one of the men working for Brett even grumbled.

Sawyer stepped toward Evan. "Where's Zane?"

Evan's green eyes narrowed, and he never looked away from his older brother as he shouted to his own men. "McCade hands, move out. I sent Zane away before it even started."

Sawyer gripped his fists tighter. "I'll see you in town."

"All right brother," Evan spat with sarcasm.

Sawyer held his gaze and then turned back to the men from both sides who were slowly dispersing. "I expect this part of the river to remain clear. Any man, from either side, will be detained if there's more trouble. No questions asked." Sawyer eyed the men who worked for Marcus Benton, though most continued to cross the river and disappear.

Wyatt pushed Johnson ahead. "If you don't kick Evan's ass for this, I will."

It was time, but he wouldn't do it in front of Evan's men. "I need to warn you all, the cattle in the area will continue to cross here as they always have, and you'll hold your tongues and your guns or the price will be heavy." Sawyer spoke to Benton's men, shoving his revolver in his holster, yet leaving his hand ready at his side.

He and Wyatt watched as the last few men left the river, some bloody as they mounted their horses. In only moments the river was clear.

Sawyer turned to Wyatt. "Take him in."

Wyatt shoved Johnson along toward their horses as gunfire exploded in the air on the other side of the river, turning them all. Sawyer drew his weapon.

Wyatt shoved Johnson aside and pulled both revolvers taking aim.

Sawyer ran toward the river with a curse, his heart in his throat. "Son of a…"

At the top of the ridge across the river, Marcus Benton stood with two of his men, one of them holding

Zane by the elbow, his hands tied behind him.

His gut clenched, and every ounce of his body shook in rage. What the hell had happened?

"Seems we've got a little trade to make, McCade. My man for yours—man that he is." Marcus Benton's evil laugh coursed across the river, and he shoved Zane toward the water.

Sawyer glared at the man he'd hated his entire life and then made eye contact with the son he now loved more than life itself. Enough was enough. He stepped toward the river only to have Wyatt grab him by the shoulder to stop him.

"The bastard wants you to cross the river, then he'll shoot you on the spot," Wyatt talked through his teeth.

"I sent Zane back to the ranch, I swear it, Sawyer," Evan whispered, trotting closer.

Sawyer only glanced at Evan and met Zane's gaze once more. Though his hands were tied behind him, he seemed unharmed, and while he was probably afraid, he didn't cower. Sawyer cursed under his breath. He couldn't lose control at this point. Nothing mattered save getting Zane away from Marcus Benton, even if he did have to release Johnson.

Benton waited, shoving Zane hard, sending him forward again, ever closer to the river. While Zane could put up little fight, he kept his footing and glared hard at the man, his face red with anger.

"Sawyer, I *did* send him back," Evan tried again.

Sawyer rounded on a dime. "Evan, just..." He held up a hand and nodded to Wyatt instead. "Remove his cuffs."

Wyatt unlocked the irons from Johnson. "Careful

brother, he's liable to hurt Zane anyway."

Brett who had remained moved closer from behind them. "Bastard's lying."

Johnson smirked with Brett's comment.

Without batting an eye, Brett sent his fist right across the man's cheek, Johnson's head jolted back and his knees buckled.

Wyatt hauled him to his feet again. "Make one wrong move, and I'll kill you myself."

Sawyer's heart thumped hard in his chest. It was all he could do not to rush the river, swim it, and take Marcus Benton's life with his bare hands.

"Come on McCade, your *son*, for Johnson." Benton's voice dripped sarcasm.

"Send my son across first." Sawyer tightened the grip on his revolver. He could take the man out in less than a second, but Zane would be at risk.

Benton laughed again. "Not a chance. Quite a family resemblance going on, sort of like looking at a young John McCade, bastard that he was."

Sawyer glared. What choice did he have? There was no assurance if he sent Johnson across that Zane would be returned. "You give me proof you'll send my son!"

"You have no proof." Evan stomped past him. "I'll get him back myself."

Brett was quick to shove Evan back. "He'll shoot you before you hit the grass on the other side."

"This isn't a *check*, but a *check mate*, McCade. Send him now or we'll have real problems." Benton jerked Zane backward by his tied hands. Zane stumbled, falling to his knees in the mud and struggling to stand but making it to his feet.

Sawyer made it to the river's edge in two steps, dragging Johnson with him and shoving him into the current. "You swim swiftly. If I don't get my son in return expect a bullet in your back before you hit the top of the ridge and you will still answer if the man you shot dies."

"Sawyer, you can't trust he'll turn Zane loose." Wyatt tried to grab Johnson as he stepped off into deeper water.

"He'll send him." Sawyer hissed. Benton wasn't here to kill Zane. He was just sending a payback for Sawyer breaking his silence over Harrison Colbert.

"He's bluffing, Sawyer," Brett added.

"No, he's not." Sawyer never took his eyes from Benton's. While he was behind a number of deaths, he didn't do his own killing and never had. He was too smart to harm Zane and find himself a wanted man.

Johnson made it to the deeper part of the river swimming hard against the current. "Good thing the bastard can swim," Wyatt whispered under his breath.

Once Johnson stood in the shallows on the far side of the river, the two men with Benton helped him up onto the shore, where he fell to his knees in exhaustion.

"Send my son!" Sawyer yelled, stepping into the shallows of the water.

Benton nodded to his men who took hold of Zane, dragging him into the water as he resisted.

Sawyer's heart sank. The men were going to throw Zane in the river, without untying his hands. He'd drown. "Cut his ties! Cut his ties now you son of a bitch!" Sawyer dropped his revolver to the ground, kicking off his boots and wading into the water, as the two men shoved Zane into the deeper water. "No!

Zane!"

Brett kicked out of his boots, following Sawyer into the water as Wyatt and Evan fired on Benton and his men who had retreated.

Zane went under but bobbed back up gulping for air.

Sawyer fought to get to him. He wouldn't lose his son, not like this. And he'd have Marcus Benton when this was over if it was the last thing he did. His socked feet sank in the muddy bottom of the river, and he dove toward Zane. He swam upriver, knowing the current would push him Zane's direction. Opening his eyes under water proved futile, the water was too dark and muddy. He surfaced and sucked in a breath, turning in the water. Brett was several yards behind him in waist-deep water, pointing. "There."

Sawyer dove the direction Brett had pointed. Surfacing again, he bumped into Zane, the current pushing them further into deep water. He grabbed Zane and pulled his head out of the water. Zane coughed and sputtered. Sawyer held the boy tight and let the current push them along toward Brett, who was holding out his hand.

Sawyer grabbed hold, and Brett began backing up to shallow water, pulling them along. Sawyer fought to keep his grip on Zane as the current pushed him under again. Growling, he pulled his son to him with all his might to get his head above the surface. His feet hit mud, and he pushed himself erect, dragging Zane upright. Brett grabbed Zane who was coughing and gagging and handed him off to Evan who was now in the water's edge.

Sawyer grabbed Wyatt's offered hand, pulling up

to the shore and bending down before Zane, who collapsed into the deep grass. Sawyer cut his ties, freeing his hands.

"Zane?"

Zane pulled himself to his knees, vomiting a large amount of water, his body heaving with the effort.

Sawyer placed a hand to his back in support as he continued to expel more water. Finally, Zane rolled to his back, his eyes closed and his breathing heavy.

Sawyer looked over his shoulder. Marcus Benton and his men were long gone and he cursed under his breath.

"I'm fine." Zane struggled to sit up, "but they took...my...horse."

Sawyer steadied him. "We'll get your horse later."

Wyatt tossed Sawyer his boots. "I'm not one for guessing, but I'd have to say this is related to that discussion that included Harrison Colbert."

He glared at his brother and pushed his muddy feet into the boots, his socks lost to the mud of the river. He stood and helped Zane up, the boy shaking in fatigue.

"Sawyer?" Evan tried.

Sawyer held up his hand. "I told you I would deal with you in town."

"Wait." Zane pulled from his grip. "Evan told me to go back to the ranch." He looked up at Sawyer with some hesitation, "I knew I shouldn't fight so I hid in the trees...thought maybe if I was needed I could shoot."

Sawyer took a moment to comprehend the story.

"I guess I wasn't hidden well enough." Zane looked down, his clothing still dripping into his mud-covered boots.

"Where's your revolver?" Sawyer ignored Evan

and placed his hands on his hips listening closely.

"Mr. Benton took that too."

Wyatt nudged Evan, and the two mounted their horses heading toward town, leaving Sawyer to his son. He waited a moment and turned back to Zane. "I've asked you not to carry that gun and to take orders from Evan. They didn't hurt you?"

"No, Pa." Zane dug his boots in the sand. "I'm sorry, I thought I could help. But I suppose you'll need to punish me, maybe even send me back to Mankato."

Sawyer was dumfounded. Was that how Zane saw things? He held eye contact long enough for the thought to sink in. His own father had never laid a hand on him, though Dodge had used a switch on all the boys from time to time.

"Zane, I would never send you back. This is your home now." Sawyer searched his mind for the right thing to say.

Zane glanced up but said nothing, his eyes glistening. He looked back at the ground again.

"I'm just glad you weren't harmed anymore than you were. You still aren't fully well, and it could have been a lot worse, but—" Sawyer waited until Zane looked up again. "Nothing. Nothing could ever make me send you away Zane. You are my son. I may not be happy with the choices you make, like this, but I would never send you back."

He stepped closer and grabbed Zane tugging him into a hug with both arms. "I love you Zane, don't forget that."

After a moment of holding his body tense, Zane let go and hugged him back whispering, "I am sorry, Pa." The boy let go and stepped back, quickly wiping his eyes.

"We'll get your horse back and maybe the revolver." Sawyer glanced across the river once more.

Zane shook his head. "Mr. Benton's men will probably be glad to give him back. They had a terrible time controlling him, but they might hurt him."

"We'll get him back. Come on, I'll get you to the ranch."

Zane didn't follow and Sawyer turned.

"Pa, could I just walk. I mean, I know you need to go to town and I'll be fine."

Sawyer gave it thought. Benton wouldn't be a worry right now, after all if he had wanted Zane, he'd still have him and the ranch was only a few miles away. "All right, but straight there. I'll see you tomorrow evening."

Zane nodded and turned to head the direction of the ranch on foot.

Sawyer watched him until he was out of sight. The boy had been through enough with the loss of his mother and his injuries, but he had stood right there expecting his punishment as any boy his age might have. Rage coursed through Sawyer. He gripped his fists tight. Benton would pay for nearly drowning his son. Hell the man would pay for a lot of things when the time came, and he'd see to that himself. He took Colonel by the reins and walked slowly along as a light rain began to fall. He'd been right, the rain had come after all. Thunder echoed to the west as surely as it did inside his chest. He turned to eye across the river, and with all that was in him, he would bring Marcus Benton to justice, even if in the process he brought down the wrath of Satan himself.

Chapter Twenty-Three

Sawyer entered the jail office, shaking off the rain and glancing at Wyatt. Thunder hinted again in the distance, but the impending storm was inside him. He met gazes with Evan, who stood arms folded, face angry and red. It was apparent he and Wyatt had already had words. Sawyer hung his hat, shrugging out of his duster, water dripping to the wooden floor, his clothes still damp from the river.

"How did it go?" Wyatt broke the silence, turned and took a step toward him.

Of course Wyatt was asking about Zane. He glanced from him to Evan and back. "Fine, he actually thought I might whip him or send him back to Mankato. But to tell you the truth, he's not the one who needs an ass whipping."

"You do it anytime you think you're man enough, brother." Evan spat, his eyes dark.

"Shut your mouth for once, Evan." Sawyer raised his voice and gripped his fists tight.

Evan didn't back down. "Any time."

Sawyer slammed across the room, grabbing Evan by the collar with both hands, slinging him toward the chairs. Enough was damn enough. Evan resisted, the two battling for the strongest hold. Sawyer shoved harder, and sent a fist to his brother's jaw. Evan's head popped back, but he righted himself, blood trickling from his mouth.

"Stop it, both of you. Sawyer, no!" Dodge ran in from outside. "Boys, stop this minute."

Sawyer jerked Evan toward him and hit him again across the cheek, cursing at the pain in his knuckles. Thunder shook the jail, and a hard rain begin to pound the roof.

Evan sent a punch across Sawyer's brow, tossing him off balance. He caught himself on the desk and turned back around.

"Stop it Sawyer, this minute. Let go of me." Dodge struggled to free herself from Wyatt, who held her back from the fight.

Sawyer hit Evan again, avoiding the next fist that drove his way. He tackled his brother, and both crashed to the hard wooden floor. Sawyer had the upper hand with Evan face down. He held his forearm to Evan's head, keeping him flat, and it took all he could muster to keep his brother in check. Evan sputtered and struggled to free himself, but to no avail.

Sawyer sucked in his own breath. "Enough damn it." He glanced at his bloody knuckles and lightened the pressure on Evan as he relaxed. It wasn't the first time he and one of his brother's had come to blows and it would likely not be the last, but damn if Evan wasn't big as grizzly and hard to handle. He tried to catch his breath.

Suddenly, Wyatt pulled Sawyer off Evan who staggered up, facing them both, wiping blood from his lip, out of breath. "This isn't done."

"Sit Evan!" It was Wyatt who shoved him toward a chair and followed making sure he sat in it.

"What in the hell is the meaning of this?" Dodge

glared at Sawyer and then Evan.

Sawyer ignored her and glanced at his youngest brother. Evan had it coming and had for a while. As sheriff, he couldn't keep order if his own brother was part of the problem. He'd a good mind to whack his brother again for good measure, but Wyatt stepped in front of him.

"He's had enough." Wyatt directed the words to him softly.

Sawyer eyed Evan, choosing his words carefully. "When are you gonna learn Evan, this isn't some dumb assed game you're playing. A man took a bullet today, and you go put on the fight...taking my son with you. *My son!* I should have kicked your ass right there in front of all your men."

"I told...you, if you were...man enough." Evan shouted and stood again.

"Man enough?" Sawyer stomped closer pointing to the door. "Man enough is my son, who knew he did wrong and asked for his punishment. Though I think he's been through plenty the last few months."

Evan only glared at him.

Sawyer fought to calm down, thinking Zane *was* more of a man than his youngest brother. "Marcus Benton was just waiting, and you gave him the opportunity. One man is shot, likely dead, and you allow your men to have an all out brawl at the river. You're lucky we aren't all dead. Holy hell, Evan, you'll never learn. I have spoken to you the last time about this kind of trouble. You lead the men on the ranch. If you can't do that the right way, I'll do it myself."

"*I* run the ranch!" Evan hissed, stepping forward only to have Wyatt stand in his way.

Sawyer never batted an eye. "Then do your job!"

Evan eyed him for a moment and grabbed his hat from the floor and slammed outside the jail. Sawyer waited, saying nothing, the remaining tension in the room scoring through him.

"I suppose I got here just in time. The man who was shot will survive." Dodge spoke softly.

Sawyer ran a hand through his dark hair. *Well at least something positive had happened.*

"Sawyer, Evan is young and still has some growing to do. We all know that." Dodge defended her youngest as usual.

"Yes, and it's damn time." He met gazes with his mother.

Dodge touched his arm. "I'll talk to him, but you can't take the ranch from him."

"He's running out of chances." He shook his head and turned a complete circle, then focused back on his mother. "I'm going to ask this as you are the only one likely to get it done. Benton took Zane's horse and revolver. I suppose the revolver is likely gone, but the horse...he can't do without."

Dodge sighed. "I'll go tomorrow."

"Take Hudson with you. He can take the warrant for Johnson." Sawyer hated involving his mother, but her hold on Marcus Benton was all he had.

"I've got him logged in the books." Wyatt was sitting at the desk and closed the logbook.

Dodge walked closer to Sawyer, taking a deep breath and sighing. "Sawyer, Evan's not like you and Wyatt, finding some kind of connection with the law. He never really found his place until Brett gave him the ranch to manage, even if he was so young. Don't take that from him because it's the only thing he knows your father gave to him though Brett."

He knew it was true. Their father had headed them into law, stayed frustrated with Dawson's lack of interest in that or the ranch, but had allowed Evan to ride with Brett as ranch foreman to learn the ropes from the time he could ride.

Dodge glanced from him to Wyatt. "You'll need to run Evan out of the saloon."

Wyatt got up. "I'll let him toss down a few and see that he heads to the ranch before too long. Good-night Dodge." He kissed his mother and exited the jail.

Dodge turned back to Sawyer, studying him for the moment. "And Zane?"

Sawyer shrugged. "Evan sent him home when the fighting started, but he didn't do as he was told. Benton's men got him. I had to trade off Johnson to get him back, and Benton tossed Zane in the river, hands still tied. Liked to of drowned. And of all things, Zane thought I would punish him by sending him back to Minnesota." Sawyer shrugged, still at a loss where his son was concerned.

Dodge's mouth dropped open in disbelief. "I'll have words with Marcus about trying to kill my grandson, the rotten scoundrel. I'll go help Tess with the injured gentleman tonight and see you in the morning." She touched his hand and smiled. The kind of smile he sometimes needed to know that things would work out. Somehow as meddling and sneaky as she could be, Dodge always found a way to smooth things over.

He glanced at his pocket watch. After eight. The growl in his stomach let him know he'd long missed dinner, the thunder roaring along with it. Never mind, he needed to check on Rose before thinking about any food. He grabbed his hat and sloshed forward in his muddy wet boots. The jail was empty, and Hudson would be on in less than an hour. He made his way across the office to the small storage room and grabbed a new shirt and trousers. He could change at Rose's. He dimmed the lantern on the side table by the door and exited. The streets of Cheyenne were dark, and rain played steady across him as he made his way to her home. The darkening sky glowed bright with lightning heading him on a trot up the stairs. He ducked out of the rain to the porch and kicked out of his wet boots.

The door opened, and in spite of his mood, he smiled. Somehow, just the sight of Rose was his reward for the incredibly hard afternoon.

"Sawyer, I was so worried." She grabbed his hand, tugging him inside and hugging him. "I saved a plate for you. You're barefooted and your clothes are damp." She giggled, backing up a step and surveying him.

"I'm quite a mess from the river." He wiggled his naked toes.

"What on earth?"

He shrugged, walking further inside. How would he go about explaining any of it, though it all still played over and over in his mind?

"Sawyer?"

"It's been a long afternoon." He sat his hat aside, on the small table at the door, adding his dry shirt and trousers. "I should just sleep. I'm..." He didn't finish. What was he? Frustrated? Tired? Hungry? Angry—or all of it? He closed his eyes and rubbed his hands across his face and through his dark hair. He was hungry, wasn't he? "Hungry."

"Come on, give me your shirt while you eat, we can let it dry by the fire." Rose began tugging at the buttons.

Sawyer took over, placing his hands with hers and letting her pull his shirt free. He removed his damp undershirt from over his head, handing it her and sat at the table, knowing it not proper to be shirtless while eating, but she didn't seem to mind. She pushed the covered plate toward him and he began to eat, watching as she hung his shirts on chair backs near the small fireplace hearth. She seemed to make a fuss over him and frankly right now, he needed it. Thunder clapped loud, the storm getting worse, but it only added to his mood.

She sat down across from him. "Pork dumplings. I hear they're your favorite."

He smiled. She'd been talking to Mei Ling again. He stabbed a dumpling, shoving it in his mouth and chewing. "Damn near better than Mei Lings."

She smiled with pride. "And the river?"

He shook his head. "I don't know. Our men were fighting with Benton's. One of Brett's hands took a bullet, but Dodge says he'll live. It never changes with Evan. He should know better."

"You fought with your brother?" She touched his brow. "You're bruised."

He gave her a slow nod. "Evan and I never see things the same. Dodge thinks I am too hard on him, but he needs a swift kick in the pants from time to time. If that weren't enough—" He stopped, pushing his plate away, not even hungry after all.

She waited, eyes showing her concern.

"It was the damndest thing. Evan sent Zane away when the fighting started, but Zane didn't leave as told. Benton's men had him, damn near drown him in the river. It was all I could do to get him to shore, the reason I'm muddy." Why was she so easy to talk to, the words seemed to keep coming? "He knew he was in trouble for not doing as he was told. My own brother can't stand up to face his responsibilities, but Zane stood right there expecting his punishment and thinking I would send him back to Mankato."

"Sawyer, you didn't whip him?" Rose let her mouth drop open.

"No." Sawyer shook his head. He wouldn't do that. Ever.

Rose remained quiet. His mind still whirled around Evan, Zane, and Marcus Benton. He couldn't focus, thinking that Benton had allowed Zane to be tossed in the river still tied. What scared him the most was that if he could have gotten to Marcus Benton, he'd have killed him right there, sheriff or not. He rarely lost control like that.

Rose stood from the table, taking his hand and tugging.

"Rose, tonight's not—"

Rose put her fingers to his lips as he done to her earlier in the day, pulling him to his feet and leading him through the door of her bedroom. Lightning brightened the room and the thunder roared again as heavy rain played across the roof.

He protested. "Rose." Before Rose, he might have found his way to the brothel to take out his frustrations, but this was the woman he planned to marry and somehow it wouldn't be right to do the same thing to her. He wanted to make love to Rose when he had his mind set on her—only her.

Rose kissed his chest and neck, letting her hands explore his torso. His arousal came to life in one second of her heated lips on his skin, but he couldn't. The heavy rain hid the sounds of her breath as she breathed soft against him in between her kisses.

"Come on Rose, I can't…" He sucked in a breath.

When she reached for his trousers, he stopped her hands and she looked up. How could the shy woman he'd known only a short time ago, be bold enough to undress him now?

"Your pants are cold and damp, and I drew a bath a little while ago. You can bathe and put on dry clothes." She continued with the buttons of his trousers and glanced at him as she slowly, tugged them to the floor where he stepped from them and let her lead him by the hand to the tub in the small wash room off her bedroom.

"Rose, this isn't a good idea. I'm frustrated and…tired."

She pushed him gently toward the tub where the water was still steaming. He slid down into the heated water reluctantly, looking back up to her as she grabbed a cloth and bent at the side of the tub. She dipped the cloth in the hot water of the tub, adding lye soap creating suds. Placing the cloth to his chest, she began washing him as he watched her.

"I'm sorry." Her soft hand continued to rub the cloth across his chest and shoulders. She moved in behind him and nudged him to lean forward, pushing the cloth across his shoulders and his back. Damn, it felt good to have someone scrub his back.

"It's all right." He shook his head and leaned back as she finished. She dipped the cloth in the water and squeezing it out over his chest, rinsing him. Roses, she smelled of roses.

"You finish up and come to bed. Only to rest and sleep mind you." She raised an eyebrow.

He could only nod, so fatigued he thought he might well fall asleep in the warm water. "Sounds nice as long as I can hold you all night."

Rose only smiled again and left him to his bath.

In no time, he found himself lying in Rose's bed, his arm wrapped around her as she snuggled in close to him. Her body was so warm and soft the thought of making love to her snuck inside his mind, but there would be time for that later. Right now what he needed was someone to hold and a place to rest, though he wondered if his whirling mind would allow it.

Rose turned on her side to face him and traced his mustache with her fingers, kissing his lips tenderly. "Close your eyes, Sawyer. There's nothing you can do now but rest my sweet sheriff."

She was right and he let go of all that plagued him for the moment, allowing her warm embrace and the light sound of her heartbeat lull him to sleep.

Chapter Twenty-Four

Sawyer sat on the rocks by the river, he and Zane fishing in the pool that collected below the rushing falls. He'd missed spending time with Zane on the ranch, with all that had taken place and with the fact he had stayed in town for a while to be with Rose. The picnic at the river had been her suggestion, and with Wyatt and Hudson on duty, he'd agreed, thinking it had been a while since he'd been fishing. The other thing was that he wanted to explain to Zane that he and Rose would be marrying very soon.

The mention of fishing had been the first smile he'd seen out of Zane since losing his horse. Dodge would in all likelihood get the horse back, but a morning of fishing had taken Zane's mind off things. At the river since long before sunrise, they'd filled a bucket with enough trout to feed the family that evening, and it was probably time he and Rose spent time doing something other than—He shook his head and smiled, glancing at her where she stood near the wagon.

"One more." Zane worked the fish to shore, lifting it and removing the hook. Sawyer dropped his current thoughts and pulled his own hook from the water. Sirius, ran along to chase after the fish, growling and barking as Zane held it out of his reach.

"That's a nice one." Sawyer watched as Zane

tossed the fish in the bucket and nodded to the rock beside him. "Come, sit for a minute."

Zane plopped down on the rock beside him and tossed his newly baited hook back in the water.

"I want to talk about Rose." Sawyer tried to remember what he'd rehearsed, but now with the moment on him he couldn't find the same words.

Zane glanced at him and then back to the rushing blue water.

"I know you've wondered about...Rose and I." This was harder than he thought.

Zane only shrugged.

"I've, uh, asked Rose to...become my wife." He sucked in a breath, waiting for Zane's reaction, but Zane paid more attention to his line in the water. It was important to him that Zane would accept Rose. Not as a mother, but at least as his wife and as someone who would care for him perhaps as much as his own mother had.

"We wanted to tell you, before telling the family." Sawyer continued. "I don't want anything to change for you and me. Neither does Rose."

Zane nodded, tugging on his line.

"The ranch is your home, and you and I will still keep doing things together like today. You, Rose, and I will be...a family." Sawyer pulled his line from the water, liking the sound of what had just come out of his mouth. While he'd always thought about a family of his own, he'd never have guessed the one right before him.

Zane finally spoke, his like gray eyes bright and his lip curling into a slight smile. "I never thought I would have a family again."

"Rose insists you play your violin at the wedding,"

Sawyer added on a lighter note, having talked with Rose in depth about what she might like in the way of a ceremony.

"Sure. Will Rose move to the ranch?" Zane asked glancing at him.

Sawyer cocked an eyebrow toward him. "Once we are wed."

"Good...she's fun." Zane's smile was genuine this time.

"She's fun?" Somehow that wasn't what he'd expected from Zane, though it was good.

Zane scooted closer on the rock to adjust where his line was lying in the water. "She plays games and laughs a lot. She makes you happy...she's fun."

"Well, I suppose that's a congratulations?" He ruffled Zane's hair, thinking it strange his son had noticed how happy Rose did make him.

"Yep." Zane jumped up to pull in another fish, Sirius barking wildly.

"I hope you men are hungry." Rose carried the basket of lunch items and set it on the rock they were sitting on. She handed Zane one of the sandwiches.

He took it with a nod and tossed a piece of the bread to Sirius, who greedily chomped it down in a gulp.

"He's growing so fast." Rose handed a sandwich to Sawyer and held his gaze for a moment.

Zane scolded the dog for trying to chew his boot, laughing as the fat puppy rolled away with his tender kick. "He's a brat."

"He's the only dog in the history of the McCade household to get to stay inside," Sawyer chided and bit into his lunch, chewing heartily.

"So your father told you our plans?" Rose asked glancing from Sawyer to Zane.

"I can play my violin at the wedding." Zane continued chewing and kicking around with the puppy.

"It's important to us that you are happy too." She held her sandwich but hadn't taken the first bite yet.

"It's all right by me." He grabbed the pup and carried him off to fish again.

"He seems fine, glad you'll be living at the ranch. He thinks you're fun." Sawyer chuckled scooting closer to her as she sat.

"And what do you think?" Her light eyebrows lifted in question.

Sawyer moved closer stealing a kiss. "Well, I can think of a bit of fun to have with you, but we have too much company for that."

"You'll just have to wait," she whispered with a giggle.

"Nope…" He smiled. "In fact, tonight after we tell everyone our plans, I have a surprise for you."

"That sounds like trouble brewing, Sheriff." Rose touched a slender hand to his cheek

"You have no idea." He kissed her again, passionate and soft, just wanting to feel the tenderness of her full lips. Sandwich forgotten.

"Perhaps we should head back early." Her voice was suggestive.

"Zane…wanna head back?" He was all for hurrying things along, and they had more than enough fish. He shoved another bite of his sandwich in his mouth and gulped it down.

Zane pulled his line from the river just as gunfire ricocheted off the rocks beside Rose. Rock and dust shattered across them. Rose shrieked, and Sawyer shoved her to the ground, pulling his revolver, shooting at the rider who remained hidden in the tree line across the shallow river.

Zane ducked for cover, grabbing Sirius who was growling and barking madly to be freed.

"Watch yourself Sheriff McCade." The voice came from the rider, whose face remained nothing but a darkened shadow.

"Stay here," Sawyer yelled at Rose and held a hand up to keep Zane where he was behind a patch of bushes.

"Sawyer…no," Rose cried trying to stop him.

He ignored her, making his way across the shallow river, climbing the bank toward the trees, his revolver poised. The rider took off on a gallop, firing at him again. Sawyer ducked and fired several rounds in return, racing further up the steep grade and with a deep guttural laugh, the lone horseman rode off through the trees and disappeared.

Sawyer froze, shaking his head in disbelief. The echo of the laughter cut him just as if a bullet had ripped through his body. He struggled to suck in a breath, gripping the handle of the revolver with all his might. *Holy hell, but the day had finally come!*

Fifteen years he'd waited. He'd only been seventeen, but he'd made eye contact with the man who took his father's life, and he'd never forgotten the haunting laughter as that man had ridden away. And now he'd heard the laughter once again. His body shook, not from fear, but from rage. Justice would be his. *Son of a bitch.* Glancing once more where the rider was long gone, he turned back, not wanting to alarm Zane or Rose any further.

Zane lowered the rifle as he returned back across the river. For a moment he thought to scold his son, but saw he'd only been protecting Rose. "Are you hurt?" He turned to her.

"No. Sawyer, who was it?" She brushed the dirt and rock from her dress as he helped her stand.

"Whoever it was knows you. He headed toward Mr. Benton's ranch didn't he?" Zane's shock was evident, his eyes wide with wonder.

"Marcus Benton?" Rose questioned, her mouth dropping open,

"It's not Benton," Sawyer reassured. He handed the basket of lunch items to Zane, who led the way to the wagon, still carrying the rifle and glancing over her shoulder. He didn't know who the man was by name, but it wasn't Benton.

"We could track him," Zane offered.

"No." He put Zane off, not needing a visit to Benton's ranch for any proof. He hadn't a doubt that Marcus Benton was somehow behind his father's death back then, and now the man who had pulled the trigger had returned—just as he'd always known he would. His father had always said as much, *Evil will return to check its damage and that's when you take evil down.*

"Let's just head back." He nodded to the wagon watching Zane jump on the back with the pup. The boy still held a rigid grip on the rifle. He climbed up on the buckboard, after helping Rose inside, his heart pounding a steady beat throughout his chest. Damn it to hell, but he could taste the revenge and had to will his body and mind to settle. He needed a moment to think clearly and some thought to put it all together. That the rider had gone the direction he had meant the only place he could be heading was Marcus Benton's ranch. If he'd been alone and had Colonel, he'd be in chase after the man this very minute.

Rose whispered, "I suppose I'll always be looking behind me, thinking Wes will find me. What if he sent that man, the bullet was aimed at me."

"Rose, it wasn't him. This one isn't about you."

"But…how do you know?" She leaned into him, taking a grip to his arm with her shaking hands.

He reassured her, knowing he needed to change the subject to regain his own composure. For the moment, it hadn't even crossed his mind that her fear wasn't related to his own. "That man wasn't Stadiar. He knew me—" *And I knew him.* "Besides, we have an announcement to make." He smiled not wanting Rose to lose the excitement of telling the family they would marry soon.

"Sawyer, you're shaking." Rose took a good look at him and held to him tighter as he took the wagon toward the ranch.

"When it was just me, there wasn't much to worry about, but thinking of you or Zane being hurt—" Fifteen years. He'd heard that same laughter in his dreams many times, and he'd hidden the truth from his family far too long. And now things had come full circle. There could only be one reason his father's murderer had returned—and now, as he'd vowed, he would bring down that man and Marcus Benton right along with him.

****

"Benton's behind it, regardless who the rider was. Dodge got Zane's horse and revolver back, but I think we need to do some investigating," Wyatt spouted his impatience as the family sat to Sunday evening dinner.

Sawyer glanced at his brother, setting his coffee aside. "We'll find out soon enough. If he wanted me dead, I would be." That he knew the rider wasn't something he could share—yet. They all thought the man who killed John McCade was dead—all except Brett, who had been with him when his father died. But until he knew more, he couldn't say anything to Brett either.

"He's got to be the same rider Brett and I saw, a few days ago." It surprised Sawyer that Evan spoke up, given he hadn't said a word to him since their fight after the river. That was how it was being brothers. Fists one day and back to brothers the next.

Brett sat stoic at the head of the table opposite him, moving his food around on his plate, but he hadn't eaten. While he was a quiet man by nature, he seemed lost in his own thoughts. Was there something Brett knew that he wasn't adding? Maybe he had recognized the rider as well.

"I've got some leads, but in the mean time, Zane and Rose are to be here on the ranch from now on." Sawyer eyed Zane, who nodded. Rose was quick to do the same. Well at least she hadn't insisted on returning to town, and that alone let him know how frightened she had been.

Wyatt shoved his empty plate aside and rested his elbows on the table. "You seen anything of this man Dawson?"

Dawson looked up from a map he was studying, folding it into one fist. "Nope, been riding back trails, nothing but a few Cheyenne along the way."

"I'll put one of the hands watching the house."

Evan leaned back in his chair, pushing away from the table

"Dodge you don't need to leave the ranch on your own either," Sawyer warned. "Leastwise until we know what he is up to."

Dodge glanced at Brett and back to him. "Well, I hardly go anywhere without at least one set of eyes on me these days, if not two."

"You had no business out there." Brett's charged tone caused Dodge to jerk her glance back in his direction.

"My grandson needed his horse. Reason enough." She raised her inquisitive eyebrows turning back at Sawyer.

Sawyer had to concentrate to focus and plan what was best for the family, but this night wasn't supposed to be about anything more than the news he and Rose now shared. He could deal with the likes of finding the rider's whereabouts tomorrow. "To change the subject..." He glanced around the table and settled his gaze on Rose. "Rose has a bit of news to share."

Rose's face glowed bright pink, but her smile was bright and sure. "Well, Sawyer...has asked me to...become his wife."

Dodge gave him an *I told you so* look of satisfaction. "That's what news I've been expecting for some time."

"She was a lot of trouble when she first got here. I couldn't let her win, so in order to tame her, I have to marry her." He glanced at Rose again and watched her posture.

"You will never tame me Sawyer McCade. I'm from the city, remember?" She beamed with pride.

349

"You've just bought yourself more trouble than he is worth." Wyatt grinned at Rose and leaned to shake Sawyer's hand in congratulations.

Sawyer only shook his head. His brother's would milk this one for all it was worth no doubts. His life would certainly never be the same with Rose, but he didn't want to imagine another day of his life without her.

Evan spoke to Rose, offering a semblance of a smile to his brother. "I know what he was thinking, but did you really think about this?"

Rose only smiled, beaming actually, and he enjoyed watching her glow if nothing else. This was her time. Her happiness scored through that slight place in his heart that no one had ever filled—or ever would.

"Congratulations, Sawyer. Rose." Dawson added from across the table, tucking the map back into the front of his leather shirt.

"Dodge I thought perhaps you and Mei Ling could help me plan for a small wedding here on the ranch." Rose squeezed his hand as she spoke.

He glanced down at her hand in his. Slight and fragile but with strength and heart. How could he have been so stupid in the beginning? He should have swept her right of that train and right to marriage. He smiled at her studying. If she knew what he had in mind for tonight, she'd know to run and fast. He stifled his chuckle and watched her enjoy herself.

Dodge smiled. "Of course. I've waited an eternity for planning one of my boys to wed, but I am afraid small is not an option. We are going to have the biggest wedding Cheyenne has ever seen."

"Now you are in trouble." Wyatt glanced at

Sawyer.

"On that note, *Mother*." Sawyer caught her full attention. "I got a nice long wire from Max Ferguson explaining a few things."

Dodge met his gaze and waited. She was all too aware that he was talking about the fact that Max had sent Rose to hide as a proposed mail-order-bride. Not the bride that Dodge had ordered for him. He should have locked her up at the time, but maybe she should get off for good behavior this time. He allowed a grin to slip.

"I am very good at what I do, am I not?" Dodge glowed as well as Rose.

Sawyer pulled the telegram from his pocket and handed it to Rose. "He also sent some information for you."

Rose opened the note and slowly read, her eyes glistening. "My father's accounts have been restored, and the horses are being brought here by a Mr. Samuel Hagen and Muriel sends her love. She's expecting." She leaned to hug Sawyer and drew the note to her chest to embrace it.

Her excitement solved a lot of her issues. It was true that Max had gotten her nothing of a marriage annulled and most of her father's shipping accounts now remained intact. And even though it mattered little to him, their marriage meant all her father's restored assets would once again be her own, including the horses she obviously adored. Max had also assured him of her safety due to Wes Stadiar being detained for theft and fraud, some of which were not even related to Rose's father.

"Samuel had the horses?" Dawson was suddenly

interested.

Sawyer nodded. Rose had agreed that he could share her story, as she wanted no more secrets between them or his family. His gut tightened at the secret he'd held too long from them all. The laughter echoed through his mind again, cold and rigid.

"Shadow came from Mr. Hagen." Zane eyes brightened, as the boy shoveled in another mouthful of dinner.

Rose wiped her eyes with her linen napkin. "Can they live here in Wyoming? I mean they have only ever known New York and the heat and winters here."

"I'll personally see to their care," Evan offered, "They'll do fine. Arabians fare well in any climate."

"Cake on porch. I tell you arrange bride best, Sawyer." Mei Ling joined them carrying a large frosted cake and leading the way outside.

"Get your violin." Sawyer made the request of Zane as he took Rose's hand assisting her to stand and following her.

Mei Ling began plating slices of cake and handing them off. Rose took hers and turned to him, taking a small bite. He could watch her all night, though thoughts in the back of his mind remained unsettled. He could hear the laughter ringing in his head, but his job right now was to make sure Rose had the kind of night she deserved. He could see to things tomorrow when he'd had a bit more time to put all the pieces together and do some investigating alone.

Rose glanced his way and sauntered over, setting her cake aside and leaning into him as they listened to Zane play his violin. He pulled her closer, wrapping his arms around her from behind. Somehow touching her calmed the storm that wanted to explode within him.

He kissed the top of her head. "Happy?"

"Yes." She pressed into him and he inhaled deeply. Her hair smelled of the sweet flowery soap she bathed with and her warm body pressed against his own kept him focused.

Dodge made her way over. "Sawyer McCade, you've been holding out on me, but at least you've gotten Rose back to the ranch for good. Rose, your room is still as you left it, though you will not be scolded for staying with Sawyer if you wish."

Rose's cheeks flushed. "I…it wouldn't be proper, until we are married."

"You have my blessing either way. Welcome to our family." Dodge hugged her again and turned to go inside.

"Dodge must surely know of us." Rose hid her face in his chest as she turned.

"Well, no sneaking in my room at night. I have a reputation to think about." Sawyer chuckled. "But if you insist on your old room, I know the way up from outside."

"Oh, you are so very bad Sawyer McCade." Rose giggled.

"Come on, I have something to show you." Sawyer took her by the hand, leaving the party behind them. He led her to the barn where he quickly saddled Colonel. Mounting up he held out his arm, pulling her up to ride behind him. "Hang on."

"What about the rider, it could be dangerous?" Rose asked hugging tightly around his middle.

"We're not going that direction." He took Colonel to a canter, west off the ranch, the sky darkening before them. He was glad for the full moon, which lit the way across the higher grasses of the prairie, but he was most grateful for her arms that she held wrapped around his middle, clinging tight.

"How far are we going?" Rose raised her voice against the wind.

"A little ways." He slowed Colonel after they had ridden a while longer. He had wanted to bring her here, his private place where he'd always come to think. He dismounted and assisted her down at the shore of a small stream.

"This is really beautiful." Rose admired, in spite of the darkness setting in around them.

Sawyer grabbed her hand, tugging Colonel behind him. "This is one of my favorite places." He stopped before a large pool of shallow water and tied off Colonel. "The water is usually warm in summer. I ride out for a swim sometimes. Gives me time to think. I wanted you to see it."

"And what do you see?" She whispered, gazing intently into his eyes, drawing closer to him.

He wrapped his arms around her. "My future wife, who I am about to lie across the rocks and make love to." He kissed her, delving inside her lips and tasting the sweetness of her.

"But we're outside." Rose pulled from the kiss as she surveyed around them.

"There's no one for miles." He trotted back to Colonel and took down his bedroll. Returning, he grabbed her hand and helped her up the ledge of rocks and laid the bedroll down, untying it and allowing it to fall open. He gestured for her to sit.

"You must have brought all your girls here?" She

sat and gazed up at him.

"Nope. Just some pushy, independent New York girl who carries a derringer." He sat beside her, pushing back the intrusion of the day that tried to return.

"Just me? Really?" She raised her voice an octave and batted her eyes.

He shrugged but held her gaze. "I brought you here to make love to you again, but I also want to make sure becoming my wife is what you really want. You left a lot behind in New York, and being a sheriff's wife can be a challenge as you have already seen. I just want you to be sure."

She thought on things and touched his cheek. "My reasons for being here were so uncertain, but my reasons for staying are more than sure, Sawyer. A life here, a real life, with you. Not about money and stocks and people of prestige. I always hated being spoiled and pampered. I like the woman you allow me to be. The woman I am when I am with you."

"There's a might problem though. I plan to spoil and pamper you as much as you'll let me." Sawyer hadn't any reservations that she was all he ever needed.

"I have a feeling I will allow it." She melted as Sawyer pulled her to rest against his chest.

"I know today frightened you, but I've got some leads that even Wyatt doesn't know about. I'll get to the bottom of it soon enough." He could still hear the laughter echoing in his mind. Tonight was for Rose, but tomorrow fifteen years of waiting would begin his bringing down the wrath of God to the renegade who'd killed his father.

"I suppose I worry Wes will return at some point and…what if he does?"

There was every possibility her ex-husband might one day find her, but when he did it would be the last day the man drew a breath. "Max mentioned he has been detained. You're safe Rose, as long as I'm here."

"I know." She hugged herself closer. "I've haven't felt like I belong anywhere for a very long time, but with you—I love you Sawyer."

Sawyer brushed her cheek with a kiss. "So much beauty, I'm afraid I may never discover it all."

She shivered as he traced his hand down her neck and shoulders. "Are you cold?"

"I don't shiver from cold, but from your touch."

Sawyer took his time unbuttoning her blouse, making each button a journey. She watched him intently, her light blue eyes glistening. He slid it from her arms and reached for her chemise, slowing manipulating the tiny pearled buttons with his thick fumbling fingers. Exposing her breasts, he dipped his head kissing and nipping at her already pert nipples. When she shivered, he sucked harder eliciting a moan from her. *Damn near perfection.*

She reached for his vest, attacking the buttons and pulling his shirt free of his pants, helping him pull both over his head. He smiled at her boldness in exploring his chest, the strain in his trousers punishing as she found his nipples with her tongue. Her bold display set him on fire, but he had something better in mind. Pushing her back to the bedroll, he helped her scoot out of her skirt and undergarments, leaving her naked on his bedroll. He was scorching, hard as a rock, but he'd see her pleasured first and he'd been thinking about that all day.

Rose sighed, running her hands in his hair, curling

her fingers into the thickness and holding him to her breasts. Sawyer obliged, using his thumb along one nipple and his heated lips against the other.

"So good." Her whisper was his encouragement.

He sucked harder, pulling her nipple deep inside his mouth and her chest bowed off the rocks as he pinched the other tightly.

"Lord, Sawyer…" She exhaled, her fingers fisting in his hair.

Sawyer switched to the other nipple, this time nipping enough for her to suck in a slight breath. He glided his hand down her belly and into the sweet slick heat of her center. So wet. He moaned when she did and sank two fingers inside her depths. Rose writhed on the bedroll, legs quivering.

He began scooting down her body, fevering hard kisses and nips along her tender skin. Rose parted her legs for him and he groaned in agony at the display of her pink satin folds. He parted her and lowered his head, tracing his tongue along her gently.

"Sawyer?" Rose spoke his name in a whisper, but let her legs fall further apart.

He grinned. He hadn't done this to her before, and her willingness surprised him. This woman would be something else when they'd had more time together. He tossed her legs over his shoulders giving her no reprieve from his demanding tongue. She tensed and began to move her hips with the motion of his mouth, her thighs tense and her breath short. Sawyer rasped against her time and again over the course of moments that remained uncounted.

"Ohhhh." It was the slightest sound that escaped her after a time and she threw her head back, pulling his hair in so tight a grip he thought about yelping, save moving his mouth from her as she rode out the pleasure.

She collapsed moments later, her legs falling away from his shoulders.

Sawyer climbed back up her body thinking that alone, had been worth the trip to the river. She was so responsive to his touch. It had taken very little for her to learn to allow her body to be pleasured. He watched her come back to earth, knowing he'd spend until his dying day finding new ways to please her. Hell, he'd be in her bed again later this night if she would allow it.

"It's something, watching you." He brushed strands of hair away from her perspiring face. *Damn beautiful as he'd ever seen in all his lifetime.*

"Muriel told me of this, but I wasn't sure what to do." She stroked his cheek.

"We'll learn together." He kicked out of his boots and pushed his trousers past his knees, juggling out of them. He lay back down beside her on the bedroll and caressed her breasts, letting her catch her breath. He took her hand, brought it to his lips, and kissed her fingers, pulling her to lie on top of him and then urging her to sit along his thighs.

Rose tensed slightly as he pressed himself into her, tugging her down to take all of him. She closed her eyes, and he groaned as the slick warm heat of her enveloped him. She held her hands to his chest for balance.

"Are you all right?" He touched her face, with one hand. She shuddered a rapid breath and a slight smile but continued the motion he'd set on her own, with his hands along her hips.

Sawyer leaned back against the bedroll, knowing beauty was measured only by her and he'd never seen anything more lovely. He reached up to pull the pins from her hair letting it fall across her shoulders and breasts. He could have watched her all night.

She opened her eyes, meeting his gaze as he traced his hands up her thighs, and the fingers of one hand continued to her center. Searching, he found her and she gasped, increasing her pace. He wanted to chuckle, the slick heat of her gripping him, taking him near to the edge of release. He raised himself again and took her mouth for himself, pumping into her with earnest. "My Rose. Mine." He spoke the muffled words in between his heated kisses.

Rose closed her eyes, biting her lip, her body gripping him so tightly he thought he might simply explode. "Yours...Sawyer," she whispered, stretching forward against his fingers, seeking his touch.

"Mine..." He gave a tender squeeze to the nub he'd been teasing, and she clamped down tight on him, gripped her hands into his hair, her body letting go with spasms that milked him, her whispered sigh's filling his ears.

Sawyer thrust upward to fill her again and again, his own climax bursting from him in spurts of heated bliss that nearly sucked the life right out of him. He continued until she fell against his chest. And he held her, kissing away the sweat that trickled from her neck, still buried deep inside her.

"I fear, I can't marry you, Sawyer. If I lie in your bed every night, I may simply die of pleasure." She clung to him as if her life depended on it.

Sawyer rolled her to her back, chuckling as he felt

much the same. "I'll let you have an evening off every now and then." He kissed her once more.

Rose pulled from the kiss, eyeing him with intensity. "I'm glad it was you Sawyer, who…showed me love like this."

Sawyer held her gaze with his own. "I'm going to show you all the love I can, Rose, each and every day." He slowly stood and lifting her into his arms. He kissed her as she placed her arms around his neck and as he walked into the cool water carrying her with him. Holding her there, he bathed her tenderly and then took her back to the bedroll where they lay together until they dried. She dozed for a little while, curled into his side and covered with his shirt and all he did was watch her. Making love to her shook him to the core of his being, but loving her—well, he'd damn well lost his heart. It was done, passed through his body and into hers…where she would hold it forever.

Chapter Twenty-Five

Sawyer rode closer to the back of the house and kissed Rose on the brow to wake her. "Hey, we're home. I'll let you down here." She'd fallen asleep against him after only a short time of riding toward the ranch. He had ridden slower than normal on the return from the river so he could hold her longer, cradling her across his lap on Colonel.

"I'm sorry." She startled to alertness, glancing around them.

"It's all right. Take the back stairs." He kissed her forehead and let her down to the ground at the back stairs. Entering through the kitchen meant she wouldn't need to explain where she had been, though it was likely no one would be concerned anyway considering the hour. She would be too tired for him to visit later tonight, but the thought was enticing. He chuckled as he watched her stagger to the house drowsily.

He circled Colonel back, rounding the corner of the house. He'd be a married man soon enough. It seemed strange but comfortable. While he'd been all too sure he'd never get past Catherine, Rose somehow filled his long empty heart with the piece of a missing puzzle. For the first time in a long time, he was content. Settled. He urged Colonel ahead on a slow canter turning toward the barn.

The blast sounded only a second before pain ripped

though his shoulder. Sawyer fell from Colonel hitting the ground, the searing pain taking what breath the impact hadn't. The smell of gunpowder filled the night, and he was confused for a moment. He fought for air and balance, trying to make sense of what had just happened. He couldn't move to get himself up, the pain scorching. He'd been shot, and in the distance a horse galloped off into the night. He tried to sit up but couldn't find his way, dizzy and confused.

Then in the moonlight, he caught a glimpse of the man's face, and heard the hearty guttural laugh that went with it. *Son of a bitch!* He tried to pull himself up again, but fell back, unable to even groan. He tried to grab his revolver, but somehow he couldn't find it. He fell back again, the bones in his shoulder grinding loudly and the warmth of coppery smelling blood saturating his shirt.

"Sawyer!" Evan slammed out onto the porch, followed by Wyatt, who jumped the railing, running toward him.

"Sawyer? It's all right, I got ya." Wyatt pulled him to sitting as he struggled to breathe normally.

"Son of...a...bitch." Sawyer growled. He couldn't take a deep breath as pain scored through him like fire. He was going to pass out. Hell, he was going to die.

"Did you see anyone?" Wyatt scanned the darkness across the ranch.

Sawyer couldn't hold himself up, "only...one." He knew who it was...damn it, he knew. He'd been a fool to think that the attack early that afternoon was only a warning. He should have taken it as a threat. Nausea plagued him, causing him to retch. He coughed and groaned at the searing pain in his shoulder as he gagged.

Evan ran across the porch as Zane exited the front door, his puppy barking at the commotion. He pushed Zane back. "Get your ass back inside." Evan cocked the rifle he carried and jumped from the porch, running to where Wyatt held Sawyer.

Zane stayed on the porch. "Pa!"

Dodge pushed past him to the stairs. "Oh my God! Sawyer!"

"Come on brother, let's get you inside. I got you." Wyatt pulled him up with Evan's assistance. Sawyer tried to help but couldn't hold his own weight. His legs felt heavy, and he couldn't breathe. The world began to blur. He should've known better. *Damn it, he hurt.*

"Get him to his room." Dodge held to his shirt, taking an intense look at his eyes. He could barely focus, but the fear was evident on her face.

Sawyer winced through the pain as his brothers got him up the stairs. He couldn't focus, blood pouring down the front of his shirt and dripping to the porch.

"Sawyer!" Rose held her hand to her mouth in shock, following as his brothers carried him toward his room inside the house.

"Rose?" He couldn't see her.

"Get the doc," Evan yelled, gripping tighter to heave him into bed with Wyatt's help.

Sawyer closed his eyes to the pain, his ear ringing. He couldn't breathe, and he wasn't sure he wouldn't pass out. His vision blurred, and he couldn't think clearly, but he heard the laughter. Damn it to hell, he heard the bastard's laugh. He knew, after all these years, he finally knew, but... "Rose?"

"I'm here, Sawyer." She took his hand in hers.

"Zane, no," Wyatt yelled, turning to follow Zane who had taken off on a run.

Sawyer glanced around the room, not seeing Zane. "Zane!" Without asking it was apparent what had happened. Zane was taking off to get the doc alone and that wasn't safe. "Go...after...him...damn it!"

"Sawyer, you must lie still." Rose tried to hold him down, but it was Evan who managed it and Dodge who began cutting his shirt away.

"Lay back, brother." Evan's deep voice was tender, but the weight of his brother stopped his fight.

"I need to get the bleeding stopped." Dodge held pressure to the wound with a large cloth, pressing with the weight of her own thin frame.

Sawyer fought the pain and the darkness that threatened to take him. He tried to relax and let Dodge see to him. It was bad. That much he knew, and while he wasn't sure he would make it, he had no intentions of dying until he could settle the score. He fought to stay conscious but gave up the fight. Evan let go and tugged his boots off one at a time.

"My back...ahhh...son of a..." He winced at the pain. He had suffered the pain of broken bones, but his shoulder burned to the point he wanted to scream had he the strength. He closed his eyes, the room beginning to spin, his ears ringing so loudly, he couldn't hear. The pain was so intense, he growled as Dodge pressed harder to stop the bleeding. He could hear the crunch of bone in his shoulder and even worse, felt it.

"This all of bandage...I boil water," Mei Ling shouted in her broken Chinese and disappeared.

Sawyer fought, trying to stay awake. "Ahhhh, damn it!" He glanced at Rose, his eyes blurred with the tears of pain. She was all right. That was all he needed to know for now. She was fine. His Rose. But Zane. He tried to rise again.

Evan pushed him back down, turning away from the wound. "Sawyer lay still...you have to, brother."

Rose placed her hands on both his cheeks to get his attention. "Sawyer, let Dodge help you. Stop fighting. It's all right; it'll be all right. You must lie still."

He focused on Rose's eyes, but the pain was enough to keep him from thinking rational. He heard her sweet voice telling him he would be fine. She was beautiful, wasn't she? She was his Rose, but she had tears. He whispered, "Don't...cry."

Tears spilled down her cheeks crushing his chest further. He gripped her hand in his, unable to let her know her tears would be his undoing. He couldn't get the laughter from his head. He was confused, but he still heard it. He was shot. He should have been on guard. Zane? The family was in danger. Rose?

"I should...never, let...my guard...down. Get the...men on...perimeter." He had to protect the ranch, his family.

"It's done, brother. I heard Wyatt telling the men." Evan had a knee on the bed, still holding him down lightly.

"Get...Brett." Sawyer was still trying to figure it all out. He was confused, but Brett would understand it all, just as he did. "Tell Brett...he...knows...the laugh."

Evan shook his head, glancing at Dodge and back. "Brett knows what?"

"Rose...you aren't...hurt." Sawyer rambled, but she was there. Zane, where had he gone? The laughter echoed in his head confusing his thoughts. Brett knew.

365

Evan? He was losing control, his breath short and his mind wasn't clear.

"No, lie still, please lie still, Sawyer," Rose pleaded with him as she handed Dodge more dressing cloths. The one's Dodge pulled away were saturated in crimson blood. Too much blood.

"Zane?" Sawyer tried to get up again. Zane didn't need to be out alone.

"Wyatt's gone to get him...lie back." Evan fought harder to keep him still.

Sawyer growled in the effort, but then Dodge was talking to him. No, she was yelling at him. "Sawyer...stop it, right now. Be still." His mother's blue eyes were serious and concerned. He let out a breath and relaxed.

"My back...I can't...breathe." His eyes rolled and he let out a sigh, trying to fight the darkness again. Things were closing in tight, but the pain never eased.

"Sawyer...don't close your eyes...stay awake. Look at me. Look at me Sawyer." Rose grabbed his face in both hands, speaking so loud his ringing ears hurt.

He opened his eyes again, her soft touch along his cheek and brow. Tender, so sweet, so damn sweet.

"Don't you dare think of leaving here, Sawyer. I love you so much," Rose scolded, not letting go.

He tried for a chuckle in spite of it all, focusing for a brief second. "I know."

Rose's eyes glistened, and the hint of a smile edged her lips.

"Gotta rest...a...minute." He closed his eyes again, his body shaking, the laughter roaring in his mind, deepening pain.

"Tess will be here soon." Dodge grabbed his wrist, counting in a whisper, using his pocket watch.

Sawyer grimaced and held to Rose's hand, trying once more to focus. She kissed his knuckles.

"Tell Brett...he'll know." Burning pain scored through his shoulder and back. He couldn't breathe and his head spun. He was floating to the fading darkness and fight as he might he was losing ground. He heard the laughter, but as he drifted, he saw his father standing tall and proud before him.

****

Muffled chatter edged through Sawyer's mind, stirring him from slumber. Where was he? What had happened? And he'd seen his father. He had been dreaming and yet, he didn't want to wake. Being with his father again brought a peace, taking away the confusion and the pain which now pulled him to consciousness. He struggled to open his eyes. The dream and his father were gone. He'd been shot and Zane—.

"Zane?" Sawyer called for his son.

"Lie still, son." Dodge held him as Tess worked above him.

"Zane?" He focused on Dodge but then saw Zane at the door as he scanned the room. The boy should never have taken off on a horse alone with all that was happening.

Zane came closer, shoving his hands in his pockets, shock in his wide gray eyes.

"Don't...ever do...something...like that...again." Sawyer scolded, as Zane's eyes filled with tears. "Damn it...you...aren't...to leave...this ranch."

Zane backed up and shook his head slowly, and ran

from the room.

"Zane! Damn it!" Sawyer winced with Tess' intrusion into his shoulder.

"Sawyer, that boy worships the ground you walk on...you had no call to do that injured or not!" Dodge handed Tess another line of readied suture. "Wyatt."

Wyatt who stood at the foot of the bed glanced from her to Sawyer and took off to see to Zane once again.

Sawyer grimaced. He'd passed out or dozed for what seemed only a moment and then Doc Tess was there. "Ahhhh...he'll get himself...killed. I can't take this...damn it."

Rose held Sawyer's hand tighter, sitting on the right side of the bed with him.

"Dodge. Chloroform." Tess, pulled the dressing back to take a look at the wound once more and dug in with the suture needle.

Sawyer yelped. No chloroform. He couldn't go to sleep again. Not now.

Dodge dampened the cloth with the clear solution.

"No! I need...to stay awake." Sawyer resisted. He had to stay awake. Giving into the darkness again meant he would likely die never knowing it. He'd seen his father only because he'd almost let go and given in to death. But, it wasn't done yet, and he was the one who needed to do it.

Dodge held the cloth in her hand and stepped closer. "Sawyer it's best son, Tess needs to work."

"Evan." Tess never glanced up from where her fingers were deep into his wound once more. The sting of the needle sent jolts of pain through to his back. *Holy hell.*

"We gotta do it, Sawyer. The doc can work and you won't hurt." Evan's voice was soft as he leaned past Rose, taking a strong hold of Sawyer's good arm.

Rose lost her grip but moved to keep her weight on his legs as he tried to resist.

"Just…get the bullet out." Sawyer pulled away as Evan grabbed him, placing the cloth over his mouth and nose. He held his breath but went numb anyway. He shook his head trying to free the cloth that Evan held steady, but he lacked strength. Damn it, he would kick Evan's ass yet again—if he lived.

"Easy brother…easy." Evan coaxed holding him tight as his thoughts blurred and he grasped one last glance at Rose, the darkness sucking him down.

****

Rose sat back in her place, next to Sawyer, picking up his limp hand again.

"He'll probably kick my ass for that." Evan backed up, washing his hands in the nearby basin just as Dodge had.

"It had to be done." Dodge stood above Tess inspecting her work and gripping Sawyer's limp wrist, counting.

Rose glanced at Sawyer, his eyes closed and his breathing shallow. He looked peaceful, though blood stained his chest and neck, covering much of the upper bed linens. He couldn't die, but there was so much blood and while it was all she could do to look, his shoulder lay wide open from the bullet. She fought more tears, wiping her eyes quickly. No, she wouldn't cry, she would do what she needed to do to help. She studied his face, so handsome with his neatly trimmed beard, squared jaw and high cheekbones. She wasn't sure at what point their relationship had changed. Perhaps she'd arrived to Cheyenne already loving him. He'd put up such a fuss and she'd been so determined to succeed without him, that it had driven them apart in a way or perhaps brought them to the realization they needed to be together. Especially after her capture by the outlaws. And now. He couldn't die, not like this, but the worried glances between Dodge and Tess told the story. Things weren't good. Tears filled her eyes and spilled down her cheeks in spite of her will. There was nothing more she could do. *Oh, please God, merciful Jesus, don't take him now.*

Evan left the room abruptly and could be heard retching on the porch. Dodge turned back to her. "Evan never handles things like this well. Rose, perhaps you should wait outside too?"

She glanced up, wiping her tears quickly. "No, I am fine. I want to be with him."

Dodge gave her a nod and threaded a needle, handing it off to Tess. She reached for Sawyer's wrist once more and held the watch up. "One-hundred sixty and twenty-eight."

Tess held out her blood-drenched hand as Dodge laid the threaded needle there. "Dodge, are you all right?" Tess continued to stitch, having only glanced at her briefly.

"You should know by now, I'm use to this." Dodge went back to counting, but Rose, like Tess, could tell she was in as much shock as they all were.

Rose touched a dark strand of Sawyer's hair that fell across his pillow. How could this have happened when he had been so sure there was no further danger? Who was it that seemed to want him dead? None of it made any sense to her.

"He's lost a lot of blood." Tess continued to work her hands inside Sawyer's wound, blotting blood and tossing aside the cloth.

Dodge turned immediately, as Dawson bolted into the room followed by Wyatt and Evan, who stayed at the door.

"Who did this?" Dawson's serious blue eyes scanned across Sawyer.

"Sawyer was at the river with Rose and Zane earlier today and a rider, probably from Benton's ranch fired at them in warning. I think the same man returned tonight." Wyatt explained, exchanging glances with Tess.

"Benton's gotta be stopped, this just goes on and on." Dawson charged, folding his arms.

"The bones in his shoulder are near shattered and while the bleeding is now less…I'm just not sure, though he is strong." Tess glanced at Rose and then continued to work.

Rose eyed the wound. There did seem to be less blood seeping from the gaping hole. If he did survive, she wondered of the use he would have of his arm and hand, but she watched as Tess worked bone into place and remove large shrapnel's of splintered pieces. Funny she had never been fond of the sight of blood, but being it was Sawyer, her belly had never knotted in response.

Tess, then began to suture the wound closed and after a time, stopped. "That's it, all I can do for now."

"Then he will live?" Rose had remained quiet, praying softly and not sure of wanting Tess' answer.

Tess got up to wash her hands in the basin nearby. "Now, we all wait and pray."

"He's always had a fierce drive in life. He won't give up so easily." Dodge was lost to tears, and Dawson wrapped his arms around her. She muffled her tears in his chest, sniffling, her body shaking.

Rose jerked her gaze to the door with the deafening thud that made her jump.

Evan lay out cold on the floor.

Tess shook her head. "Let him lay there until he comes too. Put a cold rag on his face."

"Go figure. He can birth cows and horses and take care of their wounds, but make it a person and the man falls out cold every time." Wyatt laughed in spite of it all, trotting to drag Evan further into the room by both legs.

"It's just how he is," Dodge explained, pushing from Dawson and grabbing a cool cloth.

Dawson glanced at Tess. "Sawyer?"

"The blood loss is extensive, but stopped for now. I pieced back the bones in his shoulder, but the fall must have broken the ribs along his back. It's hard to tell with his condition and all the swelling." She tucked a loose strand of hair behind her ear and wiped her damp brow with the sleeve of her blood stained blouse.

"Not gonna sit idle on this one. Who the hell is the man he saw?" Dawson glanced at Wyatt.

"I'll be finding out of short." Wyatt hissed running a hand through his short dark hair.

"Enough has been done this day; you boys will wait until we figure things out." Dodge glanced up from the floor by Evan where she remained on her knees, wiping her youngest son's brow.

Wyatt only met her gaze and then nodded, though it didn't go past Rose the intense gaze the brothers gave to each other as Wyatt motioned for Dawson to follow. How on earth would Dodge keep any of her sons from some kind of revenge?

Rose sat down by Sawyer again. He was as pale as she'd ever seen him, and his brow was full of sweat. She took a cloth, wiped his forehead, and kissed his cheek softly whispering. "I love you." If he died, she didn't know what she would do. She'd never loved someone like she loved him. It was a love she hadn't known she was even capable of experiencing.

Zane appeared at the door, leaning against the frame, hands shoved deep in the pocket of his trousers.

"Zane?" Dodge questioned, when he said nothing. She stood, leaving Evan on the floor.

"How is he?" Zane gazed at his father, his sad face solemn.

It was Tess who answered him, her voice tender, shaking her head. "He has lost blood, but I got the bullet out. We must give him some time."

Rose looked on as Zane nodded and dropped his eyes. The poor boy. She got up and walked to him, taking his hand and bringing him to Sawyer's bedside. "You sit by him for a moment."

Zane sat and slowly glanced up to study his father's still form. He'd been shaking, she thought from worry or fright.

Evan growled from the floor, pulling himself to sitting and Rose from her thoughts. "I passed out again? Sawyer?"

"Holding his own. You go drink lots of water and even a few cups of milk, Evan." Tess directed taking another look at Sawyer's dressing.

Dodge grabbed Evan by one arm as he stood but

spoke to Zane. "Zane, you need to rest after your hard ride. Evan you drink." She sent them on their way and turned back into the room.

Rose met her glance, but focused back at Sawyer, taking the chair beside him once more.

"Rose, you should rest. I'll wake you if there is any change." Dodge tried, touching her shoulder.

"I can't leave him." Rose shook her head, clinging hard to Sawyer's hand, praying silently once more.

Dodge lifted one of the blankets from the bed and wrapped it around her shoulders, hugging her in an embrace of hope she thought.

"We should have known to stay here with what happened today," Rose whispered. "I was afraid, but he said we'd be fine. What kind of man does this to another and why?" She was at a loss but there were no answers. Every ounce of her body wanted to scream at the injustice and if Sawyer died, she had no doubts that she would die right alongside him.

Chapter Twenty-Six

Sawyer urged his horse faster, trying to catch up to his father. John McCade was leading the group of men further west to show them some of the Great Plains. He knew he was dreaming, as his father slowed his horse and turned with his bright smile and like gray eyes. He coaxed his horse along, but something wanted to wake him. There was deep seated pain, but he wanted the dream. He wanted his father again.

John McCade sat his mount, tall and proud. Loud thunder echoed across the prairie. There was thunder and pain, but no rain. He was dreaming, as it hadn't rained when his father died. Riding with his father, he sensed the danger. Thunder was the gunfire that sounded. His dream darkened, and his father fell in slow motion over and over again never hitting the earth. He hit the reins, but the horse wouldn't catch up and the path seemed longer—farther—darker.

He was out of breath, and there was pain coursing through his back, but he caught his father and they were falling. The impact of the ground shook them both with thunder, deep through his body. Brett fell to his knees beside them and Sawyer pleading for his help. John McCade would die, blood pouring from mid chest and Sawyer holding him, begging for his father's will to live.

He pounded his fists to keep his father awake. He

pounded his fists to the pain and thunder that rocked through him. It all came full circle as he cried out, to keep his father with him. Sawyer clung to him and glaring at the lone horseman in the distance, he made eye contact with the man who fired at him and laughed as the burning bullet tore through his shoulder in an explosion of heat.

His dream faded and he lost his father, but he had solved the mystery. He couldn't breathe, the pain was deep, but he had to find Brett. Brett would know. He had been there too. The face of the lightning laughed at the gunfire with a deep guttural hiss, and he saw the man's eyes as the bullet scorched him again and again. And then he was falling from his horse into the darkness, seeing the scarred face of the man he couldn't name.

He gulped a small breath of air and tried to swallow across his scorched throat. He hurt so deeply, but he couldn't let anyone know he was awake, and he'd been shot. He remembered the fall and moaned, unable to move. He had to get help. He was going to bleed to death like his father, if no one found him. It was cold where he was and the thunder hurt him as much as the laughter. He had to wake up. He had to get the man, he knew…after all these years—he knew.

"Sawyer?"

Rose called his name. He tried to speak, though no words escaped him. He struggled to open his eyes, his body shaking. He had to tell them. He had to tell Brett. Damn his shoulder and back, he couldn't even breathe. He was cold in the rain, and things were foggy. He could hear the thunder and see the man laughing.

Rose was calling to him and Dodge was speaking,

but he couldn't get his voice to work or his eyes to open. Now he remembered he had been shot, his father was gone, and the man still laughed inside his head. His parched voice was choking him and his head was spinning. He forced his eyes to open, to the blurred room. Thunder rumbled outside, jarring the house, which seemed to shake right through his injuries. His eyes filled with tears, the pain unbearable.

Tess leaned over him, lifting his eyelids to take a look. "Sawyer, you're all right. I got the bullet. You are home in your own bed...you are safe. He's probably confused given the chloroform."

He tried to get up, but all he could move was his right hand, which Rose held in between both her hands. He couldn't see, but he knew without a doubt it was her touch. He had to tell them, he needed Brett. He had to get up and stop the man. His father...he had to avenge his father. After all these years he could finally do something about it. It would finally all be answered, his whole life as a lawman given some kind of justice.

"No, Sawyer, you can't get up." Rose tenderly nudged him back down, but he fought still.

"No you'll, bleed again." It was Wyatt who held him still with little effort, when he finally did open his eyes.

He struggled to speak in a parched whisper. "Brett." He had to make them see. Brett would know. Brett had been there when John McCade died, and he'd seen the man and heard the laughter—he would know.

"Brett's not here. Rest brother." Wyatt held a hand to him, but lessened his touch.

"I'm so...cold. Get Brett." Sawyer shivered hard. He still couldn't focus, like he'd been on a drunk for days. Chloroform made a man crazy and that he knew from experience.

"Sawyer, Brett's not here. What does Brett know?" Wyatt raised a questioning brow.

Rose let go of his hand and pulled another blanket across him.

He let out a loud growl of pain and struggled not to lose consciousness, his eyes rolling back and air leaving his lungs roughly. He closed his eyes, and tears streamed down the sides of his cheeks. He batted his eyes open once more.

"Sawyer, I can get you something for pain." Tess grabbed a syringe and upturned a glass vial filling it.

Sawyer didn't want something for the pain. Brett....he needed to tell Brett. "Get...Brett!" He yelled and grimaced, gritting his teeth.

Rose took his hand once more, and he pulled her closer. "Brett...knows." He said no more, the pain too much. He shook hard, chilled and spent, fighting to keep himself conscious. He couldn't hold himself where he was and let go, giving in and closing his eyes, not having the energy to keep them open.

Wyatt's heavy boots stomp across the floor. "Why is he calling for Brett?"

"He's confused Wyatt, the chloroform...he needs time," Tess answered.

"No. He knows what he's asking. Sawyer's never been a good drunk. He doesn't hallucinate well, never did. Something's wrong. I'm going for Brett." Wyatt stomped from the room.

Sawyer squeezed Rose's hand that had never let him go. Damn the pain drummed through him to the point he thought he might've wished for death, save the feel of her soft clinging fingers. She was probably frightened out of her mind, and he could do nothing save hang on.

"Rose, you need to rest. You're exhausted and you can't help him if we have to care for you. You've not slept in the entire three days." Dodge's voice filled the room.

Sawyer forced his eyes open, trying to focus on Rose. Had it been three days? He raised his hand until he cupped her cheek, wiping away the damp tears. "Rest..." He dropped his hand and closed his eyes again. Rose let go as Dodge pulled her away. It was quiet then, all but the echoing laughter he still couldn't fight. The laughter hissed, and the thunder from the storm outside shook the house, pounding his shoulder.

"Sawyer, I have something for the pain. Just a small stick." Tess jabbed the needle in his thigh before he could stop her.

He grimaced. "I need to stay awake...I have to talk to Brett."

"Rest Sawyer," Tess whispered wiping a cool cloth across his brow.

He gave up. He couldn't fight the things running through his head anymore than he could get out of the bed to take care of business at hand. His mind drifted with the medication, the thunder confused with the wind and the rain and—the terrible hissing laughter.

****

Rose burst into tears, as she followed Dodge into the kitchen. Dodge sat her in a chair and brought a cool cloth to her face. Sawyer had been in so much pain and he'd been confused, but at least he'd woken. It had been all she could do not to cry as she held his hand, but now her pent up emotions surfaced. She sucked in a few breaths, taking the cold cloth and cleaning her face and wiping her eyes. Dodge ladled stew in bowls for each of them and plopped into the chair beside her, shoving a steaming bowl her way.

"Try to eat a little. We can't care for him if we don't take care of ourselves, but it's very good he's conscious and talking." Dodge's reassurance wasn't convincing. The older woman's eyes were as tired as her own.

"He was in so much pain." Rose managed a small bite, but bile filled her throat.

Dodge nodded, dipping her spoon into the stew. "Tess will give him morphine. It's best he sleeps."

"I'm sorry to be so much trouble." She didn't mean for Dodge to have to care for her as well.

"It's all right, but after you eat a bit more, you are going to lie down. Mei Ling is making a pallet on the floor in Sawyer's room, but you will lie down and rest." Dodge scolded, taking her hand for a small squeeze.

She nodded. As long as she could be near him that would be enough. "Dodge, why?" She asked, not knowing any answers, having replayed parts of his being shot over and over in her mind. Sawyer was a sheriff, and she'd already known how dangerous things could be, but she had never expected this.

Dodge shook her head, having no words.

Rose tried for another bite but then put her spoon down. The rain continued to course across the house, thunder crashing down on the prairie. Somehow the storm added to her worry. She'd always feared storms, and now it was all coming at once.

"I love him so much. He wanted to show me his

favorite spot at the river. We should never have gone…it's my fault." Tears welled in her eyes again.

"It isn't your fault. You are the best thing that has ever happened to Sawyer," Dodge reassured her.

Rose wiped the tears that fell down her cheeks. Dodge meant well, but had he not wanted the time at the river with her this might never have happened. She willed no more tears to come, wanting to be as brave as his mother.

Zane entered the kitchen, glancing from one to the other and taking the seat across from them without a sound.

"Your father woke for a bit, which is a good sign." Dodge patted his hand and went to the stove for another bowl of stew setting it before him. "Eat sweetie, where've you been."

Zane picked up the spoon and shoved it in the bowl but hesitated. "I know Sawyer doesn't pray, but I've been out on the porch watching the storm and praying for him anyway."

Dodge studied him. "You're wrong, you know. Sawyer prays. He isn't a church going man, none of my sons are, but they all believe in God—well, all but Dawson who used to. I'm afraid his Indian infatuations have left him in awe of their ways, but I think your prayers are a good thing, and I think your father would be happy to have them right now." Dodge beamed at him with a smile.

Rose jumped as Wyatt and Brett came through the back door into the kitchen, shaking off the rain.

Wyatt slung his hat aside to the hearth by the fire and pulled off his duster, laying it over one of the chairs. Brett did the same, glancing at Dodge

"Both of you sit for some hot coffee and stew. You'll catch your death in this." Dodge went to the stove once more.

Brett leaned to kiss her cheek. "This storm'll likely go on for another day or two. How is he?"

"He could hardly speak or get a breath in, but he called for you more than once, insisting that Wyatt get you here. He kept saying *Brett knows*." Dodge shrugged and sat two more bowls of heaping hot stew on the table, but Wyatt disappeared

"Might be the medicines. He's been worried about the cattle coming across the river." Brett sipped the coffee she handed to him and leaned on the counter.

Dawson came into the kitchen, rubbing his eyes, shirtless, wearing only his buckskin trousers." Did you rest? You were awake all night again." Dodge pushed one of the bowls on the table toward him.

"Some. Wyatt said the tracks matched?" Dawson eyed Brett.

"He's at Benton's or at least whoever he is has been there, given the damp mud around the barns which didn't let the prints wash." Brett's deep voice filled the room.

"Benton's always kept questionable counterparts." Dawson brushed his long brown hair from his face tucking it behind his ear, the length of a braided in feather tucked as well.

Dodge turned to them both, slamming her fists to her narrow hips. "You were out there, that's where you, Wyatt, and Evan rode off to yesterday, isn't it? You can't tell one thing about tracks in this rain."

"Tracks matched what Sawyer saw at the river. He's there. There's a notch in the horse's left hoof, proof enough." Brett answered, setting his cup aside.

"None of you had any business out there. You know Marcus would whip you and leave you for dead if he caught you on his property. He's been looking for an excuse for years." Dodge shook her head and glared at Brett.

"I sure as hell wish he'd try." Brett's serious green eyes narrowed on her as he followed Wyatt.

****

Rose lie on a pallet beside Sawyer's bed, where she had been for several hours. She had slept on and off, but the fatigue and worry only added to her restlessness. It was dark outside now, another day passing with Sawyer sleeping through it, but at least he was alive. She climbed to her feet, glancing at him and taking the chair across from Wyatt who sat with his elbows along his knees and his chin across his folded knuckles.

"His pulse is better," Tess whispered and sat again, picking up her book.

Wyatt broke in when the silence seemed too long, staring at his brother as he spoke. "When we were young, maybe under twelve, Sawyer was always figuring things out and teaching us. He was never one of those big brothers that picked fights. Once, I got mad and told him he didn't know everything and ran off. I was gonna ride to Chicago and work with the railroad. I rode my horse for days and realized in no time I was lost." He chuckled softly, and Rose had to smile, taking Sawyer's lifeless hand in hers.

"Your father didn't come for you?" Tess folded her book closed and glanced at him.

"He didn't know, but Sawyer followed me. Found me lost and hungry. He got a fire started, fed us both,

383

and headed us home. Neither Father nor Dodge said a thing. I assumed I'd be punished. That went on for days, and Sawyer never said a word to them. Just made sure I got home. He always protected us. Still does." He shook his head. "I should've been there."

Rose glanced at him. "You couldn't have known, but perhaps we all should have heeded the warning of the shots at the river."

Wyatt glanced at her and back at his brother. "That wasn't a warning. Likely he missed earlier at the river on what he really wanted to do."

That idea sent a bolt of cold electricity through Rose's center. Perhaps the man had been shooting at her, but Sawyer had insisted it wasn't Wes. "I asked Dodge why. With Mr. Benton so angry over the cattle and river, is it him?" Rose had thought on it for a time now. All the hours of watching Sawyer, she had tried to piece together parts of the story, but there were so many things she was unsure about.

Wyatt raised his brows and studied her for a long moment. "Marcus Benton didn't pull the trigger, but he's connected to the one that did this. Tracks matched, just gotta figure out who the hell he is and God help him when I do."

Tess shook her head. "Wyatt, you can't take on the world alone."

"I'm not alone in this fight." He shook his head and gripped his fists tight.

Rose held Wyatt's gaze. Even in the dimmed room, his deep blue eyes were fierce. He resembled Sawyer, only a hint taller, but with the same dark locks he kept short and neat. His jaw line was the same, but he favored Dodge through the eyes and facial features if she had to say.

"Leastwise I've got some checking to do on a few things. Got a couple of leads, but I figure Sawyer wanting to talk to Brett, might clear up some of it." He leaned back in his chair and glanced at Tess.

"Getting yourself hurt in the process will only worsen things, Wyatt, and you know better than to go to Benton's ranch. He's an evil man, best left alone." Tess scolded, her eyes glistening.

He folded his arms, cutting his eyes her direction. "And he's reined over the people of this town just a little too long, and I won't sit idle and let him have this done to my brother."

"I'm not asking you to do that, but getting yourself killed in the process—" Tess gave up, clearly frustrated.

Rose turned back to Sawyer. Wyatt's comments were justified, though Tess was right. Adding more violence to the situation seemed futile to her. She needed to figure the story as that was what she was best at, and right now she only had a few bits and pieces to put together. With what Wyatt, Dodge, and even Sawyer had told her, it was looking as Wyatt had said that Marcus Benton might very well be behind it all. And if he was, how did they stop a man of such wealth and power? It was the same in New York. Evil doers had their money and men behind them and cared little for the havoc they left in their wake. She trembled.

"I've got work to do." Wyatt stood and made a hasty exit, not looking back at either of them or his brother.

"Some things never change." Tess took a deep breath and let it out.

Rose glanced at her, folding her other hand around

the current one already holding tightly to Sawyer. "You and Wyatt?" She hadn't questioned Tess about their relationship until now, though she knew there was an interest on both their parts.

Tess glanced at Sawyer and back to her. "There is no Wyatt and I. At least not until he can rein in that temper. He's so full of fight. I don't know. There are just so many things…"

Rose gave her a nod, catching a hint of disappointment in Tess that she hadn't noticed before. She gazed back at Sawyer. "The men here in Cheyenne. So rough sometimes it can be frightening."

"I've been here for years now, and it's less and less civilized. Wyatt and Sawyer both believe Mr. Benton to have killed their father long ago, or at least that he is behind it. I don't know who shot Sawyer but Wyatt, Evan, nor Brett have ever stepped foot on Benton's land. He is really a terrible man. Call me if you need me, I'll be resting for a bit in the parlor."

Rose sighed heavily when she was gone. She glanced back at Sawyer, his breathing slow and steady. Tess had changed his dressing earlier, and while the wound was closed, the scars would plague his body the rest of his life. Never mind that. He was alive, but that he had lived, he would be just as his brother, set on revenge for himself and still for the father he'd lost.

Dodge had told her that Colonel McCade had been gunned down years ago, and that man had been killed. Something didn't add up somewhere. And if Marcus Benton were involved, then why had the McCade brothers waited to see to it that the man paid for his crimes, long before now. That was how men like Sawyer were, not killers but seeing that justice was done. Sawyer had mentioned Mr. Benton's mile long list of crimes and had warned her to stay away from him and she had, but none of this made any sense.

She touched Sawyer's brow. He was warm to touch, but she pulled the blankets higher on him anyway, tucking them. She then placed a tender kiss to his forehead and sat back down, placing her hand across his once more. It was very early morning and with everyone else sleeping, she relished the quiet with just she and Sawyer.

"Mrs. Sawyer Zane McCade." It was only a whisper and all she had ever wanted in her life. A place where she meant something other than money and where she was safe from the past she had left behind. He had to get better, though Tess still said it would take time to know for sure. He couldn't die, not after all they had shared and all they might share in a lifetime. She thought of the river, where he'd made love to her out in the open, so attentive to her every need, lifting her to that place where they mingled as one, her body yielding in a passion so strong all she could do was cling to him.

And now, it might be months before they could marry, if at all. The tears began, the silent ones that had haunted her since before escaping New York. And if Sawyer didn't recover what would become of her? Well, she wasn't going to go back to New York, not now or ever and she simply wasn't going to let Sawyer die—Not now or ever.

****

Sawyer batted his eyes open, unbearable pain coursing through his shoulder and back. He remembered where he was, from the pain alone. He'd dreamed restlessly over and over about the man who shot him, the same man who had shot and killed his father.

"Ahhh." He hurt so bad it took his breath and moving only deepened the hurt.

"Easy." Wyatt hovered over him, his brother's blurry face concerned.

Rose jumped up from the chair beside him and took his hand. "Sawyer. It's all right."

Sawyer blinked his eyes trying his best to focus on her. "Bring...Zane." He closed his eyes to the spinning nausea, but he was thinking more clearly. He'd hurt Zane and needed to talk to him.

Wyatt slipped from the room, returning a moment later with Zane and Dodge.

Zane stopped before his bed. Sawyer watched him shove his hands in his pockets and try for a smile.

"I'm...sorry son." It had worried him, and he needed to make things right after yelling so horribly at his son.

Zane shook his head. "It's fine, Pa."

"But just...the same, keep your...hind end...on the ranch." Sawyer let a chuckle slip and held his breath to the searing pain in his shoulder.

"I'll get some morphine, Sawyer." Dodge turned to the dresser.

Sawyer grimaced, tugging his hand from Rose's to grasp to his shoulder. "No! Wyatt? I need to...talk to Brett?"

His brother narrowed his gaze. "He's here."

Sawyer waited to catch his breath. "I want...to talk...to him...alone."

"I'll send Brett in." Dodge put the medication back on the dresser and nodded for Rose and Zane to follow, both doing so quietly.

Sawyer struggled for a breath, meeting Wyatt's gaze and without a doubt his brother was asking questions best left unsaid. Wyatt studied him for a moment and then turned to go. He closed his eyes to the pain, fighting the nausea.

"Sawyer?" Brett touched his arm lightly.

Sawyer glanced around the room, and back to Brett, gathering what strength he could muster. "Do...you remember, when...Father died?" he started but winced in pain. "Ahhh! Damn it."

Brett gripped his arm. "Take it easy. Go slow."

Sawyer blinked hard and took another shallow breath. "Father was riding...and then the gunshot sounded. I got to...him."

Brett leaned closer.

"He knew he'd die." Sawyer growled through his pain again. "The man that shot him rode...off and all he did was laugh. I've never forgotten...how he sounded."

Brett cursed. "And the son of a bitch is here isn't he? I didn't say anything, but he's the same man Evan and I saw a few days ago, nosing around the river. His face is scarred now, a burn or the like, but I couldn't place him."

"It's him...he must have connections...with Benton. I saw him and I...heard his laugh when he got me. But Benton...knew Father had died, before it was common news." His strength ebbed, and he closed his eyes and then opened them once more.

Brett spoke, "Benton knew it but never admitted a thing."

"He knew. Harrison Colbert somehow...knew Benton had father killed, and Harrison died for it.

Benton knows he'll hang for it if I can prove it."
Sawyer closed his eyes, fighting the pain and his
emotions.

"I'll slit the bastard's throat myself." Brett
narrowed his eyes, gripping his fists.

"The family…still thinks we killed…the man that
got father—we can't tell them. I knew…he'd come
back one day and I've waited…so damn long." Sawyer
tried to adjust in bed and yelped, giving up.

"You rest. That rat's ass bastard. I should have
known, well the son of a bitch will pay now." Brett
stood. "Don't you worry none about that."

"No, he's mine. I'll…do…it." Sawyer growled in
anger, hurting like hell. He felt close to passing out and
he knew he couldn't get up, but he'd damn well try.

Brett shook his head, pushing him back to the bed.
"You're in no condition. You lie still, do your healing.
I'll see what I can find out, and you'll have your
revenge come hell or high water, and I'll watch you
have it."

Sawyer nodded and glanced at the doorway long
after Brett was gone. He could hear his father's last
words. *Justice, not revenge,* but it was revenge he
wanted. He had waited fifteen years for this, and now
he wasn't in any condition to do what needed to be
done. But he'd see to it soon. Very, very soon.

****

Sawyer woke to find Rose sitting beside him. It
looked to be morning by the bright sunlight beaming
across the room. His shoulder pained in spite of the
effects of the medication Doc Tess had stuck into his
leg earlier, and he wasn't too sure he wanted much
more of that. He felt like a pin cushion at a quilting

circle. No he felt like he'd been run down by a herd of wild horses. The medicine made him crazy, with dreams that haunted him, and he'd woken during the night confused only to have Rose touch his hand and whisper all was well.

"Sawyer?" She touched his cheek.

He tried for a smile, but the effort was too much. His back throbbed in a searing pain that didn't let up and was worse with a deep breath. Maybe it would have been better if he had died. This was hell all except for her touch.

"My back...I need to move." He tried but only grimaced.

"Wait, Dawson can help. I can't move you by myself." Rose scampered from the room and returned with Zane and Dawson in only a matter of moments.

"You want up higher brother?" Dawson walked to the bed, his blue eyes fatigued. He'd likely been just like the rest of the family in worry over him.

Sawyer groaned, trying again.

"Wait, let us move you. Zane get on his good side." Dawson pulled the blankets back. "Rose, come on this side. Don't tense, let us move you...it's gonna hurt, but relax."

"One, two, three." All pulled on him together. Sawyer gritted his teeth tossing his head back and crying out with a loud yell. When they settled him, he still had yet to take a breath his body called for. He gulped, and tears fell down the sides of his cheeks.

"Relax, it's all right now. Shhhh." Rose's voice was so sweet. She soothed a hand across his brow.

"Never...hurt...like this." He finally spoke, not wanting to scare her or Zane more than he probably already had.

"You're going to hurt brother. The bullet tore your upper chest and shoulder apart. It was all the doc could do to patch up the bleeding. She thinks the fall from Colonel, broke several ribs in your back." Dawson covered him again.

"How many days...has it been?" He was losing track of time. Confusion plagued him each time he woke, or maybe it was the medicine. He knew it had been several days more, but he didn't know how many. Frankly, he had thought he would die the first few hours.

"Seven." Rose sat on the bed gently.

"Wyatt's in town?" Dawson folded his arms and stepped closer. "Hudson's had his hands full with Benton's men lingering in the saloon. And Evan left for the cattle yesterday."

Sawyer's eyes widened. "They should have waited...you have to get the men in town to watch the river."

Dawson touched his leg, giving a slight squeeze. "Calm down. Wyatt has a team together. Everyone will stand up against Benton and his men. The other ranch's are on board too. Everyone's tired of it."

Sawyer shook his head. "You'll have to keep Wyatt grounded and Evan from mouthing off. You tell Wyatt to make...Brett take the...oath." The men assisting Wyatt would be deputized, and Brett was a man of honor. If he took the oath, he'd do right by the law. But it was highly unlikely Brett would want the oath, given Marcus Benton was on the other side of the river.

"I'll try, but Brett's a mind of his own. Wyatt can

do this brother, but I'll be there," Dawson reassured him.

Sawyer asked, "The doc?"

"She had rounds to check on others. She'll be back." Rose rubbed his arm.

"I can't take this pain." He hated how the medication confused his dreams, but right now he needed it.

"Tess left the laudanum for you." She got up, but Dawson motioned her to stay and went for Dodge instead.

"Is there anything more I can do, Sawyer?" Rose sat beside him on the bed once more.

Sawyer squeezed his eyes closed and shook his head. Nothing helped much at all, save touching her...he must have survived for that alone. He lifted his hand and touched her cheek.

"Pa...I've been brushing Colonel every day. He was pretty startled when...it happened, but I think he's fine. I've been helping Evan with the chores." Zane beamed with pride and the hint of a smile.

"Good, son. I was worried about him." Sawyer tried for his own smile and watched as Zane turned to go.

"He's really been keeping busy. He is so tired at night, he goes to bed right after dinner." Rose leaned into his hand, holding it in place.

"I know...I scared him."

"He's sat by your bed a lot of hours and slept on the floor sometimes, just to be near you." Her eyes were puffy. She'd likely had more tears or no sleep, probably both.

"He's a good...boy." Sawyer closed his eyes again.

"I know…you were here too."

"Sawyer, I've got the pain medication." Dodge lifted the covers, and he opened his eyes, bracing as she injected his hip. "I'll be back in a little while to check on you."

Sawyer nodded and glanced at Rose again.

"The medicine should help soon." She put his hand back on the bed.

"It just makes me dream…restless. But I'm tired…so damn tired." He closed his eyes but ran his hand across the bed in search of hers, which she placed in his. He held on until the medication started taking effect. "So damn beautiful and if I had died, I would have died…that night a happy man." His speech slurred but his lips curled slightly.

"Sawyer McCade. If you would have died, I would have simply died with you," she whispered and kissed his hand and held onto him until the medication had taken him once more.

Chapter Twenty-Seven

Sawyer lay propped on pillows, agitated at the news. He could move a little better, but he hadn't the ability to do what he needed to do.

"Wyatt sent a rider. They're on schedule, maybe around noon." Dawson leaned hard on the post at the foot of the bed and folded his arms. "I've told Zane to go to the herds east and put the fear of Indian torture on him to stay there. I threatened Dodge just the same."

"You...make sure." Sawyer didn't want to have to worry about Zane or for that matter Dodge when the cattle crossed the river. His pulse raced in thinking on the day's events. "I should be there."

"No, you can't possibly do that," Rose scolded. Setting aside the shirt she had been mending.

He grimaced trying to adjust in bed. "Keep an eye on Evan. Wyatt's good under pressure, but Evan..."

"I got it brother...Rose you keep him right here, not that you could make it onto a horse anyway," Dawson teased, holding his gaze.

Sawyer eyed his brother, no words needed. Dawson was smart, as his father had once reminded him. He thought things out, always wise beyond his years. Wyatt was the tough one, quick tempered, who feared no one, and Evan was the one who reacted without a thought to the consequences. And he was their brother, always determined as the first born to be their protector. "Watch...yourself."

Dawson grabbed Sawyer's big toe through the blanket. "I plan to." He turned to go after a quick nod to Rose.

"This really is frightening. Isn't there a better way? Dodge and Mei Ling are going into town for most of the day. I suppose Dodge is glad to stay busy." Rose picked the shirt up again.

"Don't be fooled. Dodge will show at the river. I should have had Wyatt arrest her for the duration." Sawyer swore under his breath.

"Surely not."

"Dodge doesn't sit idle." Sawyer shook his head, knowing the least of his worries today was Dodge—at least he hoped so. But he didn't doubt for a minute she would make it to the crossing, though in her case, she was probably safer than the rest, given Marcus Benton's fondness for her.

"This feud and you being shot, that strange man on a horse, and Mr. Benton's suspected involvement... Sawyer, there is more, isn't there?" Rose jumped up and placed her hands on the rounded curves of her slender hips waiting.

"There are a lot of things..." He avoided answering in full. Only he and Brett really knew the details, but Brett hadn't gone with the men to bring the cattle in. Word had it he was down with his back. That was to keep Dodge off his trail if he knew anything about it. Brett was out on his own searching for the answers that Sawyer should be finding himself.

"I see you lay here each day thinking hard on it all. Sawyer, I am going to be your wife and..." She paced around the room, slinging her arms and raising her voice. "I did finally tell you about me. I told you my reasons for becoming your mail-order-bride. I didn't hold back, not one thing." She was stomping her feet hard now and he let a smile cross his lips at that bit of feistiness that had returned.

She turned around to face him again. "I told you about my marriage that wasn't a marriage and how bad it seemed that my own husband didn't desire me. Do you know how hard it was to tell you that?" She stopped and glared at him, narrowing her eyes. "I let you know every detail because I love you. I shared it Sawyer, all of it." She moseyed closer to the bed and folded her arms, taping one toe. "And if we are to be married, you must confide in me. I want to be who you confide in."

Sawyer groaned and sat himself up, still leaning on the pillows and protecting his shoulder. Well, she was certainly something to reckon with when angered and he'd rather deal with the likes of Marcus Benton than her when she got into this state. And she was right. So he answered her. "All right."

Rose stopped in her tracks, gazing hard at him. "All right?" She lowered her voice with the question, clearly shocked at his positive response.

"Sit down, but promise you won't do that again." He gave her a smile, shaking his head and letting go of the grin.

She sat on the bed beside him, arms still folded. "I'm sorry, but this whole thing scares me, and I do not understand any of it."

It was time, and he needed to tell her. "The man who shot me has a connection to Benton, but I don't know what that is. I've read all I can find on the

Ashburn brothers and Benton, but I don't know this man's reasons for shooting me."

"I know you have thought Mr. Benton behind things indirectly?" She took his hand, and he relished in the bit of forgiveness.

"He's behind it, but if Marcus Benton wanted me dead, I think he's had plenty of opportunity. What you don't know, neither do my brothers or Dodge is that the man who shot me…also killed my father." Sawyer waited. Even saying it brought it all to the surface. His body was tense and he hurt, but the pain justified his feelings somehow.

"That man was killed. You and Brett saw him killed…" She stopped when he shook his head.

"When father died, the man got away, but Brett and I agreed we didn't need Dodge or my brothers out seeking revenge. It seemed best at the time."

"But how do you know it's him?" she questioned, with a giant shrug of her shoulders, her blue eyes intense with question.

"I got a look at him, but I'll never forget how he laughed after he killed Father. I tried to go after him then, but Brett stopped me. I would have been killed, young and wanting revenge. Hell, I still do." His pulse raced and his pain intensified.

"That's why you and Catherine. She knew one day this would happen."

He nodded. "Maybe. I'm not sure of anything there. I was full of spitfire back then…more like Wyatt, fighting just to fight. She couldn't live with me and wasn't interested in a marriage, but I didn't know about Zane."

Compassion glistened in her eyes, and he thought

for a moment she might have tears, but he continued. "But I've waited fifteen years and I knew one day...the man who shot Father would be back. I saw his eyes that day and he saw mine...and he's here and he almost got me...but I'll see it done!" He hissed in pain, jerking his hand from hers and holding his shoulder.

"Sawyer, you can't do it alone." She moved closer wrapping her arms around him gently.

Sawyer wanted his chance to take the man down, whoever the hell he was. But Rose was holding him so tenderly and her soft smell permeated his mind to the point, if he could have, he'd have simply rolled her beneath him to forget the coming day.

"I don't want my brothers or Dodge to know. Brett knows, and he and I can handle it when the time comes, like we should have done back then." He lay back in frustration, letting her go, his body weary.

"I won't tell them, but this man, even when you are well. You almost died, Sawyer." Tears welled in her eyes. "I wouldn't have survived that."

"I'm not going anywhere," he whispered gazing at her.

"But I know if you could be up, you would be there and I would go out of my mind with worry, just as I will anyway worrying of your brothers." She stood again. "I'm going to be in the kitchen, preparing the evening meal. I know once this is over, everyone will likely be hungry. I'll be back in a bit to help you with bathing."

"One day I'll return the favor." Sawyer offered her a slight smile.

"Sheriff McCade...you have already bathed me in the stream, and I'm afraid it will be some time before you can try that again." Rose lingered at the doorway, with an enticing smile that suggested he hurry his recovery.

"Well, I'll nap and dream of it." He locked gazes with her and then she was gone. He settled back in bed. Hell he couldn't nap with all that was happening without his being there, but he hadn't woken once when she hadn't soothed him through the pain that he thought would eventually kill him. And now the pain was still there, though the deeper part of it was in his consciousness over not being at the river.

****

Wyatt brought his cantering horse to a stop alongside Dawson, who sat his painted horse Viho. Men were gathering around the McCade side of the river, and his brother had been keeping an eye on things. He glanced into the scorching mid-day sun, judging the time and looking on as Brett rode up on a gallop from the direction of his own ranch. The man he'd known most all his life and the man who'd taught he and his brothers the business of running a ranch, stopped his mount beside them with a nod.

"You want credentials?" Dawson spoke to Brett and waited with narrowed brows.

Wyatt thought to chuckle but stifled it. Dawson was well aware Brett wouldn't swear an oath of following any law but his own.

"Nope." Brett spat tobacco away from the wind.

"Sawyer wanted you legal." Wyatt met the hard green eyes of wisdom knowing it was wasted breath.

Brett pulled out his pocket watch, avoiding the question. "About an hour to go."

"Chad Harper was found whipped and left for

dead. You know anything about that? I saw the two of you talking a few days ago, outside Benton's ranch." Wyatt didn't hesitate asking. Harper's body had been dumped along the river's edge.

Brett spat his plug of tobacco to the ground. "You scouting around following me, or were you just taking a look at Benton's?"

"You know what I was doing. Same as you. The man that shot Sawyer is still there. So Harper had information for you?" Wyatt held tighter to still his restless horse. Brett hadn't killed the man, but he knew a mite more than he was telling.

"Yep. Harper was a good man, no doubts that he was whipped by who did it. It's Benton's calling card, the bastard. I paid Harper enough money to get on the damn train this morning, reckon he didn't make it." Brett's face remained stoic as usual.

"He should know better than to work for the likes of Benton, they all should, but what did he tell you?" Dawson pulled his long brown hair back, tying it in a leather band,

"Not what I wanted to hear." Brett changed the subject eyeing the yellow paint on Dawson's biceps. "Wearin' war paint this morning?"

Dawson glanced down at his arms and back up with a grin. "Protection."

"For God's sake, don't wear it home and remind Dodge you worship some god other than the one found at the church in town." Brett pulled his revolver, opened the cylinder, and rolled the loaded barrel.

Wyatt met gazes with his brother, who often wore the colors of war in a fight and that is exactly what this was as far as he was concerned. Right now they could use all the help they could get, and if Dawson brought the issue to the darn Cheyenne gods then he'd have nothing more to say of it.

"You and I both know Dodge doesn't attend church except to keep up with the latest gossip." Dawson shook his head and nodded to Brett.

More of Benton's men rode into the area on the other side of the river, finding cover, but making no secret of their arrival. Wyatt turned his horse to watch as the men found cover, guns poised.

"So we're supposed to think that's all he is sending?" Brett pulled a pouch from his vest pocket and tucked a chaw of tobacco in his jaw.

"Look close at the tree line. They've been there since dawn." Dawson nodded toward the trees in the distance, where a number of Benton's men splayed in and among the thickness.

Wyatt shook his head. Sawyer had warned him about Benton having men in the woods around them.

Brett pulled his scope. "Sneaky bastard, thinks we're stupid."

Wyatt turned, eyeing a horseman coming in from the south, hooves stirring up dust behind his pace. "They're on the way."

It was Billy who rode rapidly toward them and stopped, his horse, circling them. "They're about three miles out." The boy fought to catch his breath.

"All right. You're to ride back to the eastern herds as the men will need help." Wyatt nodded that direction.

"I can help out here if needed," Billy said and while Wyatt noted the pistol strapped to his side, he was far too young for such.

"I need you with the herds, there aren't enough men out there. Go on." He gave the young man a stern glare and with a nod, Billy turned his horse and took it to a slow gallop, doing as told.

"It was all I could do to keep Zane away today. I sent him to the east herds as well." Dawson glanced at Billy and back.

"This ain't no place for either boy. Hell, it isn't a place for any of these men." Brett growled and spat to the ground again.

"You didn't take the oath. Sawyer would advise you to watch yourself." Wyatt warned, but the movement at the top of the ridge caught his attention. "We've got company."

"Well at least the bastard showed, though he's out of shooting range. Coward!" Brett cursed under his breath.

"Our men know not to fire until instructed, but maybe it won't come to that." Wyatt adjusted his boots in the stirrups and tugged on the reins. "Cover this side of the river. I'll meet up with Evan on the far side."

Dawson nodded, blue eyes serious and cold, setting the mood that was already crushing in on him. Wyatt took his horse toward the water, not looking back. This wouldn't be pretty, no matter how it started or ended and without Sawyer it was up to him. The fate of the men from both sides were at his discretion.

He glanced at Benton and entered the water crossing to the other side and taking off on a gallop, only moments later to meet up with the herds his brother was driving. Dust and the smell of animal and earth wafted around him, filling his nostrils with dirt. He tugged the bandana from around his neck across his face. He hated this shit. The dirt and grime and the damn cattle. But what he hated worse was playing sheriff. He wasn't as patient as Sawyer, and would just as soon arrest the lot of them.

He'd had a quick chat with Sawyer, who was fit to be tied, earlier that morning. His brother was moving a bit better and had been out of bed with help, but he was nowhere near well. The slightest effort wore him to a frazzle, but he'd still warned Wyatt to keep things calm and read the order they had received from Washington the very day before.

And he'd had words with Evan weeks ago about following orders and letting him handle the river. His younger brother had given him a reluctant nod and ridden off toward Kansas with the other hands.

And now as Evan, the hands, and the cattle approached the last ridge before the river, his heart thundered in his chest. While he could handle things, he was already on edge and some deep seated part of his confidence wished Sawyer was here. He took a deep breath and urged his horse to a canter further ahead.

He scanned the river behind him and the cattle closing in and turned his horse back again. He met glances with Dawson as he stopped his horse. His brother knew to ready the men. He pulled his bandana away from his face, eyeing Marcus Benton and the two men protecting him.

He pulled a thick paper from his shirt and unfolded it and then shouted as loudly as he could muster. "These cattle will cross by the order of the Federal Marshal's office in Washington." He held up the paper and folded it once again, tucking it inside his shirt.

With that said, Benton's men began to line the

river in the path of the cattle, rifles and pistols raised.

"Marcus Benton...I order you to call your men off!" Wyatt raised his voice, meeting the man's constant glare.

Benton never moved, though the two men beside him raised their rifles.

Dawson rode toward him, crossing the river, which hit the horses' shoulders at mid-river. He ushered the horse up the bank and stopped alongside him, turning the animal to face him.

"He's not budging." Wyatt met his brother's blue eyes and tightened the reins in his hand. He hadn't expected Benton to back down.

"Nope. The men have their orders. Watch yourself." Dawson shrugged.

Wyatt held his ground for another moment, glancing at his brother. "Benton! Call your men off. You men working for Benton's ranch, you will be jailed for murder if anyone is killed!" A few of Benton's men eyed each other nervously, but not a one of them moved. *Son of a bitch!*

"The first man to fire on either side will hang!" At his last word, rapid fire came from across the southern ridge above the river, spreading a spray of bullets across the water as a warning from Benton's side.

Dawson's horse reared on hind legs, and he struggled to steady the animal. "A Gatling gun!"

Wyatt turned his horse. Leave it to Marcus Benton. The man on the wagon with the smoking gun stopped his firing and hazy white smoked mingled with dirt as the cattle neared the river.

Dawson dropped from his spooked horse, gripping the reins to control the frightened animal. "I'm going to

405

circle and come in behind them. He'll calm if I run him."

"Wait Dawson." Wyatt stopped his brother from mounting again.

"What?" Dawson held steady.

"Benton, call it off!" Wyatt dismounted, pulling the long rifle from his saddle

"Or you will be the first to die today!" He cocked the rifle and laid it over his horse's saddle, glancing at his brother. In the same second, the two men mounted on horses beside Benton took aim directly at him, though he had the advantage of the long rifle.

Marcus Benton tipped his dark hat, and Wyatt cursed. "Bastard. You know this long rifle, don't make me use it."

Dawson drew the tomahawk from his horse and tucked it into his belt. "Careful Wyatt, they've got you sighted."

Before any of the men could react further, the Gatling gun went off again in a long shower of random bullets from one side of the river to the other. Men on both sides, ducked for cover in the blinding confusion, smoke filling the air.

Wyatt stopped, eyeing the woman on the wagon at the Gatling gun. "Holy mother of…"

"Dodge!" Dawson finished for him. "She said she was going to town. I should have known better."

There she was for all the men at the river to see, standing in the back of the wagon, aiming randomly, moving the gun about with little control. The man who'd been on the gun earlier was now on the nearby ground, out cold.

Wyatt cursed, eyeing his brother. "Shit! Should

have locked her hind end right up!"

"Too late." Dawson mounted up as did Wyatt.

"I've got her." Wyatt took off in her direction, but before he could get there, Dodge stopped the gun and yelled for all to hear. "Marcus...this is the end of it. The cattle are not stopping. I am not going to sit here while all these men kill each other, and I am not going to watch my sons die. Call off your men, let the cattle through."

Silence plagued the river, though the sounds of cattle echoed in the distance. "Eleanor, how lovely to see you, but this is really no place for a lady," Benton yelled sarcastically.

"I'm not here to beg, Marcus...move your men now," Dodge yelled at the top of her lungs, juggling the aim of the Gatling gun once more.

"Not very becoming of a lady, Eleanor, but then, you haven't been a lady for some time, considering the company you keep," Benton spouted and laughed.

Wyatt watched from his horse as Brett made it to Dodge, taking her from the gun and manning it himself. And then all hell broke loose, men firing from both sides, anxious confused cattle breaking through the water and smoke so thick in the air it was hard to breathe. Wyatt caught sight of Evan leading a stray section of cattle in to tighten the herd.

A hiss of bullets flew passed him as men from both sides continued firing through the haze of dust, smoke, and cattle. Wyatt dismounted and took cover behind his horse once more. Cattle rushed around him, but it was clear Benton's two guards were firing at him directly. He carefully placed the long rifle over his horse's saddle once more and took aim. He fired once and snared one of the men with Marcus Benton. The man fell dead, though Benton never flinched or pulled his own gun.

Wyatt mounted his horse again as Evan rode past him, shouting orders at his men. "Keep them going. Don't stop the herds!"

Wyatt met his brother's glance but turned his horse as Brett rode up alongside him, smoking revolver in the air.

"Dodge is under the wagon." Brett was winded as he'd dismounted and took cover in the small area of trees with Wyatt who followed, tugging his horse along.

"Where's Dawson?" Wyatt shouted. Holy shit but he was better as a bounty hunter, one or a few more men at a time instead of the fiasco before him. How could he fight trying to keep his brothers out of trouble? Suddenly it crossed his mind just how Sawyer must have felt all along. Damn he wished Sawyer was here.

"Not sure." Brett fired again and a man from across the river fell into the muddy water cursing, cattle all around him.

"This is falling apart. Son of a…cover me! Evan!" Wyatt shouted and mounted up once again. Evan rode toward Marcus Benton. Wyatt urged his horse to a gallop keeping sight of his brother. He couldn't get there, fighting to ride his way around straying cattle. He urged his horse faster toward Evan who was in the clear on his own mount and getting ever closer to where Benton remained. Then Benton's man stepped forward, no longer sitting his horse, but taking aim at his brother.

Wyatt was too far for his revolvers to do any good, and the long rifle would take him too long now that it was holstered to the saddle once more. He took his horse to a full run. The firing continued to echo and suddenly Evan fell from his horse.

"Evvvvvaaaaaannnnn!" he yelled, riding hard toward where his brother went down.

Gunfire continued to sound, and a smoky haze covered the river as he raced his horse further, hearing the hiss of bullets spray his direction. And out of nowhere, his horse halted in its tracks and spilled him forward, throwing him in the dirt where he rolled to miss the impact of the animal falling. The horse had taken a bullet to the chest and lay there snorting hard in the dust, cattle all around them. He took a look at the wound and the animal's dilated eyes. "Shit!" He spat the dust he'd eaten to the ground.

He took his revolver and, still on his knees, quickly pulled the bandana from his neck over his head. He placed it over the struggling animal's eye and put the revolver to its temple. He pulled the trigger, the gunshot ending the horse's misery. *Son of a bitch!*

"I never gave you a name…" He stood. It was true, he'd quit naming his horses years ago. He took a deep breath, remembering Evan and squinted in search of his brother. Hiding behind wet cattle, he grabbed the long rifle from the saddle, holding it at his side. As he made his way up river, he saw Evan's horse ahead of him and went that direction, scampering through cattle and spotting his brother on the ground cursing at the top of his lungs.

"Evan!" Wyatt ducked crawling closer, cattle merging around them.

"Get me back on the horse, I can ride…shit!" Evan held a blood covered hand to his thigh, growling in pain as he tried to rise.

"That's not gonna happen." Wyatt pulled back the torn part of Evan's trouser to eye the wound. It was a good one, and he was bleeding heavily. "Give me your belt."

Evan growled again and unbuckled his belt, pulling hard to free it of his trousers.

Wyatt wrapped it around his leg, sending it through the buckle and pulling tightly. He tucked it to keep it in place and grabbed Evan to drag him along to the safety of the trees. The cattle were enough of a barrier to hide them as he struggled to lift his limping brother.

"Holy hell, brother, Mei Ling's gotta stop feeding your ass so much." He dumped Evan along the ground handing him the long rifle.

Evan grimaced, straightening his leg to a better position. He leaned his head against the tree behind him, trying to catch his breath—his eyes closed.

Wyatt smacked his face hard to get his attention. "Oh no you don't…you can't pass out now. I told you to stay with the herds, now this is a real mess…stay alert and keep this gun on Benton!" He shoved the large rifle at his brother.

Wyatt grabbed a random horse, wandering with the herds, nodding at the convenience and took off on a gallop.

It seemed now the gunfire was a mix of random shots, echoing across the water, smoke still filling the air, but the cattle were moving and right now that was enough. He cursed under his breath again and turned the horse back. "Hold the river!"

The men on the McCade side worked into place as the last of the cattle came up the banks, several more hands following. So the cattle were on their way, but

Marcus Benton still held the ridge, and his men were moving in closer. "Son of a bitch!"

Chapter Twenty-Eight

Wyatt remained hidden in the trees watching Marcus Benton from behind. He'd moved quiet and swift to gain the proximity he now held, knowing of all those at the river the man was looking for him. Benton held his revolver at his side having dismounted from his own horse moments ago. The coward stood idle, gazing at the happenings along the river, the man Wyatt had shot lying dead and his remaining side-kick aiming his rifle below.

Wyatt steadied the knife in his left hand. No damn time like the present. He took off on a run, boots swift along the earth. Before Benton knew what hit him, Wyatt had grabbed the man, placing the knife to his throat. "Drop it."

Benton didn't move but after a slight hesitation, let the revolver fall to the ground. It landed with a thud in the high grass.

"Hey…drop your rifle." Wyatt yelled, kicking the revolver behind him, out of reach.

Benton's man turned and met his gaze, lifting the rifle toward him.

"It's a hell of a way to die. One crisp slice, a rapid spray of blood and two minutes." Wyatt pressed the knife harder against Benton's throat, a trickle of blood dripping down the blade to his own hand. He'd a good mind to just do it anyway, the bastard.

Benton's man held stance and eyed his boss.

"Now would be a good time." Wyatt never raised his voice, but held the knife steady.

"Drop it!" Benton's voice was a scratchy whisper, his hands held in the air before him.

Benton's man held steady. "Boss?"

"Do it, he'll kill me," Benton spat.

Damn right he would if there was one wrong move. Wyatt waited, not even allowing a blink. The man dropped his rifle and raised his own hands.

"Call it all off." Wyatt pushed the knife harder against Benton's throat, forcing him to walk forward out into the open. It crossed his mind that one slip and both men would kill him, no doubt with hidden weapons, but he had the upper hand for now.

"Surrender you weapons!" He held his position as the gunfire ceased, Benton signaling his men with simply his own gaze. And with that the last of the herds wandered off toward the southern pastures, only a scattering of hands with them.

"Order all your men to drop their weapons and dismount." Wyatt held his voice steady, thinking his heart raced hard enough to hear it, yet he remained calm and steady. He pulled his revolver and sheathed the large knife in his belt. He should just kill the bastard for good measure if nothing else, though some deep seated part of him could hear his father's voice. *Justice pays the devil, not men.*

Benton hesitated for only a moment. "Dismount and drop your weapons...now! You'll pay for this McCade. Actually, all of you will pay soon enough." Benton gave an evil laugh.

"Keep your mouth shut. This never had to happen

like a lot of things." Wyatt shoved him forward and tied his hands behind his back, doing the same to the man with him.

Men on Benton's side of the river, followed orders and dropped their weapons. Hudson, who'd left town in spite of orders, was below gathering guns and ammunition along with the other deputized men. Evan was on the ground in the distance with Dodge rendering care to his leg.

Brett rode up the steep ridge and dismounted nearby, pacing toward them swift and steady. He never stopped until he planted a right hook across Benton's jaw. Wyatt had to fight to keep himself and Benton upright, the revolver he'd kept on the man still in his grip.

Benton eyed Brett spitting blood to the ground and holding himself steady.

Wyatt grabbed Benton by the shirt, sending a warning to the rage he saw in Brett and pulling the man back a step.

Dawson emerged from the woods on a trot, belting his tomahawk and stopping Brett by grabbing him. "Brett, no!"

"Where's your brother?" Brett shucked away from Dawson's grasp and confronted Benton with a swift shove, knocking him back.

Benton said nothing but kept his evil smirk as Brett waited for an answer. "I know he is back, and I aim to have some answers, right damn now." Brett gave him a swift kick to the knee. Benton yelped as his knee buckled, and he hopped trying to keep his stance.

"I have no brother." Benton regained his footing, narrowing his dark eyes.

"All right then I suppose you would know nothing about Chad Harper found dead?" Brett spat tobacco and cursed under his breath.

Benton's lip curled into a smile. "Some men choose their own fate."

"So I will ask you again, where's your brother?" Brett punched him hard across the left cheek, breaking the skin, blood seeping down his jaw. "Martin Hickman, ring a bell? I know he's here, and he's the one that shot Sawyer, and you know the rest of the story! I'm not asking again!" Brett struck him again, and Benton's head bobbled as he struggled to keep himself up. He spat blood on the ground and staggered.

Wyatt couldn't believe Brett's words and stepped forward, grabbing Marcus Benton by the collar. "You had Sawyer taken down?"

Brett shoved Wyatt out of the way with a growl. "No he didn't do it directly, the son of a bitch. He's too much of a coward for doing his own dirty work." Brett grabbed and shoved his revolver in Benton's face, pulling the man from Wyatt's grasp.

"Start talking!" Brett twisted his collar further.

Benton said nothing, eyes dark.

"All right then. I'll talk you coward." Brett holstered his gun once more and grabbed Benton's shirt with both fists. "He's here, brother or not and Sawyer and I both know him, from way back. You would have us think he is here to avenge the Ashburn brothers. I knew you were a low life from the first day I ever met you, acting all high and mighty, damn state of Wyoming, city of Cheyenne, bottom shelf."

Brett's large body shook as he continued slinging the man back and forth as he yelled. "And you had

Sawyer shot for what? Surely not these damn cattle and not the Ashburns, but to finish what you started over fifteen years ago. John McCade did right by you, and you had him killed for the land you hoped to own, but never will. I was there, and I saw your brother's face. Sawyer was just a boy, who got to watch his father die, you fucking bastard! Admit it!" Brett scowled and punched the man again, Benton's head snapping back.

"What?" Wyatt spun around glaring at Brett.

Dawson shook his head, his gaze catching Benton's. "You did this to Sawyer and...Father?"

Wyatt couldn't believe what he had just heard. They had all long suspected Benton, but it had been years, and no one had gained any proof. How had Brett and Sawyer figured to keep all this from them? Wyatt shook his head, a roar emerging as he tackled Benton to the ground, beating his face repeatedly. "Father trusted you..."

It was Dawson who pulled him away still swinging. Wyatt kept his bloody fists balled trying to focus and figure on the details.

Brett drug Benton to his feet once more, the man barely able to stand. "Where is your brother now?"

Benton said nothing as he stood on legs that would hardly hold him up and of all things, he gave into an evil smile.

"The ranch?" Dawson glanced Wyatt's direction and ran, mounting his horse and racing off that direction.

Wyatt cursed again. How had they not known this day might simply be a trap, and Rose was home with Sawyer alone. "I'll see you in hell before this is over."

Brett grabbed Wyatt and threw him aside. "Get to

the ranch!"

****

Rose spent the morning cooking for the evening meal, worried with no news about the happenings at the river. Surely the cattle had made it across by now. It was past noon, and she'd helped Sawyer bathe and fed him a short time ago, and while he'd been reluctant to sleep, he had finally dozed off. She stirred the pot of beans and pork and lifted it with both hands to set it to the side of the wood burning stove to cool. She could warm it later when it was time to eat. With Mei Ling and Dodge in town, she was proud of having the pot waiting and ready along with several batches of bread, a large bowl of field peas, and two blackberry pies that were now cooling on the table.

When she'd first arrived, it had taken Dodge and Mei Ling and lots of practice for her to handle cooking the amount that happened on the ranch for one evening meal. Now, it seemed easier, and if she kept focused, she no longer burned the bread. She smiled, thinking it was time to check on Sawyer once more.

Entering Sawyer's room, she found he was still sleeping and watched him for a long moment. She loved him so much, and while he still had a long way to go in healing, she was simply grateful he was alive. He was still weak, and he had suffered violent dreams most nights, but he was getting better. He was able to walk with help, but most of the time, he only did so when one of his brothers or Zane could assist him.

She spent a lot of time each day thinking about their wedding and how it would feel to finally be Mrs. Sawyer McCade. He was a beautiful man, so strong he scared her at times, but so gentle she melted into him when he made love to her. She shivered and smiled to herself, looking at him once more. This was love, and for the first time in her life, she knew it for certain. And with her father's horses safe and most of the money returned to her accounts, the marriage to Sawyer would restore them all to her. And even though she had tried to explain the extravagant amount of her assets to Sawyer, he'd told her all that he ever wanted was her alone.

She smiled and turned to head back to the kitchen to finish the meal preparations. Out the window over the sink, she noticed the barn door swinging and Colonel loose outside the corral. She grinned. The clever horse had probably let himself out of his stall, either that or Zane had returned. She wiped her hands, heading outside calling to Colonel who all but ignored her. She moved toward him slow and deliberate, petting along his side and scolding him.

"You silly horse, let's get you back to the corral. I know you miss him, but he'll be well soon. Come on, Colonel. Come on boy." She led him inside the barn and to the side gate to put him out into the corral. "There you go." She watched as he galloped ahead and turned to look at her, ears perked. "He'll be well very soon, boy."

Turning to go inside, she reached the door of the barn, sensing someone there and turned. She screamed as a hand covered her mouth and nose, almost to the point she couldn't breathe. She resisted, unable to free herself, fighting hard to suck in air, thinking the worst. The man was large, but she couldn't see his face. She fought, placing her hands on his trying to pull it away from so she could breathe.

"No sense resisting little lady, you walked right into this trap, and I'm going to need you to accomplish a few things." The man laughed. "Now if you know what's good for you, you will keep real quiet. Understand?"

Rose froze, his hand still covering her mouth. He had such a grip on her arm, it hurt, and she tried to pull his hand away to no avail, but she nodded. Maybe if she cooperated she could free herself.

"I know the sheriff's inside, and I want to know if there is anyone else in the house." He gripped her harder. Rose bit her lower lip to the pain, shaking her head.

The cold steel of a gun poked into the skin of her side. She wanted to scream, but that would bring Sawyer. Oh God. This man would likely kill them both, and Zane was due in soon. At first she had thought it might be Wes, but she figured this man to be the one who had shot Sawyer, and there was only one reason he had returned—to finish what he started. A plague of fear bolted through her. Sawyer was much too weak to fight.

Oh, Lord God, please. The only way she could keep Sawyer safe was to struggle and resist, putting her own life on the line, figuring she would be dead either way. Fear gripped her until she could barely move. Surely she had not endured all that had happened to meet her end with Sawyer, like this. Maybe one of the hands would return soon, or someone would come.

"I'm here alone. Everyone is at the cattle drive." She lied, and struggled again to free herself.

The man gave a hard deep laugh. He shoved her against the barn wall hard enough to knock the breath from her. She clutched her side, struggling to breathe as he held her there with his body and whispered in her ear. "I know the sheriff is inside, and if you lie to me, you'll get yourself killed. How is the sheriff...heard he like to have died?" The man pushed her harder to the wall, gripping her arm enough for her to yelp.

"Shut up!" He squeezed even harder pulling her along outside the barn.

Rose dragged her feet to slow him. If she resisted, she could stall him and maybe one of the hands would return or someone would see and help her. He pulled her hard, dragging her, her feet skirting through the sandy ground, stirring up dust. He outweighed her by far, and she sat down, making it harder for him. If he thought she would allow him to Sawyer so easily, he was sorely mistaken. She dug in her heels.

He cocked the gun and shoved it against her neck and pulled her hair to get her standing again. "Come on little lady, this will be painless for you."

She was reliving the incident at the bank, but this time Sawyer couldn't save her. She had to try and save him. She pulled harder, and the man drew back his hand and slapped her across the face. She fell to her knees, tasting blood, senseless for a moment. She had never been hit by anyone, and the burn stung the side of her face. But before she could clearly think anything further, the man grabbed her wrist and tugged her to her feet.

It appeared he was heading them in the direction of the house. If he went inside, he would kill Sawyer. She resisted, and when she made no progress, she leaned down and bit his dirty hand. It worked, he cursed and let go of her. She ran and got as far as the inside of the barn again, thinking she might get to one of the horses. Before she could open the first stall, the man tackled her, the weight of his body pinning her to the hard earth of the barn. The air left her lungs, and dust encircled them, making her cough.

"Do you have any idea...no, you don't, but you will once I take care of the sheriff. I've not had a woman in some time, and might appreciate one as fancy as you, but you are worth more to me in good condition. Wes has been looking very forward to seeing you again. Seems you have some money and horses that belong to him, and he'd paid me a good price to round you up." He held her tightly and ran a hand to her breast and squeezed. Rose screamed, and he slapped a hand over her mouth and pumped his body against her several times. How did this man who shot Sawyer know anything about Wes? He might violate her, but she would die before she went back with Wes. Oh God, please bring someone to help, but she had screamed and Sawyer...no, she had to fight and against her better judgment, she bit down hard on his hand once more.

The man jerked his hand away and slapped her again, pulling her to her feet, "You'll pay for that later...little lady. I bite too."

For a moment, Rose lost her way, trying to think what to do next. She wobbled on unsteady feet, but gained her footing as he stomped forward. She leaned back dragging her feet with all her weight.

"Feisty huh! No wonder the sheriff's hanging on tight to the likes of you. Well, he'll be dead shortly and you and I will be meeting Wesley in Council Bluffs. We'll finish this bit of business a bit later on. I like myself a woman with a little fight...makes it interesting." He laughed again, and Rose continued to resist. She couldn't let him get to Sawyer even if she lost her own life in the process.

Chapter Twenty-Nine

Sawyer jumped and grabbed his shoulder. Rose's scream came from outside, and he was sure of it, even though he had been dreaming. He struggled to get himself up. It was all he could do to sit on the side of the bed, without help. It took great effort to get that far and then, out of breath he opened the drawer next to the bed. He grabbed his revolver and checked. It was loaded. He reached his trousers and fought to get them on, stifling a yelp at his shoulder, his arm still hanging in the sling. He pulled the right suspender strap over his right shoulder, to keep his trousers up, and struggled to step into his boots quickly, ignoring the pain as he stood.

His shoulder burned with the movement, and his eyes watered as he tried to remain standing. The sling held his arm, but any movement was unbearable, his breath short. He held onto the bedpost, fearing he might pass out, but then made his way to the window to peer outside. He cursed under his breath. "Son of a bitch!"

He'd only heard Martin Hicks name from Brett a few days before, and they had yet to tell his brothers. Now the man had Rose and no one was at the ranch to help them. He sucked in a long breath, ignoring the pain to his ribs.

"Damn it." They'd been foolish not to keep one of the men at the ranch, but it seemed they would need every extra man at the river. No doubt Hicks had come to finish things—him for starters. But now Rose was at risk. He moved quietly to the front door, hanging onto the wall for support. He wouldn't be any good in a fight. Hell, he wasn't even sure he could fire his revolver, he was so weak.

He opened the front door and crept onto the porch, revolver cocked and heavy. His breath was short, and a thin layer of sweat collected along his brow. He blinked hard to clear his mind and got to the stairs, stopping for a moment. He wasn't sure he could even manage them as hard as he was already shaking. He hadn't a choice and took them one at a time, his shoulder jolting as he got to the ground. Stifling a growl, his eyes watering he forged ahead. *Holy Hell!*

Neither Rose nor Hickman had yet to see him as he crept to the side of the house to intercept them. What the hell was the man planning and what in the hell was he to do in his condition?

Gaining his momentum, he turned the corner. There was no point in stalling; his energy was going fast. Rose was digging her feet in the sand, resisting. There would be no playing games now, not like with the Ashburns. "Let her go!"

The same laugh that had haunted him since his father had died carried to him across the short distance. "Well, Sheriff, it looks like you are healing quite nicely. What a shame." Hickman laughed again, and Rose hissed trying to loosen the grip he had of her wrist.

"I said let her go." Sawyer held his revolver toward the man, doing his best to keep it steady. He might not be accurate, but he wouldn't miss. His hand shook, his body trembled, and sweat poured down his naked back.

He didn't know if he could shoot, but seeing Rose once again in jeopardy, he'd sure as hell try.

"Well, now why would I want to do a thing like that? She and I were just getting acquainted. Right pretty little thing, but she's wanted back in New York. Horse thief. Reckon she'll hang? Been paid a pretty price to return her to her husband." Hickman cackled and glanced at Rose. "You should'a stayed away from sending those telegrams back and forth. Wes has a lot of friend in low places." He roared in a guttural laugh once more.

Sawyer met gazes with Rose, and there was blood at the corner of her swollen mouth. *Son of a Bitch.* He knew he might die this very day, but the man before him would pay right now for a lot of years, his father and—Rose.

"Sheriff, it looks like to me you are still a little under the weather. A shaking man doesn't have a steady hand. Miss and this little lady will take the next bullet. What a darn shame that would be." Hickman riled further, kissing Rose on the neck, the gun in her back.

Every ounce of Sawyer's being shook with rage, not pain. "I'm giving you until the count of *three* to let her go."

Hickman eyed him hard. "You're shaking, Sheriff...I can see that from here."

"One." Sawyer spoke loud and clear and wiggled the fingers of the hand in the sling. Rose knew about the counting of fingers, and he hoped she played along once more.

The man pulled Rose in front of him to shield his body, laughing. "John McCade thought he was invincible, running the war and his men as if he were God himself, all high and mighty. Well, he found out different." Hickman snarled and tugged Rose closer. "He might have run the war, but he didn't run the West, not like he wanted. That's right, I know you were there. I remember you trying to ride after me...well, here I am. After all this time, here I am big Sheriff Sawyer McCade." Hickman stirred the pot. It was all Sawyer could do not too shoot him dead, but he'd risk Rose further if he didn't maintain control.

"Two." Sawyer didn't back down, glancing at Rose. He didn't have the strength to fight more than what he was about to do.

"John McCade thought he could settle the West with law, not quite the man he boasted. War hero they called him, well, he was a liar, and a cheat." Hickman laughed once more.

Sawyer steadied his hand as best he could. "My father was a better man than you or your brother will ever be." He fought to steady his hand, fatigue plaguing him but the fear of losing Rose keeping him on his feet. "That's right. I know who you are, Marcus Benton's half brother, I've waited fifteen years for this day." Sawyer took a step closer. Rose could read him, she had before.

Hickman eyed him and laughed. "You're shaking, Sheriff, and you'll likely miss." He rubbed his gun along Rose's temple.

Sawyer braced the revolver in his hand tightly, raised it a bit further to steady it, and moved the fingers of his left hand three times. On the third time, the world began to move in slow motion. *Three.*

Rose pulled away from Hickman and Sawyer fired,

hitting the man in the abdomen and sending him back a step.

The shot jolted pain through his own shoulder and back. Sawyer sucked in a breath and fought to stand, but fell to his knees in the sand.

Rose crawled quickly out of the way, trying to get to him.

Hickman raised his gun again. Sawyer jostled to move and raise his revolver once more, the pain unforgiving as the bullet hit the dirt beside his knees. The cloud of dust choked him, shortening his breath further. He lost sight of Rose, coughing at the dust and glancing up. Hickman looked down at the blood spurting from his belly and poised his gun again.

Sawyer's heart dropped. This was it. On the wrong end of the fight for once in his life. No escape. And Rose would die right along with him. He froze, glaring at Hickman, waiting on his fate, unable to raise his gun, exhausted. There was nothing more he could do. Had he been able to stand, he would have rushed Hickman in a last effort, gun or not. He saw his father, felt his father—"law, not revenge."

Hickman laughed again, ignoring the blood dripping to the ground across his boots. "I've waited as long as you for this day. I'll give you a second to get right with your maker, Sheriff McCade."

Rose jumped from the ground and ran toward Hickman, screaming.

Sawyer tried to get up, but could only crawl that way. "Rose, no!" He scrambled further as Hickman took aim at him. He waited for impact but kept crawling, closing his eyes and then opening them once more. His last moment would be viewing Rose who still ran. He'd tried with all he had, and even if he had fight left, he couldn't make his legs work. The pain from his shoulder, took his breath, but he kept going forward.

And then the blast sounded. Sawyer braced himself but never felt the burn of the bullet and glared back at Hickman who stood dazed. Rose had stopped in her tracks with a scream, her hands covering her face.

Hickman looked down where blood spurted from a gaping hole in his middle chest. He dropped to his knees, as the crimson liquid gurgled from his mouth and nose. His body jolted from a second blast, and he raised his revolver once more aiming at Sawyer. The gun went off, the random bullet straying. Then the man fell forward, facedown and moved no more.

What the hell had happened? Sawyer struggled to make some kind of sense out of it. Hickman was dead, and Rose dropped before him, wrapping her arms around him.

The dust cleared, and Sawyer strained to see past her, not believing his eyes. Behind Hickman, near the barn stood Zane, his face white with shock. The boy lowered the rifle in his hands and met Sawyer's gaze.

"Zane?" Sawyer called to him, but he stood frozen.

"Sawyer?" Rose settled him in her lap, holding his upper body against her chest as he struggled to sit upright.

"I'm...all right...just...can't stand up...any longer. Zane!" He closed his eyes and tried to breathe slowly. He'd probably broken the bones in his shoulder again, leastwise it felt as if things were ripped apart once more.

"Zane, it's all right." Rose turned and called to Zane who wandered closer, looking at Hickman's unmoving body as he passed, still carrying the smoking rifle.

Sawyer forced himself to sit up as Zane bent before him. He hugged him close. "You did good…son."

"I came back. Shadow lost a shoe and I saw." Zane's voice shook as he carefully laid the rifle on the ground.

"You did what you had to do. Are you all right?" Rose pulled him to her, hugging both of them.

Zane only nodded, glancing back at the dead man, tugging away.

"He hit you?" Sawyer asked, touching Rose's face, still leaning against her. He had yet to catch his breath, and while he hadn't had laudanum in a while, he was sure he would need it soon.

"I'm fine." She brushed the hair back from his face.

And suddenly the impact of it all set the weight of the world on his shoulders. Sawyer began to shake. Maybe it was rage, maybe it was the pain. and maybe it was his father and his son. *Hell, holy holy hell!* "I waited fifteen years…for this—" Tears escaped his lids, rolling down the sides of his cheeks. Finally, his father had been avenged, and it was his son, the son he never expected that had done it. It was as it should be.

"Oh Sawyer, I'm sorry, so very sorry." She held him tighter and tugged Zane in closer to them both once more.

Sawyer placed a hand along his son's arm and closed his eyes. While he had wanted the kill for himself, he'd never been so proud. He opened his eyes again and met gazes with Zane and then Rose and in spite of the pain and fatigue spoke. "I love you both and this day is finally done. It's done."

"We need to get you back to bed, Pa." Zane spoke softly, hanging on to his good arm and tugging.

Sawyer opened his eyes again and shook his head. "Can't. Need to rest."

A rider approached from the west, the horse's hooves pounding across the earth and dust wafting behind him.

Zane glanced that direction. "It's Dawson."

Moments later, his brother dismounted on a run, leaving the horse and falling to his knees beside them, huffing and out of breath. "Sawyer?"

"He's all right, just exhaustion." Rose held Sawyer tightly.

"The cattle? Benton...you have to get him." Sawyer focused on Dawson, but he read his brother's eyes.

"We got him, but you should have told us about Benton and his brother. The cattle have crossed and will be a few more hours to the southern pastures." Dawson who rarely showed his anger did so now. "Why, Sawyer, after all these years?"

Sawyer studied him, pulling up to sit once more, favoring his paining shoulder. "You, were all...full of anger...you didn't need to know. Didn't need you, Wyatt...or Evan out on...some quest of revenge." He groaned at the effort. The pain was scorching through him now, and he hadn't the strength for much more. How would his brothers or Dodge ever understand?

"Sawyer." Rose leaned in to support him again.

"I'm fine." He turned back to his brother. "I figured it out when Benton's men killed Harrison Colbert years ago. Harrison...was with us when Father died…and he must…have known…Benton was behind it. He lost his life for it…and so I waited. I knew one day…I'd…get Benton. I didn't know how he fit in…until now. The Ashburn brothers…worked for Hickman." He sucked in a breath. "Tired, so damn tired."

Dawson nodded, digging a small stick into the dirt and then raising his head." You and Brett told us you killed that man. That's a hell of a secret to keep right along with Benton killing father for the land Brett got."

"Dawson, not now. He needs rest," Rose scolded, brushing a strand of hair away from Sawyer's face.

Dawson sighed and shook his head.

"Where are Wyatt and Evan?" Sawyer needed to know where they were. He didn't need them out hanging Marcus Benton.

"Benton's been detained. Brett liked to have killed him, but he'll go to justice. Wyatt's on the way." Dawson turned to look behind him, scanning for Wyatt. "Evan took a hit to the leg, but he'll be fine."

Sawyer closed his eyes for a moment. So Benton was in hand and yes, he would answer for all he'd done now and in the past. And Hickman had now paid the price for his father's death. Somehow he had thought there might be some kind of peace about it all when it was done, but maybe peace never came for men like him, set on revenge. His father had been right. When he opened his eyes again, Wyatt was dismounting and trotting their way.

"He's good, just had a little too much excitement for one day." Dawson stood and placed himself in between Sawyer and Wyatt.

By the look in Wyatt's eyes, he was glad for the

moment of protection.

Wyatt glanced at Hickman's dead body and back, his deep blue eyes full of anger. "It's true then, he's Benton's brother, and Benton had him kill Father?"

"Wyatt, it's...done." Dawson pushed him back but he glared at Sawyer, stepping closer.

"No, it's not done as long as Benton walks this earth. It should have been done long before now!" Wyatt cursed and kicked the dirt, walking away.

"No Wyatt! We're...the law...he'll hang." Sawyer grimaced in pain at raising his voice to make his brother understand.

"Always the damn law. I'm a bounty hunter for God's sake. I hunt down men like that and never knew I needed to avenge my own father!" Wyatt ripped the badge from his chest and threw the deputy star in the dirt by Sawyer, stomping toward his horse once again.

"Ahhhh...Wyatt...Father taught you law...he's been avenged, we got Hickman and Benton...it's over." Sawyer growled in pain making it to his feet and staggering with Rose and Zane helping.

"Sawyer." Rose held to him tighter, but he wanted to stand on his own two feet and brushed her away, tugging from Zane.

Wyatt scowled and kicked the dirt again, yelling. "You owed us the truth! Well, I'll take care of Benton right now. I just wanted to hear it from you." He pulled his horse forward, preparing to mount the animal.

"Stop him." Sawyer tried, but it was Dawson who caught up, halting Wyatt from mounting the horse again.

Wyatt jerked around, pulling free. "He knew it was Benton all this time...and we've lived here, dealing with the likes of him all these years!"

"But it's over now...it's finished." Dawson tried, their voices echoing across the ranch.

"No...it's not finished. Not until Benton hangs...and I'll see to that myself, right damn now." Wyatt tried again to mount the horse, but Dawson pushed him away from the animal that trotted off.

"You son of a—" Wyatt swung at Dawson making contact with his cheek. Dawson tackled him, both falling to the ground and rolling.

Sawyer couldn't stop them anymore than he could stand on his own. "Wyatt...no!"

Dawson dodged a fist and hugged Wyatt around the middle, wrestling his brother to his side.

"Stop it Wyatt, Damn it....I'm your brother!" Dawson rolled him to his back keeping a forearm under his chin. "I'm your brother." This time it was a whisper and Wyatt froze, stopping the fight, gazing hard at his brother, both men breathless from the fight.

Wyatt jerked himself free and hauled himself up to his feet. He glanced at Sawyer, blue eyes dark and glistening. "You should have told us." He shoved Dawson once more and turned to walk toward the bunk houses, never looking back and leaving the horse behind.

"Let him go." Sawyer stopped Dawson from following, holding his shoulder, his large frame shaking. Wyatt was a hard man and had to deal with things his own way, but his brother's tears had nearly crushed him. He hadn't seen his brother cry since the death of their father all those years ago.

Dawson wiped the blood from his lip with the back of his hand. "Let's get you inside."

"I'll take care of the horses." Zane eyed the dead man, but Sawyer touched his sleeve.

Zane turned and held his gaze.

Sawyer smiled. If he knew anything, John McCade was smiling too at the grandson he'd never met. Sawyer pulled him close once more for a hug. "I'm proud, so very proud to be your father."

Zane's face flushed, but he gave the hint of a smile and turned to tend the horses.

Dawson grabbed Sawyer's arm and lifted it over his shoulder. "Hang on, can you make the stairs?"

Sawyer nodded as Rose wrapped her arm around his middle and supported his arm bound by the sling. It took some effort to get him lying comfortable again in bed, his fatigue so great. The soft bed was a welcome relief, though the intense pain never stopped and neither did the anguish that tore through him over what he'd caused his family.

Rose touched his hand. "I hope your shoulder is all right. Doc Tess was to come by tonight, but with so many injured at the fighting at the river, I am sure she was needed there." She pulled the blanket up on him, her nervous chatter evident of her concern.

"I'm not hurt, just tired." Sawyer adjusted again with a groan, wondering at the woman before him once more. As brave as he'd ever seen. Between her and his son, he wondered if God in heaven was trying to teach him a thing or two on humility.

"There are a few men on each side wounded. Milner's dead and a few of Benton's men—Briggs and Johnson. Hudson's got the names." Dawson sighed. "I'll go see to the body outside and head into town to sit watch with Hudson."

Sawyer met his gaze, and he turned to go, shaking his head. Sawyer let out a deep breath, wondering if he'd ever find forgiveness from any of his brothers ever again. Rose sat on the edge of the bed. He touched her swollen lip. Holy hell, that anyone had hurt her. It was a good damn thing the bastard was dead.

"It will heal." She smiled taking Sawyer's hand away and kissing his fist.

"When I saw he'd hit you—" The rage surfaced again, but she held it at bay.

"I'm fine…really."

"I'm sorry…I brought all this to you."

Rose had tears; he supposed that were of relief. "I'm getting used to being at risk, being a law man's wife." She sniffled, and wiped them away.

"Lay with me, I know what you are thinking." Sawyer pulled her beside him and Rose settled in, tugging the quilt up again.

"What if he comes? Hickman was taking me to Council Bluffs, and that's not so far away." She whispered, hugging his arm tighter. He'd been right. She was thinking about Wes Stadiar, that part still wasn't over for her.

"He's not coming here. Not when word of this hits the papers. Likely he'll be on the run to avoid his connection to Hickman." He rubbed her shoulder.

"Then I shall put the first story out as soon as it's morning." Rose offered.

Sawyer chuckled. He had no doubt she was writing those words now, right inside that pretty head of hers. He yawned and groaned at his paining shoulder.

Rose turned gently to face him. "Rest my sweet sheriff, you can hardly hold your eyes open."

Sawyer pulled her to him and in spite of his pain and fatigued kissed her lightly and held her, taking in the sweet rose smells of her perfume. He was tired and some part of him was broken at hurting his brothers and then there was still Dodge who would want explanations when she returned from helping Tess with all those who had suffered injury. Disappointing her was the worst, but he had it coming. He closed his eyes. He could deal with his brothers, Dodge, and the rest of the world when he woke.

****

Dodge sat on the porch, long after midnight, slowly breathing the cool night air into her lungs. The stars were bright and the moon full, casting shadows across the barn and corrals. The house was quiet after the events of the day, and she was left alone to her thoughts. So many years. So many things in her past she had not been proud of, but that was life and things happened in one's life sometimes with the best of intentions.

Brett climbed up the porch, startling her from her thoughts. His dark eyes were serious as he leaned on the railing. "I've done a lot of wrong in my life, but suppose I know better than to ask about your actions with the Gatling gun."

"I liked to have never got the safety pin out, and I think I might have lost a bit of my hearing right along with the spray across the river. Sit." She patted the chair beside her. He'd probably come seeking some kind of forgiveness, but if he knew her as well as he did, he needn't ask.

He hesitantly walked over, spurs clinking along the hardwoods of the porch. He tugged his hat away and held it in his hands as he sat beside her, looking across the ranch. The silence was understood for a time.

"How's Evan?" His concern was apparent.

"Resting. He'll be fine…they'll all be fine…eventually." She shrugged and wrapped her arms around herself. Would they all heal from so much at one time? Sawyer and Brett had held the secret of Hickman for more years then humanly possible, and there was hurt in that alone for them and her other sons. Funny, for her that part wasn't so painful. John was dead, and it mattered little who or how to her anymore. There were times she had wondered what her life would have been, had he lived, but life was full of all such questions, the ones never answered and the ones best left unanswered.

"I don't rightly know how to fix things. You have every right to be as angry as the boys." Brett fiddled with the hat in his hands. "At the time, it seemed best; Sawyer had seen enough as a youngster."

Dodge glanced at him and back into the darkened sky. Brett's explanation wasn't needed. "John knew, about me and you, yet he never said anything. I suppose he loved these boys enough to bypass the hurt for all."

"He loved you." Brett's voice was deep and soft.

"Yes…" Dodge leaned back and folded her hands in her lap. "But that is what made his death…all the more painful." John had loved her but not more than he loved his work which took him away and allowed them to grow apart. And he had known of her and Brett, early on. She'd clearly expected him to drive her away, confront her and fight Brett for her, but he hadn't. Maybe that was his way of punishing her.

Brett nodded.

"I caused this, the sins of my past. And my sons…have paid the full price for it." She glanced at him and looked back across the ranch that John had created with his bare hands.

"No…Marcus Benton caused all this." Brett's tone wasn't a surprise.

Dodge shook her head. "You and Sawyer held this secret all these years. I knew Sawyer struggled but never understood it fully. And this is all because Marcus wanted the plot of land John deeded to you?"

"Yep. He'll hang for killing John. Benton only wanted to open the copper mines on my west property. He wanted to fill his pockets with the mines given the railroad was coming. I think John figured it out, and that's why Hickman got him. They were using railroad funds illegally, and he knew it."

"You didn't know Hickman was his brother?" Dodge asked.

"No, though I have no doubts he is the one that…killed John." Brett glanced at her.

"I saw Hickman with Marcus at times. Sawyer said he was under John's command in the war. I never knew that. I just thought he worked for Marcus back then." Dodge shook her head. It all made sense. Marcus Benton was a swindler, and he had been angry over the land division when he had worked under John for a time. She hadn't known it was related to wanting the mines.

"John had Hickman court-martialed from what I could find out…he was after revenge. Not being in the army lost him his railroad plans." Brett cleared his voice and held her gaze. "I should have killed Benton, all those years ago, ended this for all of us."

Dodge only looked at him. He'd come so close back then, and it had been her that had stopped him. Maybe she shouldn't have, and maybe things happened as they were supposed to.

"I'll be at the bunkhouse here on the ranch, if you need anything—" He stood and touched her hand before leaving the porch and walking off into the darkness of the night. She turned back toward the ranch before her. So it was as it was supposed to be, how it was destined to happen. Brett and Sawyer had held their secret until now. Brett had walked away with his forgiveness of sorts, and Sawyer would eventually find the words to tame his brothers. Wyatt, well he would steam for a while, but he would come around. Dawson would ride off into the woods, light a fire, and dance and chant for some Cheyenne god's understanding and Evan would mend. And for herself, she would be fine, but live with the regrets.

Chapter Thirty

Sawyer sat on the bed in his room, his mind rambling over all that had taken place. He was sore and still exhausted, but it was Sunday dinner and as Dodge expected, all her sons were home. It was time he explained things. Then and only then could he rest and heal.

"I need to do this." Fifteen years he'd waited to avenge his father, and fifteen years his brothers and Dodge had remained in the dark. He owed them more than a simple explanation. They now deserved the truth. All of it.

"Well, you aren't well, and this last escapade has knocked you back several days in healing, but leastwise you aren't bleeding any further," Tess scolded putting her stethoscope away.

"I'll make sure he rests." Rose's face still showed its own bruising to her cheek and lip.

"I'll be fine, but I want you there as well Tess." Sawyer glanced at her, working to get his good arm through his shirtsleeve.

Tess shook her head. "Sawyer, this is family and I—"

He stood on his own, growling through it, being careful of his shoulder. "Tess, whether you like it or not and whether or not you and Wyatt—"

"All right. Really…Sawyer." Tess cut him short,

and his guess was so he wouldn't finish his thoughts on her and his brother.

"It's no secret Tess, but you *are* family, come on." Sawyer looked at her until she rolled her eyes and headed to the dining room, leaving him alone with Rose.

Rose helped him finish with his shirt. "Well, that is as good as it gets. We can't button you until we get your arm free of the sling." The long sleeve white shirt fitted to his right arm but hung across his chest and left arm.

He touched her, and she glanced at him. "I love you Rose. I knew you were frightened, but you were— so damn brave once again."

Rose shivered. "I knew he would kill us and thank God Zane came home."

"It's finally over, except for making sure my family can move past it and with Wesley Stadiar behind bars, you have no more worries there either." He still couldn't believe it himself, but he'd managed to have Stadiar picked up by the sheriff in Council Bluffs, and there would be enough on the man to keep him jailed for years.

He sucked in a deep breath and let it out slowly. So many things plagued his mind. He'd thought so much about his father and how he had lived and how he'd died. Maybe avenging his father hadn't been the answer anymore than living as his father had lived.

"They love you, but you must give them time." Rose read his mind and placed her arms around his middle to help him along.

He owed his brothers an explanation, and this one would be a hard one for Dodge as well as Brett. He hadn't wanted to talk to any of them until he could have them all together.

They entered the dining room, and Sawyer urged her to her seat, standing on his own surveying the room. All were quiet except for a growl from Evan as he adjusted his leg for comfort. Wyatt stood nearby with arms folded, glaring at him. Well, some things never changed, but at least he was here as was Brett and he hadn't been sure of that either.

He took a deep breath. "I want you all to sit. I want to talk before we eat while I can get it out. I know there are a lot of feelings, rightly so." He waited a moment and sat gingerly, adjusting his shoulder, gritting his teeth as everyone found their place.

Wyatt sat last, slamming down in his seat with Tess beside him, though he avoided looking directly at either of them. Dawson sat beside Evan, pulling out a chair for Dodge, who smiled at Sawyer in spite of it all. He knew it was to encourage him. Hell if nothing else, she was good at that and finding the best in a situation, but he was sure there was no best here and now.

"I'm going to tell you what I have to say and then this family, as a whole is moving forward—together." He glanced around the room at all the faces of those he loved more than life itself. He worried about Wyatt as he wasn't so forgiving, but he and even Evan would come around—eventually. And there was Rose and Zane. His son. It occurred to him again that his father would be proud. Life did indeed come full circle and that Zane had saved their lives was surreal.

With one more deep breath, he began. "I took that last trip out with Father, at the last minute. I hadn't planned it, and he asked that I go. I sometimes think he knew. It was a good trip at first. He and I talked and planned things and all those officials from back east were there. I was young, but he made sure I was included in the discussions." He smiled remembering.

Wyatt adjusted in his chair, still not making eye contact.

"I was there when it happened and so was Brett. Ambushed when we three were taking the lead, Father just ahead of us. I never told you all about the last moments—" His throat tightened, "—to spare you the pain. He was shot before I knew it. I didn't know what had happen, but I heard the shot and saw Father…jolt…and I raced my horse to him. He held on to his horse and fell as I got there to catch him."

Dodge bowed her head, and Brett placed his hand on hers.

"I'm sorry, Dodge." Sawyer shook his head, his throat tight.

She looked up in spite of her tears. "Go on."

He continued as best he could, living it all as he had thousands of times in the past. "I got him to the ground, and he knew he wasn't going to make it. He spoke to me, telling me to take care of all of you, naming each of you. He didn't struggle, just looked at me and even smiled, telling me how proud he was of all of us, and how much he loved us." Sawyer's eyes filled with tears, and he gulped the lack of saliva in his mouth.

"He said to keep the ranch as a family, and we have. He never suffered or showed that he did, never even grimaced once. Just sat for a while after he was done talking, and he was gone." Sawyer struggled to gain his emotions once more, his eyes clouded with tears that streaked his cheeks. There was no point in wiping them away, but he again found the words.

"The last thing I remember about that day has haunted me...all these years. Brett and I saw the man, Hickman, who shot Father. I'll never forget...how he laughed as he rode away. He just laughed. I've heard that laugh a lot in my dreams, when I was angry over losing Father and when I thought hard about revenge. Then when I was hit, I saw Hickman, knew his face and knew his laugh once more. I had to tell Brett because I knew I would not be able to stop you...my brothers from revenge of your own. I couldn't risk that then or now." He finally brushed the tears away with his sleeve and noticed Mei Ling sitting near Dodge had her own tears.

"And that Benton still lives, there will be no need to avenge Father's death, or you are going to deal with me and go against everything Father stood for." Sawyer stopped, glancing at each brother in turn.

Dawson and Evan nodded but Wyatt had yet to even look at him.

"Wyatt?" Sawyer waited his voice weak. "Wyatt, it'll be done...he'll hang."

Wyatt finally gave a reluctant nod and looked up his deep blue eyes showing the hurt.

"Hickman met his maker a few days ago, years in getting what he had coming. I knew Benton had something to do with Father's death, but I didn't figure it out until Harrison Colbert was killed. He was with us when Father died. I suppose he challenged Benton and ended up on the wrong end of that challenge. He knew about Benton and his brother's misuse of railroad funds."

Sawyer was tiring, and it was harder than he had thought, his tense body hurting. "So I waited. I knew I would catch Benton at some point, and I waited all these years for Hickman to return, it was bound to happen. When the Ashburn brothers came to town, I did some research, but nothing connected until later on." Sawyer had to stop, completely winded. He closed his eyes for a moment, his large body shaking.

"Sawyer, you need to lie back down," Tess spoke softly.

Sawyer nodded. "In a minute...Brett, I know it took a lot for you to hold back. I'm asking you also to let the law handle Marcus Benton."

Brett gave a stern glare, nodding reluctantly.

Sawyer went on, cramps plaguing his back. "When we returned after Father died, I didn't want to let you all know that Hickman had gotten away. I think I held myself responsible for keeping you safe...as Father told me. All this time, I've felt it was my fault, and I should have been able to...do something. That's why I...took the law so seriously. I knew Father did. I think this is the first time I've been able to forgive myself." Sawyer stopped, tears dropping from his eyes in saying it.

Evan growled adjusting his position again, holding his leg to move it.

Sawyer took a long breath and gripped the table for support. "As a lawman, there are times it's hard to forgive yourself...killing someone because you have no other choice. Father struggled with that and I remember him saying, '*Men will answer to God on both sides of a gun, a war and a battle for love, but only when he forgives himself and offers himself mercy, does he truly find the forgiveness that God holds.*'" He glanced at

Zane's solemn gray eyes. "Zane, I do believe in God. You've renewed that for me, and you have no call to feel bad about what you had to do."

Zane who had not uttered a word offered a smile to his father.

"And…" He took Rose by the hand. "I've also messed up some really nice plans for a wedding by getting myself shot. So, Rose…I've had Dodge and Mei Ling work to re-plan the wedding in a few weeks. Doc says I should be able to wear a shirt by then. That is if you think this life as a lawman's wife might still work out for you." He teased his voice fading.

"Yes," Rose whispered and took his hand.

"Wyatt, help get your brother back to bed." Tess gave Wyatt a nudge.

Wyatt stood and helped him stand but said nothing on the way to his room. He lay back on the bed, Wyatt lifting his legs and plopping them down. He groaned adjusting the pillows behind him and eyed his brother. He wasn't sure what he was reading in Wyatt. "You all right?"

Wyatt nodded.

"Father was worried about you. He said you were most like him and told me to keep you focused."

"I argued with him before that trip…angry words, because I wanted to go." Wyatt turned away from Sawyer facing the window. "Said things I shouldn't have said."

"Wyatt, those kinds of things don't mean much, he loved you…you are the most like him. That's why the two of you fought from time to time." Sawyer tried. It was true. Wyatt was his father made over again.

"I was young and stupid. He would pull me aside

and nearly take a fist to me when I smarted off—" Wyatt shook his head and turned back around to face his brother. "But he never hit me."

"Father had a terrible temper, but we never really were the brunt of it. I hardly ever saw it in him, but his men did. Maybe that's what Hickman got from Father for his behavior as a soldier. Father loved you Wyatt, you were the son he saw the potential in...you were. I was too passive for Father's way of reining the law. That's why I am sheriff, and you are the best bounty hunter there is. He taught you that. Hell, he didn't have to teach you. It was born in you." Sawyer shook his head.

Wyatt ran his hands through his dark hair. "Maybe I went after all the bounties, hoping it would one day be enough to win his approval."

"That's just it; you never had to win it." Sawyer tried again, "He said you would make more with your life than any man he knew. He said for us both to listen to Dawson, that he was smart about things and to make sure Evan always knew he was a McCade and to keep him out of trouble."

Wyatt finally grinned for all of a second. "We'll all pay hell keeping Evan out of trouble."

Sawyer lay back. "Benton will hang. Justice will be done. Here ya go." He held out his closed fist.

Wyatt moved closer and reached hesitantly.

"It's hard to be a lawman or bounty hunter without one." Sawyer pushed Wyatt's badge back into his hand. Wyatt looked down and touched the badge, gripping it tight and glancing at his brother once more before leaving the room.

****

Sawyer reached for Rose and pulled her to him in their bed. He'd made love to her earlier and afterward she'd lay in his arms, quiet and content. He, however wasn't content any longer. In fact, now that he was well enough to see to her needs in more ways than one, he'd probably never be content again.

"Sheriff McCade, I've already serviced you once this night." She smiled and rolled against him, allowing him the kiss and sighing at his tenderness.

"Yes, but tomorrow is Sunday, and we've nowhere to be. If you let me keep you up late, I'll let you sleep in the morning." He kissed her, and his hands roamed her still naked body as he raised himself up to look at her.

"You never allow me a quiet morning of sleep." Rose laughed but then sighed as he climbed between her legs once more. She wrapped her legs around his hips as he thrust inside her and began pumping slowly.

"Mrs. McCade...it is a husband's right to see to it his wife is pleasured time and again and again and again." Sawyer growled as he continued, knowing he'd never get enough of her—ever.

"I've only been Mrs. McCade for around a month, and you've kept me your captive in this bed, day and night, Sheriff." Rose sighed and gripped her hands tight against his now healed ribs.

"Well, with the men taking the cattle to market, Zane out with the herds and all quiet...what else is there for us to do?" He kissed her neck, growling, and kicked the covers free where he could move above her, spreading her legs nice and wide.

"Sawyer...your...shoulder." She pressed against him, breathless.

"My shoulder is fine...how's this?" He thrust

deeper.

"Yes…" Rose leaned her head back and sighed.

Sawyer concentrated on his efforts until her muscles began to tighten along him, increasing his own pleasure. In no time, he could feel her gripping hard to his sides pulling him, urging his pace. He obliged and thrust fervently until her body bowed, arching as she rode along the edge of her pleasure.

"So beautiful…" he whispered, continuing the motion of his body until she was spent. Only then did he take his own release, pulling her hard against him as he came. He groaned as his body quivered through. "Damn sweet."

After catching her breath, Rose rolled to lie across his chest. "I never knew love was like this." She looked toward the window with the neighing of horses. Grabbing her robe, she got up and covered herself, trotting to the window and pulling back the curtain.

Sawyer rolled on his side to watch her. "They're fine." He had to grin.

"I know, I just can't believe they are all here." She smiled looking out the window to the main corral, where her father's horses were now being kept.

"Samuel Hagen is a good man, said he didn't want to keep a lady waiting for her prize horses." He chuckled at her excitement.

Rose turned gazing at him. "You planned for them to be brought here by Mr. Hagen."

"Maybe."

She lay back down beside him. "You make me so happy, Sawyer. I so wish there was more I could do for you." She kissed his cheek.

"You do plenty for me, but I'll let you rest

tomorrow." He was out of breath, and his shoulder did hurt like hell. Likely it always would.

"Oh, you will wake me in the morning to finish more of what you gave me this night, Sawyer McCade. I'll only get relief when I go into the paper each Monday and Thursday." She lay back against the pillow, looking at the ceiling.

"Monday and Thursday?" He was used to her working most days but Sunday, as she loved her writing. He hadn't preferred her to work, but he had to admit having her in town with him each day was nice.

"Yes, well, I let Mr. McDonald know today that Doc Tess suggested less hours until the baby arrives." She couldn't hide her grin.

Had he heard her right? She was pregnant? He shook his head. "You saw the doc?"

"Yes, this morning, and she says it's true."

"You're having a baby? Maybe, we shouldn't have—" He was almost speechless, his mind whirling.

"It is perfectly fine to love my husband as long as it remains comfortable from what Doc Tess says." She smiled and touched his cheek.

Sawyer rolled her beneath him kissing her and then just looking at her and smiling. "A baby."

"I suppose if we have a daughter, she will ride and shoot as well as any man, including pulling cows out of the mud," Rose teased and ran her hands in his hair.

"Well, Zane and I can teach her to shoot and ride, you can teach her to behave like a lady, and we'll hope Dodge teaches her nothing more than what a lady should know." Sawyer laughed, brushing a strand of hair from her face. "I love you."

"At least this explains why I've been so tired," she

added. "I had thought it was you keeping me up nights."

"Well, now a baby is going to keep this whole house up. That's some combination, a mixture of McCade and Parker," Sawyer teased, wrapping his arms around her.

"Well, she should certainly be some kind of feisty then." Rose looked at him in question, but saw his smile.

"She?"

"You have one son, so you need a daughter, to tame you a bit." Rose yawned and closed her eyes.

"Sleep. I won't wake you in the morning." He pulled her along the curve of him.

"You are happy then?" she whispered, looking at him again.

"Yes."

"You've helped me find myself again Sawyer. When I left New York, I was so broken. I almost got off the train in Chicago, but something was drawing me here. I kept saying your name over and over and somehow I knew."

Sawyer kissed her forehead. "I knew when you got off that train, but I was too damn scared to…love someone."

"I love you, Sawyer." She closed her eyes, snuggling into him.

In no time her breathing was slow and even. Rose was having a baby. His baby. He'd missed this part of Zane being on the way and then being born and growing up. He didn't plan on missing a thing about this child. He laid his hand across her low belly thinking of the life there. It occurred to him that he'd

451

finally put the past behind him and reached for this happiness before him, and there would only be good things to come in loving this woman for a lifetime.

"Sawyer," she whispered placing her hand on his. "It's too early to feel anything, it will be months."

"Shhh. The baby is sleeping. Let me enjoy." He spoke softly, snuggling closer and kissing her neck. He listened to her peaceful breathing long into the night. Who would have thought when he was waiting on that train for a mail-order-bride things would have turned out like this? She had seamlessly woven her way into his heart and life, and that was exactly where he planned to keep her forever.

Epilogue

Nine months later…

Sawyer paced along the front porch, heavy boots and spurs clinking along the wooden planks. Waiting word on Rose was putting him through a slow and agonizing death. Doc Tess, Dodge, and Mei Ling were with her, though he was stuck with Zane and his brothers riling him as they waited. He'd found it impossible to try and sit while Rose was giving birth to their child.

"Sawyer sit down; you can't rush this kind of thing. Babies get here when they're ready. I've birthed enough animals to know how it goes." Evan was more than amused at his expense.

Sawyer kept pacing. "This is my child, not some damn horse."

Evan shrugged. "Same principle."

"Cheat. No one wins that much. Good thing we are playing for beans." Wyatt blew out a puff of smoke from a skinny cigar riding his lips.

"I don't cheat, it's called skill and you uncles around here just don't have it." Zane raked the pile of beans in the middle of the table his direction with a sly grin.

"No baby yet?" Dawson tied his horse and moseyed over.

Sawyer shook his head, leaning on the porch railing. "About an hour ago, they said soon." He shook his head and paced some more. He didn't know it was this hard to wait on a child, and he didn't know he would be so nervous. He worried about Rose, his heart nearly beating out of his chest every time he heard her cry in pain.

"Jacob and Lang are taking bets at the saloon, on it being a boy." Dawson chuckled. "Some things never change."

"Sit and watch. Sawyer is slowing losing his mind," Evan teased as Dawson stepped up to the porch.

Sawyer glared a warning his direction, but the likes had been going on since early morning. It wasn't every day a baby was born on the McCade ranch, and it wasn't every day it was his baby. Damn, something had to be wrong. He wanted to be with Rose, but Doc Tess had scolded the idea.

Rose had enjoyed an uneventful pregnancy, and he'd enjoyed the journey with her, but now was the hard part. He heard Rose cry again, this time in a half stifled scream. She was probably fine, but he was seriously wondering if he would survive it.

Brett came back out of the house, having been instructed by Dodge to get more water for Mei Ling to boil. "Sawyer you're as white as a ghost. She's doing fine."

"You saw her?" Sawyer didn't think it fair.

"Only for a second, they are all hovering around her, and things were getting too tense for me." Brett said. "Might not be long now."

Sawyer paced again, and it was only seconds later that a baby cried, stopping him dead in his tracks.

Cheers erupted from the men on the porch. He looked toward the door and waited. So the baby was here. Now was Rose all right? It seemed to take forever for someone to come and let him know, but then Dodge appeared at the door all smiles.

"Rose?" Sawyer asked.

"Rose is fine. Come on, Papa." Dodge had to grab Sawyer's hand to lead him in the house. He felt like his legs wouldn't take him one step, but he made it inside the room where Rose was sitting up in bed. She smiled, holding the baby wrapped in a bundle of blankets.

"Congratulations." Tess glanced up with a hearty smile as she washed instruments in the large porcelain bowl on the table by the bed.

Managing even a word wasn't something he could do, but he edged closer and sat on the bed, taking in the beautiful sight of Rose—his Rose.

"Well, Papa?" She handed the baby to him. She looked tired but smiled her blue eyes bright and as sure as ever.

Sawyer took the bundle looking down into the tiny face of his child. It had been years since he had held a baby, and this one was sucking its fingers. He touched the tiny hand and glanced back at her.

"He has your eyes, just like Zane and your father." Rose pulled the blanket back so he could see his son's face better.

"He?" Sawyer didn't care one way or the other, his child...was beautiful, boy or girl.

"A son." Her smile melted his heart.

Sawyer shook his head. "Shouldn't you lay back and rest...it took so long."

"First births can take a while, but she did

beautifully, and she is fine to move around as she likes. But, Rose." Tess dropped her gaze to Rose. "You do need to rest for several weeks, only taking care of the baby and let everyone else take care of you."

Rose nodded in understanding, but never took her eyes from him.

"He's a healthy eight pounds Sawyer." Tess gathered the instruments into her bag, turning back to him.

"Eight pounds, a big boy." Sawyer admired the bundle in his arms.

"It was so hard." Rose took his hand.

"You did good." He looked at his son again. "John Nicholas McCade—Nick."

Rose smiled. "Nicholas for Papa and John for your father."

"If it's all right, Dodge." Sawyer glanced at Dodge, who stood nearby.

"I think your father would be proud." She smiled her approval, and if he didn't know better, he thought he might have seen a twinkle of a tear.

Rose clasped her arms around him. "Why don't you go and introduce him to his uncles and big brother."

Sawyer kissed her cheek. "I love you, Rose."

He stood, carrying the baby as if he were precious as gold, but then he was. He made his way out onto the porch.

"All right, let's hear it." Wyatt threw down his cards.

"Gentleman, I'd like you to meet my son, John Nicholas McCade." Sawyer glanced at Zane who got up to come closer.

"Fitting name." Dawson climbed back up the stairs for a closer look as did Evan. Brett even leaned to have a look and disappeared back inside after a strong slap to Sawyer's shoulder.

Sawyer thought his chest might swell with such pride his heart would burst. "Father used to say a man has to leave a legacy…and now I've got two. You boys better get to work on creating your own."

"I don't do wagons." Wyatt was quick to answer, slapping his hat on his head.

Dawson held his hands up. "Not me, brother."

"Well, when I can get to it I'll take about ten of 'em." Evan laughed loudly.

"Why don't you hold him?" Sawyer handed the baby to Zane.

"No, well, I mean I can. I'm not afraid or anything." Zane held out his arms, and the two struggled with the hand off of the priceless merchandise.

Zane gazed at his new brother full of pride. "He's so tiny."

"My first thoughts, too," Sawyer said. "But Doc Tess says he is a good size, eight pounds by her scale."

"Well, I suppose with the lot around here I'll have to teach him to shoot, ride, and play poker." Zane riled, glaring at Wyatt and Evan.

"Idle talk, wasted breath…hand him over." Wyatt took the baby into the crook of his arm as Tess stepped outside to leave. "Well, I'll be…he has your eyes Sawyer."

"Wyatt McCade, hand that baby to someone else, you probably smell like those darn cigars you smoke all the time," she scolded, glaring hard his way.

Wyatt was quick to hand the baby to Dawson. "Well, an uncle deserves a good smoke."

Tess pulled her coat on bouncing down the stairs. "I need a ride back to town."

Wyatt scampered down behind her, following her to the barn.

Dawson held his nephew and laughed. "He'll be the next one married if I know anything. He's a handsome boy, Sawyer."

Sawyer figured Dawson was right, and he listened as Wyatt and Tess bickered over hitching Dodge's buggy. Maybe Wyatt would be next, but it would certainly take a bit of work.

Dawson handed the baby to Evan who held him to his chest, rocking slightly in the large porch chair. "Yep and if your big brother has the poker, horses, and guns handled, I'll teach you about women and how to stay clear of them."

Zane stopped at the stairs. "I'm going for a ride, care to race."

Evan handed the baby back to Sawyer. "You're on."

"Congratulations brother." Dawson patted Sawyer's back and followed Evan and Zane toward the corral.

Sawyer returned inside, carrying his son and meeting Dodge in the hallway.

"She's sleeping, let her rest. Let me know if you need anything." Dodge hugged him and kissed the top of the baby's head.

Sawyer walked quietly in the room where Rose slept. He sat in the chair beside their bed, staring into the baby's face.

"And what did Zane think?" she whispered, opening her drowsy eyes.

"He held him for a minute...all of them took a turn." Sawyer touched his son's tender head.

"He looks so like you." Rose spoke softly.

"I think, maybe the eyes, but he has your nose and mouth." Sawyer juggled the baby who wrinkled up his face and let out a squeak.

Rose smiled and patted the bed. Sawyer handed her the baby and lay down on his belly beside her to watch her feed their son. She seemed to know just what to do to coax the baby to nurse, but her eyes widened as he took to it.

"Are you all right?"

"Tired but relieved he is well. I was getting so miserable and cranky, I know." Rose offered an apology.

"Expectant women have that right." Sawyer scooted closer to her so he could watch his son nurse.

Rose glanced up "Did you think he was a boy? You never would say or guess."

"Boy or girl as long as you were all right, nothing else much mattered." Sawyer rolled to his back and scooted up beside her, leaning back on the headboard and crossing his boots at the ankle.

"Oh, I suppose we can have a daughter later on...much later on." She shook her head.

Sawyer chuckled, but pitied her. "There's no hurry there. I think you are going to have your hands full with this one."

She stirred Nick to keep him nursing. "Come on sweet boy."

"He's giving up to sleep, and I think you need to

do the same. My turn. You rest. I'll be right here." And he would be. He took his son once more and waited on her to settle back.

"I love you, Sawyer." She closed her eyes.

"I know." He flinched as she gave him a mild punch to the thigh. "I love you...more than you will ever know." Smiling at her, he tucked the blankets around her. "Sleep."

Sawyer held his son long into the night, listening to his rapid breathing. Was he dreaming of riding some horse across the plains after a band of renegades? He chuckled at the thought. He needed no more dreams, himself, just moments like this where all that mattered was his family—his wife and sons. Hugging the small bundle closely, he gazed at Rose and brushed a tendril of hair away from her face. God he loved her, with a love he'd never thought possible and with a love he knew would never end.

A word about the author...

Kim Turner writes western historical romance and discovered her passion of writing at the age of eight by writing poems, short stories, and journals. Kim graduated from Clayton State University with a Bachelor of Science in Nursing and holds a Master's Degree in Adult Education from Central Michigan University.

Working as a registered nurse educator for over twenty-six years, she enjoys studying the medical treatments of the old west as well as keeping up with the latest western movies and television series.

While she loves reading anything from highlanders to pirates, she claims to have an unquenchable thirst for the American cowboy when choosing her reads. Kim lives south of Atlanta with her husband and calls her greatest accomplishments the birth of one daughter and the adoption of another from China—neither of which came easy.

Kim is a member of Romance Writers of America and Georgia Romance Writers and says her critique group from Southside Scribes is the best thing that ever happened to her writing—that and a pretty wonderful group of beta readers.

Kim's Motto: *It's All About A Cowboy and the Woman He Loves*.

Thank you for purchasing
this publication of The Wild Rose Press, Inc.

If you enjoyed the story, we would appreciate your
letting others know by leaving a review.

For other wonderful stories,
please visit our on-line bookstore at
www.thewildrosepress.com.

For questions or more information
contact us at
info@thewildrosepress.com.

The Wild Rose Press, Inc.
www.thewildrosepress.com

Stay current with The Wild Rose Press, Inc.

Like us on Facebook

https://www.facebook.com/TheWildRosePress

And Follow us on Twitter
https://twitter.com/WildRosePress